MONUMENTAL LIES

WILBUR S. SHEPPERSON SERIES IN NEVADA HISTORY

Series Editor, Michael Green (UNLV)

Nevada is known politically as a swing state and culturally as a swinging state. Politically, its electoral votes have gone to the winning presidential candidate in all but two elections since 1912 (it missed in 1976 and 2016). Its geographic location in the Sun Belt; an ethnically diverse, heavily urban, and fast-growing population; and an economy based on tourism and mining make it a laboratory for understanding the growth and development of postwar America and post-industrial society. Culturally, Nevada has been associated with legal gambling, easy divorce, and social permissiveness. Yet the state also exemplifies conflicts between image and reality: It is also a conservative state yet depends heavily on the federal government. Its gaming regulatory system is the envy of the world but resulted from long and difficult experience with organized crime. And its bright lights often obscure the role of organized religion in Nevada affairs. To some who have emphasized the impact of globalization and celebrated or deplored changing moral standards, Nevada reflects America and the world; to others, it affects them.

This series is named in honor of one of the state's most distinguished historians, author of numerous books on the state's immigrants and cultural development, a longtime educator, and an advocate for history and the humanities. The series welcomes manuscripts on any and all aspects of Nevada that offer insight into how the state has developed and how its development has been connected to the region, the nation, and the world.

Charcoal and Blood: Italian Immigrants in Eureka,
Nevada and the Fish Creek Massacre
by Silvio Manno

A Great Basin Mosaic: The Cultures of Rural Nevada
by James W. Hulse

Gambling with Lives: A History of Occupational Health in Greater Las Vegas
by Michelle Follette Turk

The Sagebrush State: Nevada's History, Government, and Politics, Sixth Edition
by Michael Bowers

The Westside Slugger: Joe Neal's Lifelong Fight for Social Justice
by John L. Smith

Monumental Lies: Early Nevada Folklore of the Wild West
by Ronald M. James

MONUMENTAL LIES

Early Nevada Folklore of the Wild West

RONALD M. JAMES

UNIVERSITY OF NEVADA PRESS | *Reno & Las Vegas*

University of Nevada Press | Reno, Nevada 89557 USA
www.unpress.nevada.edu
Copyright © 2023 by University of Nevada Press
All rights reserved
Manufactured in the United States of America

FIRST PRINTING

Cover photographs from the author's private collection and the Special Collections and
University Archives Department, University of Nevada, Reno, Libraries.

LIBRARY OF CONGRESS CATALOGING-IN-PUBLICATION DATA
Names: James, Ronald M. (Ronald Michael), 1955– author.
Title: Monumental lies : early Nevada folklore of the Wild West / Ronald M. James.
Other titles: Wilbur S. Shepperson series in Nevada history.
Description: Reno, Nevada : University of Nevada Press, [2023] |Series: Shepperson series
    in Nevada history | Includes bibliographical references and index. |
Summary: "*Monumental Lies* explores early western folklore complete with its playful
    embrace of tall tales and exaggeration, a brand of deceit woven into diverse traditions by
    people placing their mark on the region. Examining a wide variety of sources ranging
    from private journals, books, newspaper articles and archaeological remains, this con-
    siders how folklore took root in rocky soil during the nineteenth century and then how
    modern perspective regards the popularized Wild West."—Provided by publisher.
Identifiers: LCCN 2023002006 | ISBN 9781647791162 (paperback) | ISBN
    9781647791179 (ebook)
Subjects: LCSH: Folklore—Nevada. | Tall tales—Nevada—History and criticism. |
    American wit and humor—Nevada—History and criticism. | Nevada—Social life and
    customs.
Classification: LCC GR110.N38 J36 2023 | DDC 398.209793—dc23/eng/20230227
LC record available at https://lccn.loc.gov/2023002006

The paper used in this book meets the requirements of American National Standard for
Information Sciences—Permanence of Paper for Printed Library Materials, ANSI/NISO
Z39.48–1992 (R2002).

Dedicated to all the liars with a gift for monumental

artistry, thereby distinguishing their talent from

the deceit practiced by all the rest of you

Contents

Acknowledgments

I HOPE TO HAVE succeeded in putting down on paper the most honest pack of lies that any westerner has ever assembled, but such a bombastic claim only hints at the help and support I have received along the way. In 1980, fellow graduate student Paul Strickland gave me his seminar paper "The Folklore of the Comstock Lode and Surrounding Regions: 1850–1900." Besides its valuable oral testimony from longtime Nevadan Ty Cobb (1915–97), the paper became an inspiration and a burden. Strickland's survey demonstrated the need for a book-length treatment grounded in the discipline of folklore. My training, however, was in European oral tradition, ill suited for a topic dealing with the Intermountain West.

When the International Telephone and Telegraph Corporation (ITT) funded a year's research in Ireland (1981–82), I went to consider medieval diffusion of folklore. I nevertheless carried Nevada traditions with me and continued to ponder them. What I did not fully appreciate was how my Irish sojourn set the stage for dealing with the American West. My research there took an unexpected turn, leading me to a question about recent literary influences. In addition, while exploring the immense library of the Irish Folklore Commission, I found material that contributed to a first publication addressing western traditions. That article, on the transformation of the Cornish knocker into the tommyknocker of North American mines, appeared in *Western Folklore* in 1992.[1] ITT and the Institute of International Education consequently deserve acknowledgment.

Throughout subsequent years, I recalled the topic of western folklore when I stumbled upon Paul's paper in my files or when I dutifully tucked away relevant material. Years passed, all with gnawing disappointment due to a lack of proper focus. An exploration of Virginia City's unblindfolded statue of Lady Justice represented another unexpected step forward, granting insights into regional tradition. The result appeared in numerous publications, finally discussed in my 1994 look at Nevada courthouses. Thanks to the University of Nevada Press for the publication of that, my first book.[2]

While I continued writing about European traditions, I began publishing brief pieces on western folklore on the website Folklore Thursday, and my thanks go to its creators and caretakers, Dee Dee Chainey and Willow

Winsham. I also presented a paper on western folklore for the first online conference of Reddit's renowned site AskHistorians. Both patrons with great questions and fellow moderators and "flairs" of that website community have provided a decade of stimulating opportunities to consider worldwide perspectives.

Despite these small steps, it was not until 2017 that I published another major article on western folklore, this time on the famous story of Horace Greeley and teamster Hank Monk. A subsequent article, dealing with folklore in the writings of Alfred Doten and Dan De Quille, finally set the stage for crafting this book. The many editors and peer reviewers of these various venues warrant acknowledgment for assistance, support, and feedback as this research coalesced over the years, but I especially thank Tok Thompson and William Rowley for thoughtful comments. In addition, I owe a great deal to the helpful suggestions and dialogue with Michael Dylan Foster and Jeffrey A. Tolbert, editors of the seminal collection of essays that coined the term "folkloresque," which became key in my framing much of what has happened with western traditions.[3]

AT THE HEART OF pondering the form this book might take was whether it should be a collection of stories or a means to understand them. While inclined toward the latter, I realized that a presentation of stories with brief introductions would be an easier way to address an inspiration dating to 1980. Although he was not a folklorist, Richard Erdoes (1912–2008) published so often in the genre that his intuition is valuable. In 1991, he presented a celebration of western folklore by reprinting—and often retelling—stories of the West.[4] The narratives clearly enchanted the author, who shared his enthusiasm. *Monumental Lies,* however, is an attempt to understand. Those who seek an unencumbered path to the richness of the stories should turn to Erdoes and others who offer similar compendiums. For readers wishing to unravel the inner workings of this aspect of the West, the following may offer insight.

While my ambition to write on early Nevada folklore dates to 1980, my interest in the topic can be traced roughly to 1960, when I was five and becoming dimly aware of circulating legends. That year, my parents first took me to Virginia City, where I heard stories that continue to resonate. In chapter 11, I discuss how I stumbled into the legend of Julia Bulette, but that was not all. I also have a vivid recollection of standing at the edge of an open-pit mine in Gold Hill and being told that this was the "glory hole" of Sandy and Eilley Bowers where they retrieved untold riches from the earth. I knew of Bowers Mansion because it was my favorite place to go swimming. The idea of "untold riches" conjured an image of colorful, faceted, sparkling jewels, something I likely borrowed from Disney's *Snow White and the Seven Dwarfs*. I may not have understood the sexual commerce of Bulette or the process of precious metal mining and milling, but the poignant sorrow of glamorous death and the quest for wealth of mythic proportion both enthralled me.

Years later, this early inspiration motivated at least some of my writing. With a sputtering start followed by the gathering of material for decades, I insinuated references to regional folklore into my various history publications. I have also integrated history into my work on folklore. Given my debt to both fields, I wish to acknowledge my mentor, Sven Liljeblad, and his five years of private tutorial nearly a half century ago, informing me in the Swedish method of folklore studies. At the same time, I thank Frank Hartigan for his patience while instructing me in the Annales approach to history. Without the generosity of these kind souls, this would not be my closest attempt at a balanced synthesis of two disciplines. Perhaps it can stand as a model for how this might be achieved elsewhere.

Over the years while I picked away at this topic—and in 2021 when I undertook to address it systematically—many assisted me. Importantly, I wish to remember my old friend the late John McCarthy who made his grandfather's diary (and so much more) available for my use. Other honorable Comstockers include Joe Curtis and Ron Gallagher who keep the flag of history waving proudly (and thanks to Joe for his help with one of the images presented here). The first half of this book's dedication is with them and their ilk in mind.

Thanks to Laura Rocke at the University of Nevada, Reno, Special Collections and Archives for assistance with images. I am also in debt to Richard Etulain for taking the time to look at the manuscript; his encouragement is much appreciated. In addition, the late Lawrence Berkove was always kind to a younger associate. Larry anticipated much of what is contained in this volume by pursuing the idea of a Sagebrush School of writers and advocating the literary importance of William Wright.

Always available with friendship and answers include Jessica Axsom, Alice Baldrica, Michael "Bert" Bedeau, Tamara Buzich, Donnelyn Curtis, Mike Green, Mella Harmon, Gene Hattori, Susie Kastens, Barbara Mackay, and Candace Rossi Wheeler. With Gene, I also wish to remember his late wife, Lauri Sheehan, with thanks to both for the first edition of De Quille's book, the lithographs from which are featured throughout this volume. Mike Makley, whom I am proud to regard as a colleague and friend, did remarkable heavy lifting with this manuscript. I owe him a lot. Mentioned last because of their importance to me, I am grateful for the friendship and support of Bill Kersten (thanks for all the suggestions!) and Ann Ebner as well as Jim Hattori.

The internet allowed for stirring international discussions, including a conversation spanning recent years with Simon Young, who has my gratitude. In addition, there is the matter of two decades of archaeological programs that shed light on western folklore, warranting my thanks to Don Hardesty and Kelly Dixon.

I am also grateful to all the talented, dedicated staff at the University of Nevada Press, including JoAnne Banducci, Curtis Vickers, Jinni Fontana, Caroline Dickens, and Caddie Dufurrena, as well as my copyeditor, Annette Wenda. They are the best. In addition, I thank my longtime friend Margaret Dalrymple, who had previously helped shepherd so much of my work to print. Without her encouragement, I would not have submitted this manuscript to Nevada. As *Monumental Lies* begins its final journey toward print, I regret that a shadow is cast over this acknowledgment: we all mourn the passing of our beloved Margaret. Her remarkable career spanning many decades contributed to countless publications, a process she assisted with extraordinary intelligence and delightful humor. She relished all aspects of book birthing, and it is an honor to consider that this volume is perhaps the last to bear her gifted imprint.

It goes without saying but nevertheless needs to be affirmed: my wife, Susan James, is always an amazing source of love, support, and perspective. Thanks to her for editing this book (doing far more than anyone else), but also for listening to my contemplations of this subject for four decades. Much the same can be said of Reed James, our brilliant son, who is quick with valuable observations and incisive if not vexing questions. Profound thanks to you both. I might have dedicated this book to the two of you, but this is about lying, and you are both shockingly honest. No offense intended.

MONUMENTAL LIES

Introduction

FOLKLORIST C. GRANT LOOMIS (1901–63) introduced an article about Nevada journalist Dan De Quille (a.k.a. William Wright [1829–98]) with the following quip taken from the *Virginia Daily Union*, December 2, 1864:

> *Here lies the famous Dan De Quille,*
> *He lied on earth; now he lies still,*
> *His F-lying soul somewhere did soar,*
> *There to lie forevermore.*[1]

The report of De Quille's demise was facetious; he would continue to write for another three decades. At the heart of his fictitious obituary is something central to western folklore: the lie. Westerners lied for entertainment. They lied for comic exaggeration. They lied to dupe their companions with hoaxes. They competed in efforts to tell the greatest lies, and those who won these contests earned the title of "Monumental Liar." Or so the story goes, for not even the notion that there was a Monumental Liar award can be taken, strictly, at face value. For westerners, the occasions for deceit knew no bounds. Lying was sport and Dan De Quille an Olympian, but at the same time, others strived to match his level of triumph.

Even before Sam Clemens came to Nevada in 1861, his family regarded him as a natural liar, but it took the experience of the West to hone his skill, allowing him to realize its full potential. Clemens studied with the best, including De Quille, and discovered the freedom to tell his yarns with greater purpose. As Clemens transformed into Twain, he soared from local talent to national icon. During that journey, he was well served by Nevada's lessons about deceit and storytelling.

Although western folklore has many dimensions, the art of deception has always been key, a first cornerstone of the region's traditions: many westerners found liberation in their careless attitude toward facts.

DEFINING NEVADA FOLKLORE OF any period is complicated by the transience of the region, a second cornerstone of the West's traditions. Those who arrived brought their own cultural assumptions, beliefs, and narratives.

Indeed, explosive population growth, compounded by the way people drifted in and out of the area, shaped Nevada, adding another essential part of its early folklore.

A third factor affecting local traditions was diversity. Those who arrived in Nevada were from a wide range of places. The juxtaposition of arrivals from throughout the world makes the state's folklore in any decade complex and difficult to discuss as it defies generalization.

Of course, none of this would have been possible without mining, a fourth essential factor. The industry dominated the economy of nineteenth-century Nevada and defined its culture. Ranching and other endeavors had deep roots during the state's first period, but those occupations attracted hundreds, while mining lured tens of thousands. Many of those who came for mining soon left, intermittently replaced by others. The fluctuation of the industry was at the heart of a developing character. Regardless of whether people remained or came and went, mining was a constant theme, the subject of much of the oral tradition of the earliest period.

THESE FOUR FACTORS WERE at the heart of how early Nevada folklore took form. Identifying this aspect of culture in a historical setting is another matter. One of the first obstacles to understand the nineteenth-century layers of tradition is that most arrivals lived in a small part of what constitutes the modern state. This included Virginia City and the other communities of the Comstock Mining District, and it extended into a few valleys along the eastern slope of the Sierra Nevada, up to Lake Tahoe and back down to the Truckee Meadows, the modern Reno-Sparks area. Most sources useful in this context originated there. Those living elsewhere had folklore, but there are scant resources to cast light into those shadows.

Challenges are compounded by the expansive sweep of the Great Basin together with the southern reaches of Nevada. The seventh-largest state in the nation encompasses many different places, resulting in islands in the great "sagebrush ocean." Geography created a situation that defied any trend toward forming a single bedrock culture. Towns, including Pioche, Austin, Eureka, Belmont, Aurora, Tuscarora, Unionville, Elko, Winnemucca, and the small settlement of Las Vegas far to the south, as well as many others, each had their own traditions. With the immense landscape, they were far removed from the largest population centers to the west.

Today, while talking about these local regions within the state, it is important to concede that those living in the various communities are likely to object to being lumped together, protesting that their traditions are far removed from those of distant neighbors. In addition, the two larger

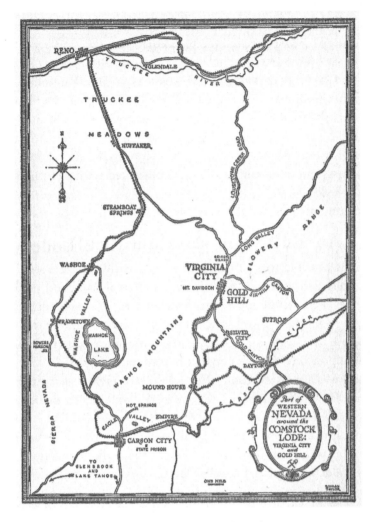

In 1936, Wells Drury published his memoir about being a newspaperman in nineteenth-century Nevada. The map he provided captures the region where most of early Nevada's population resided. Because of the concentration of people and documents, the folklore discussed in this book draws heavily from this area. From the author's private collection.

urbanized parts of the state, the Las Vegas metropolis and the Reno-Sparks area, stand apart from the rural expanse, where many have their own distinct traditions, often grounded in ranching and mining.

A modern scholar seeking to describe what constitutes today's "Nevada folklore" faces challenges that are not easily overcome. The effort to reconstruct historic predecessors encounters vast geography filled with diverse, scattered people. These obstacles create impediments that were largely the same in the past as they are today, but nineteenth-century sources require careful evaluation, compounding the problem.

FOR THE FIRST NEWCOMERS in the 1850s, the small communities were tightly bound geographically.[2] Whatever went before, there was a seismic shift in 1859. The gold and silver strikes of that year resulted in the formation of the Comstock Mining District. Thousands subsequently arrived during the "Rush to Washoe," a tidal wave that reshaped the western Great Basin. A new stratum of folklore all but obliterated whatever might have been taking hold.

The demographic stew of early Nevada aside, there is a challenge in understanding who was documenting the period's folklore. Traditions can seem invisible in nineteenth-century documents, yet with an appropriate lens, it is possible to find evidence locked within diverse sources. In fact, some popular narratives were intentionally collected and published, although they were not necessarily recognized then—or now—as folklore.

After surveying the possibilities, it struck me how one writer in particular would have been a recognized folklorist under different circumstances. With an intuitive ear for folk narratives, William Wright—Dan De Quille—was a masterful storyteller, often recounting tales that he had heard. Had De Quille published similar works while living in Britain, he would be acclaimed today as a valued founder of regional folklore studies.

It is reasonable, then, to contemplate why historians do not regard Wright in this way. At most, many see him as the author of a flawed Comstock history, eclipsed by the more accurate work of Eliot Lord, *Comstock Mining and Miners*, which appeared in 1883. De Quille's 1876 *History of the Big Bonanza* is subsequently reduced to the whimsical literary jaunt of Mark Twain's lesser-known colleague. The consideration here, however, elevates De Quille, recognizing him as an astute cultural observer.[3]

Considering a British analogy, Cornwall's William Bottrell (1816–81) collected his homeland's folklore, publishing three volumes between 1870 and 1880, precisely when De Quille was working. Bottrell added his own literary flair and can be counted as both folklorist and storyteller. What distinguishes De Quille from Bottrell are geography and circumstance. While Bottrell worked in the context of European folklore collecting and publishing, honoring a legacy with potentially deep roots, De Quille did much the same, but the traditions he considered were only then coalescing.[4]

It is important to concede that De Quille probably would not have seen himself as a folklorist. We can imagine that he was affected by the common perception that folklore was an inheritance from a distant past. De Quille

William Wright took the pen name Dan De Quille before he began submitting articles to the *Territorial Enterprise* in late 1861. He became the dean of Comstock journalism during the nineteenth century, reporting on the mining district for nearly forty years. Courtesy of Special Collections and University Archives Department, University of Nevada, Reno, Libraries.

was fascinated with Paiute folklore, the traditions of the local Indigenous people, but he likely saw the narratives told among the new arrivals to the region as something different. In this case, his focus was not on recording folklore; rather, what he documented reflected his unabashed interest in a good story.

De Quille is not without his advocates, especially in recognition of his literary talent, something that Lawrence Berkove advanced during his long career as a scholar on western writers.[5] In addition, in the 1940s, Loomis lauded De Quille from a folklorist's perspective, recognizing this early expert practitioner of the western tall tale. Nevertheless, a new marker is set down here as I celebrate De Quille's folklore collecting. He is not, of course, the only author considered in these pages. Many others contributed valuable material on this subject, but recognizing De Quille as a folklorist is part of a new assessment of western history.

Of course, De Quille might have understood the word "folklore" in a way removed from modern readers. An English antiquarian, William Thoms (1803–85), invented the term in 1846, little more than a dozen years before De Quille began his career as a writer.[6] Even today, many devoted to the study of folklore cannot agree on what the term means. Among the features of popular culture included are oral traditions as well as a range of folk arts, crafts, and even vernacular architecture. Although nineteenth-century narratives dominate the pages that follow, other forms of folklore appear as well.

WITH VARIOUS SOURCES IN hand, it is possible to begin the process of reconstructing the early folklore of the region. The first two chapters deal with the beginning of the Nevada Territory and state. The early events and characters are well documented in histories, but it is another matter to find evidence of the period's oral traditions. Because of the importance of precious metal mining, it should come as no surprise that the industry was key to the earliest traditions.[7]

Chapter 3 focuses on the journals of Alfred Doten. Containing nearly two million words and spanning more than a half century (1849–1903), this valuable resource includes diverse observations by a journalist. Tucked within the multitude of pages are references to folklore. Doten's comments about traditions are brought to the fore when viewed with the proper filter. The exercise also provides a reminder that given the diverse origins of people populating early Nevada, beliefs and customs were equally varied. The discussion consequently addresses the problem of developing an understanding of folk traditions for a society that is transient and dominated by newcomers from many places.[8]

The following chapter explores the rich material that De Quille preserved in his publications. As indicated previously, De Quille is pivotal to understanding the region's early folklore. This chapter explores the evidence that demonstrates his importance to the field.[9]

Chapter 5, dealing with the hoax, and chapter 6, addressing other genres of deception, explore the role of deceit in western folklore. Hoaxes, tall tales, burlesque lies, and practical jokes each expressed an entangled tradition that was essential to western amusements. The celebration of exaggeration and trickery as entertainment was one of the region's more obvious cultural hallmarks.

The western "tall tale" infused itself into many contemporary stories, and it was imitated in other written works. This often sets up a quandary for folklore studies: the specific content of everything from hoaxes to practical jokes may have been individual creations, but the genres that they employed were a matter of tradition. In addition, a well-played lie or joke could feature in a popular narrative.

An exploration of a range of disjointed elements of folklore is the subject of chapter 7. Isolated examples of tradition and belief can thrive but are easily overlooked because they often pass before the reader in an almost subliminal way. Topics include legends about underground rivers, mining folklore, remnants of magic found in archaeological excavations, jokes about ethnicity, performances by a group called the Horribles, and a way to treat a severed finger.

Chapter 8 addresses characters who figured in nineteenth-century Nevada folklore, among them Sandy and Eilley Bowers, as well as the intrepid miners who later discovered the acclaimed Big Bonanza. Many of those discussed here are still remembered as part of the lore of the state. Others have drifted into a lesser-known status, largely forgotten even though they were celebrated in the nineteenth century.

The subject of ghosts is considered in two distinct sections of this book. The first, chapter 9, compares early hauntings of the community with those beneath the ground. Many miners believed in the lingering spirits of those who had died below, but this idea was easily confused with tommyknockers, elfin sprites who migrated with the Cornish miners to the New World. Sorting out ghost from fairy and comparing these with spirits on the surface reveal complex perspectives as well as traditions in transition.[10] The subject here considers how there was a gray zone in the western mines vaguely separating underground ghosts and the knocker/fairy folklore.

Chapter 10 deals with an important early western legend, the famous story of Hank Monk and Horace Greeley. With Mark Twain's help, a tall tale about remarkable characters and a breathtaking setting combined to form a foundation for folklore about folklore, a meta-approach to the subject. While traditions from the past several decades are the subject of the following two chapters, roots of the modern can be seen in how the exploits of Hank Monk were handled in the nineteenth century.[11]

The final two chapters look at more recent traditions and how subsequent generations have considered the period of the Wild West, a now mythical place viewed from a modern perspective. With a population in constant flux, new generations frequently had little direct connection with the region's past, but they did not ignore the stories about Nevada's earliest characters. Instead, folklore about the first decades continues to resonate, adding new shades to an exceptional legacy. Chapter 11 addresses everything from a sex worker named Julia Bulette to camel races and a new generation of monumental lies. In the mix of all of this is an eastern folklorist,

Duncan Emrich, whose fascination with the West inspired his documentation of some of what was occurring in the middle of the twentieth century.[12]

With a second look at ghosts, chapter 12 explores evidence of tradition from the second half of the twentieth century to the present. It discusses how earlier accounts of seeing the spirits of the recently departed have often been nudged aside by classic ghost stories, narratives about encountering phantoms from a more distant past. This transformation is part of how modern Nevadans have employed folklore to consider their heritage. Legends of ghosts thrill a new audience, especially those intrigued with exploring old buildings and their perceived Wild West legacy.

WHILE CONSIDERING EARLY NEVADA, it is important to acknowledge that the western Great Basin had rich, thriving Indigenous traditions. Native Americans had lived there for thousands of years, and although newcomers disrupted their lives in ways that are difficult if not horrible to contemplate, Indigenous people strived to maintain their culture. Native American folklore survived and continues to flourish, changing as all traditions do to meet new circumstances. Their folklore is best addressed with Native voices and by specialists.[13] Here, the emphasis is on those who newly arrived in the region and made it their home.

In addition, much of the diversity of new arrivals that enriched early Nevada is not given much space in this book. Thousands of Chinese Americans called Nevada home in the nineteenth century. There were also hundreds of speakers of Spanish, many of whom were born on the Pacific Coast before the Mexican-American War (1846–48). The turmoil of the time redefined the place of their birth, transforming residents of California into foreigners in their own land. Asians and Mexicans, together with those from South America, added their own traditions to Nevada as it took shape. Many "Americans" commented on how people from various places filled the calendar with joyful celebrations, occasions that typically welcomed everyone. Too often, however, available sources are silent when it comes to some aspects of folklore that helped define these and other distinct communities.

Yet another concession is appropriate here: although poetry and song were no doubt important to early Nevada folklore, sources are lacking. Aside from the example of "Baldy Green," featured in chapter 8, this volume does not tackle the rich, complex subject of rhyme and song. As a lifelong musician, Alfred Doten made many references to music in his journals, but what he described involves the acquisition of sheet music and the playing and singing of songs that were featured in the national repertoire.[14] Doten's journals as with many other sources do little to cast light on early Nevada folk traditions in this regard.

The lack of song and poetry here is particularly conspicuous since the National Cowboy Poetry Gathering, held annually in Elko, Nevada, has been an important expression of the state's heritage since 1985.[15] There is little doubt that this festival celebrates traditions with deep roots, but for the most part little more can be done than to imagine what existed in the past, lacking adequate documentation.

A larger problem when it comes to song and poetry is the role of mining. Emrich points out that miners, as opposed to those dealing with cattle, were less apt to craft these expressions of folk culture: "The heavy work of the mines, the sound of pick and shovel, and the drilling and blasting gave him no opportunity for making music. And when he left the mine, he went to the local saloons to be entertained, not to entertain himself."[16] This affected how song and ballad would establish itself in Nevada's various cultures.

ALTHOUGH IT MIGHT SEEM that oral traditions should take time to form, even in a recently—and quickly—settled land, this element of culture thrived. If we accept that folklore is the sum of time-honored beliefs and practices, we might conclude that new arrivals to the western Great Basin in the 1860s would have traditions only to the extent that emigrants brought what they could carry from elsewhere. The early West, however, was much more than this. The region was fluid and might seem unlikely soil for folklore to take root. Yet it did.

Nevada is an excellent setting to consider how folklore comes into being when fortune seekers from all over the world converge to form a society. Newness did not deprive the young territory of traditions. It merely set the stage for a period of explosive creativity. Considering early Nevada provides a means to understand the culture of an emerging people. Western ideals offered the foundation for coalescing folklore even as traditions blended with the international array of emigrants, all settling in that dynamic place known as the West.

CHAPTER I

Lost Mines and the First Strikes

GOLD! THE VERY WORD fuels the imagination, and when that furnace is stoked, folklore is not far behind.

Even before fully understanding the mineral potential of the western Great Basin, outsiders began settling in the region. The few who arrived by 1850 no doubt brought their own beliefs, customs, and narratives, but the communities they established were about to be overwhelmed by a tsunami of newcomers. In 1859, gold and silver strikes attracted thousands to what would transform into Nevada. The resulting cultural mix profoundly affected the emerging traditions of the transient population.

Communities in their infancy were not obvious places for folklore to be found. Despite that, traditions took hold quickly while responding to impermanence. This observation may run counter to intuition: nineteenth-century scholars were drawn to folklore, perceiving its roots as reaching back hundreds if not thousands of years. Deep soil seemed best to cultivate traditions, beliefs, and oral narratives.[1]

Running against this perception, a dynamic process in the western Great Basin fostered folklore. Constant change transformed events into remote, distant memories after only a few years. Before too much time passed, people were telling legends about the first characters who lived in the region, how they made their discoveries and how their quirks set a tone for what followed. Initially, the parched landscape was home to scattered placer miners retrieving gold in the same manner as in the California gold country. This approach focused on dispersed, modest deposits on or near the surface.

Miners dug promising soil from riverbeds or elsewhere and "washed" the material in rockers or other wooden structures. The method depended on the weight of gold: because it was so heavy, it sank to the bottom of these boxes, and worthless sand and dirt drifted away with the flow of water. The process revealed small particles of the precious metal together with an occasional nugget. Miners could use tweezers to gather the proceeds of their labor, but mercury also proved expedient since it combines with gold,

One of the few early depictions of James "Old Virginny" Finney, an 1850s placer miner of the western Great Basin. The lithograph from De Quille's 1876 book does not match the image of Finney presented elsewhere in the volume. Finney uses a rocker to wash away worthless soil so gold could settle at the bottom. Wright, *History of the Big Bonanza* (1876); from the author's private collection.

forming an amalgam. Miners could then cook off the mercury, leaving the treasure they sought.

Nineteenth-century placer mining required minimal training and investment, meaning that anyone could participate. In 1859, discoveries of concentrated deposits in the western Great Basin demonstrated that mineral wealth occurred in veins that extended underground. Self-employed placer miners gave way to a few mine owners employing hundreds and then thousands of wageworkers. The first prospectors and their primitive wooden boxes became part of a receding memory, representing fertile soil for the seeding of folklore.[2]

A story about a lost mine was one of the first of a widespread tradition to take hold in the region. These narratives, often attached to the earliest settlers, were typically set in situations where it is not possible to retrace one's steps to find important claims. Although Nevada was not noted for discoveries made and then lost, this motif was too powerful not to find a place to take root.

Among the earliest characters, whose story resonated for years, were brothers Hosea B. and Edgar Allen Grosh. These two California placer gold miners crossed the Sierra Nevada several times in the 1850s, inspired by a rumor of an underground vein of silver. Frank Antonio, a prospector who had worked in South America, told the young men that he had found evidence of just such a deposit, and so they endeavored to locate it.[3]

The brothers set up housekeeping in a small cabin near the convergence of Gold Canyon and American Ravine, just below Grizzly Hill in the vicinity of what would become Silver City. In letters home to Pennsylvania, they wrote of digging and taking samples, which they assayed. What the prospectors found encouraged them enough to write of their promising discovery. Ever the optimists, there was hope that their years of labor in the West, beginning in 1849, would finally be rewarded.

Sadly, Hosea Grosh struck his ankle with a pick in August 1857. Although he seemed to be recovering, a fatal infection claimed his life. This left his grieving brother to attempt a mountain crossing back to California as winter encroached. A snowstorm caught Allen Grosh and a companion in the mountains, and they barely managed to reach a settlement on the western slope. Grosh thought he would survive his severe frostbite and penned a confident final letter, but then he succumbed, taking with him knowledge of whatever discovery they had made. It was all too easy to join the ranks of the many who tested fate in the mining West, only to perish.

After the 1859 strikes of a nearby enormous deposit of gold and silver, the district was named after a living local miner, Henry Comstock. It would also be called a "lode," using a traditional term for orebody employed by Cornish miners. To be clear, the Grosh brothers were not digging in the best spot to find what would be lauded as one of the world's greatest silver and gold deposits. Without the discoveries of the Comstock Lode, it is possible that they would have been forgotten, but the events transformed memories into folklore. The romantic urge to see the tragic plight of Hosea and Allen Grosh through the lens of the legend of the lost mine proved irresistible. Tradition celebrated their tale of sorrow, inspiring people to imagine that these early prospectors had found the bonanza (using a traditional Spanish word for an abundance of wealth), only to take its location and significance to the grave.[4]

As is often the case, Dan De Quille is essential for tracking this aspect of Nevada folklore. His *History of the Big Bonanza* documented "a story current among the miners, in 1860, that before starting on the trip over the Sierra Nevada which resulted in his death, Allen Grosh boxed up the library and all the chemical and assaying apparatus and *cached* the whole some-where about Grizzly Hill, the mountain at the base of which stood the cabin occupied by the brothers."[5]

De Quille documented how people believed the Grosh brothers may have found something richer than anything before or since in the Silver City area. Removed from the great mines, Silver City was humble compared with Virginia City and Gold Hill, so the idea of an abandoned prospect was enticing. With this motivation, many searched for the hidden Grosh doc-uments, hoping it would yield information about the location of a rich lost mine. An alternative version of the Grosh story maintained that they had climbed the mountain and found the heart of the Comstock Lode, only to forfeit their discovery.

Popular attraction to the story of Hosea and Allen Grosh was twofold. The idea of lost mines was captivating. Because information of anything the brothers found died with them, local memory of what they allegedly uncov-ered gained significance with the 1859 strikes higher on the mountain. After that, westerners could look back in awe at what might have been. The pros-pectors were, after all, the first to be well known for searching for silver in the vicinity. Also, it was a fascinating notion that prosperity can be within reach, but fate can take everything away. Mining folklore often explores the prospect of touching wealth only to lose it all. Tragedy always makes for a good story, and the Grosh brothers were the earliest local evidence of the widespread tradition that having treasure at one's fingertips did not always lead to success and happiness.

GOLD, GREED, AND DREAMS of sudden wealth are at the center of legends of lost mines. Tales of rich deposits won and lost are international, but they are especially common in the North American West. Narratives often fea-ture a confused old prospector who emerges from the wilderness with gold in his pockets. In some accounts, he cannot remember where he found the treasure, but other stories describe him as delirious with sunstroke. Either way, he dies after revealing only a few clues about where he had been. This inspires subsequent explorers who attempt to retrace the old man's steps, to find the vein of gold that had been found, but then was lost. Many of the later efforts become woven into a larger legend complex.

The most famous of these is the Lost Dutchman Mine, usually asso-ciated with the Superstition Mountains east of Phoenix, Arizona, in the American Southwest. Indeed, the state is at the center of a complex of sto-ries dealing with lost mines. The Dutchman featured in the most famous of these legends is Jacob Waltz (ca. 1810–91), a German—or "Deutsch"—immigrant. Some accounts include a second German, evidence that the narrative has circulated for decades and evolved into distinct variants.[6]

Alternatively, a young "tenderfoot"—someone new to the West—takes the place of the old coot. In this case, an inexperienced stranger walks out of the wilderness with gold ore in his pockets. Sometimes the story involves a snowstorm covering his trail. He is not aware that he found anything significant until others tell him the value of his specimens, but then it is too late: he cannot retrace his steps back to the bullion he had found, and the wealth remains lost. There are many other variants, but they all share the motif of a spectacularly rich gold deposit having been discovered, only to have the claimant unable to find it again or dying before disclosing the exact location. This initial discovery is frequently followed by accounts of other people attempting to find the lost gold mine, sometimes resulting in more deaths and additional episodes attached to the core narrative.[7]

The western Great Basin presented a problem that restricted the spread of legends of the lost mine. Folklorist Caroline Bancroft suggests that only regions with "remoteness and great distances" easily foster and perpetuate these stories. In Colorado, she notes that narratives about discoveries of precious metals that could not be relocated often inspired thorough prospecting where geography was limited. Because of this, fabled lost deposits of ore were rediscovered or proven fictional. Either way, the stories died out. Despite the thorough search of the Comstock region, the idea of lost mines was so powerful, it enhanced the Grosh story.[8]

In places where expanses defy easy reconnaissance, legends of lost mines can persist. Historically, one of the oldest lingering rumors of a phantom gold mine centered on Ophir, the fabulous excavations of King Solomon in the Bible. Although the fascination with Solomon's epic wealth is centuries old, much of the modern perception of this lost treasure draws from an 1885 novel by Sir H. Rider Haggard, featuring the hero-adventurer Allan Quatermain. Because of the allure of these riches, many mines took the name "Ophir" to suggest that they boasted gold on an epic scale. It comes as no surprise that this was the name given to the company founded at one of the 1859 strikes that identified the Comstock Lode.

Similarly, belief in El Dorado, the mythical New World city of gold, inspired Spanish explorers for many decades. It also lured Sir Walter Raleigh, the English adventurer, to a final fateful expedition: In 1617, he sought El Dorado in Guiana and sent his son to find the treasure, resulting in the young man's death. Raleigh returned to England, and King James

I had him beheaded for the consequences of his pursuit of elusive gold. As with the name "Ophir," the West is filled with places called "Eldorado."

In "Eldorado," Edgar Allan Poe (1809–49) addresses the romantic but often futile quest for legendary wealth. Poe wrote the poem as news of California's vast reserves of gold captured worldwide attention, attracting tens of thousands with the same emotional chord of easy gold and sudden wealth. He concludes with an otherworldly assertion that finding lost treasure requires bold persistence, yet Poe's warning also hints that El Dorado might be found not in this world, but rather in the "Valley of the Shadow," using a biblical reference to the land of death. "Eldorado" proved to be one of the poet's final works, a fitting close to his own transitory but brilliant quest for poetic gold.[9]

BANCROFT FURTHER POINTS OUT that legends of lost mines are closely related to two other types of narrative. One features stories about "lucky strikes," the peculiar circumstances of how rich ore was discovered, a motif that echoes in early Nevada folklore. Often accounts of lost mines have a remarkable discovery as an introduction, but not all lucky strikes are lost. Some examples of this device stand alone as a narrative that describes how a prosperous mining district was founded. The initial discovery is commonly tied to an animal: a dog running off, leading its owner on an untrodden path, or a donkey kicking a rock that reveals the gleam of gold. Sometimes, the frustrated owner, often fighting an illness, pursues the animal, and in the chase, he stumbles upon an outcropping of ore.[10]

This is behind the account of the turn-of-the-century discovery of the Mizpah Ledge near what would be Tonopah, setting off a momentous gold and silver rush to central Nevada. Many explored the area, inspired by the legend of the Lost Breyfogle Mine, a discovery that supposedly occurred in the 1860s. Jim Butler's story tells of how he was camping with two donkeys on a cold, stormy night in central Nevada. One of his beasts wandered off and the prospector picked up a rock to throw at it, but he was immediately struck by the stone's unusual weight. He chipped samples from a protruding ledge, which were eventually assayed as being rich with silver.[11]

The specifics of Butler's burro tale are often contested. The incident may have happened, but its veracity is not the issue here as much as its popularity. More important, there has been a persistent fascination with the notion of a donkey participating in the discovery of the famed Tonopah ledge. The image of Butler and his burro has become iconic, celebrated with "Jim Butler Days" held annually in Tonopah in honor of the first strike.

Coincidentally, a lost donkey is central to the story of how the mining district of Kellogg, Idaho, began. Death Valley's Lost Burro Mine in Inyo County, California, takes its name from an account that describes a prospector who was trying to round up stray burros and accidentally discovered a rich outcropping of gold in 1907. In Grass Valley, California, an errant cow is credited with the discovery of a quartz vein of gold in 1850. A similar story from Cornwall has a horse kicking up the edge of an orebody. De Quille recorded yet another story of this kind involving the search for a goat in Peru resulting in the discovery of the famed Potosi Mine.[12]

The motif of the stray animal is ubiquitous. Charles Howard Shinn considered the device in his 1910 book, *The Story of the Mine*, when he mentioned that "Old Frank" Antonio identified the Comstock Lode's silver ore in 1853 before telling the Grosh brothers about it. Shinn wrote that Antonio made the find while searching for a horse that had been stolen.[13] Coincidentally, when placer miners Peter O'Riley and Patrick McLaughlin made the second of the 1859 strikes, yet another miner, a fast talker named Henry Comstock, came upon their work after searching for a horse that had wandered away.

At the heart of the legends, and the related accounts of hidden or lost treasures, is the realization that many people yearn to "win the lottery," to stumble into wealth. As the eminent mining historian Duane A. Smith (b. 1937) once proclaimed, "The American dream is NOT to work hard and get rich; the American dream is to NOT work hard and get rich."[14] Nothing speaks to that embedded aspiration more than the idea of finding a lost mine, the location of a treasure or a fabulously rich orebody that was found, lost, and now awaits a new adventurer to claim the wealth.

THOSE WHO TOOK PART in the strikes of 1859 fared only a little better than Hosea and Allen Grosh. Like the brothers, the 1859 claimants found their place in local oral tradition and reinforced the theme that life and wealth are fleeting. Comstock and James "Old Virginny" Finney were among the placer miners who rose to prominence with the events of that year. Regardless of the real nature of these and the other early participants, Finney was remembered as a perpetual drunk and Comstock as a lazy liar, known as "Pancake," because he was not inclined to use his flour in the time-consuming method needed to bake bread. This became the quintessential way early Nevada folklore depicted the two, even as the accounts of the discoveries, the events themselves, became the focus of the Nevada origin story.[15]

In January 1859, prospectors climbing up Gold Canyon from the south decided to work the soil of a small hill overlooking the canyon below. There was a general assumption among miners that gold-bearing placer sands in drainage systems acquired precious metals through the erosion of a "mother lode" somewhere above. These fortune seekers were reticent to spend their time trying to find such a deposit because they might not be able to exploit it even if they knew where it was: underground ore potentially drifted deep in concentrated veins. While tempting to consider the possibilities, placer miners, with their simple tools and lack of expertise in working beneath the surface, realized that they could not accomplish or support a prolonged, expensive excavation. Besides, the vein might pinch out before justifying the effort.

Fortunately for those who worked the deposit, the knoll at the head of Gold Canyon consisted of friable rock, material that easily crumbled to the touch. When Finney, Comstock, and others washed away the worthless debris, they found that this was a rich claim, easily exploited with their shovels and rockers. Those who had been considering the need to move on to other districts far from Gold Canyon now realized that the area might provide for at least one more profitable season. Even so, they recognized nothing in what they found that January to suggest the even greater potential unseen below.

During the spring of 1859, two other placer miners, Patrick McLaughlin and Peter O'Riley, hiked up Six Mile Canyon from the east, seeking a good place to open a digging. They climbed to the head of the canyon, a few miles north of what had become known as Gold Hill, the location where Finney, Comstock, and others were working. Six Mile Canyon had not been preferred for placer mining because its gold was sparse compared with what was found in Gold Canyon. Nevertheless, times were tough, so even modest sands warranted consideration. With other deposits exhausted, new diggings needed to be found.

On June 8, McLaughlin and O'Riley found a small spring up on the mountain slope at a point where Six Mile Canyon began. In placer works, water was essential for washing away soil to reveal gold, so they dug a hole and created a little dam. Without much consideration—so the story goes—they threw some of the dirt into their rocker, just to see if it would yield any "color." The result astounded the miners. It seemed the ground was full of gold. They worked for the rest of the day, retrieving more than a dozen ounces of the precious metal. Key to the day's events and for those that followed, the process of extracting the gold was aggravated by a heavy bluish-black mud weighing nearly as much as the gold, challenging efforts to wash away the worthless dirt. This came to occupy its own place in the folklore that emerged, but more on that later.

What occurred at dusk of that first day of the strike is etched into the region's folklore, and it consistently became a fixture in early histories of Nevada. Having arrived from Iowa by way of California in 1860, De Quille offers an account of what happened the year before. His version is likely as close as any to how the story was told:

In the evening of the day on which the grand discovery was made by O'Riley and McLaughlin, H. T. P. Comstock made his appearance upon the scene.

"Old Pancake," who was then looking after his Gold Hill mines, which were beginning to yield largely, had strolled northward up the mountain, toward evening, in search of a mustang pony that he had for prospecting for a living among the hills. He had found his pony, had mounted him, and with his long legs dragging the tops of sagebrush, came riding up just as the lucky miners were making the last clean-up of their rockers for the day.

Comstock, who had a keen eye for all that was going on in the way of mining in any place he might visit, saw at a glance the unusual quantity of gold that was in sight.

When the gold caught his eye, he was off the back of his pony in an instant. He was soon down in the thick of it all—"hefting" and running his fingers through the gold, and picking into and probing the mass of strange-looking "stuff" exposed.

Conceiving at once that a wonderful discovery of some kind had been made, "Old Pancake" straightened himself up, as he arose from a critical examination of the black mass in the cut, wherein he had observed the glittering spangles of gold, and coolly proceeded to inform the astonished miners that they were on ground that belonged to him.

He asserted that he had some time before taken up 160 acres of land at this point, for a ranche; also that he owned the water they were using in mining. . . .

Suspecting that they were working in a decomposed quartz vein, McLaughlin and O'Riley had written out and posted up a notice, calling for a claim of 300 feet for each and a third claim for the discovery; which extra claim they were entitled to under the mining laws.

Having soon ascertained all this from the men before him, Comstock would have "none of it." He boisterously declared that they should not work there at all unless they would agree to locate himself and his friend Manny (Emmanuel) Penrod in the claim. In case he and Penrod were given interest, there should be no further trouble about the ground.

After consulting together, the discoverers concluded that, rather than have a great row about the matter, they would put the names of Comstock and Penrod in their notice of location.[16]

As mentioned, the story includes the motif of a lost animal leading its owner to a discovery. At its heart, the narrative promotes the depiction of Comstock as a fast-talking charlatan, who swindled the hardworking O'Riley and McLaughlin out of half their claim and insisted that they also include his friend Penrod. In fact, all parties benefited: the region's accepted rules meant that prospectors were restricted in the number of feet of an orebody that they could claim. Additional partners meant that O'Riley and McLaughlin could claim several hundred additional feet of the ledge, the rock outcropping that proved to be so valuable. Despite this aspect of how the encounter was resolved, the technicalities of early mining customs were easily forgotten or misunderstood as subsequent people told this story.

There is no way to determine what really happened on June 8, 1859, but authors soon after the incident gave credence to the account as presented here. At the same time, it seems clear that the narrative was perpetuated by word of mouth. Even after writers published their versions, the story likely continued to reverberate orally. Indeed, it is still possible to hear people tell this part of local history to tourists on the streets of Virginia City. Truth is not in question here. What matters in this context is whether the narrative survived—and survives—as a recounted anecdote.

Insight into one aspect of how this legend functioned can be found in the work of Danish folklorist Axel Olrik (1864–1917). In the first decade of the twentieth century, his "Epic Laws of Folk Narrative" presented the idea that at one or more key points, a narrative brings the characters and action together in a way that is so memorable and powerful that it often finds itself depicted in art: Olrik asserted that the story "invariably rises to peaks in the form of one or more *tableaux scenes* . . . [when] the actors draw near to each other: the hero and his horse; the hero and the monster," and so forth.[17] This precisely describes how storytellers and artists have considered the moment of Comstock's arrival and his swindling of the naive placer miners. The scene became a point of fascination and was irresistible for local painters and lithographers, who captured the moment.

Just as the Gold Hill discovery in January 1859 did not initially change the community of placer miners who had worked the region, so too the strike in June on the eastern slope of what was early on called Sun Mountain

COMSTOCK DISCOVERING SILVER.

The story of Henry Comstock confronting Peter O'Riley and Patrick McLaughlin framed a powerful moment in local folklore, an event that inspired numerous local artists. This lithograph capturing the scene is from De Quille's account of the Comstock Mining District. Wright, *History of the Big Bonanza* (1876); from the author's private collection.

had little effect on the business of the day, at least at first. Nevertheless, a transformation was about to occur. A crucial part of this story is the way the heavy blue mud was cursed and cast aside for a few weeks—until it was found to be concentrated silver ore.

In 1934, George Lyman in his fictional quasi-history oddly suggested that the "damned 'blue stuff'" was present in rockers throughout the 1850s. Perhaps in response to this, later folklore described the noisome presence for a decade, extending it both before and well after the first strikes. The idea of discarded silver ore fitted into a much later tradition that the streets of Virginia City were paved with this scorned waste rock. The motif of the blue mud and the paving of streets is picked up with the modern perspective discussed in chapter 11, but here the focus is on how nineteenth-century Nevadans told of this episode.[18]

Early on, the troublesome nature of the blue mud captured the imagination and made for a good story. Again, De Quille recalled the pivotal incident in a way that is still recounted among Comstockers. He explained how miners discarded the annoying mud, "throwing it anywhere to get it out of the way of the rockers," and that despite the hindrance, the site was yielding "a thousand dollars or more per day" in gold. News of diggings this prosperous could not be contained for long.

Miners who had been working modest deposits in the vicinity, previously managing on three or four dollars a day, came up the mountain to stake their own claims. The activity at Gold Hill and now at this new discovery became the subject of increased scrutiny. Once more, De Quille captured the moment: "It was not long before other companies had found pay, and soon there was in the place quite a lively little camp," but still, the general tenor of the area had not changed significantly. Many were the same people who had worked nearby for the past few years. That said, the dam was about to break.[19]

Ever attuned to the telling of a good story, De Quille exhibited his grace with a pen:

> About the 1st of July, 1859 August Harrison, a ranchman living on the Truckee Meadows, visited the new diggings about which so much was then said in the several settlements. He took a piece of the ore and going to California shortly afterwards carried it to Grass Valley, Nevada County. . . . The ore was assayed and yielded at the rate of several thousand dollars per ton, in gold and silver.
>
> All were astonished and not a little excited when it was ascertained that the black-looking rock which the miners over in Washoe—as the region about the Comstock lode was called—considered worthless, and were throwing away, was almost a solid mass of silver. . . . It was agreed among the few who knew the result of the assay, that the matter should, for the time being, be kept a profound secret; meantime they would arrange to cross the Sierras and secure as much ground as possible on the line of the newly-discovered silver lode.
>
> But each man had intimate friends in whom he had the utmost confidence in every respect, and these bosom friends soon knew that a silver-mine of wonderful richness had been discovered over in the Washoe country. These again had their friends, and, although the result of the assay . . . was not ascertained until late at night, by nine o'clock the next morning half the town of Grass Valley knew the wonderful news.[20]

This event came to play a pivotal role in the origin story of the Comstock and early Nevada. Occurring not even a month after the initial strike by McLaughlin and O'Riley, tradition often stretches the time separating the day of the initial discovery and the remarkable assay. Regardless of when the events occurred, they inspired an onslaught of newcomers. The region that would be known as Nevada was forever altered. Whatever oral traditions existed there before July 1859 were affected if not obliterated.

This, then, is the first indication of a key aspect of the region's early folklore: throughout the first two decades after these discoveries, people would come and go by the thousands. The effect of this demographic pulse shaped narratives and the traditions that took root. The following chapter picks up the story as it unfolded in the first months and years. Swift and profound population change continued to be a factor in Nevada history and folklore, influencing the way subsequent arrivals viewed the events of 1859.

CHAPTER 2

The Earliest Characters

WITH THE "RUSH TO Washoe," as the excitement over the new claims was called, communities began to take root in the western Great Basin. Miners organized and established rules to govern their newly commissioned Comstock Mining District. The town of Silver City coalesced near the Grosh prospect. The aptly named Gold Hill had grown up around the mound of ore that was, in fact, an outcropping of the Comstock Lode, discovered in January 1859. The O'Riley-McLaughlin strike had inspired the founding of a settlement, and by the end of the year, it took the name of Virginia City in honor of James "Old Virginny" Finney.

As the mining district was established, the arrival of hundreds had a profound effect on the region. Most original claimants, who knew little of underground mining, sold their interests for prices that rarely exceeded $10,000. Most then departed the scene, leaving the new towns to others. Later folklore would deride the first to sell, accusing them of being fools, drunks, or insane, but the issues were more complex.[1]

Without solid documentation, understanding how change in the summer of 1859 affected local folklore requires speculation, but some things are clear. The established small colony of placer miners was numerically overwhelmed by a minor rush that occurred that summer and autumn. Many of these original workers "cashed out" because they believed the lode would not last. This was a reasonable assumption, since anyone familiar with mining knew that promises of fabulous wealth almost always fizzled. The West, after all, was littered with abandoned discoveries that once attracted dreamers, who had their hopes dashed by failed prospects even as everyone hurried to the next promise of El Dorado.

The winter of 1859–60 was brutal, isolating the young mining district as mountain passes closed, threatening to smother the new communities. As soon as spring opened routes over the Sierra Nevada, entrepreneurs conveyed desperately needed supplies, traveling alongside a flood of new fortune seekers. Many of those present in 1859 or before sold their interests and left, all with the effect of making the original placer miners and their first strikes a distant memory.

For those who reached the diggings in this second wave, the preceding events were knowable only through what others said. New arrivals continued the transformation of the region as they acquired secondhand knowledge of the first strikes. Because of this process, most residents in the late 1860s at best had only a thirdhand understanding of the founders of their communities in 1859.

Properties and claims changed hands quickly during the first years, documented in one of the oldest volumes curated in the Storey County Recorders vault. Record Book C begins with mining and real-estate transactions in June 1859.[2] The makeshift governing body of the new mining district was attempting to establish order by keeping evidence of what transpired. Even so, the pages are replete with names crossed out and other inked-in amendments.

As nineteenth-century Comstock historian Eliot Lord noted, "The book was kept by the recorder in a saloon, where it lay on a shelf behind the bar, and was taken up by any one who wished to alter the course of his boundary lines or make such insertions as might please him."[3] While flawed documentation of the first transactions represented weak legal evidence, those pages capture the upheavals that dominated the beginning of the district. De Quille also described the record book, by the 1870s viewed as a relic of a fabled earlier time:

> The "boys" were in the habit of taking it from behind the bar whenever they desired to consult it, and if they thought a location made by them was not advantageously bounded they altered the course of their lines and fixed the whole thing up in good shape, in accordance with the latest developments.
>
> When the book was not wanted for this use, those lounging about the saloon were in the habit of snatching it up and "batting" each other over the head with it.
>
> The old book is now in the office of the County Recorder, at Virginia City, and is beginning to be regarded as quite the curiosity.[4]

The record book, then, had become evidence that supported the emerging popular perception of a lawless time. This was complete with careless recordkeeping and the violence and hard drinking attributed to the first days. As with the records, so too the community oral history of the earliest events increasingly featured "names crossed out and other amendments." It was an ideal environment for the growth of folklore.

Turmoil dominated the first months of the Comstock as people came and went. Ever-vigilant investors watched for signs that the time of bonanza was slumping into the inevitable borrasca, using the widely understood Spanish term for bad times: in this fluid society, a mixture of language and traditions was inevitable. Fortunately, the bonanza lasted longer than most expected, yet the cautious were always ready to pull out.

By late 1863, rumors began to spread that the orebodies were nearly exhausted. Many fled, seeing signs of the inevitable collapse of a mining-based economy. It is easy to imagine that among those who lingered, there was a pervasive, sickening feeling that anyone holding declining stocks would be caught with worthless paper. Change was again in the wind, inspiring a harvest of what could be salvaged by selling investments followed by departures. The mining district led the way as much of the Nevada Territory fell into decline.

Against reasonable expectations, the mines returned to bonanza following Nevada statehood in the autumn of 1864. Yet another wave of hopefuls was drawn to the region. Then the mines slumped once more in the final years of the decade. With more discoveries in 1869, prosperity returned, but borrasca again followed, always with a similar pattern of departures. In 1873 all this was eclipsed in popular memory with the location of the so-called Big Bonanza, one of history's richest discoveries of gold and silver. Thousands responded, hoping to gain a share of wealth so epic in scale that it seemed to flood the streets.

Perhaps the single most remarkable thing about early Nevada was that for two decades, repeated depressions were each succeeded by new discoveries and new periods of bonanza. The mines did not die as predicted, and the region shared in that prosperity. The effect of the subsequent demographic tidal action on the state and its folklore was huge.

Many left during the hard times, but more replaced them with subsequent phases of affluence. In addition, each high tide established a community that was larger and wealthier than before. The peak was in the mid-1870s when Gold Hill and Virginia City reached close to twenty-five thousand people; later folklore would exaggerate this figure considerably. Even so, because of the constant influx and departures, those who claimed the Comstock as home at one time or another was far greater. There is no way to be certain, but it is easy to imagine that as many as ten times the twenty-five thousand who lived there at its height had called the place home for six months or more between 1859 and 1880.

This is the historical backdrop, the setting, to grapple with what was happening as Nevada traditions evolved after 1859. Contemporary documentation about traditions is scarce, but some things are easily deduced. Because everyone has folklore, clearly each of the diverse arrivals in the successive waves brought what they knew. Some cultural traits—language, beliefs, skills, and stories—were shared, while much was not, making for a complex kaleidoscope of possibilities that was constantly changing.

In addition, there was the matter of emerging local narratives. By looking at the assorted stories about the establishment of the mining district, it is possible to understand some of what took root as oral tradition. With the repeated turnover of the population, the first participants and the initial events became part of the folk memory. Because few lingered who had been there in the spring of 1859, not many could "correct the record" as stories drifted away from facts and the earliest claimants gained mythic status.

The mining West often stands in contrast with a neighboring region: in midwestern agricultural communities, settlers tended to remain and establish farms, many of which would stay in families for generations. Others followed and towns took shape. Relatively slow, stable growth occurred as children were born. Typically, newcomers were scattered over the years. In this idyllic portrait of farming towns, many if not most of the founders stayed and could tell of the earliest days. It often took several decades for communities to lose touch with these aging eyewitnesses of the beginnings. A century or more might pass before the deaths of the last of those who knew the first to arrive. This was true of De Quille's southeastern Iowa, for example, even as he did so much to document the disrupted beginnings of Nevada.[5]

On the Comstock, the loss of people remembering events before 1859 became a factor within months. Whatever folk culture that existed among the placer miners was washed away by hundreds of fortune seekers in July of that year, followed by thousands more in the spring of 1860. As many sold out and left, firsthand memories of the initial events became scarce. Late among this second wave was William Wright, who had already taken the pen name Dan De Quille as he wrote letters to publishing outlets. He settled in the small town of Silver City and prospected in the hinterland, hoping for his own bonanza. It was not until later that he became a professional reporter, moving to Virginia City, the center of activity. If he knew a few of the first claimants and placer miners, he likely did not know many of them well, and this was generally the case for those who came on the scene as each month passed.[6]

With the perspective of the 1860 cohort, De Quille eloquently described changes he observed in a letter dated December 16 of that year, addressed to San Francisco's *Golden Era*. It had been only a few months since he had come to the western Great Basin, yet he was astonished by the transformation:

> I took my 4th of July dinner under drooping branches of a willow in the S. Fork of Gold Canyon with not a single house in sight; now *my* willow tree is gone; there are quartz mills near the spot, and a long street of adobe, frame and stone houses on either side of the ravine, where whole droves of *musical* jackasses were wont to graze and frolic not "land syne." Hotels, saloons, stores and dwellings are constantly being erected, and though we are not given to boast we cannot help feeling that Silver City is going to be *the* place. Our mills are not little "one horse" concerns, but large and substantially constructed buildings, filled with the best and latest style of quartz reducing machinery.[7]

The initial waves of people did not signal the end of demographic turmoil. Repeated cycles of bonanza and borrasca obliterated most of whatever came before. Soon, there were few who knew what really happened even in 1860. Folk traditions emerged to explain a place that was becoming internationally famous for its wealth even as its deepest roots had not been witnessed by most. That is not to say that the stories that circulated were false. Some of them may have been completely or largely true. The point here is that knowledge of the past depended on word of mouth, and almost everyone relied on what they had heard, not what they had observed.

IN THE EARLY 1860s, a new chapter unfolded regarding the role of Hosea and Allen Grosh, once again reinforcing local tradition. A Grosh family lawsuit against some of the richest mines contended that the brothers were the original claimants. Fought out between 1863 and 1865, the challenge to the ownership of the Comstock Lode proved unsuccessful. The courts could not easily agree with an effort to change ownerships worth millions, but the deliberation put the Grosh tragedy before many who may not have heard of the brothers. By then, Nevada was far removed from what happened in 1857 when they died.[8] The legal contest may have reminded a few, including De Quille, of the accounts that had circulated earlier. For most, however, the trial over ownership could have been their first introduction to the Grosh story, allowing the chord of the legend of the lost mine to be struck and securing it in Comstock folklore.

The lawsuit likely also played a part in making people aware of how Frank Antonio reputedly told the Grosh brothers to search for silver in the area. Although sometimes remembered as Brazilian or Portuguese, Antonio is generally identified as Mexican, and with this, he fitted in with another motif that was fancied at the time: De Quille wrote of a Mexican American who was in the Gold Canyon area in 1853, asserting that it was roughly the same time that Antonio had been there. De Quille noted "that he was of the opinion that there were silver-mines in the mountains above them. The man spoke no English, therefore was unable at the time to make himself understood." De Quille went on to recount the incident:

> Pointing to the large fragments of quartz rock lying along the bed of the cañon, the Mexican said: "Bueno!"—good! Then pointing toward the mountain peaks about the head of the cañon, and giving his hand a general wave over them all, he cried emphatically: "*Mucho plata! mucho plata!*" "Much silver! much silver! all above you in those hills," was what the Mexican said by word and gesture.
>
> The men who were at work with the Mexican remember this, because during the two or three days he was at work with them he several times uttered the same words and went through the same pantomime. All that the miners understood of what the fellow was driving at was, "lots of money, gold," somewhere above them in the mountains.
>
> The fact is, that silver was so little in the minds of the early miners, and they knew so little about any ore of silver, that when they at last found it, they did not know what it was and cursed it.[9]

The knowledgeable—and misunderstood—Mexican American miner is a fixture of western lore, often linked to missed opportunities and lost mines. Here, De Quille preserved a story that he likely did not hear from any eyewitness. It is implausible that years afterward, placer miners in 1853 would have been able to recall the unintelligible foreign words of this phantom Mexican miner. In addition, it is unlikely that a witness would have been around in the 1860s so he could recount the story firsthand.

This element of local folklore is also in keeping with a widespread western tradition that linked speakers of Spanish with silver mining. As Comstock writer Henry DeGroot noted in 1876, "There were Spanish legends ascribing to [the region] a great wealth of this kind, stories of successful expeditions thither in search of the precious metals having come down to us from former times."[10] It was easy for this motif to be attached to the

Comstock, and it may have been reinforced by the Spanish-speaking prospector who provided the tip to the Grosh brothers.

Vaguely remembered events involving Mexican Americans or the Grosh brothers in the 1850s easily folded into local tradition. Other miners, those who were in the area long enough to participate in the great 1859 strikes, took a more direct route into the folklore of the area. They were incorporated into oral narratives about the first days with word of mouth shaping their legacy.

As the inspiration of two prominent place-names, James "Old Virginny" Finney and Henry T. P. "Pancake" Comstock were easily remembered. After they departed the scene, the process of describing them and their roles depended on what was said rather than what was known. They became leading characters in the drama about the founding of mining in Nevada.

James Finney—or sometimes Fennimore—was born in Virginia in about 1817, hence his nickname, "Old Virginny." He was well liked and remembered for his generosity, fulfilling a cliché of the old West of the simple, honest prospector. Records indicate that Finney was illiterate and could not even sign his name.[11] He had been one of the first who worked the placer sands in Gold Canyon during the 1850s, and he was apparently part of the original group that started exploring the outcropping that would be known as Gold Hill. Although Alec Henderson, Jack Yount, and John Bishop were his partners, they linger as little more than names, failing to become fully developed characters in local tradition.

Of the original Gold Hill claimants, Finney is one of the few remembered in legends. He is the focus, for example, of a brief anecdote about the naming of Virginia City, a story that one still hears in the community. Wells Drury (1851–1932) recalled the incident in his memoir, having arrived on the Comstock in 1874 and working there as a journalist for fourteen years. Because of his profession, Drury had a keen eye for sources and veracity. He makes it clear he did not necessarily accept some of the stories he documented, indicating that although they were popular, he perceived them as leaning toward legend more than fact.

For the account of the naming of Virginia City, Drury's source is unclear, yet his story is close to what appears elsewhere. He belonged to the generation after the incident happened, lending credence to the idea that it continued to circulate in oral tradition. As is often the case, it is difficult to be certain whether he acquired the text from word of mouth or another

NAMING VIRGINIA CITY.

People continue to tell the story of James "Old Virginny" Finney christening the ground with whiskey, giving the emerging community the name of Virginia City. Wright, *History of the Big Bonanza* (1876); from the author's private collection.

printed source. Either way, the story likely drifted back and forth: "On one of his sprees, while carrying a precious bottle from saloon to cabin, he [that is, Old Virginny] fell down and broke the bottle on a rock. Always a man of ready resource, he arose with the dripping bottle and proclaimed, so loud that the whole camp might hear, 'I Christen this ground Virginia!' And thus came the name Virginia City."[12]

As indicated, the veracity of an account does not exclude it from being considered as an expression of folklore. This incident may or may not have happened. As mid-twentieth-century folklorist Duncan Emrich notes, legends like this existed throughout the West.[13] What is important here is that the story circulated. That Finney's nickname was applied to a city of fabulous wealth guaranteed him a place in folklore, but this was not the only account about him. Many narratives associated with him focused on his hard drinking and his careless attitude toward his claims, property that would eventually produce tens of millions of dollars.

For example, De Quille noted that people maintained that Old Virginny sold his interest in the lode "for an old horse, a pair of blankets, and a bottle of whisky." By the time photojournalists and authors Lucius Beebe and Charles Clegg recounted the story in 1950, Old Virginny "sold out for a quart of whiskey and a stone-blind mustang."[14] Narratives about trans-actions were ubiquitous in the early lore of the region. To enhance their absurdity, stories often describe horses, bottles of whiskey, or other mun-dane things as being part of the purchase price. This is not to say that real exchanges did not in fact feature these things, but a popular fascination focused on them because of the contrast between the humble objects as opposed to the tremendous wealth that would be eventually drawn from the ground.[15]

Henry DeGroot related a similar story about Old Virginny in articles he published in 1876.[16] De Quille also maintained that Finney sold "a third interest in the sluices, water, and diggings in the cañon to John Bishop, for $25." At the same time, a man named John Hart, "who had an interest in the sluices and diggings in the cañon, sold his right to be 'considered in' on the big discovery to J. D. Winters, of Washoe Valley, for a horse and $20 in coin." Winters raised horses, so it is easy to imagine that the animal was a fine one. De Quille concluded that "in this way Winters got into the Ophir as one of the locators, and from this came the 'old horse' story that has always been saddled upon Old Virginia—to fix it still more firmly upon the old fellow, the bottle of whiskey was added."[17]

De Quille, ever the keen observer of tradition, often attempted to describe how local folklore evolved, while making it clear that he was skep-tical about its accuracy. This sort of detective work reveals his appreciation of the way oral tradition could distance itself from history. The author's attempt to unravel the sequence of misunderstandings and misattributions reinforces his role as folklorist, at least on an intuitive level. He was clearly interested in the process by which stories could tangle and bleed into one another.

In his most important publication, *History of the Big Bonanza*, De Quille hoped to replicate the success of Mark Twain's 1872 reminiscence of his western sojourn, *Roughing It*. The two were friends, and Twain helped with De Quille's book. Although Twain drew on his experiences in Virginia City with little consideration for accuracy, *Roughing It*, written nearly a decade after leaving the Comstock, tends to be removed from oral tradi-tion. It often seems that Twain was more interested in being a storyteller and story creator than in the narratives told by others. All this makes Twain less useful than De Quille when it comes to reconstructing the folklore of early Nevada. Nevertheless, there are times when Twain struck directly into the rich vein of western oral tradition, and his publication cannot be com-pletely dismissed in this context.

For example, Twain elaborated on the sale of mining claims for horses, an indication of the importance of this motif while he was in the Nevada Territory between 1861 and 1864. Twain also stressed the foolishness of claimants who allowed what would become wealth-producing mines to slip through their fingers. The revered American author wrote:

> An individual who owned twenty feet in the Ophir mine before its great riches were revealed to men, traded it for a horse, and a very sorry-looking brute he was, too. A year or so afterward, when Ophir stock went up to three thousand dollars a foot, this man, who had not a cent, used to say he was the most startling example of magnificence and misery the world had ever seen—because he was able to ride a sixty-thousand-dollar horse—yet could not scrape up cash enough to buy a saddle, and was obliged to borrow one or ride bareback. He said if fortune were to give him another sixty-thousand-dollar horse it would ruin him.[18]

This is clearly literary elaboration more than oral tradition, but it seems Twain was captivated by the absurd yet powerful nature of the story. The idea that someone would sell a valuable claim for a horse, a bottle of whiskey, and twenty dollars was part of the standard stock of a Comstock storyteller, and the motif drifted in attribution from one early character to the next.

De Quille astutely suggested how other details became attached to Old Virginny. For example, he recounted a story about how the prospector was always too drunk to reveal the location of an original notice paper for a claim he had sold to a group of investors. They subsequently locked him in a tunnel and then returned the following morning to find "Old Virginia sober, but very savage. He would say nor do nothing until they had taken him down town and given him half a tumbler of whisky."[19] After this, Old Virginny took them to a spot where he had hidden his original claim notice, according to the custom of the time.

Even in his final act, Finney became the subject of oral tradition. On June 20, 1861, Old Virginny, who had known four decades, was thrown from a horse and died. Accounts maintain that he was drunk, and he may have been, but even if he was not, the oral narrative would have imposed it upon him because of his legendary alcoholism.[20] Having departed the stage two years after the first strikes, Finney entered the realm of folklore.

Henry T. P. "Pancake" Comstock was another 1850s placer miner who came to figure prominently in local folklore, assuming a role in even more legends than those featured in the previous chapter. Besides those narratives, De Quille recounted an incident about women visiting the new diggings that would eventually organize as the settlement of Virginia City. The story was set after the first strike, and like so many others, it seems to be drawn from oral tradition. He documented the episode as follows:

> About this time some ladies from Genoa visited the mine. . . . Comstock was delighted, showed them everything and very gallantly offered each lady a pan of dirt, a piece of politeness customary in California in the early days when ladies visited a mine. "Old Pancake" was anxious that each of the ladies should get something worth carrying home, therefore by means of sly nods and winks gave one of the workmen to understand that he was to fill the pans from the richest spot.
>
> One of the ladies was young and very pretty. Although the other ladies had each obtained from $150 to $200 in her pan, Comstock was determined that something still handsomer should be done for this one. Therefore, when her pan of dirt was being handed up out of the cut . . . , he stepped forward to receive it, and as he did so, slyly slipped into it a large handful of gold which he had taken out of his private purse. The result was a pan that went over $300, and "Old Pancake" was happy all the rest of the day.[21]

This was not the end of Comstock's fixation with women, as depicted in oral tradition. De Quille recorded another story about the object of this early miner's desires. In this case, "Comstock was smitten by the tender passion and made a venture in the matrimonial line." The inspiration was the wife of a Mormon named Carter. A newcomer to the mining district, Carter desperately needed employment. Comstock hired him at the Ophir Mine, where he was the superintendent, using the ploy to keep the woman nearby.[22]

Although De Quille frequently disclosed the source of his stories, in this case there is no clue. Lacking evidence that the incident occurred, the account of Comstock's foray into marriage reads as though it was borrowed from contemporary oral narrative. In addition, the story is too entertaining not to have been retold by those who heard it. Nevertheless, it is possible only to speculate about a relationship with folklore. Sadly, this is often the situation with nineteenth-century sources.

De Quille provided hints that indicate the incident occurred in the autumn of 1859, bringing the saga to a close in the spring of 1860:

The Mormon pair made their home in their wagon, and in the course of a week or two it was observed that Comstock spent most of his time in the neighborhood of the vehicle, was all the time hanging about it. Finally he was one day seen seated upon the wagon tongue, smiling upon all nature, with the Mormon wife engaged in combing his hair. The next morning both Comstock and the wife were missing. The hair-combing had meant business—showed the sealing of a compact of some kind. The pair had made a bee-line for Washoe Valley, where a preacher acquaintance of Comstock's . . . married them after the manner of the "Gentiles."

The next day Comstock and bride went to Carson City, and while there receiving the congratulations of friends, the Mormon husband suddenly appeared upon the scene.

There was for a time a considerable amount of blowing on both sides, Comstock producing his certificate of marriage and asserting that it was the right he stood upon. Finally, to settle the difficulty, Comstock agreed to give the ex-husband a horse, a revolver, and $60 in money for the woman, and so have no more bother.

This was agreed to and Carter took the "consideration" and started off. After he was gone a distance of two or three hundred yards, Comstock shouted after him and told him to come back. When he had returned, Comstock demanded of him a bill of sale for his wife, saying that the right way to do business was "up and up"; he wanted no "after-claps"—didn't wish to be obliged to pay for the woman a dozen times over.

Carter then made out and signed a regular bill of sale, which Comstock put in his wallet and then waved the man away.

In a few days Comstock had business at San Francisco. He left his bride at Carson City and started over the mountains. When he had reached Sacramento, word was sent him that his wife had run away with a seductive youth of the town, and that the pair were on their way to California by the Placerville route.

Comstock was all activity as soon as this news reached him. He engaged the services of half a dozen Washoe friends whom he found at Sacramento, and all hands hastened to Placerville, where they waited for the runaways, who were on foot, to come in.[23]

De Quille then described how the woman and her lover were captured, after which Comstock believed he was able to reach an agreement with her not to leave. When he excused himself to inform his friends of her compliance, she escaped and again left with her companion.

> "To horse! To horse!" was then the cry, and soon Comstock's friends had mounted and were away. Not a moment was to be lost if the fugitives were to be captured. . . . Comstock himself was not idle. He went forth into the town and offered $100 reward for the capture and return of the runaways. . . . The next day [a California miner] walked the runaways into Placerville in front of his six-shooter. Comstock was delighted, and at once paid the man the $100 reward.[24]

Comstock then locked his wife in a hotel room, and her young suitor was also held under guard. His warden told him that it was decided that he should be hanged, but he also expressed regret over the idea of a lynching: the guard said that he would be visiting a saloon, and he let the prisoner know that he would have an opportunity to escape, adding that "if I find you here when I come back it will be your own fault." The young man fled and was not seen again. Comstock kept his wife during the winter, but when the season turned to warmer weather, she left again, this time successfully fleeing with another man.[25]

While well crafted, the story of the runaway spouse is offensive: treating a woman as chattel and threatening to lynch an innocent man are hardly acceptable in the twenty-first century, and today a story like this would easily be scorned as inappropriate humor. The nineteenth century is often found wanting by modern standards, but the traditions of early Nevada fitted the times, which were rife with sexism, racism, and a range of other expressions of cruelty and objectionable perspectives. Books could be written on this aspect of Nevada's past, but the intent here is to consider the period's folklore, understanding it in its context and allowing for the fact that "the past is a foreign country: they do things differently there," as novelist Leslie P. Hartley tells us.[26]

There is a remarkable verification that purchasing the runaway wife was indeed part of local folklore. Mary McNair Mathews, new to Nevada in 1869, wrote a memoir of her nearly ten years of living on the Comstock. She credited hearing of the incident from "an old Comstocker, Mr. Brown, who roomed at my house." According to Mathews, she recorded the story "as it was related to me; and if it is not strictly true, I am not to blame. I have no doubt but it is true." She recounted the story as follows:

COMSTOCK'S AFFINITY.

RETURN OF COMSTOCK'S WIFE.

De Quille's *History of the Big Bonanza* included a depiction of Henry Comstock attempting to obtain—and keep—a wife. Wright, *History of the Big Bonanza* (1876); from the author's private collection.

Comstock was a miner of early days. He was poor when he discovered the ledge. He was rather a reckless man, but would have done well had he stuck to his ledge, and drank less. But was foolish enough to sell his mine, which he had located on the ledge, to a man for his handsome wife, a horse, and a silk handkerchief, and $2,000 in gold coin.

He hitched up his horse and started for Carson City with the woman he had bought. At Carson City she jumped out of a window and ran off. He got her back, but she left him again. He became disheartened, and gambled off his money, and is to-day a poor man, if living.[27]

What is important here is that the story was clearly circulating and taking a variety of forms. The ubiquitous horse, so often part of narratives describing early transactions on the Comstock, crops up in this tale as the price for a bride, together with "a silk handkerchief" for added flair.

After the incident with his would-be wife, Comstock left the mining district that bore his name. He opened a store in Carson City, but his business quickly failed. The old-time placer miner then abandoned western Nevada in search of the next bonanza, leaving his legacy to be defined more by folklore than factual history. He traveled to Idaho and Montana where he met with a series of failures, apparently committing suicide in 1870.

The Grosh brothers were part of the 1850s placer-miner era, but their exploration for underground veins of precious metals anticipated the future. Their lives ended with tragic death before the 1859 strikes, so they could not figure directly in the story of the founding of the mining district. Finney and Comstock were also miners from the 1850s. They were present during the initial transition to working underground, what the industry called quartz or hard-rock mining, but both men failed as the new phase unfolded. Finney and Comstock lingered long enough to witness the first and second waves of new arrivals in 1859 and 1860, but they soon departed the scene. Like the Grosh brothers, it remained for them to play a role in the early folklore of Nevada. Except for a letter from Comstock, with its deranged hazy view of the past, these players were unable to provide after-the-fact eyewitness testimony about the founding of the district.

Untethered by accurate accounts of the early actors, narratives coalesced, depicting the explosive first period of mining in Nevada. A collective memory emerged, forming a mutually held perception of the past. The chapter that follows serves as a reminder of the diversity of the Intermountain West. Many components of folklore are not typically understood as such, for even as we are all bearers of beliefs, narratives, and customs, we do not necessarily recognize these aspects of our lives as having cultural significance as we interact with them in a passive way. The folklore of the West included a range of possibilities given a population that was truly international. Newspaperman Alfred Doten's private journals from the last half of the nineteenth century provide an opportunity to understand how every person who called Nevada home at one time or another bore a cultural imprint that was not necessarily held in common.

CHAPTER 3

The Kaleidoscope of Western Folklore

ON JULY 20, 1896, NEVADA newspaperman Alfred Doten noted in his journals that he "found an old horseshoe, with three nails remaining in it, & fastened it up over the door to my room, No 13." With a header for the page, he declared that the horseshoe was "for Luck."[1] The account offers an example of a folklore practice that may seem familiar to many: horseshoes are lucky, and when placed over doorways they convey good fortune.

The detail that Doten included, namely, that the iron still had three nails in it, may be obscure for some today. For many of his contemporaries, the number of nails in a horseshoe enhanced its luck, and the specific mention of this indicates that he knew the full tradition.[2] The brief reference is one of many examples that illustrate how Doten's journals grant modern readers an understanding into the culture of his time. It is important to remember, however, that what the private diary reveals are his beliefs and traditions, which were not necessarily shared by others.

Some North American communities were established by mass migration from another country or from another region on the continent. Such places can exhibit a degree of cultural homogeneity, including a shared folklore, drawing heavily from the same homeland. Even regions settled largely by Americans from several eastern states can have a bedrock of at least some similar traditions. They may come from different towns, but these early arrivals often held much in common. The West, on the other hand, attracted people from many locations.

Nineteenth-century Nevada had more foreign-born residents per capita than elsewhere in the United States.[3] As Mark Twain observed about the Nevada he knew while there between 1861 and 1864, "All the peoples of the earth had representative adventurers in the Silverland, and as each adventurer had brought the slang of his nation or his locality with him, the combination made the slang of Nevada the richest and the most infinitely varied and copious that has ever existed anywhere in the world, perhaps except in the mines of California in the 'early days.'"[4] As with slang and language in general, so too with folklore.

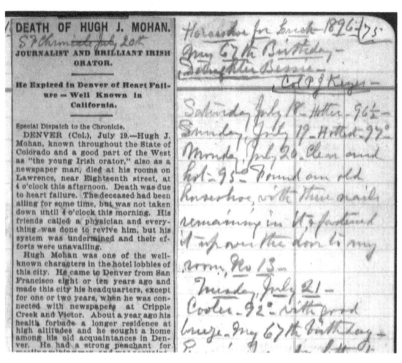

Doten's journal for July 20, 1896 (book 72, page 79), includes information about the luck of horseshoes. Typical of his daily notes, the page features a clipping. Courtesy of Special Collections and University Archives Department, University of Nevada, Reno, Libraries.

Among those who followed their various paths to Nevada was Alfred Doten (1829–1903). He would not be much remembered except for his remarkable journals that he kept, writing something every day since leaving Plymouth, Massachusetts, on March 18, 1849, until his death on November 12, 1903. With more than twenty thousand entries and over 1.6 million words, Doten described a remarkably diverse West, detailing whatever he regarded as noteworthy. His legacy is one of the most extensive daily records left by anyone in the region in the nineteenth century. As a thorough documentarian, Doten wrote about his world in many ways, often providing insight into one person's beliefs and traditions. Certainly, it was not his intent to mention the folklore, yet indications of his beliefs from the East as well as the traditions he encountered in the West survive on those pages.[5]

This chapter considers how a cultural perspective became embedded in Doten's journals; what follows compares Doten's writing with that of his fellow newspaperman Dan De Quille. Assessing the two writers presents an opportunity to examine how distinct bodies of work reveal shared as well as

Alfred "Alf" Doten became a respected Nevada journalist, reporting the news for four decades. His daily journal began in 1849 and ended with a final note written hours before his death, November 12, 1903. Courtesy of Special Collections and University Archives Department, University of Nevada, Reno, Libraries.

individual traditions and beliefs. Further, this analysis demonstrates the way folkloric content is often expressed in primary sources. By seeking insights from what they wrote, it is possible to grasp an important part of western history, namely, how folklore took shape among a diverse population.

Doten with his expansive journals and De Quille with his extensive publications, present contrasting problems in attempting to understand the folklore of nineteenth-century Nevada. Both wrote during the same general period, but their legacies are different, requiring separate tactics. Nevertheless, instances when folklore appears in the text open the door to understanding those traditions.

IN 1849, DOTEN JOINED the tens of thousands from throughout the world traveling to the Pacific Coast, enticed by the famed California Gold Rush.[6] Born in 1829, he had not yet turned twenty as he sailed away from the East Coast, never to return. Doten tried mining and then farming in California, but neither occupation proved prosperous, so in 1863 he decided to give mining another chance. He relocated to the Nevada Territory, settling in Como in what is now Lyon County. Like De Quille, Doten found his calling when he began working as a reporter, in this case writing for the *Como Sentinel*. Before long, he moved to the Comstock, employed by the *Virginia Daily Union*, the *Territorial Enterprise*, and the *Gold Hill Daily News*; he finally purchased the last of these, serving as its editor. Doten then moved on, writing for newspapers in Austin in central Nevada and in Reno and Carson City.

Doten's career fluoresced and declined with the mines of Nevada. At his most prosperous, he was a prominent business owner, wielding the power of an important newspaper, and he succeeded in establishing a family and a life that seemed unassailable. Unfortunately, as mining waned in the 1880s, Doten's fortunes failed him, and he sank into poverty and alcoholism, working piecemeal as best he could, ultimately separated from his wife and children.

Doten's daily record of items he found interesting is written in stark, matter-of-fact prose, resulting in fewer passages related to folklore than one might hope. In addition, when he mentioned something that was linked to this aspect of culture, it is often merely a few words without explanation. Nevertheless, among the enormous quantity of his words are many nods to tradition.

The example of the horseshoe cited earlier draws from one of three of Doten's references to the luck associated with this type of object. Of further importance is the observation that his room was "that unlucky number 13."[7] It was enough of a concern to appear in his journals when he moved there on May 7, 1896. This illustrates how even a few words can correspond to folk belief, in this case the well-known idea that thirteen is bad luck.

In 1897, Doten recorded how he removed the horseshoe when changing residence so he could install it above his new door. That year, he found and pocketed another "old horseshoe lying by the roadside."[8] With these examples, we can glimpse the possibilities within Doten's thousands of pages.

While Doten often included mere allusions to nineteenth-century folklore, these can help build an understanding of the range of possibilities. For example, two expressions of traditions about the weather from Doten's journals further illustrate the wealth of material represented. On March 14, 1882, he described a storm as being an "Equinoctial Gale." He made a similar observation on March 22 and 23, 1887. This refers to a popular belief that winds are more furious at the spring and autumn equinoxes. There is no evidence that this tradition is based on fact, but folklore often defies science.[9]

Doten wrote about another aspect of weather folklore on May 12, 1891:

"Lots of angle worms made their appearance crawling on the streets and sidewalks—evidently rained down—clouds must be wormy." At this point, he was drawing on the belief that rain can contain animals of various sorts. The notion that creatures can precipitate from rain is based on a flawed deductive reasoning not uncommon in folklore: various species emerge after it has rained; therefore, they must have dropped from the clouds. The correct observation is that rain simply causes some creatures to be on the ground. The folk belief has nevertheless inspired scientific inquiry to find real-life inspirations for the tradition, drawing on a form of modern folklore that all legends have a basis in truth. According to this line of thought, people believe animals precipitate from clouds; therefore, sometimes this must really occur to have inspired the idea. While such incidents are rare and real events can reinforce belief, it is more likely that the commonplace effect of rain on things that live on or in soil inspired the tradition.[10]

Doten also referred to two folkloric themes regarding footwear. At several points, he discussed the importance of removing a dying man's boots to avoid being scorned as someone who died "with his boots on." For example, when Ben Ballou was shot on March 2, 1866, in a Virginia City saloon, Doten wrote, "His boots were pulled off at once like Tom Peasley's, that he 'might not die in them.'" The assertion suggests that Doten joined others in feeling that it was undesirable to die wearing one's boots and that the same approach was taken when Peasley, a Virginia City favorite, was shot in Carson City earlier in the year.[11]

Dying with one's boots on has become a cliché in film and literature. Projecting backward with modern folk tradition associated with the Wild West, people have found inspiration in the idea that only bad men died wearing boots. They then framed forlorn, once-respectable frontier graveyards with the name "Boot Hill." This process became tangled with Virginia City's Flowery Hill Cemetery, one of the earliest proper final resting places of the community; in the twentieth century, it became "Boot Hill," as described in chapter 11. This emerged as a folk tradition intended to provide the lens through which to peer at the past.

Doten revealed how dying while wearing boots manifested in the nineteenth century in real terms. At the same time, it is important to point out that the assumption that it is undesirable to die in this way has not been universal even in the English-speaking world. It is a tradition that has transformed over time, for folklore constantly changes.

Shakespeare's Macbeth declares that "at least we'll die with harness on our back," meaning the armor worn in battle. Here and in other instances, to die in armor, or often with one's boots on, indicated an honorable death in battle as opposed to a soldier who dies in bed. These phrases also applied to people who worked at an occupation until death, again something seen as admirable. Conversely, to "die with his boots on" was a way to scorn hanged criminals, so the phrase was not used consistently. In the American West, the concept was traditionally negative, associated with a violent death in uncommendable circumstance, hence the rush to remove a victim's boots.[12]

On the day when Doten wrote about the death of Ballou, there was a second passage concerning footwear in the context of folklore. From his journals we know he said farewell to friends by throwing "an old shoe after them for luck."[13] The custom of tossing shoes after someone who is departing on a trip was once widespread in Europe and North America. The tradition has largely faded, but it survives in the practice of tying footwear to the back of a vehicle as newlyweds leave on a honeymoon. While not thrown, the shoes nevertheless pursue the couple as a wish for good luck.[14]

Coincidentally, two additional expressions of Doten's belief system deal with weddings. On March 26, 1867, he recorded that he slept with a piece of wedding cake "under my pillow." Folk tradition held that this could inspire a dream of a future marriage partner. Usually reserved for women, Doten demonstrated that men could also engage in this form of love divination.[15]

Then on July 24, 1874, a year after marrying Mary Stoddard (1845–1914), Doten noted that he had worn his wedding coat every day since his wedding, "but it being worn out, I burned it"; he then cited an "old saying [that] I wont [*sic*] have any luck till you wear out your wedding coat—don't bother me now—Will have lots of luck now, no doubt." Doten was responding to a contemporary tradition that a wedding coat must be worn out before a couple would know true happiness and good fortune.[16]

Doten also described the use of divining rods: divining, witching, or dowsing with a rod is a means of locating certain things, ranging from underground water and precious metals to graves and lost items. In what persists into the present, practitioners use a dowsing rod (or rods) or a forked stick. The belief in the efficacy of dowsing has deep roots in European folklore, appearing, for example, in Georgius Agricola's sixteenth-century monograph on mining, *De re metallica*. The dowser uses a forked implement or separate metal rods to point to the object of the search. The dowser maintains that the device moves independent of any human effort and is effective in "divining" the location of things.[17]

Twice in 1890, Doten provided evidence of a saying shared among his peers, but unlike the subject of divining rods, this had shallow roots: he made a reference to a now-obscure phrase, "Wild Night on Treasure Hill & Poor Milligan Busted." Lawrence Berkove, an authority on early Nevada literature, identified this as "a popular expression in Nevada mining communities used to indicate an abrupt onset of bad luck that doomed whatever enterprise one had been pursuing."[18] It was western slang, a part of folklore before it faded from existence.

Doten also documented a cycle of narratives of a sort now often called urban legends. In 1896, he wrote of "a mythical air ship being seen in the heavens all over the Pacific coast." These stories originated in northern California and quickly crossed into Nevada. By 1897, accounts of the phantom vessel had spread throughout the nation. People suggested it was the work of some secretive, eccentric inventor or that the craft carried explorers from Mars. In a few reports, the airship landed with human or near-human crew members walking out to offer greetings. This early cycle of modern popular narratives faded away after 1897 and left no lingering imprint on popular culture; they are significant, nevertheless, in the way they anticipated the UFO excitement following World War II. The stories can also be seen as a form of late nineteenth-century folklore without deep roots in tradition. Rather, they emerged in an increasingly modernized world, anticipating the way that many popular narratives have spread in recent decades, relying heavily on media.[19]

There are many other examples of Doten referring to belief and tradition, but two more will suffice, both dealing with death and bodies of water. On May 22, 1902, he noted a search along the Carson River for the body of someone who was thought to have drowned: "plenty of boats, hooks and drags, dynamite and cannon, but didn't accomplish anything." Nineteenth-century British and American folklore included the idea that a submerged body would surface in response to a cannon fired over the water. This appeared in North American literature as early as 1842 with Edgar Allan Poe's story "The Mystery of Marie Rogêt" and four decades later in Mark Twain's classic *Adventures of Huckleberry Finn* (1884). People concluded that the explosion would burst the gallbladder of the corpse, and this would somehow cause the body to rise. Rare instances when the method seemed effective were likely because the concussion dislodged someone's remains snagged at the bottom. In general, this pervasive tradition is not confirmed by reality, but it nevertheless persisted as folklore.[20]

Another of Doten's references to belief about the dead and bodies of water is a matter of local tradition. On April 18, 1897, he asserted that "Lake Tahoe Gives not up her Dead." It is a common fixture of folklore that nearby lakes keep those who drown there, the corpse never to be found. Various North American lakes have acquired this reputation, famously including Lake Superior. In Nevada, this notion was and continues to be associated with Pyramid Lake and Tahoe. Historically, the liminal nature of water has represented a place where the terrestrial world ends in a significant way, and those lost in water, or more often at sea, retain a status different from those given burial on land.[21]

The persistent tradition of corpse retention for Pyramid and Tahoe is an unusual example of early Nevada folklore surviving decades to the present. The process of population fluctuation and change was not strictly a phenomenon of the first two decades of territory and statehood. Relentless, dramatic change among those who have called the state home continues to the present, yet the folklore about these two lakes not giving up their dead endures.

DOTEN'S ISOLATED PASSAGES RELATED to folklore in his journals capture his privately expressed point of view. Had he kept such a daily record while never leaving his home on the East Coast, folklorists could use this material to understand nineteenth-century culture in Massachusetts during the second half of the nineteenth century. Removed from that context, his perspective must be seen as unique rather than necessarily shared.

Predictably, most of Doten's references to folklore reflect what he imported from the East to the West. It is the expected exclusivity of someone recording thoughts for himself. Considering one person's comments only hints at the larger possibilities. While each of the thousands of newcomers had their own distinct range of traditions, some things were held in common before arriving. Others became a matter of shared culture as the region assumed its own identity. Consequently, while Doten primarily described what he brought with him, he also alluded to facets of folklore that were forming, new to the West. His journals capture the process of cultural migration, isolation, diffusion, and rebirth.

IN ADDITION, DOTEN YIELDS insight into yet another aspect of nineteenth-century beliefs and traditions. His notes include observations of various approaches to pseudoscience. These were often promoted in newspapers, so their link to folklore becomes tenuous and entwined with the written word. Folklore has always been influenced by what is written—just as traditions have influenced literature—but the two became increasingly intimate partners as the decades progressed into the modern world. Now popular belief and narratives are embedded in everything from the printed word to television and the internet, but even in Doten's world, understanding the diffusion and complex interactions between publications and folklore can be challenging.

On January 28, 1866, Doten sent a lock of his hair to an address in Wisconsin. He added a sample from a woman who had captured his fancy, all this in response to a couple in the "Badger State" who advertised that for a fee, they would diagnose psychiatric traits based on the samples. The underpinning of this practice is old: the notion that human character can be calculated from various physical features was based on folk belief. Measurements and observation of head shapes, lines on hands, and the nature of hair have long been part of this tradition. The enthusiasm for science and technology during the nineteenth century inspired some to add a scientific veneer to the examination of physical traits to diagnose a person's psychological profile. The promotion of the "scientific" application of an old belief, using newsprint for advertising, anticipates how folklore would be shaped and transmitted in the modern world.[22]

Besides this, Doten made extensive references to spiritualism. Considering this topic presents yet another type of problem in the context of folklore studies. Doten's participation in séances relied on his belief in spirits in the afterworld and in their ability—and desire—to communicate with the living. The specifics of what occurred in many instances were guided by the American spiritualist movement, which began to take form in the mid-nineteenth century, gaining adherents in the wake of the Civil War. Advocates organized meetings, printed books and pamphlets, and gave lectures while occasionally hosting private séances. Spiritualists organized in ways akin to religion. All this made the spiritualist movement seem a step apart from folk belief and tradition.[23]

Nevertheless, the participation that Doten repeatedly described also drew upon a popular "ground-up" enthusiasm for the belief in ghosts. There were specific means of communicating with the dead, a shared tradition that blended with the emerging excitement gripping many people. While some methods to conjure spirits were in imitation of stage presentations or were outlined in publications, specific practices were sometimes spread by word of mouth, placing Doten's participation in the spiritualist movement in the realm of folklore.

Doten's descriptions of séances, beginning in the mid-1860s, provide details about everyday events. Most of the efforts he documented took the form of interpreting rapping sounds, "which were evidently under the floor, near our feet." Sometimes there was also spirit writing, as occurred on October 24, 1867, with a spiritualist named Ada Hoyt Foye, who claimed to be in communication with Samuel Doten, the father of the journalist:

Got note from Ada Hoyt Foye at Enterprise Office, requesting me to call a& [etc.] see her at her room—went—had sitting with her. . . . I wrote the names of Samuel Doten, and Capt Fred Morton, on separate ballots, folded each & laid them on the little table between us—Then she took one ballot after the other, asking if there was a spirit present who would answer to either of them; three raps were given for "yes"— The spirit then caused her to write with a pencil: "I will try to answer you. Samuel Doten"—This was written bottom up, & from right to left, & quicker than I ever saw writing done. . . . The Following are the answers elicited: "I was your father—I was 78 years old when I died—I died of heart disease—There were nine brothers & sisters of you in the family—8 are them now living—a sister is dead."[24]

Doten, apparently acknowledging that it was his father, then described how this spirit gave additional information about a variety of things, including prospects in finances and love. For several years, Doten made repeated attempts to communicate with the dead, always seeking verification that the spirit was real by confirming basic information and then attempting to gain insight into matters of the heart. He was also interested in stock investments or other things pressing at the time.

One of the common techniques that Doten identified as being used during séances was "table tipping" to communicate with the departed. The first reference to this occurred on December 11, 1867, a time when lawyer, newspaper publisher, suffragist, and spiritualist Laura De Force Gordon (1838–1907) was lecturing in Virginia City. Back in Massachusetts, she became a friend of fellow spiritualist Lizzie Doten, the sister of the Nevada newspaperman. Because of this connection, Gordon had entrée to Virginia City and had reason to speak with Alf Doten. Perhaps because of this connection, he went to a house on North A Street where "about 12 or 15 . . . ladies & gents" and Gordon had gathered for a session.[25]

Claiming some success, Doten was less clear about their approach, but it is possible to imagine the process as he knew it. Typically, table-tipping participants would place their hands on a table and wait for it to move, rotate, or lift into the air. Various examples of fraud were eventually exposed, but this method to reach the realm of the dead remained popular in the 1850s and 1860s.

Besides believing that spirits could communicate with the living, Doten also considered the dead as able to affect the world. In 1867, he described how he saw the importance of spirits in relation to the career of Peter O'Riley, one of the first discoverers of the deposit that inspired the founding of

Virginia City, discussed earlier. Doten wrote: "Peter O'Reilly [*sic*] was the old man of my story—O'Reilly was one of the first discoverers of the Comstock, & is an eccentric, visionary genius—He is now working prospecting after some imaginary ledge in the low hills near Carson river, just south of Carson City—The 'spirits' told him about this ledge, & he expects to strike it rich."[26] In this case, O'Riley looked to the otherworld for help to find gold. Doten usually approached ghosts for answers about matters of the heart or concerning greater philosophical questions, including issues of faith. Nevertheless, he was also sometimes interested in stock tips from the deceased.

OVERALL, DOTEN'S BELIEF IN an active, communicative spirit world folded in with other thoughts that he recorded in his journals. Together, spiritualism augmented the rich body of folklore that he alluded to throughout this remarkable document. While some of Doten's personal folklore was held in private, spiritualism was a tradition that he shared with his neighbors. This was an example of something that was new and, by its nature, held in common nationally. At the same time, there were emerging expressions of western folklore that were making the region distinct.

Various factors contributed to the kaleidoscope of folklore that enriched early Nevada. People brought their own beliefs and narratives, sometimes sharing traditions and sometimes not. In addition, there was the growth of new expressions of western folklore. All these combined in references in the primary record. Sometimes meaning is clear and sometimes it is not, but either way, when attempting to reconstruct the folklore of the period, it is essential to attempt to understand the context and intent of the author.

For the most part, Doten's isolated, often unintentional nods to folklore are without elaboration, and it is necessary to fill in where only shadows exist. At the same time, his journals call to mind the issues that can occur when using historical documents to understand traditions from the past. Occasionally, the nature of the written record makes it easy to identify folkloric content, and at other times perception is clouded by vague or unspoken details.[27] The following chapter deals with the work of Dan De Quille. His writings present a different type of primary source, with its own combination of opportunities and challenges.

CHAPTER 4

Dan De Quille the Folklorist

Corresponding from Silver City to Iowa's *Cedar Falls Gazette* on March 28, 1861, William Wright made use of an oral narrative he had heard. He had been publishing articles for more than a year, employing the name Dan De Quille, but now he was writing from the Nevada Territory, signed into existence by President James Buchanan only days before. A brief story tucked away in this letter is revealing about De Quille's natural inclination to conduct himself as a folklorist.[1]

De Quille described the circumstance of how he collected the tale, thereby providing valuable information: "I heard a big story here the other day of the sagacity of the Iowa horse. The story was told by a Dr. Pollock of this place, an Iowa man, and said to be strictly true; if it is there can be no harm in your knowing it, and if it ain't, why I can't help it." With this, the journalist provided Pollock's name and homeland, and De Quille also indicated that it was told in Silver City. He then proceeded to identify the anecdote as a legend, for it was told to be believed. De Quille went further with his skepticism, making it clear that this was not ordinary news that could be confirmed.

The narrative is about a horse being kept near a well with a windlass and a curb, the short circular stone wall designed to keep people and animals from falling down the open shaft. As De Quille wrote,

> The horse was in the habit of going to the well and drawing whenever he became thirsty. You will wonder how he could do this and imagine that he worked the crank by seizing it in his teeth—no such thing. How then could he do it? I hear you ask. . . . He would go to the well and if the bucket was not down in the well he would push it off its resting place on the curb with his nose, then after it had filled he would seize hold on the rope with his teeth and walk backwards until he found that the bucket had reached the curb. . . . He puts down first one of his fore feet, then the other on the rope, as it lies on the ground,

and thus walks up to the well, lifts the bucket to its place on the curb, and helps himself, like a smart horse, as he was![2]

De Quille then added the observation, "This is said to be a solemn fact, and is not impossible." He used the telling of this unlikely incident to transition to another, writing that "Now, as we are a little 'on it,' I will consider it my 'put in' and tell one of the same stamp." In this case, another Iowa horse presumably knew how to pump water. He followed this with a third narrative about a Nevada horse owned by a drunk, which he suggested had also been circulating. This features a courageous animal defending its intoxicated owner who had fallen to the ground and slumbered where he fell. A large rattlesnake was approaching the man, and the horse, in a fury, attacked the venomous creature, stomping it to death.[3]

As often happens with storytelling sessions, one narrative leads to another. In the first case, De Quille indicated that this was from oral tradition, identifying the source and circumstance of the telling. It is easy to imagine these three tales being told, one after another, as people gathered in Silver City in early 1861, and it is reasonably clear that the accounts were, indeed, being told. Too often, however, this is not obvious, and a degree of speculation must be applied.

The problem a folklorist encounters with many works by Wright is determining whether he was borrowing from oral tradition or writing his own stories. Gleaning references to folklore in Doten's journals is a challenge, but his intent is usually obvious. For Wright, it is another matter. He was, after all, an accomplished storyteller, both recounting what he had heard and creating his own narratives. Distinguishing between the two can be a challenge.

De Quille was one of the more famous nineteenth-century Nevada authors, with many valuable publications to his credit. Of these, his monumental book, *History of the Big Bonanza,* offers a particularly important window onto early Nevada. He became a journalist even as the Nevada Territory was establishing itself in the early 1860s. He then spent a lifetime reporting on the famed Comstock Mining District during the years of its greatest prosperity followed by its decline, beginning in the 1880s. His book is essential here because it relies heavily on anecdotes that offer hints about narratives that were popular at the time. No other writer was poised to know early Nevada better, and few could boast of having such a fine ear for the stories of the day.

Raised in Ohio, William Wright and his family moved to West Liberty, Iowa, when he was eighteen. In 1853, he married and began tending to his own family with three children who would survive infancy. Four years later in 1857, Wright went to California, hoping to find gold, but his efforts failed. In June 1860, he crossed the Sierra Nevada, attracted by the newly founded Comstock Mining District on the western edge of the enormous Utah Territory. As before, Wright was unsuccessful at mining. Instead, he fell upon his future career. He had written pieces for Iowa newspapers, and he even landed his work in the prestigious New York publication *Knicker-bocker Magazine.* Wright drew on that experience and began writing about the new diggings, submitting articles to the lauded San Francisco literary magazine the *Golden Era.*

Wright explored various pen names, and by 1860 he was using "Dan De Quille," which would serve him for nearly four decades. The moniker drew on the term "nom de plume," literally, "name of the feather or quill." Wright's choice can read as "Dandy Quille" (that is, a fine pen) or "Dan of the Quille" (that is, Dan of the pen). In addition, "De Quille" plays on his last name, a homophone, which sounds the same as "write." By late 1861, Wright attracted the attention of Joseph T. "Joe" Goodman, co-owner of Virginia City's *Territorial Enterprise,* where he soon became a full-time reporter.[4]

Although he was often troubled by alcoholism, De Quille's career was long and prolific. By the late 1880s, however, his personal life began to reflect the downturn in the Nevada mining economy, much as had happened with Doten. De Quille had extended periods of unemployment as editors waited for him to "dry out." At the same time, he found outlets in national news-papers for his work on the Comstock, and he began writing novellas, which went unnoticed during his lifetime. The effects of alcohol and age eventually combined to cause De Quille's health to decline, and in 1897 he returned to his family in Iowa, where he died the following year.[5]

In much of his writings, De Quille hoped to entertain rather than simply present information, and so he often documented narratives, which may have derived from contemporary oral tradition. Complicating matters from the perspective of folklore, De Quille was a celebrated master of the hoax in newspapers, the subject of the following chapter. These were exag-gerations or pure fabrications intended to lure people to believe, making them the butt of the joke. For the sake of parsing De Quille's *History of the Big Bonanza,* it is fortunate that he generally did not use this device in his book, intending it as a factual overview of the Comstock Mining Dis-trict. When he recorded narratives he had heard, it appears that they were told with the assumption of being true, meeting the folkloric definition of a local legend.[6]

De Quille's book is an obvious source of early western folklore, and his published letters from the beginning of his career demonstrate that his instinct to gather popular stories dated to his earliest writing. Several posts in the *Golden Era* capture what was apparently circulating at the time. In late 1860, he recorded an incident that supposedly occurred while the conflict between Paiutes and white settlers raged during the Pyramid Lake War in May. De Quille indicated, "I tell it as 'twas told to me,' not vouching for its truth in any particular," suggesting that the narrative was presented as truth, but that he had reason to doubt its veracity.[7] In the story, a pair of prospectors, unaware of the unfolding conflict, encountered some Paiutes who allow the miners to proceed unharmed because they deduced the men were not involved in the fight.

Similarly, De Quille wrote in the *Golden Era* in late 1861, reporting on something he had heard, an account about an attempt to cross the Sierra Nevada a year earlier.[8] While this contributes to an understanding of early folklore, De Quille's description of the storytelling session is of equal value:

> After supper we were all perfectly willing to stretch our weary limbs on blankets and packs about our camp-fire, and smoke and rest. As a matter of course, where there are a half-dozen old miners and mountaineers around a camp-fire, stories of the hard-ships endured and scenes witnessed in various parts of California, are sure to be told; and now Bob (Mr. Payne) spun us a yarn—a *true one*, mind; many who read this will recall the time and circumstance—of being caught in a terrible storm in the Sierras in the spring of '60.[9]

De Quille packed his accounts with details. It is rare for one of his European contemporaries, those who collected and published folklore in the nineteenth century, to have included this amount of information about the storyteller and the setting. According to De Quille, the narrator, Bob Payne, was a participant in the incident, but that is not to be trusted since people often relate legends as having been told firsthand by "a friend," even when further investigation often reveals that it was first told by "a friend of a friend," removing it from any reliable first-person original. Truth can evaporate, yet veracity does not matter when it comes to understanding how tales were told. What is important here is that De Quille painted a detailed portrait of a storytelling session.

The narrative itself involves about thirty men attempting to travel from Nevada City on the California side of the mountains to the mines of the Comstock. The winter of 1859–60 was notoriously harsh, and as soon as it seemed the snow would relent, would-be fortune seekers attempted the crossing, but as De Quille recounted, a late-spring storm could easily prove life-threatening. What could have been a tale of heroics transformed into a comedy at the expense of a German Jew, the sort of vicious ethnic humor that was a mainstay of American folklore and an opportunity to ridicule an immigrant's dialect. The "Dutcher" (Deutsch man; that is, a German) is never named, an indication that this is a generic figure rather than one who was part of a real adventure. He refused to allow others to drink from his bottle of whiskey even though whatever everyone had was shared. Because of this stinginess, the others took the bottle and distributed it among themselves, causing the immigrant to become sullen.

The troupe was caught in a snowstorm and struggled to proceed and make camp, fearful that some of their numbers might be lost and that they would be stranded without enough food. Their fire was under constant threat of being extinguished by snowmelt, and they were all obliged to gather wood so they would not freeze. The Dutcher, however, refused. The only food among them was owned by one of them, but he willingly shared the meager fare with all, who accepted their portions quietly, all except the Dutcher, who greedily demanded what he felt was owed to him.

Bob Payne subsequently gave him more than his fair share, and when others complained, Payne told them privately—but in a fashion that was loud enough for the Dutcher to hear—that they needed to keep their troublesome companion fat and alive. He was, after all, the fattest of them, and Payne asserted that it might be necessary to kill and butcher one of their party and that there was no better candidate than the disgruntled German traveler.

Hearing this, the Dutcher refused to eat, hoping that in due time he might no longer be the fattest of them. When he continued to refuse to retrieve wood, the others openly threatened him, suggesting that they might as well "harvest" him then and there. He subsequently spent the rest of the night retrieving wood to avoid the fate of being eaten. The next day, the group managed to retreat down the mountain, and the Dutcher revealed to Payne, who he felt had been his savior, that he still had two bottles of "schnapps," which he was willing to share privately. What unfolded is an offensive expression of anti-Semitism, but it illustrates De Quille's early interest in gathering stories. It also demonstrates the sort of ethnic humor that was common at the time, understanding that comedy focusing on race or religion invariably turns cruel.

De Quille's fascination with contemporary oral traditions is even better expressed in his later writings. He was untrained, yet he was a natural folklorist who frequently let readers know that he was relaying something he had heard. Unfortunately, his source is often unclear. The problem arises specifically when De Quille dealt with events from the earliest days of the mining district. He lived on the Comstock for many years and witnessed a great deal. Separating incidents that he recalled from stories he heard is consequently difficult.

In the case of De Quille's treatment of the famed teamster Hank Monk (1826–83) in *History of the Big Bonanza*, he provided insight into how the author dealt with local circulating stories. Monk was nationally famous for giving a stagecoach ride to New York journalist Horace Greeley (1811–72) in 1859, taking his ward over the Sierra Nevada. In De Quille's own words:

> Mr. Greeley was anxious to reach Placerville [California] as early as possible, as he was expected to make a speech to the people of the town, and once or twice expressed a fear that he should be behind time. Monk said nothing, as he was then on a long up-grade. At length the top of the mountain was reached, and Monk started on the down-grade at a fearful rate of speed. Mr. Greeley bounded about the coach like a bean in a gourd, and soon became greatly alarmed. He thrust his head out at the coach window and tried to remonstrate, but Monk only cried: "Keep your seat, Horace, I'll take you through on time!"[10]

De Quille's description of Greeley's initial objections is understated perhaps for comic effect, playing to those who already knew about the incident. The Monk-Greeley encounter was typically far more exaggerated than what De Quille slipped in, as he was merely establishing the setting for another narrative about Monk that apparently was popular at the time.

The Monk-Greeley anecdote was too ingrained in western lore for De Quille to ignore it in *History of the Big Bonanza*. Fortunately, he followed with another tale, and in doing so, he reveals something important about transitions in nineteenth-century western folklore: the humiliation of Greeley put the spotlight on Monk, making him a popular subject in other legends. Indeed, an article in the *Gold Hill Evening News* declared that "many amusing stories are told of Hank."[11]

De Quille gave truth to that assertion when he included a narrative involving a traveling lady with a "Saratoga bandbox." According to De Quille, this was an enormous trunk with three compartments, "about as long and wide as a first-class spring mattress and seven or eight feet high." The customer used the rail system to get it to Carson City, but then she wanted to take it to Lake Tahoe by stage. Its transport was a great burden, and so Monk procrastinated, repeatedly promising delivery on "the next trip." Monk eventually arrived at a means to turn the task into a joke. Finally, he gave a different answer to the lady when she once again asked for her luggage:

> "No, marm, I haven't brought it, but I think some of it will be up on the next stage."
> "Some of it!" cried the lady.
> "Yes; maybe half of it, or such a matter."
> "Half of it?" fairly shrieked the owner of the Saratoga.
> "Yes, marm; half to-morrow and the rest of it next day or the day after."
> "Why, how in the name of common sense can they bring half of it?"
> "Well, when I left they were sawing it in two, and—"
> "Sawing it in two! Sawing *my* trunk in two?"
> "That was what I said," coolly answered Monk. "Two men had a big cross-cut saw, and were working down through it—had got down about to the middle, I think."
> "Sawing my trunk in two in the middle!" groaned the lady. "Sawing it in two and all my best clothes in it! God help the man that saws *my* trunk!" . . . and in a flood of tears and a towering passion she rushed indoors, threatening the hotel-keeper, the stage-line, the railroad company, the town of Carson, and the State of Nevada with suits for damages. It was in vain that she was assured that there was no truth in the story of the sawing—that she was told that Monk was a great joker—she would not believe but that her trunk had been cut in two until it arrived intact; even then she had first to examine its contents most thoroughly, so strongly had the story of the sawing impressed itself on her mind.[12]

De Quille indicated that the "joke is still remembered and told at Lake Tahoe, but the ladies all say that they can't see that there is 'one bit of fun in it.'"[13]

With De Quille's assertion that the story circulated, it appears that it had become part of Tahoe folklore. Indeed, given Monk's popularity, it is easy to imagine that the narrative was told in the surrounding region. It is likely that the account of Greeley's wild ride promoted the popularity of the second story, satisfying a hunger for additional Monk tales.

Monk apparently played at least one other role in regional folklore, which maintained he inspired Levi Strauss to use rivets for his jeans. Wells

Drury, mentioned earlier as a second-generation Comstock journalist, wrote, "Hank Monk was wont to mend his clothing with copper harness-rivets in lieu of buttons. The legend recounts that a San Francisco clothing manufacturer, Levi Strauss . . . learned of . . . Hank's ingenious method; certain it is that he made a fortune in copper riveted overalls."[14] Monk did not inspire the rivets in Levi's jeans; instead, the teamster's fame wrongly caused credit for the trousers' copper-rivet hallmark to be attached to him. Using an abbreviated description of the Greeley incident, De Quille documented the process of how regional fame attracted further attention in the mid-1870s. Drury's account illustrates Monk's continued role as the subject of legend.

While De Quille's book offers many narratives apparently drawn from regional folklore, one of these focuses on the endemic dangers of living amid the mining industry. The story has the feel of being taken from oral tradition, but at the same time it serves as an example of how it is not always easy to evaluate De Quille's work. He claimed what followed really happened, yet he must have heard about it from someone. The setting describes a teamster who unhitched his oxen from a wagon so they could graze.

> They were fastened together in a string by a heavy log chain which passed through their several yokes. . . . In picking along they reached an old shaft, round which those on the lead had passed; then moving forward had so straightened the line as to pull a middle yoke into the mouth of the shaft. All then followed, going down like links of sausage. The shaft was three hundred feet in depth, and that bonanza of beef still remains unworked at its bottom.[15]

There may have been an actual event at the heart of this, but that does not disqualify its classification as folklore. Key, here, is whether people were telling a story.

A similar anecdote from De Quille involves someone in search of a lost goat. The man followed the tracks of his animal into an old adit.

> In walking back along the tunnel in the darkness he fell into a shaft in its bottom. The shaft was about eighty feet in depth, and he would probably have been instantly killed, but that there were at the bottom the bodies of four or five dead goats; as it was, he had an arm and a leg broken.
>
> The man being missed, his neighbors turned out in search of him. They found his tracks leading into the tunnel and went in after him, in Indian file. Suddenly the head man disappeared, he having in the dim

A BONANZA OF BEEF.

In 1876, Dan De Quille published an account of oxen being pulled into a mining shaft. The story likely circulated in local oral tradition. Wright, *History of the Big Bonanza* (1876); from the author's private collection.

light of the place, stepped into the mouth of the old shaft. From the groans heard below his friends knew that he had not been killed, and at once procured a windlass and rope and descended to his rescue, when, to their surprise, they found that they had two men in the bottom of the shaft. The man who last fell in had a leg broken, and by his fall came so near jolting the life out of the man of whom they at first came in search, that when first taken out it was thought he was dead.[16]

Tales of the danger of shafts left by industry balanced stories about the wealth produced. Perhaps because of the enormous amount of riches yielded by early Nevada mines, gold and silver bullion dominates much of early Nevada folklore. Reports of robberies and stashes of ill-gotten gains are also scattered throughout *History of the Big Bonanza* and resonate to this day.

De Quille devoted several pages to the subject of robberies on the Divide, the relatively uninhabited stretch of land between Gold Hill and Virginia City. There is ample evidence that robberies did occur there, and most, by their mundane nature, would not have been subjects of conversation for long afterward. A few of the incidents, real or imagined, presented unusual circumstances, and these figured into oral tradition. In two of these accounts, the anonymity of the players and the style of presentation suggest, once again, that the author may have borrowed from folklore.

One of these involves someone from Virginia City returning home from Gold Hill with three twenty-dollar gold pieces in his pocket. As De Quille described,

[He happened] to be sauntering along with his hands in his pockets [and] had the coin in his hand. Suddenly a masked man stepped before him and thrusting a pistol into his face, cried: "Hold up your hands, sir!" The gentleman held both hands high above his head, when the footpad searched his pockets and found nothing. The gentleman had closed his hand upon his three "twenties" and held them above his head while submitting to the search. The footpad was evidently much disappointed, as he said: "If you ever come along here again without any money, I'll take you a lick under the butt of the ear. That's what I'll do with you!"[17]

A second of these stories exploits ethnic humor. This narrative features "a stout young German" who was confronted by two robbers on the Divide,

one of whom placed a six-shooter at his head. The level-headed German just reached out and twisted the pistol out of the robber's hand; whereupon he and his partner in the business of collecting tolls from belated travelers took to their heels, zigzagging and dodging industriously in the expectation that a bullet would be sent after them. Some one asked the young German what put it into his head to go for the pistol. "Py dunder," said he, "I did vant him; because in der spring, you see, I goes to der Bannock country!"[18]

While this depicts the German immigrant as clever and resolute, not all stories about the foreign born were that generous.

For example, De Quille published a "Pat and Mike" joke focusing on an ethnic group that like many others suffered from cruelty in the early West. Because of the improbable content, this has the feel of having circulated orally at the time, even though, again, De Quille is not forthcoming with this detail. The story features two Irish miners, unemployed because a judicial injunction stopped work on an excavation until the owners could survey the property boundary and "bust the injunction." Walking home, Pat and

BUSTIN' THE INJUNCTION.

With people drawn to the West from throughout the world, racism and prejudice inspired vicious narratives about various groups. This illustration, and its accompanying text by Dan De Quille, ridicules Irish immigrants. Wright, *History of the Big Bonanza* (1876); from the author's private collection.

Mike encountered a costly piece of survey equipment near the mine, and they concluded (expressed in a painful mockery of their dialect to underscore their perceived stupidity) that this piece of sophisticated technology was, in fact, the guilty party. They attacked it with their tools, "bustin' up the injunction," with the hope of resolving the problem and being able to return to work.[19]

No matter how hurtful, immigrant stories were part of the give-and-take among the diverse population drawn by the discovery of mineral wealth. Folklorists throughout the mining West have documented similar traditions, but they can also be found elsewhere. American folklorist Richard Dorson recorded some of this humor in his book on immigrant stories from Michigan's Upper Peninsula and its copper mines.[20]

Similarly, in an immigrant or settler society, the last to arrive often became the most scorned in oral traditions. Another of De Quille's stories plays on just such a newcomer, a "pilgrim." A neophyte's unfamiliarity with the setting could present an opportunity for laughter. This fellow was drunk and had fallen asleep on a bench in front of an undertaker's business. The story has all the improbable hallmarks needed to question its veracity and to classify it as folklore. De Quille's account has a policeman who waking the man and telling him to find a room for sleeping or he would throw him in jail.

> The pilgrim sat up, and rubbing his eyes, explained to the officer that he was a stranger in the town; that he had but fifty cents in his pocket, and, the night being warm, he had concluded to sleep out of doors, and save his money to pay for a breakfast the next morning. Not being a hard-hearted man the officer told the fellow that he might finish his sleep, provided he would get up and move out of sight before people were astir in the streets.
>
> Passing the same way, in the course of an hour or two, the officer found that his man had rolled off the bench, and was lying at full length in the empty case of a coffin that was standing at the edge of the sidewalk close behind the bench. Rousing his "pilgrim" again, the officer told him he must "get out of that!"
>
> "Out o' what?" growled the fellow.
>
> "Why, out of that coffin!" said the officer—though it was only one of those coffin-shaped cases in which coffins are shipped.
>
> "Who's in a coffin?" asked the fellow, evidently becoming somewhat interested.[21]

What follows is an absurd dialogue involving the pilgrim's disbelief that he was asleep in a coffin. The officer warned him that if the undertakers caught anyone asleep in their coffins, they would put a lid on it, bury the victim, then send the bill to the county. The pilgrim responded, "I'd like to know what sort of dod-rotted set of undertakers you've got out here in this country, anyway, that go and set rows of coffins 'longside the sidewalks, fur to ketch corpses."[22]

Another anecdote takes advantage of the western distinction between one-bit saloons and those charging twice that amount. Patrons paid either a quarter (two bits) or ten to fifteen cents (a short bit or a long bit) for a beer, a whiskey, or a cigar, depending on the quality of the place and its offerings. Finer businesses prided themselves for being able to charge the higher prices because of their elegant appointments and excellent products.

De Quille's story features a man visiting a two-bit saloon for a drink. The man drank then placed a dime, a short bit, on the counter and turned to leave.

"This is a two-bit house, sir," said the proprietor, in a tone which showed that he felt some pride in the establishment.

"Ah!" said the customer. "Two-bit house, eh? Well, I thought so when I first came in, but after I had tasted your whiskey I concluded it was a bit house."[23]

This humorous anecdote about a saloon and drinking has the appearance of the sort of joke that would be told, perhaps at bars, whether charging one or two bits.

THESE, THEN, ARE SOME examples of stories from *History of the Big Bonanza* that appear to have been taken from oral tradition. After considering De Quille and Doten, it is possible to proceed with an understanding of how insights can be retrieved from primary sources and how they can cast light on the nineteenth-century West. At the same time, exposing the ways folklore insinuated itself into these two radically different documents serves as a reminder that this fundamental aspect of culture and daily life was as much a part of the past as it is in the present.

The opportunities and challenges of De Quille's book are distinct from those of Doten's journals. *History of the Big Bonanza* offers more than obscure references to contemporary culture. De Quille's writing is extroverted and geared for a broad readership with stories crafted to command attention. The challenge for the folklore researcher is to determine whether the author's narratives circulated orally or were his own invention. Sometimes De Quille generously mentioned that an account was part of conversation. Elsewhere, he was less helpful, allowing only hints about this.

De Quille's stories capture the essence of early Nevada folklore, preserved in the same way that many early European collectors recorded oral traditions. Just as their work was flawed, lacking modern recording devices, De Quille likely altered what he heard. Regardless, *History of the Big Bonanza* provides an opportunity to "hear" some of the voices of nineteenth-century westerners as they talked about their world. De Quille offered not only anecdotes but also a sense of the circumstance of storytelling sessions. It is easy to imagine that he captured some of the style of the telling and that the flair of local raconteurs affected his own prose.

Doten contrasts with De Quille in this regard. His journal drops references without the eloquence of the spoken word delivering a narrative. Indeed, the differences go deeper than this as the two sources drew on separate aspects of early western folklore. Doten's text serves as a reminder that each of the tens of thousands who arrived in the area brought their own cultural perspectives from somewhere else. Their distinct backgrounds confronted one another. Sometimes there were clashes, and occasionally some traditions blended.[24] With a handful of words, Doten revealed his personal ideas about belief and tradition, and occasionally he recorded something taken from emerging local folklore. This is true of the belief that Lake Tahoe would not yield its dead, a motif that can also be found elsewhere, and this is what occurred when Doten wrote of the mysterious flying vessel of the West, stories that were new and developing in the region.

De Quille's work offers a clearer view of the birth of western traditions. He documented stories as a fresh, commonly held folklore coalesced in the nineteenth-century West. Developing a shared oral tradition was, no doubt, a complicated process, and there is no way to know how many among the diverse residents and transients on the Comstock interacted with De Quille's stories. It is easy to imagine those born in the United States enjoying the anecdotes, but whether they were shared by all, including those from the many places in Europe or from China or by Native Americans, cannot be known. Fluency in English was no doubt a factor. Nevertheless, taken together, De Quille and Doten offer an opportunity to glimpse something of the unfolding folklore that would define early Nevada.

The legacies of Doten and De Quille serve as a reminder of how folklore is ubiquitous. At the risk of asserting that it is all folklore, the two journalists represent extreme possibilities: De Quille published a collection of stories, an obvious source of nineteenth-century western oral narrative, while Doten left a record of disparate information. Yet expressions of belief and tradition in both underscore how documents, regardless of their nature, can offer clues about the folklore of the past. And in the instances presented here and in the previous chapter, there is the opportunity to glimpse something fundamental that helped define early Nevada.

The literary legacy of De Quille is remarkable in the way that it recalls the valuable material published by nineteenth-century European folklore collectors. Had he and his contemporaries understood the nature of Nevada's early folklore, he might have been seen in that context. Despite being overlooked in this regard, Dan De Quille has been celebrated for his "quaints," the expertly conceived hoaxes that fooled so many. That aspect of his career is considered in the following two chapters, dealing with the spectrum of western folkloric expressions that relied on deceit in various forms.

CHAPTER 5

The Hoax as Folklore

Samuel Clemens came to work for the *Territorial Enterprise* in September 1862, his first full-time position as a writer.[1] Despite the occasional journalistic prank, the newspaper had gained a reputation for important, reliable reporting on the mines. For Clemens, authoring hoaxes was a natural thing. He enjoyed high jinks and placed little value on truth-telling. It would be several months before he picked his famous pen name, "Mark Twain," but he did not need that to begin exploring his brand of humor and deceit.

Within a few weeks of joining the *Enterprise staff,* Clemens wrote an article named "Petrified Man." With this, he unveiled the supposed discovery of a "stony mummy," perfect in its preservation. Clemens later indicated the device was intended to ridicule a craze in western papers for stories about petrified objects, and he also hoped to mock a local judge who found himself the object of the author's attention:

A petrified man was found some time ago in the mountains south of Gravelly Ford. Every limb and feature of the stony mummy was perfect, not even excepting the left leg, which has evidently been a wooden one during the lifetime of the owner—which lifetime, by the way, came to a close about a century ago, in the opinion of a savan who has examined the defunct. The body was in a sitting posture, and leaning against a huge mass of croppings; the attitude was pensive, the right thumb resting against the side of the nose; the left thumb partially supported the chin, the fore-finger pressing the inner corner of the left eye and drawing it partly open; the right eye was closed, and the fingers of the right hand spread apart. This strange freak of nature created a profound sensation in the vicinity, and our informant states that by request, Justice Sewell or Sowell, of Humboldt City, at once proceeded to the spot and held an inquest on the body. The verdict of the jury was that "deceased came to his death from protracted exposure," etc. The people of the neighborhood volunteered to bury the poor unfortunate, and were even anxious to do so; but it was discovered, when they

Samuel Clemens was still in the process of inventing himself as Mark Twain when he wrote his satirical article about a petrified man in 1862. After he left Nevada in May 1864, he arrived at a more familiar look, shown here in 1867. Photograph by Abdullah Fréres. Courtesy of the Library of Congress.

attempted to remove him, that the water which had dripped upon him for ages from the crag above, had coursed down his back and deposited a limestone sediment under him which had glued him to the bed rock upon which he sat, as with a cement of adamant, and Judge S. refused to allow the charitable citizens to blast him from his position. The opinion expressed by his Honor that such a course would be little less than sacrilege, was eminently just and proper. Everybody goes to see the stone man, as many as three hundred having visited the hardened creature during the past five or six weeks.[2]

Some outlets reprinted Twain's piece without suggesting that it was a hoax, while others revealed it to be just that. The *Virginia City Evening Bulletin*, for example, referred to it as "A Washoe Joke."[3]

Although the content of the article was the author's invention rather than a matter of tradition, the genre of the hoax has attracted the attention of folklorists who regard it as part of their domain. While Loomis underscored the importance of deception in the region's oral tradition, even he had to acknowledge the paradox in western journalistic hoaxes: they did not initially circulate orally, even though this type of western humor, including its structure, was something governed by folklore. To complicate matters, a well-played published deception could be recounted for years afterward, becoming its own traditional narrative.[4]

The western hoax, the focus here, is entwined with tall tales, briefer burlesque lies, and practical jokes, all of which are discussed in the following chapter. These related approaches to humor share an element of deception and often exaggeration. Falsehood in its various forms often built upon itself until the absurdity is clear to most, establishing a dynamic of a storyteller, the insiders who understand the prank, and the outsiders who are oblivious. Humor is found in the tension between these three players, typically leaving the last ones failing to realize what is intended as the brunt of the prank.[5]

The hoax was by no means strictly a western genre, but applying the term widely is problematic because it implies that the various early manifestations were similar. The word "hoax" was relatively young when articles labeled in this way appeared in western newspapers in the 1860s. The term likely derives from the phrase "hocus pocus" and first appeared in the English language at the end of the eighteenth century.[6] A benchmark early hoax was little more than a swindle, an attempt in February 1814 to manipulate the London Stock Exchange with a false report of Napoleon's defeat. As a journalistic device in North America, the hoax manifested on the East Coast by the 1830s.[7] In the West, deceptions in newspapers played out differently, with any overlap in eastern and western hoaxes sometimes seeming more a matter of a shared term than of belonging to the same species.

Loomis treated the deception-related work of western writers as tall tales. Dan De Quille called his articles fitting into this genre "quaints." Twain sometimes referred to his efforts as satire, an observation that hoax authority Lynda Walsh echoes when she writes, "In a satire the audience is 'in' on the joke, whereas in a hoax the reader is a victim of the joke."[8] A gray zone exists in that some of the western audience was in on the joke while others were not. In early Nevada, a hoax depended on walking a fine line where a reasonable number of readers understood the prank. If only a few grasped the humorous intent, it might fail, but if there were too many who recognized the ruse, the writing was easily assessed as flat and uninteresting. Whether termed tall tale, quaint, satire, or hoax, what was happening in the West was distinct from hoaxes as they unfolded on the East Coast.

Edgar Allan Poe famously employed this form of deceit with his balloon hoax of 1844. Nine years earlier, the *New York Sun* had captivated thousands with an account about an astronomer using an extremely powerful tele-scope to observe lunar inhabitants, including "Man-Bats," who seemed to rival humanity for intellectual capacity. The *Sun* exploited the opportunity to increase readership and profit. Poe hoped to replicate the success, but a duped readership was wary of another deception. Although his story about a transatlantic journey by balloonists was brilliant, he wanted acclaim for his genius. He quickly revealed the trick, so its life span was brief.[9]

These expressions of the fantastic in journalism are a step removed from what would happen in the West. Eastern journalistic hoaxes sought sustained increased readership. They were not as much of a swindle as the English one in 1814, but they were, nevertheless, a type of financial scam. The longer people believed a series of articles, the better, for that would result in more sales and subscriptions. The *Sun* even produced a special booklet with lithographs for its 1835 moon hoax, increasing profits significantly. That ruse, like Poe's later transatlantic balloon story, was written to be as convincing as possible. Eastern authors took great care to use technical jargon and math-ematical computations so that even some scientists wondered about the veracity of the stories.[10]

The journalistic hoax of the West was a species apart. These were del-icately crafted pieces that blended the realistic with the absurd to achieve humor. Editors were, of course, glad to have more readers purchasing news-papers, but proceeds did not depend on duping the readers. Success was measured by the degree that humor was achieved, and editors hoped that an appreciation of ingenuity would increase subscriptions. Western journal-ists felt they had succeeded when those who understood the deception were balanced against the victims caught believing the account. Secondarily, the western hoax could also function as a humorous way to ridicule someone.[11] For either purpose, it became a revered institution in the West.

"Petrified Man," by Clemens, is an excellent example of how a western hoax functioned. Key to the tradition was that it must have a "tell," an indi-cation of why the story could not be true and should not be accepted as fact. The best hoaxes had one or more precisely placed clues that a thoughtful reader could understand and thereby recognize the article for what it was, a falsehood sufficiently obscure to trick the gullible.[12] An obvious tell in "Petrified Man" was the intricate description of the corpse's hands. A care-ful reader who replicated what Clemens was describing would find that the so-called fossil was thumbing his nose at someone. In this case, the point of ridicule was apparently the judge.

A year later with the publication of "A Bloody Massacre near Carson," Clemens, now writing as Mark Twain, found himself attacked for a poorly played hoax. Editors who reprinted the article—together with many readers—felt Twain had violated the important rule that required a conspicuous clue, a tip that it was an intended joke. There were calls for Twain's dismissal because this horrifying effort was too believable. People maintained that it had ceased to be satire and was merely a revolting lie deprived of humor.[13]

"A Bloody Massacre near Carson" featured a despondent investor who had lost everything, bilked by a California developer in the Bay Area, the intended object of ridicule. Twain maintained that the fraudulent nature of the story should have been obvious because the killings were in a forest situated at Empire to the east of Carson City where barely a tree could grow. He also had the father of the family, the murderer of his wife and children, riding into Carson City after slashing his own throat, an injury that would have quickly killed him.

Learning of his explanation, critics nevertheless pointed out that the clues were less apparent than the author maintained and that most readers were so repulsed by the blood-soaked description that they did not realize the deception. In addition, misdirection about the location would not have been recognized by California editors who reprinted the article in good faith, and the murderer's wound to the neck might not have been that deep and immediately fatal. Although Twain protested that the subterfuge was obvious, he violated an honored rule in comedy, namely, that if a joke needs to be explained, it is not funny.[14]

Compared with his disastrous final effort at deceit while reporting for the *Territorial Enterprise,* the shortcomings of "A Bloody Massacre near Carson" seem minor. In May 1864, Twain authored a scurrilous attack on Carson City women—including his own sister-in-law—who raised money for wounded Union soldiers through the Sanitary Fund, a precursor of the Red Cross. His full article does not survive, but what is clear is that he insinuated the women considered using funds to support miscegenation, marriage between the races. In a weak ploy to soften the scandalous uproar that was certain to follow, Twain wrote that the accusation "was a hoax, but not all a hoax, for an effort is being made to divert those funds from their proper course."[15]

Many have addressed how Twain's failed effort nearly ended in a duel, forcing him to flee Nevada. The episode is typically celebrated as a necessary thing, the impetus for moving on to greater things. The point here is to understand how the western genre of the humorous hoax was implemented and how it could easily fail. The term "miscegenation" was invented with the December 1863 publication of a pamphlet: *Miscegenation: The Theory of the Blending of the Races, Applied to the American White Man and Negro.* This bigoted deception was intended to persuade voters to believe that Lincoln and the Republican Party supported intermarriage between the races. The pamphlet was put forward in the fashion of eastern hoaxes, humorless and without clues about its falsehood. In keeping with eastern practices, the point was to keep the story alive as long as possible. A testament to its success, the fraud was not fully discredited until after the presidential election of November 1864. That aside, the pamphlet managed to introduce a venom-laced term into the English language.[16]

The controversy of the political miscegenation deceit was in full bloom when Twain, much to his discredit, decided to put his oar in those treacherous, racist waters. His response to the libelous pamphlet of 1863 was more akin to the eastern genre of the hoax, lacking humor or a cleverly crafted clue about its falsehood. Twain later insisted that he had been toying with humorous satire and that on the advice of Dan De Quille, he realized it failed as a joke, after which he decided to discard it. He contended that a printer for the *Enterprise* subsequently found the document and published it. Again, what exactly happened is subject to conjecture; here it merely serves to illustrate how soft the boundary between the eastern and western hoaxes could be.

Drawn in by a political fraud in the East, Twain weakly attempted to transform a mean-spirited political attack into a humorous prank. His effort at comedy lacked a clear clue about its deception. Once again as happened with "A Bloody Massacre near Carson," Twain's toying with this western genre failed.

WHEN IT CAME TO exploiting the western hoax, De Quille had far more success than his colleague. Even Twain made it clear that his colleague's understanding of the regional genre deserved respect. He recalled his conversation with De Quille about the failed miscegenation article in the following way: "I wrote & laid that item before Dan when I was not sober . . . and said he, 'Is this a joke?' I told him 'Yes.' He said he would not like such a joke as that to be perpetrated upon him, & that it would wound the feelings of the ladies of Carson. He asked me if I wanted to do that, & I said, 'No, of course not.'"[17] De Quille appreciated the fact that the heart of the western hoax was humor, and this separated it from its more malicious eastern cousin; Twain's failures took him on a darker path.

In 1954, journalistic pundit Lucius Beebe summarized his impressions of the work of Twain and De Quille with this genre: "De Quille's hoaxes . . . had none of the aspect of personal malice which characterized the imitative

Constructed in 1863, the *Territorial Enterprise* building on the west side of North C Street served the famed newspaper until it burned in 1875. With access to the second-floor offices from B Street, Nevada's most famous journalistic hoaxers, including Mark Twain and Dan De Quille, worked at this location. Courtesy of Special Collections and University Archives Department, University of Nevada, Reno, Libraries.

stories of Mark Twain. [De Quille's] were meticulously devised and so altogether preposterous as to rank as masterpieces of American folklore."[18] Key here is Beebe's word "preposterous," for without that element, the manifestations in the West would have been little more than the frauds put forward in the East. One approaches Twain's hoaxes, occasionally successful but often stumbling, as literary curiosities because of the heights that he would achieve later in life writing novels. De Quille's quaints, on the other hand, typify a western genre so well that they can be taken as its ideal expression.

Loomis explored several of De Quille's quaints, including "A Bug Mine," "The Silver Man," and "The Solar Armor." The last of these, also appearing as "Sad Fate of an Inventor," serves as an excellent example of De Quille's expertise. On July 2, 1874, the *Territorial Enterprise* published De Quille's account of Jonathan Newhouse's invention of "Solar Armor." This simple, direct article described how Newhouse had devised a suit and hood made of "common sponge . . . about an inch in thickness," designed to protect the wearer from the worst that a summer sun could inflict upon a traveler. De Quille then wrote how,

> Before starting across the desert, this armor was to be saturated with water. Under the right arm was suspended an Indian rubber sack filled with water and having a small . . . tube leading to the top of the hood. In order to keep the armor moist, all that was necessary to be done by the traveler as he progressed over the burning sands, was to press the sack occasionally, when a small quantity of water would be forced up and thoroughly saturate the hood and the jacket before.[19]

De Quille explained that by controlling the evaporation of the moisture, "any degree of cold" could be achieved. Newhouse tested his equipment in Death Valley, letting those at his camp know that he would return in two days. The following day, a Native American came to the place where Newhouse's friends waited, telling them to follow. He then led the party "to a human figure seated against a rock. Approaching they found it to be Newhouse still in his armor. He was dead and frozen stiff. His beard was covered with frost and—though the noonday sun poured down its fiercest rays—an icicle over a foot in length hung from his nose. There he had perished miserably, because his armor had worked but too well."[20]

The clue that proves the hoax is the absurd idea that water evaporation could freeze someone in the summer of Death Valley, and more so that he would still be frozen a day later. As Walsh describes, news of the "report" reached London, where the *Daily Telegraph* attempted to evaluate the invention and the tragic results of its application. That article concluded with suspicion, but according to the rules of the genre there were three potential reactions: belief, skepticism, and understanding the joke within. Only the last of these is the way to emerge unscathed; to engage in the other two is to fall susceptible to the web of deceit and to become the object of the joke. Even if skepticism is a step removed from total gullibility, it still indicates a failure to appreciate the humor.[21]

De Quille could not ignore the opportunity presented, so he fashioned a new article with additional "information." He indicated that more details of the incident had reached Virginia City, suggesting that the substance that Newhouse had used was not water alone but rather a solution of assorted chemicals that enhanced the evaporation process, creating the freezing effect. De Quille added a new scientific layer to the hoax, making it slightly more plausible, but this was merely a matter of reeling in fish that were already hooked. It remained an impossibility for someone in the 1870s to carry the equipment needed to produce such a deep freeze, lasting a day or more in that hottest of environments. This was especially hard to believe given that after he had died, he could no longer operate the mechanism.

For a western audience to see others—particularly those from the East or from Europe—falling for a hoax increased the delight. As Wells Drury noted, "When the newspapers of the Coast took Dan [De Quille] to task for his trifling, Dan only laughed and resolved never to do it again, but the next time that items were scarce he was tempted and fell from grace. These diversions, of course, were only occasional. . . . In his regular work Dan was a model of method and accuracy. This made his hoaxes all the more dangerous."[22]

A test of the folkloric strength of a hoax can be seen in its ability to transform into oral tradition as its own narrative, which others repeated as a story. Drury recounted the example of "The Solar Armor," but his details were different from De Quille's work, suggesting that his recollection was surviving outside written documentation. Similarly, Loomis mentions others who recounted the anecdote, each with variation, again a good indication that the hoax was continuing in conversation, garnering laughter after the original articles were published.[23]

These examples give expression to the tradition and to the rules that governed the genre. While a hoax in the West was false, it had to walk a narrow path separating the believable from the unlikely. Anything that was incorrect but entirely plausible was merely a lie, and there was no fun in that. Craftsmanship was in the execution, delivering the joke with a careful balance between the possible and the inconceivable. As a western hoax appeared in eastern newspapers or crossed the Atlantic, the "play" was in many ways unfair since that audience did not necessarily understand the rules of the game. Nevertheless, westerners laughed when a ruse endured.

THE MOST FAMOUS OF De Quille's quaints, "The Traveling Stones of Pahranagat Valley," resonated for the longest time on the international stage. It has been acclaimed as an expression of De Quille's genius with the genre, yet there can be some question about intent. Exactly what De Quille had in mind when he wrote the initial newspaper article cannot be known, but a careful examination of the original text indicates that this may not have begun as a hoax. Rather, De Quille may have been taken in by a legend he had heard.

There is no shame if De Quille took something at face value and then wrote about it. Modern newspapers regularly publish urban legends, presented as truth until they are exposed as folklore. If honesty were to rule the day, there is likely no folklorist who can profess never to have been caught by one of these stories. Legends are honed to be entirely believable, unlike the western hoax, which should be crafted with a clear clue about its false character.

The *Territorial Enterprise* published De Quille's original account of "The Traveling Stones of Pahranagat Valley" on October 26, 1867. He wrote about something observed in a remote valley of the state: A prospector in the Pahranagat area, "the wildest and most sterile portion of southeastern Nevada," collected round stones, which De Quille identified as being "of an irony nature." These were attracted to one another, presumably because they were "formed of a loadstone or magnetic iron ore." De Quille described the behavior of the curiosities: "When scattered about on the floor, on a table, or other level surface, within two or three feet of each other, they immediately began traveling toward a common center, and then huddled up in a bunch like a lot of eggs in a nest. A single stone removed to a distance of a yard, upon being released, at once started off with wonderful and somewhat comical celerity to rejoin its fellows; but if taken away four or five feet, it remained motionless." De Quille went on to say that the prospector had told him how these rolling stones could be found in "little basins, from a few feet to two or three rods in diameter, and it is in the bottom of these basins that the rolling stones are found."[24]

Lacking any clue that this might be false, De Quille's 1867 article fails as a hoax, at least as it was practiced in the West. Walsh suggests that there was a "wink-and-nudge" when he wrote of the ore as being "of an irony nature." She contends the term served as the clue that this was intended as a joke, yet De Quille may have been merely referring to the iron-like nature of the objects.[25] In addition, according to the "rules" of the western hoax, something this vague was insufficient to serve as a tip that something was afoot. What he wrote was, in fact, completely credible, and indeed, diverse people, apparently including P. T. Barnum and some German scientists, corresponded with the *Enterprise*, asking De Quille for some of the rocks.[26]

De Quille responded that he did not have the stones in his possession. Perhaps he reevaluated what he had written in 1867 and, according to this interpretation, realized either that his quaint was a failure or that he, himself, had been duped. He addressed the situation at least four more times, twice shifting more obviously into the realm of a hoax. In 1872, in answer to an inquiry from Colorado, De Quille wrote of his original story, "The item has been going the rounds ever since without any one being able to suggest any plan by which money might be made out of them. A request has recently come to the local postmaster for five pounds of the stones . . . We have none of said rolling stones in this city at present but would refer our Colorado speculator to Mark Twain, who probably has still on hand fifteen or twenty bushels of assorted sizes."[27]

With this, De Quille revealed an intent to see the traveling stones as one of his quaints. His clue is in directing the inquiry to Mark Twain, the comic effect of which would have been obvious to most. By distancing himself from the first report, he could claim that he had originally intended it as a joke, perhaps avoiding the need to admit that he had wrongly accepted the original account.

De Quille employed the traveling stones once again, this time in 1876 in his *History of the Big Bonanza*; in this case, he provided a frame with a new clue that allowed the original article to shift even more into the realm of the hoax. In his book, he wrote how a man from Missouri named Pike had climbed Grizzly Hill, overlooking Silver City. He came rushing back full of excitement, claiming he found "millions of tons" of "the stuff they make compasses of." Pike then explained that he considered the rock to be so valuable that it could serve as a new form of transportation, where ships could use its attractive power to move across oceans.

De Quille went on to describe, "Pike had several assays of his 'find' made, and it was weeks before he could be made to believe that it was not something of more value than magnetic iron ore." De Quille then transitioned, reprinting the text of his original 1867 article, with the following introduction: "Some years after Pike's great discovery, a prospector who had been roaming through the Pahranagat Mountains . . ."[28]

With this, De Quille gave Comstockers a clue that everything about the traveling stones was to be questioned. Anyone familiar with the mineral deposits within the mining district would know that there was no sizable vein of magnetite on Grizzly Hill. In addition, and as discussed in the following chapter, the generic name "Pike" referred to simple country folk of northeastern Missouri; De Quille's peers were likely to recognize that this character was being presented as a fictional, humorous device. These were ways of letting Nevadans in on the joke, but it completely transformed the original matter-of-fact report, solidly turning it, now, into a hoax, just as it is understood to this day.

There was, however, something that continued to rouse De Quille's interest in the topic. In 1879, he declared in the *Territorial Enterprise* that "in an idle moment, some fifteen years ago," he "concocted and wrote an item entitled 'Traveling Stones.'" He now framed the entire incident as a quaint of his invention, writing, "We desire to throw up the sponge and acknowledge the corn; therefore we solemnly affirm that we never saw or heard of any such diabolical cobbles as the traveling stones of Pahranagat." Through each of his declarations, De Quille never pointed out the "tell" in the original article that should have tipped off the careful reader, the clue that would separate the insiders from those left believing.

In addition, as Walsh notes, the account of these marvelous objects was the only one of his hoaxes that De Quille revealed in print.[29] Indeed, this is also the only one of his quaints without a readily discernible clue to identify it as false. If this were intended as a western hoax, it fails. De Quille was too talented to stumble this profoundly.

De Quille's statement in 1879 enhances the idea that the original treatment of the subject was credible; he wrote of the traveling stones that "we still think there ought to be something of the kind somewhere in the world." With this, he attested to the plausibility of his 1867 article.[30] Adding to the believability of moving stones in the Pahranagat is the fact that something like this exists to the west in Death Valley. Rocks there are well documented for leaving paths etched across the playa, representing a curiosity for decades. The movement is apparently caused by a combination of ice, water, and wind, but that recent conclusion was unknown in the nineteenth century.[31] The phenomenon from Death Valley could have given strength to a legend about moving magnetic stones in the Pahranagat region.

A connection with Death Valley can be found in an expedition of Nevada governor Henry Blasdel from Carson City, through the Death Valley area to Pahranagat, to consider mining discoveries in the area. The trip during the spring of 1866 nearly turned to disaster as the travelers encountered life-threatening environments. After the group safely returned to Carson City, news from the Pahranagat Valley circulated.[32] One can easily imagine that there were also reports of the traveling stones of Death Valley, easily confused with Pahranagat, the ultimate objective of the expedition. There is no way to know if this inspired a local legend about magnetic stones, but it is not impossible, and the timing with De Quille's 1867 article seems more than coincidence.

Finally, in 1892, De Quille wrote of the traveling stones again, this time for the *Salt Lake Daily Tribune*. With this, he provided yet another explanation of his original intent. De Quille described how word of the wonders of the Pahranagat Valley had inspired people to tell him about how they had also encountered remarkable rocks. Whatever De Quille hoped to achieve, his discussions of traveling stones piqued curiosity, and people were responding with their own accounts of similar phenomena. More important, he indicated that the object of his initial article "was to set the many prospectors then ranging the country to looking for such things."[33]

This reinforces the idea that De Quille may have considered his initial article to be true. Nevertheless, Walsh sees this as further evidence that De Quille was creating an elaborate deception, which unfolded over a quarter century.[34] At the same time, Walsh astutely observes that another author of hoaxes, Edgar Allan Poe, may not have intended his short work of fiction "The Facts in the Case of M. Valdemar" as a deception, but when readers assumed it to be true, Poe "began referring to the story as a 'hoax' to pump up its celebrity."[35] The same thing may have happened with De Quille's account of the stones from Pahranagat.

Whatever the case, there are two possibilities, both entwined with the folklore of the West. The first article was either a legend that De Quille had heard or a poorly executed hoax, itself an aspect of western folklore. He may have been a victim of his own success: De Quille had often exhibited literary genius with his quaints, and coincidentally, his traveling stones had reached an international audience.

For a Nevada journalist to "pull one over" on the world was a clear path to fame. If this was originally something he thought was true and then placed in the *Enterprise,* he became trapped. He would not easily admit that he had been fooled by his own quaint.

WELLS DRURY PERPETUATED THE perception of the Pahranagat story in his memoir, published decades later in 1936: "Who of the old-timers will forget [De Quille's] pseudo-erudite account of 'The Traveling Stones of Pahranagat Valley'? With feigned scientific minuteness he showed how these traveling stones were by some mysterious power drawn together and then scattered wide apart, only to be returned in moving, quivering masses to what appeared to be the magnetic center of the valley."[36]

Despite the celebration of De Quille's most famous ruse, its shortcomings cannot be overlooked. Embedded in the folk tradition of the West, a hoax without a "tell" is merely a lie. Even though the two are cousins, a hoax and a lie should manifest differently. Writers like De Quille and Mark Twain celebrated the western hoax, but the simple burlesque lie and its lengthier sibling, the tall tale, represent slightly different brands of trickery in the region's folklore. So too with the practical joke, which is yet another distinct species. A fine line distinguished the two camps: a hoax had to be believable but for a detail or two that pointed clearly to its being false.

Burlesque lies and tall tales succeed by extending into such incredible exaggeration that their increasing absurdity is laughable. As Carolyn Brown explains, tall tales often begin with the plausible, quickly turning "from the mildly improbable, through the physically impossible, to the mind-jarringly illogical."[37] Like the hoax, tall tales and burlesque lies can be told with insiders who understand the premise of the performance and outsiders who are left bewildered, unsure what to think as the story unfolds. This, then, is the subject of the following chapter.

CHAPTER 6

Tall Tales and Other
Deceptions as Folklore

BEGINNING IN THE 1960s and occasionally over the course of subsequent decades, some old hand would invite me to try smart pills. I never accepted them and perhaps consequently remain a shade short of smart. Indeed, some might assert the shortcoming is more than slight. A smart pill is a folk remedy for stupidity. How and when smart pills entered Nevada folklore is not easy to determine, but the motif has roots that reach back at least to the Italian Renaissance, so it may have been in Nevada long before I first heard of the cure.[1]

In 1977, folklorist Richard Bauman recorded a story about a smart pill in Oklahoma. In the narrative, someone was selling dupes rolled-up pieces of dog dung, telling his victims that if taken, the pill would make them smarter. A fool purchased and swallowed several pills, repeatedly indicating that he did not feel any smarter. The cycle repeats until he finally realizes what the pills are, at which point he objects, but the trickster declares that since the man has realized the ploy, he has, indeed, become smarter, so the pills have worked.[2]

My invitations to become smarter have occurred in the wide-open Nevada terrain, with joking offers of rabbit or deer pellets. The point here is the role of deception as part of western folklore. Besides being an essential element of the hoax, deceit is also at the heart of tall tales, burlesque lies, and practical jokes, all of which are important to regional traditions. The smart pill ranks among these, but as Bauman demonstrates, the device does not merely consist of the execution of such a deception. Like hoaxes, a practical joke can take on its own life if it becomes a traditional story. Indeed, some were immortalized as celebrated narratives. Others may have been nothing more than that.

At the outset, it is important to acknowledge that deception is not unique to western or even American folklore. It enjoys a time-honored place internationally. The tall tale, for example, can be found in the work of the

Greek writer Plutarch (ca. 46–119), who described a remote land where the temperature can become so cold that words freeze and cannot be heard until they thaw in spring. In 1528, a similar story of the exaggerated effect of frozen words appeared in Count Baldassare Castiglione's *The Book of the Courtier.*[3] Ludicrous exaggeration has long been a device in both oral and written versions.

One of the more famous examples of hyperbolic stories was the late eighteenth-century classic by Hanover-born Rudolf Erich Raspe (ca. 1736–94), who first published his *Baron Munchausen's Narrative of His Marvellous Travels and Campaigns in Russia* in 1786. His book was based on the overstated accounts of a real person, Baron Hieronymus Karl Friedrich von Münchhausen (1720–97). Despite having a life of adventure, including fighting in the Russo-Turkish War (1735–39), he nevertheless inflated his experiences.

Raspe found inspiration in von Münchhausen's embellishments, and he subsequently exaggerated the exaggerations, while also adding new adventures. With Raspe's eloquent pen, his fictional Munchausen (with a slightly different spelling) fought a gigantic crocodile, twice journeyed to the moon, survived escapades underwater within and outside a whale, rode a half horse, and traveled on a cannonball through the air. The stories became literary tall tales, the object of humor because of their absurdity. The publication of Raspe's mocking book resulted in a furious von Münchhausen, who threatened a lawsuit.[4] The fictitious adventures of Baron Munchausen set a high bar for those who would seek humor in overstatement, but many rose to the challenge.

While living in London, Benjamin Franklin famously wrote a letter to the *Public Advertiser* about American sheep being so thick with wool that farmers had to use four-wheeled wagons to carry their heavy tails. Franklin's portrait of a remarkable America had many other astounding features, including whales leaping up Niagara Falls, a phenomenon that "is esteemed, by all who have seen it, as one of the finest spectacles in nature."[5] The correspondence was in answer to another note, likely also penned by Franklin, who was using the names "The Spectator" and "The Traveller" for an epistolary feud of his own making. The letters offered an opportunity to address misconceptions and to exhibit aspects of the American colonies. Most of all, it was a chance for Franklin to demonstrate that Americans could join the ranks of Raspe and other Europeans when it came to the entertaining use of exaggeration.[6]

Franklin's foray into the tall tale underscores a fundamental truth about the expression of deceit as humor: stories that rely on absurd exaggeration have deep roots in Europe, but it would soon become a natural realm to explore in North America. What follows underscores that while the genre was not unique to the West, the tall tale became essential to the region's folklore. As author Richard Erdoes commented in his collection from the West, "The essence of American legends, particularly of western tales, is exaggeration. Nowhere else in the world can one find boastful grandiloquence like this. . . . In western tales everything is larger than life, blown up out of all proportions." Indeed, the tall tale is popularly associated with the Wild West, even though it is widespread elsewhere.[7]

Distinguishing hoaxes from tall tales—and from practical jokes and briefer burlesque lies—is a challenge. Walsh suggests that a difference can be found in the hoax being written, while the tall tale is oral, but published examples of the genre by Raspe and Franklin challenge this.[8] It is probably better to consider how the tall tale and the literary hoax occupy space on the same spectrum of stories exploiting deception. It is easier to distinguish between the two in the East. Regardless of the location, the tall tale is typified by its absurdity, often escalating with exaggeration or logical inconsistencies. This is distinct from the eastern hoax, which attempts to present a falsehood as cleverly as possible, devoid of clues about the deception.

In the West, the distinction is less clear. At times it seems possible to separate the two with the matter of newspaper publication, the journalistic hoax being a creature of print, while the tall tale was usually a spoken narrative. Even so, the latter sometimes also filled space in a newspaper's columns. A less obvious distinction is that the growing absurdity of a tall tale was different from the concealed irrationality of a literary western hoax. In the latter, the trick was discovered with careful reading, while for the tall tale, the increasing levels of farce inspired a growing share of the audience to understand the nature of the joke.

THE BEST DEFINITIONS GROW from examples. Perhaps more than anyone, James William Emery Townsend (1838–1900) came to epitomize the art of the tall tale in early western folklore. He learned to be a printer while still living in New Hampshire, the place of his birth. Townsend traveled to California with the excitement of the 1849 Gold Rush and eventually became involved in Pacific Coast journalism. There, he worked as a typesetter, printer, and editor, all the while gaining fame as a humorist.

Mostly, Townsend was known as a notable liar, an assessment meant in the most honorific of ways, for he was affectionately referred to as Lying Jim.[9] Alluding to a typesetter's case of letters used to create a sheet of newsprint, Wells Drury commented that Townsend was "by all odds the most original writer and versatile liar that the west coast, or any other coast, ever produced. He kept the West laughing for years with his quaint sayings which he set up from the case as they came to mind. They never saw manuscript. He simply set the type when he felt like expressing an idea."[10]

A hard-drinking journalist, Townsend worked in Virginia City, Carson City, and Reno in Nevada and Bodie and Lundy in California. For a short time beginning in 1859, he was with famed California author Bret Harte, serving on the staff of San Francisco's prestigious literary publication the *Golden Era*.[11] Harte apparently used Lying Jim as his inspiration for Truthful James, a fictional character bearing an ironic twist on a celebrated moniker.[12]

Mark Twain knew Lying Jim well. The two worked at the *Territorial Enterprise* at the same time, earning Townsend a place in *Roughing It*. More important, it is likely that Twain took inspiration from Lying Jim's tall tales. In fact, Townsend published an early version of the jumping-frog story in the *Sonora Herald* in 1853, long before Samuel Clemens came to the West and eventually transformed the competitive Calaveras amphibian into a ticket to national fame.[13] By all accounts, Townsend's best expressions of the tall tale were during verbal performances in saloons rather than with articles in newspapers—although the latter impressed a wide readership for many years.

The *Virginia Chronicle* reported on May 27, 1882, that Townsend had secured employment with Reno's *Gazette*. It became an opportunity to summarize Lying Jim's life to that point, in keeping with Townsend's own manner of elaboration. Virginia City's newspaper provided a biography that would have outcompeted anything attributed to the famed, fictional Baron Munchausen. The article asserted that Townsend's mother, a woman of English nobility, was the only survivor of a shipwreck, after which she gave birth to her son.[14]

The newspaper proceeded to describe how Townsend's mother was eaten by cannibals, who then raised the baby, hoping to fatten him for a later feast. At twelve, he escaped by paddling a log through the Straits of Magellan at which point a whaling ship rescued him and brought him to New Bedford, Massachusetts. He subsequently became a Methodist minister for a decade and then went to Hawaii as a missionary, serving there for another twenty years. "Then he reformed and returned to New York and opened a saloon, which he ran successfully and made a large fortune."

The account continued with how Townsend then tried his hand at journalism, and although it was "to the world's advantage," the change of occupations led him back to preaching, leaving him once more impoverished. He persevered for three decades before resuming his work in the saloon trade, spending an additional eighteen years on the East Coast before traveling to the West in 1849. "For several years Mr. Townsend simultaneously ran eight saloons, five newspapers and an immense cattle ranch in various parts of the Golden State."

The article then asserted that in 1859, he suffered from a disease that forced him to remain in bed for several months, for which he was known by the nickname "Lying Jim," a moniker that had nothing to do with deceit, if we are to believe the contents of the article. Townsend subsequently spent a decade in journalism, leaving him once again in poverty. The article concluded with a summary of Lying Jim's extensive experiences: "Some of his friends who are of a mathematical turn have ascertained from data furnished them by Mr. Townsend in various conversations the remarkable fact that he is 384 years old. Notwithstanding his great age, however, the gentleman still writes with the vigor of youth, and his shrewd humor is making for the Gazette more than a local reputation."[15]

It would be easy to proclaim Lying Jim Townsend as the Baron von Münchhausen of the West, but there is a critical difference here. The real baron was a blowhard who exaggerated his life of adventure, but he apparently meant for his stories to be believed. Raspe's literary tall tale was about a fictional, ridiculous Baron Munchausen. The real von Münchhausen evidently wished to be taken seriously, even as many snickered behind his back.

Lying Jim, on the other hand, was in on the joke. He understood the value of the tall tale in his regional context, as did everyone else. In the West, his exploitation of the genre drew on what was truly an oral tradition. Townsend was Baron von Münchhausen with a wink. He did not need a Raspe to have his embroideries recast as literature. Rather, Lying Jim framed himself with the ridiculous, with exploits that drew upon deceit in the folklore of the West.

Besides his extended non sequitur ramblings, Townsend also gained fame for his shorter stories and his witticisms. He told of a man who ran one hundred miles in a single night and said he would have run farther, but that for a while during the journey one leg ran faster than the other, causing him to run in circles for four hours. Lying Jim also asserted that "the waters of Mono Lake are so buoyant that the bottom has to be bolted down, and boys paddle about on granite boulders." Townsend amended what appears to have been a traditional proverb, "When thieves fall out, honest men get their dues"; to this he added, "But when honest men fall out, lawyers get their fees."[16]

Townsend was a brilliant orator, a teller of tall tales and witty quips, and while his surviving texts are a testament to his abilities, they only hint at the power of his spoken word. Because of this, Lying Jim is remembered more for his catchy nickname than for anything he wrote. As Drury concluded his summation of the raconteur, "He was called 'Lying Jim' Townsend to the day of his death and could he have had his way it would have been graven on his tombstone."[17]

This underscores a greater problem that confronts those who would attempt to reconstruct the folklore of the past: as is often the case, the most one can hope for is to hear whispers from long-dead voices, obscured echoes of what oral tradition was really like. Many authors, including Twain, are celebrated for their exaggerated narratives, and there is no question that he had command of the written word and expressed genius as an orator on the stage. For Townsend, the situation was different. All acknowledged that when it came to banter in the saloon, Lying Jim ranked among the best. His greatest work was as an impromptu storyteller specializing in tall tales. Surviving texts about him provide hints of all that was lost, what must have been remarkable expressions of early western folklore.

THE TALL TALE IS distinct from yet another type of deceit-based folk tradition, that of the absurd or "burlesque" lie, a falsehood that was typically brief. Carolyn Brown notes the parallels shared by tall tales and these "unplotted whoppers." She perceives these lies as like tall tales except that they are not presented as narratives, and she suggests that they could as easily be called "tall lying."[18]

One of the best Nevada manifestations of the lie as a type of trickery comes in the form of the Sazerac Lying Club, the likely invention of writer Fred H. Hart. Working as the editor of the *Reese River Reveille* in central Nevada's mining town of Austin, he invented the club in 1873; it is not clear if the organization existed, or if it was itself a deception.[19] Indeed, it is possible that what began as a hoax in turn inspired the creation of a real lying club. Hart wrote about the meetings of the organization in the Sazerac Saloon in Austin. There, members competed, attempting to outdo one another in the telling of outlandish lies, thereby winning the title "Monumental Liar of America." Those who were so acclaimed were given a small gold hatchet that could be worn on one's lapel, at least according to the story.[20]

In 1876, the *Territorial Enterprise* reprinted an article from the *Reese River Reveille* detailing the proceedings of the Austin club, describing a steady escalation of exaggerations about hemp by various members. It provides an excellent example of how meetings would unfold:

THE CLUB IN SESSION.

Fred Hart published *The Sazerac Lying Club: A Nevada Book* in 1878. The Austin-based club, if it truly existed, was reputed to have inspired a similar institution in Virginia City. On the wall, there is an illustration of young George Washington chopping down a cherry tree, an ironic backdrop for the session. According to legend, when his father questioned the boy about the deed, young Washington confessed with the preface, "I cannot tell a lie." Fred Hart, *The Sazerac Lying Club* (1878); from the author's private collection.

One modest liar said that in East Tennessee, where he came from, the hemp stalks grow to a hight [*sic*] of fifteen feet, and stalks grow to the diameter of a wagon-tongue, and they gathered about a bushel and a half of seed from each stalk. A more ambitious liar said that in North Carolina they used the stalks for flagstaffs for Fourth of July celebrations, and for ridge-poles for the big tents at camp meetings. As for seed, there was generally a wagon-load to each stalk. Then spoke up a liar from Missouri. He said that "back thar" they used to send down from St. Louis for hemp-stalks to put across the Missouri river for foot-logs, and that once when he chopped down a stalk it fell in three counties. There was something reasonable in this last statement, and all present were inclined to believe it, till the liar stated that the seed fell on the ground to such a depth as to bury tall pine trees. Then a couple of members expressed some doubt, which violation of the rules of the Club was promptly punished by the President.[21]

There is no way to know if this session of lying occurred since deception is essential to the account. Nevertheless, its approach to humor is distinct from that of the tall tale as expressed by Lying Jim Townsend. Here the lies are brief and crisp, intended to outdo the previous lie until someone is judged to have gone too far in this version of deceit-based musical chairs. One could certainly refer to the lies about hemp as tall tales, but while they are long on "tall," they are short on "tale." If there is a distinction to be made, it rests on that point, namely, the length of the telling. Otherwise, both tall tales and these burlesque lies stand on the same platform, a structure built upon falsehood, which is revealed by absurdity.[22]

Lying clubs have existed elsewhere in the nation and indeed in the world, but as is the case with tall tales and the hoax, it would be difficult to find a place where deceit has been more essential to a body of folklore than in the West.[23] Austin's Sazerac Lying Club and the honorary title "Monumental Liar" fitted early Nevada so well that the institution was apparently borrowed and came into practice in Virginia City, where monumental lies became the fashion.

Yet another form of traditional western humor based on deception was practical jokes, including those centered on April Fools' Day. Drury commented on the practical joke in early Nevada, suggesting that it would be inappropriate to "think of doing anything more serious than breaking a man's leg."[24] That, then, can be regarded as the limit that guided many as they considered the possibilities of using this device to gain a good laugh, although, plainly, Drury was exaggerating.

When Hank Monk took Horace Greeley on his wild ride across the mountains, it became one of the most celebrated practical jokes in the West. The oft-recounted event served to demonstrate that a skilled teamster did not need coaching from a greenhorn. The resulting local legend illustrates how a truly great practical joke could have a second life as a popular story.

In the case of Monk's decision to play a trick on Greeley, the joke was impromptu.[25] Many other practical jokes were better planned, and the cleverer the device, the better. While the Monk account became famous in part because Greeley was so well known, most practical jokes that transformed into stories were celebrated because of their craft, not the fame of the participants.

PRACTICAL JOKES—AND NARRATIVES RELATING to these ingenious traps—became a fixture of early Nevada folklore. Everyone was keenly aware that executing a practical joke was a matter of delicate balance, for it could easily backfire with anger, leading to violence. On April 5, 1861, in a letter to the *Cedar Falls Gazette,* De Quille noted,

In this country people *must* mind their own business.—"Jokes among friends"—be *sure you know them well*. But this rather savage picture is only meant to apply to the population of these mines *en masse* and when mingling promiscuously. There are groups of friends who have by degrees ventured together, who laugh and tell yarns and to a certain point and in certain conditions "poke sly fun" at each other, but *never* to the same degree that I have often seen it done in the States. A certain degree of dignity is accorded to every man and maintained by every man.—If a man is used as a butt for the wit of others it must be in such a manner as not to *crowd his dignity,* but rather give him an elevated opinion of himself; and a human being thus inflated often yields quite as much sport to full grown men as his toy balloon does to the boy.[26]

De Quille featured a cycle of practical jokes at the end of his *History of the Big Bonanza;* these involved the man named Pike, who also played a role connected to "The Traveling Stones of Pahranagat." In early letters, De Quille used the name "Pike" generically, employing a caricature of a rural Missourian in the fictional strike of an orebody that did not exist. Another Nevada journalist, C. C. Goodwin, confirms that the use of the name for people from the state was more than a personal anomaly of De Quille.[27]

The name "Pike" refers to Pike County, which once extended across much of the northeastern part of Missouri, bordering southeast Iowa, where De Quille had lived. In a letter dated January 31, 1862, to Iowa's *Cedar Falls Gazette*, De Quille wrote, "A family of Missourians started from here this morning. Pike is always ready to be on the move. . . . [T]hen with 'his gun on his shoulder,' a broad grin upon his countenance and a 'yaller dog' by 'his side' he is ready to 'wo haw' and be happy all day long."[28] Goodwin joined De Quille in viewing "Pikes" as affable, simple country folk.

Following Pike's introduction in the traveling-stones story, De Quille wrote of escalating practical jokes involving the Missourian. This cycle of pranks may represent something that was circulating, but it could also be the author's creation, a digression to explore humor as it was expressed in early Nevada.

De Quille's account begins with a trip south of the Comstock, in search of gold. De Quille, Pike, and a man named Tom Lovel were the last of the party to cross the Carson River, flowing strongly with the spring runoff. De Quille waded across, but Tom said he would pay Pike a half dollar if he'd carry him to the other side, "which offer Pike gladly accepted." Tom climbed on Pike's back. In midstream, Pike started screaming that "a snake is biting me all to pieces!" and he demanded that Tom dismount.[29]

THE STORY OF PIKE AND TOM.

De Quille's *History of the Big Bonanza* included this illustration of "The Story of Pike and Tom" to complement the author's elaborate telling of practical jokes traded by two men on a prospecting trip. The montage depicts the sequence of the incidents. Wright, *History of the Big Bonanza* (1876); from the author's private collection.

Tom refused, and Pike continued to protest. Finally, Pike realized that Tom's spurs were digging into his flesh, but before he could say a word, Tom hit him, and they both tumbled into the water. When they emerged, Tom threatened to shoot Pike, but the latter explained about the spurs, and the matter was settled. That did not prevent others from ridiculing Pike, who consequently retained a grudge over the harsh treatment he had received from Tom.[30]

Later during their prospecting expedition, Pike was the first to rise in the camp, and Tom was one of the last. When Tom put his second boot on, he began to howl with pain, screaming, "There is a scorpion in it!" Pike rushed over and with great theatrics tried to remove the boot, but he kept insisting it would not budge because Tom's foot was swollen. Finally, Pike cut the boot down to the ankle so Tom could get his foot out, only to find that his anguish was caused by a prickly pear rather than a scorpion.[31]

Now the joke was on Tom, who suffered in silence. His subdued reaction terrified Pike, who feared revenge, and he had reason to be concerned. With everyone else's cooperation, Tom staged an elaborate imaginary attack by Paiutes. Panic stricken, Pike fled camp into the night and was not found until the next day. The others convinced Pike that he had dreamed the whole thing, and fool that he was, he believed them, thus ending an escalating cycle of practical jokes.[32]

ONE OF THE MORE famous nineteenth-century Nevada practical jokes was played on Mark Twain on the night of November 10, 1866. Friends disguised themselves and staged a robbery to scare him as he was walking across the Divide, the open area separating Virginia City and Gold Hill. Twain wrote about it in *Roughing It*, claiming to have been less frightened than seems to have been the case. In truth, Twain was apparently upset by the incident and became angry when he realized it was a practical joke. His possessions were returned, and his former colleagues had a good laugh, but Twain never enjoyed being the brunt of these escapades, even though he was a well-known trickster. Twain ended his account of the episode by writing in *Roughing It*, "Since then I play no practical jokes on people and generally lose my temper when one is played upon me."[33]

The fake robbery of Twain is celebrated because of the victim's fame; other practical jokes are less well remembered but also inspired narratives that circulated in early Nevada. Drury documented a prank involving Pat Holland, who happened to be one of the "thieves" who had staged the robbery of Twain. Holland operated the Music Hall in Virginia City and was well known as a practical joker. Elliston Trevillian O'Neil, an itinerant eastern actor desperate for work, auditioned. Although Holland said he had no need for O'Neil's services, he suggested that there might be room for his talents in one of the theater's specialty acts. "Say, did ye ever try to wear the Professor Morse slippers?"[34] Holland asked, and O'Neil said he had not heard of them.

Holland explained that they were metal shoes attached to electric wires and a battery. There was a challenge for people to wear them without dancing about, and the theater owner said that many had tried and failed. He also indicated that there was considerable money at stake if someone could manage the task, and that if successful, the traveling actor would split the proceeds with the theater.

O'Neil said he was willing to try, so Holland proposed a test before marketing a performance with the slippers. O'Neil put on the slippers and Holland had them hooked up to the battery, but the actor said he could not feel a thing. Holland and his assistant worked some more on the wiring and then affirmed that they were turning the voltage on to full, but all "O'Neil felt [was] the pleasant warmth of a gentle stream of electricity tickling the soles of his feet. He walked about with perfect freedom, and would have danced had he not been cautioned that this was the thing of all others which he must guard against."[35]

Holland indicated his delight with O'Neil and told the actor that the following evening they would stage the event and earn the prize for being able to wear the device without dancing about. The theater owner gave the actor $100 in gold and told him to take care of himself until the performance. Holland put up posters about town advertising the show, and word circulated that the theater owner was to stage a joke on an easterner and that he needed everyone's cooperation.

The next night, the theater was packed, and Holland offered to take bets that he had finally found someone who could wear the Professor Morse slippers for five minutes without dancing about. The audience played their part, offering wagers, which an accountant pretended to collect, amounting to $10,000. To make certain that all was fair, a respected member of the community verified that the slippers were properly fastened and that wires were connected to the battery.

When they were ready and the timer set, Holland indicated to his assistant that the electricity should be turned on, but as before, only a partial current was sent through the wires. O'Neil walked about the stage calmly. "Do I dance?' he said turning to [Holland]. 'Well, I guess not. All that wealth is ours, or I'm a goat.'"[36]

The timekeeper counted off the minutes, and O'Neil began to taunt the audience, telling them, "You fellers must've been a weak-kneed lot o' cattle if you couldn't stand more than— . . ." But at that moment, the timekeeper interrupted the actor, calling out the completion of the fourth minute. O'Neil continued with his oration:

> "More than this. I've only a minute longer to stand here, and I'd like to bet a thousand dollars that I can last all night till broad daylight and go home with the gals in the morning. Just to make it an object, I'll call it two thou–
>
> "Whoop! Whoopee! Wow! Wow! Help! Help! Take 'em off! Murder! Wow! Wow!". . . the tenderfoot began turning flipflops and doing double song and dance business with himself. . . . The stage-manager at last had "turned on the heat."[37]

The audience roared with laughter at a practical joke well played. The electricity was turned off, and the actor was unharmed, even if his high hopes and pride had been shattered. The electric slippers were removed, and

O'Neil was putting his boots back on when Holland came at him with a Navy Colt revolver, threatening to kill him for costing him $10,000. O'Neil protested that he was out $5,000 and had been humiliated, but Holland pretended to accept nothing of that and told him to run or he would kill him. The actor fled with Holland firing his pistol into the air.

It may seem like a cruel prank, but an unemployed actor received $100 and the theater made $500 in ticket sales, while also entertaining the community and giving Virginia City a story to tell. Understanding the place of the practical joke is a means to fit it into early Nevada folklore, both in execution of the trick and in the later recounting. Practical jokes were tailored to the situation, but as a group, they were part of a traditional genre. The fact that they depended on deceit linked them to the western hoax, the tall tale, and the burlesque extravagant lie.

In 1949, Duncan Emrich devoted several pages to practical jokes in his far-reaching book *It's an Old Wild West Custom*. Seeking examples from throughout the region, it is unlikely that Emrich witnessed the jokes being executed. He may have heard accounts, or he may have relied on written texts. His work underscores a problem, namely, that of sorting out whether events, real or invented, ever became part of oral tradition.[38]

DESPITE THE CELEBRATIONS OF cruelty, pranks were not always so rough-and-tumble: Drury recounted a story, likely from the 1870s, about Antoinette "Aunty" Adams, who believed she was a great singer. As testimony to its survival in local oral tradition, Emrich recorded a reference to the incident when he collected folklore in Virginia City's Delta Saloon in the mid-twentieth century. Alluding to a Nevada donkey, Drury maintained that Aunty's voice was "a cross between that of a Washoe canary and a squeaky wheelbarrow."[39] Max Walter, a German immigrant who managed the Music Hall, had booked her, and while she was there, better performances would not be available. A group of Gold Hill men devised a plan to send Aunty on her way with plenty of money but never to sing on a Comstock stage again.

As Drury described it, "The boys were out for a jinks!" While only a few understood how the trap would be set, many others joined in, sensing something was to happen. In the slang of the day, they wanted "to see which way the cat was going to hop," and they all soon caught on. When Aunty Adams appeared on the stage, there was a loud cheer for her, a reception more positive than she had previously known. After she sang the only selection she apparently knew, "the gang began to applaud, wild with pretended enthusiasm. They whooped and stamped, and hammered the floor with canes and sticks and barrel-staves with which they had provided themselves for the occasion. . . . [H]alf-dollars were shied onto the stage by the handful."[40]

Aunty Adams was stunned but appreciative of the enthusiasm, so she sang her selection again, "though her upper register began to show weakness." The response was the same. She then attempted to retire from the stage, having exhausted her limited repertoire. The audience loudly demanded her return for another repeat of her song, which she finally did. Once more there was thunderous applause and cheering until Aunty Adams left the stage, having sung herself hoarse.[41]

When the audience refused to quiet, Walter appeared on the stage to explain that Adams was no longer able to sing, but the crowd refused to listen, continuing their demand for yet another encore. Aunty Adams finally returned and attempted to sing, but her voice cracked, having nothing more to give. Adams retreated, and Walter appeared once again to say that while the singer could perform no more, other acts would take the stage. At that, the audience stood as one and left the theater.

Adams, seeing the enthusiasm for her performance, demanded a well-paid salaried position, which Walter gave her, ranking her "as a blazing star." The following night, the crowd returned, led by none other than Doten, or so Drury recounted the legend. Doten, who is silent on this in his journals, allegedly asked the theater manager if he would arrange the program to suit the audience, allowing Aunty Adams to sing uninterrupted by any other performer.[42]

Drury quoted Walter's response with a mocking rendition of his German accent. "Vell, shentemen, certainly Miss Antoinette vill sing shoost so long as her preath holds out, but she can't sing all nacht, of course." To this, Doten called out an "about face," and the entire would-be audience left, leaving the theater empty for the night.[43]

Walter was bewildered by the turn of events until someone finally explained that the audience had only pretended appreciation, but in fact, they wanted Adams replaced with better acts. The manager released Adams from her contract, sending her on her way. The would-be "prima donna" left with sacks full of half dollars, "enough to last her the rest of her natural life."[44]

APRIL FOOLS' DAY OFFERED an opportunity for less extravagant practical jokes, yet this day in spring is also part of a larger folk calendar tradition. Like other expressions of the practical joke genre, there are international counterparts. Nevertheless, it was in the West that the day found commemoration in keeping with a broader appreciation for the humor of duplicity.

Doten mentioned April Fools' Day many times in his journal, identifying what tricks were typical in recognition of the occasion. These included "an old hat placed on sidewalk with a big stone under it," so people would kick the hat and find themselves kicking a rock. In 1866, Doten put a note in a newspaper about a bear and her cubs that had been captured and were in a house behind Piper's Old Corner Bar, inspiring people to go to the house, only to realize that they had been fooled. Other stunts included coins nailed to floors or with strings attached, to be pulled when people attempted to claim the prize.[45] These were, however, small matters and not the equal of the elaborately contrived practical jokes that were often executed.

Fred Hart described a more extravagant, hurtful April Fools' joke played in Austin when "Uncle" John Gibbons, a supposed member of the Sazerac Lying Club, heated a half dollar on a stove in a saloon. When a fellow member of the club came in, Gibbons took the coin in his buckskin glove and called the man over, explaining that he wanted to buy him a drink. He added that if others saw him do that, they would also demand a round, so he asked his would-be fool to take the coin "and treat me." The man took the piece, and "in about the seventeenth part of a second from the time he grasped it, that half-dollar went crashing through the glass in the front door." The image of "the American eagle, which was branded on the palm" of the April fool's hand, inspired the victim to swear that he would "get even."[46]

PRACTICAL JOKES, TALL TALES, and burlesque lies are cousins of the western hoax, and together they are part of folk tradition both in their execution and in the stories that were subsequently told about them. While each relies on falsehood, they play their cards differently: hoaxes and practical jokes set a trap with a believable situation and their deception hidden. Tall tales and burlesque lies wear their absurd deceit on their sleeves. Exaggeration makes them laughable. Incidents drawing from all four of these subgenres were crafted to catch the gullible by toying with the truth. Expressions of this sort of humor and the subsequent stories about them proved essential to the folk tradition of the region.

Credit can be given to this cultural bedrock as being important to the career of Mark Twain, and certainly he learned a great deal about deceit as humor during his western sojourn. He had been notorious for his "stretchers" while growing up in Missouri, but in Nevada he worked with experts, gaining the skill to integrate deception as comedy into his literary masterpieces. Without the Comstock, it is difficult to imagine Clemens becoming Twain. A region that valued—even celebrated—falsehoods provided the perfect environment to foster both folklore and a literary giant. Because of the fame of his many achievements, Twain's writings are seen as some of the best expressions of deceit as humor in the West. The examples of Dan De Quille, Lying Jim Townsend, and Pat Holland demonstrate that talented rivals also mastered this facet of folklore.

There is some irony, perhaps, in the West's celebrated love for the tall tale since the region's brand of deception was far more diverse. Of course, a good storyteller could expand an outlandish lie into a tall tale, but journalistic hoaxes also expressed the regional appreciation for deceit. In addition, there were practical jokes, yet another celebrated dimension of trickery embedded in early Nevada folklore. Carolyn Brown's summary of the tall tale can be applied to all western manifestations of deception: whether hoax, tall tale, burlesque lie, or practical joke, they played out in "an atmosphere in which the line between fact and fiction is hazy and the manipulation of that boundary is a source of humor."[47]

The diverse expressions of deceit-related folklore in Nevada are reminders that not all tradition consists of elaborate narratives. Compendiums of the folklore of the "Wild West" typically include an assortment of "tall tales," for that is what often comes to mind when the subject of folklore of the region is raised. While the tall tale played an important role beneath the umbrella of the region's traditions, many other aspects of culture manifested as well. These include legends, beliefs, magical practices, and additional features of folklore that are discussed in the following chapter.

CHAPTER 7

A Severed Finger and
Other Disjointed Items

ONE OF THE OLDEST examples of Nevada folklore I can remember is a story from 1960. My father brought the account home, having heard it from someone else. It is a legend about a man lost while fishing at Pyramid Lake in northern Nevada. Months later, the drowned man and his boat appeared in a lake in South America. Not only that, but besides Pyramid this distant body of water was the only other home of the unusual cui-ui sucker fish. The surfacing of the dead man and his vessel established a reason that a distinct species occurred in only those two places in the world: there is an underground river connecting the bodies of water across the continents, and the man and his boat had been swept along in that subterranean current from the Nevada lake to the one a world away.[1]

I was fascinated by this story, and I would have given anything to explore that underground river. The power of folklore inspired me to attempt a model of the phenomenon in my kindergarten sandbox. Several buckets of water later, I was in a lot of trouble. Of course, the anecdote about Pyramid's underground waterway was not true; there are no South American cui-ui, which in fact swim only in the Nevada desert lake. The motif of a fisherman lost in Pyramid's waters is related to a complex of narratives, mentioned by Doten, that describe the drowned as lost forever. That said, the legend of the underground river adds the flair of discovering the corpse thousands of miles to the south.

There is evidence of a nineteenth-century notion of an underground river beginning in Lake Tahoe and leading to the Comstock mines, antici-pating the account I had heard. Samuel P. "Sam" Davis (1850–1918) authored an important expression of the story at the turn of the century. Arriving on the Comstock as a journalist in 1875, he was part of the second genera-tion of Nevada writers. He eventually became editor and part owner of the *Carson Morning Appeal*, stepping away from the job in 1898 to serve as the state controller. In 1913, Davis published an important two-volume history of Nevada.[2]

In 1901, while he was the state controller, Davis wrote an imaginative take on underground rivers in Nevada. His "The Mystery of the Savage Sump" appeared in the *Black Cat*, a national literary magazine.[3] He indicated that the story dated to the 1870s, when the Comstock mines were at the height of their prosperity and he had just arrived to work there. Davis told of a man who discovered a hole in the bed of Lake Tahoe near Carnelian Bay to the north. The man speculated that it might connect to the Comstock, so he dropped a stick carved with his initials into the hole, secured a job working in the Savage Mine sump, and found the stick he had carved while at the lake.

As the story unfolds, the man obtained the support of an investor, and together, they devised a means to plug the hole, causing water levels to decline in the depths of the Savage Mine. This allowed rich ore to be retrieved less expensively, and stock prices consequently rose. The two men purchased and sold stocks at highs and lows, which only they could predict since they determined when the mine would be flooded or would prove free of water.

When the investor was satisfied with his profit, he clubbed his partner, the discoverer of the hole. He then lowered his victim into the cavity, and the body was subsequently found in the sump of the Savage Mine. The corpse was badly mangled by the journey, and the hot water of the Comstock had further corrupted its flesh. What remained included fine shoes and clothing, making it clear that this man was not working in the mine. In addition, management could not identify anyone—miner or visitor—who had gone missing. The source of the body remained a mystery, the truth being known only to the investor who had succeeded in getting away with murder and millions of stock-swindled dollars.

Unfortunately, there are often too few clues to indicate what is behind a published account like this. Sorting out whether it drew on folklore or was an original composition that later affected oral tradition is a challenge. There are some remarkable leaps at the outset: it is improbable that anyone could guess that the Comstock was the destination of water flowing into a hole in the floor of Lake Tahoe, let alone the idea that of all the possibilities, it would terminate in the Savage Mine where the man just happened to search for his carved stick. Although this is not definitive evidence, a far-fetched premise can be an indication that a folk legend is at play as a source of inspiration.

In fact, what Davis drew upon is not clear. His story is sometimes held up as a hoax, but it was published in a magazine that specialized in fiction, so it does not seem that the author was trying to "pull one off." Davis did not exaggerate as needed with a tall tale. Although he framed the incident as something that happened, it is more likely that it was intended as fiction and that is the way it was taken. Nevertheless, Davis certainly knew of similar anecdotes that were presented as truth, even if they were cloaked with a certain amount of skepticism.

For example, his own newspaper in Carson City had published an article in 1883 with the title "Tahoe's Subterranean Outlet." This described much of the same circumstance: fishermen near Carnelian Bay discovered water draining from a three-foot hole in the lake's solid-rock floor. The reporter speculated that what was lost to Tahoe might be responsible for the flooding of the Comstock mines, and the article proposed plugging the drain to save the lake's water and to decrease the need for pumping of the mines.[4]

This article may have been intended as a hoax, but again there is no clue to allow astute readers to conclude that this was the case. Rather, it seems to be an account presented to be believed. Davis was likely influenced by this or similar anecdotes for the story he published in 1901.

In February 1876, De Quille wrote a hoax that also drew on the idea of a subsurface connection between one of the region's bodies of water and the Comstock mines. He announced the discovery of five eyeless fish, three to four inches in length, found in the shared sump of the Savage and the Hale and Norcross Mines after they were flooded. The creatures were bloodred in color and resembled goldfish. Aside from the lack of eyes, they were also remarkable for their habitat: the fish were thriving in scalding water recorded at 128 degrees Fahrenheit. When captured and put in cooler water, they immediately died. Conjecture suggested that they had arrived in the sump by way of an underground river connected with Tahoe.[5]

De Quille explained the dynamics of flooding in the mines:

> The water by which the mines are flooded broke in at a depth of 2,200 feet in a drift that was getting pushed to the northward in the Savage. It rose in the mine—also in the Hale and Norcross, the two mines being connected—to the height of 400 feet; that is, up to the 1,800 foot level. This would seem to prove that a great subterranean reservoir or lake has been tapped, and from this lake doubtless came the fish hoisted from the mine last evening.
>
> Eyeless fishes are frequently found in the lakes of large caves, but we have never before heard of their existence in either surface or

subterranean water the temperature of which was so high as is the water in those mines. The lower workings of the Savage mine are far below the bed of the Carson River, below the bottom of the Washoe lake—below any water running or standing anywhere within a distance of ten miles of the mine.[6]

De Quille described an excavation pushing northward from the Savage Mine toward the Hale and Norcross. He was also alluding to some of the deepest works in 1876, which easily played with the imagination. Ultimately, Comstock mines reached depths of more than three thousand feet, well over a half mile beneath the surface.

The clue to the hoax was the absurdity of the fish being able to survive at that temperature.[7] De Quille published several more articles dealing with his blind fish, relying on the idea of an underground passage from a lake to the Comstock mines. These articles, together with the one in 1883, are evidence of a persistent belief in the possibility of an underground river.[8] In 1954, Lucius Beebe, a raconteur himself and ever the unreliable source, wrote that De Quille's article persisted in snagging believers "almost a hundred years after it was written."[9] De Quille's contribution to the lingering tradition is difficult to evaluate, but in this case, Beebe is likely correct that the reporter's quaint in 1876 was a factor.

Belief in a subterranean river was reinforced by the notion that Lake Tahoe did not give up its dead, and it is worth repeating that this idea was applied to Pyramid Lake as well. People could imagine that corpses disappeared in either body of water because of widespread speculation that they may have been sucked into the entrance of an underground river. Combined with the evidence that I was told an account like Davis's short story published some six decades earlier suggests that this is a long-lasting bedrock of Nevada folklore.[10]

ACCOUNTS OF UNDERGROUND RIVERS demonstrate the challenges and opportunities presented by nineteenth-century documents when it comes to understanding their relationship with contemporary tradition. Many aspects of belief and custom besides stories also provide texture to life. Finding the fingerprints of this facet of culture in the record of another century offers hints of the possible. For example, when Mary McNair Mathews brought up the "Horribles" in her Nevada memoir of the 1870s, she gave a nod to an aspect of folklife that is not part of oral narrative. She observed the Horribles in a parade where, according to her, they were "the same that the Eastern people call 'Fantastics,' only both animals and men are represented, being the most grotesque objects ever witnessed."[11] An article dating to 1887, appearing in the *Nevada State Journal*, portrayed them as terrifying "youngsters, and [creating] immense merriment for all concerned."[12] Doten also wrote about them in his journal, as appearing in a Virginia City play, the afternoon of the Fourth of July 1879.[13]

Mathews helpfully compared the Horribles with the Fantastics, providing a road map to understand what she was describing. Mathews was, in fact, acting as an intuitive folklorist, recognizing similarities and attempting to grapple with what existed in the West. Following her direction, it is possible to see the Horribles in a larger context.

Appearing in the East as both Horribles and Fantasticals (or Fantastics), these groups of men dressed in grotesque outfits, and sometimes their costumes leaned toward political satire. The practice recalls British mummers, although any connection between the two continents is unclear. Fantasticals were common in the East in the early nineteenth century, with a few groups surviving into the turn of the century. Some communities have even resurrected the institution. Appearances were traditionally associated with winter holidays, but most groups selected a single event for their focus, typically New Year's Day or Christmas or a parade such as the one on Independence Day. The celebration of the institution in Nevada is testimony to the ability of traditions from the East to take root in the West.[14]

Mathews documented many other traditions that she encountered during her stay in Nevada. For example, she wrote about a folk legend, a narrative that she heard and then claimed to be recording, "exactly as it was given to me."[15] The anecdote was told in the context of the many holdups that were plaguing the region. A young man boasted that if he were ever robbed, he would not put his hands up, but instead would defy the criminals. Friends decided to set a trap for him the next time he took a carriage for a ride with his sweetheart. They ambushed him as it was growing dark and demanded that he put his hands up so his valuables could be taken. He complied without hesitation, and when he returned home, he found everything that had been taken, waiting for him, together with a note warning him not to be so boastful about resisting robbers.

Continuing with an exploration of what a single source can yield, Mathews also mentioned a children's game she called "Queen Dido's dead." This consisted of children sitting on a bench. "The first one says 'Queen Dido is dead.' The second one then says, 'How did she die?' 'Doing just so,' says the first, shaking her head. The question is repeated and answered till the head, feet, and hands are in motion. And the whole crowd resembles so many jumping-jacks."[16] A variation of this appears in a book of children's games dating to 1852; the name Queen Dido is a reference to a monarch of Greek legend who ended her life to avoid an unwanted marriage.[17]

This brief reference corresponds to the wealth of material associated with children's oral traditions and beliefs that exists internationally. John Waldorf's remarkable memoir, *A Kid on the Comstock*, points to the possibilities, as do the many artifacts uncovered by Nevada archaeologists.[18] Too often, however, both documents and objects miss the mark when it comes to folklore. Marbles, shattered parts of dolls, and metal toys testify to the existence of children, but that does not automatically yield insight into songs, jokes, or games that circulated among the young.

Although aspects of folklore held by children of the mining district are embedded within Waldorf's text, many of his references are vague. Occasionally, he documented a story he heard while growing up, but usually with scant detail. Like so many aspects of early Nevada folklore, the traditions of childhood warrant further exploration beyond what is possible with this overview.

Finally, Mathews mentioned the Washoe Zephyrs, which blew with such intensity that not only were these winds given a distinct name, but they also became the subject of legend. De Quille maintained that gusts were so powerful they sent hats down Six Mile Canyon, far below Virginia City. He suggested that one zephyr created, "it is said, drifts of hats fully fifteen feet in depth."[19] Whether this falls within the genre of tall tale or is an account that was popularly told to be believed is difficult to say. Either way, it fits the realm of folklore.

Recalling something clearly drawn from oral tradition, Mathews described how in response to a recounting of the damage to roofs during a wind, a woman responded, "That is nothing. I saw a man sawing wood on a piece of sidewalk that was fastened together perfectly solid. The sidewalk was taken up and carried two or three hundred feet through the air—the man sawing wood all the time, and never let up." Mathews importantly commented: "I could hardly give this credit. But I have since heard the same story from several persons." This insight reveals a great deal about early Nevada storytelling traditions, and fortunately she further noted the inclination of Comstockers to answer one anecdote with another: "The Virginia City people never allow any person to get the start of them on a good story. The one who tells the last has the advantage of the rest."[20]

There is a similar account dealing with a particularly powerful zephyr that sent a donkey aloft and sailing above town, braying in fright. In 1876, De Quille specifically attributed this event to the spring of 1863, writing that the animal was "five or six hundred feet above the houses, finally landing near the Sugar-Loaf Mountain, nearly five miles away." He added that "a tradition in Virginia City [asserts that] as the poor beast was hurried away over the town, his neck was stretched out to its greatest length, and he was shrieking in the most despairing and heart-rending tones ever heard from any living creature." De Quille further evaluated the tradition by adding, "The oldest inhabitant sometimes tries to spoil this story by saying that what was seen was an old gander, the leader of a flock of wild geese . . . but most folks along the Comstock cling to the donkey and sneer at the gander."[21]

Besides being featured in legends about Washoe Zephyrs, beasts of burden have played an important role in the folklore of the mining world. Chapter 1 describes how they frequently became ingrained into traditions about lost mines and about the discovery of new ones. Indeed, the image of the prospector and his burro is permanently etched into the folklore of the American West, becoming one of the region's most enduring symbols. Donkeys were known as "Desert Canaries," in recognition of their noisy braying, but in early Nevada, the burro was more specifically called a "Washoe Canary."[22]

A monument to a mule, located at the entrance to the Silver Terrace Cemeteries of Virginia City, is a testament to the significance attributed to a beast of burden. In 1992, the group known as E. Clampus Vitus, the "Clampers," erected a marker above the supposed grave of Mary Jane Simpson, a prized mule that had worked in the mines and then was killed by the fire of 1875. The tombstone drew on the text of an original marker, quoted in a local paper, which read, "Sacred to the memory of Mary Jane Simpson. The within was only a mule still she was nobody's fule. Stranger, tread lightly."[23]

The Clampers are themselves something of a phenomenon of folklore, celebrating a Wild West of their definition with their own brand of nostalgia and contributing to ubiquitous markers that are sometimes wedded more to celebration than veracity. In whatever way the tombstone for Mary Jane Simpson is viewed, the object serves as a reminder that mules and donkeys were important in industry and for those who possessed them. Today, these creatures serve as symbols of a West the way it should have been.

The idea of wandering the desert with one's donkey, enjoying the open air and hoping for that once-in-a-lifetime strike, conveys a carefree feel that continues to resonate. Deep, hard-rock mining created a different reality. It is another matter altogether to walk deep into a mine and to turn around to see the last gleam of sunlight eclipsed by the next turn. This can conjure the feeling of overwhelming weight bearing down from above, the true burden

An eerie, life-threatening mine has the power to inspire folklore. Documented by archaeologists in 1990, this Virginia City adit—a term for a horizontal excavation—dates to the 1880s. The site revealed a simple approach to digging one thousand feet into the mountainside. The miners relied on a traditional understanding of their trade rather than state-of-the-art nineteenth-century industrial science. Photograph by Ronald M. James.

of the nineteenth-century miner. When all signs of the outside world are gone, the bulk of the mountain above seems even more menacing, as it threatens to crush the wooden supports that keep miners alive. The terrifying danger of the subterranean world echoes with every drip of water, every creak of timber, and every pebble shifting within the excavation.

Being underground is unnatural, and mines consequently inspire a rich body of folklore. Traditions fluoresce, no doubt, because peril coincides with wealth. The chance to discover rich, concentrated deposits encased in rock captured the imagination. Balancing the wish to gain good luck and to avert misfortune, miners sometimes tapped into their traditions to turn things in a favorable direction. At the same time, while workers' "laborlore" was and is shared exclusively by miners, there were also community beliefs and narratives about the industry.[24]

OBJECTS CAN BE ANOTHER way that folk traditions find expressions. Miners used iron candlestick holders with one or more hooks and points so that they could be stuck into timbers or the wall of a mine at convenient locations and angles. Although there were some designs that appear consistently, homemade versions allowed for the variation of folk art.

The miner's lunch pail could also be an expression of tradition, especially regarding what it contained. Images in nineteenth-century photographs of groups of miners invariably show them holding their lunch pails. These were tin cylinders that had several levels. A miner would eat each "course" of his lunch and then remove its tray so he could proceed to the next layer. The mining West commonly attributed this device to the Cornish miners, who may indeed have been the source of the innovation.

Similarly, the Cornish pasty is a typical ethnic food associated with miners. This consisted of a pastry shell that was folded over a stew-like combination of beef, potatoes, rutabaga, and onions, although ingredients varied. The pasties' Cornish origin seems clear, but they quickly became popular throughout mining communities. A common story involves a means of testing the abilities of a pasty baker: according to tradition, a pasty should be able to withstand a drop down a shaft. If it remained intact, the cook was competent.

Other objects hint at folklore removed from the mining industry, but like all artifacts, they can remain stubbornly silent unless coaxed to speak. Altered coins, the skeleton of a small animal, and various items including a boot represent another opportunity to approach beliefs and practices likely implemented in secret. Archaeologists in Virginia City have found these objects, placed beneath buildings or inside walls during the nineteenth century. Although they seem to be hidden attempts to increase good fortune, without written clues, all that remains is to surmise their meaning.

Most people who entered the structures would not have known what had been concealed in secluded shadows. Excavations in Virginia City have identified three examples of this practice from the nineteenth century. Because the act of depositing objects was similar, it would be easy to assume that these were expressions of a shared culture, but this was almost certainly not the case. People worlds apart inhabited the structures, and while they fell upon analogous strategies to manipulate the supernatural, their acts were in response to distinct traditions.

Two altered coins found beneath the floorboards of the Boston Saloon are probably the oldest of these. This property was operated by William A. G. Brown, a freeborn African American native of Massachusetts. He came to Virginia City in roughly 1863 and soon opened a saloon. By 1866, he moved his business to D Street, across from the community's most important theater. The coins seem to have been placed there about the time that

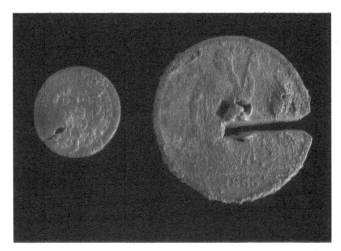

Archaeologists found an altered dime and half dollar beneath the charred floor-boards of the African American Boston Saloon in Virginia City. The building was destroyed in the Great Fire of October 26, 1875. The coins were likely hidden in 1866 when William A. G. Brown moved his business to that location. The tradition of hiding mutilated coins beneath a building has roots in West Africa. Photograph by Ronald M. James.

Brown occupied the building, but this cannot be certain. He managed his saloon until about 1875, after which it burned. During an excavation in 2000, archaeologists found a dime and a half dollar beneath charred floorboards. Both had been cut and punctured.

Archaeologist Kelly Dixon expertly interpreted the coins as evidence of a magical practice with roots in southern African American culture, ultimately reaching back to West Africa. The dime, minted between 1853 and 1860, had a hole drilled into it, causing a fracture; the half dollar, bearing the date 1865, had two punched holes as well as a wide cut from one of the holes to the edge of the coin. There is evidence that they had been heated, perhaps to facilitate these modifications.[25] Although Brown was from New England, most of his patrons were southerners. As is so often the case with archaeology when lacking written records, conjecture must play a factor. Following whatever path, the tradition of putting altered coins beneath a structure found its way into practice, hidden by the floorboards of Brown's Boston Saloon.

Another archaeologist, Jessica Axsom, uncovered the skeleton of a small mammal beneath a foundation stone of a mercantile store in Virginia City's Chinatown. It appears that the caustic content of the mortar dissolved many of the animal's delicate bones, for what remained was too decomposed to identify. Nevertheless, the creature was likely to have been a cat or small dog. The foundation was apparently constructed after the 1875 fire. Like the altered coins beneath the Boston Saloon, no records exist concerning what was intended, but the placement of an animal—or its remains—beneath a foundation of a building was a widespread practice typically intended to confer a level of protection on those using the structure.[26]

Within the remains of a doctor's house, which also served as a private hospital, archaeologist Julie Schablitsky found evidence of several items that were either beneath the building or in one of its walls. These include a worn Civil War–era boot, a padlock, a bottle, some worked leather, and a hat. Here, it is not clear who might have left these objects because the builder and original owners are unknown. The structure was on the western edge of Chinatown, but there is no reason to assume that Chinese Americans lived there. Intent is even more difficult to assess in this case, but the placement of the items is, again, consistent with a pervasive practice of attempting to confer good fortune by hiding objects in or beneath a building.[27]

People of diverse backgrounds left objects within walls or beneath buildings. Although unrelated historically, these practices drew on similar ideas that objects could grant luck to those living or working there. In addition, concealing the things was not a communal activity. Often, they were hidden secretly, and practices conducted in private are equally obscure in the historical record.

SIMILARLY, MARY MCNAIR MATHEWS was acting on her own when she dealt with her young son's loss of a finger. Applying what she regarded as sound medical practice, she placed the digit in a jar filled with brandy, thereby preventing it from "ever bothering him after it healed up." Mathews believed that if the severed digit were not treated properly, it could give her son pain in the future. With this, she was drawing on a tradition found in western Europe and North America: if a severed appendage were to be burned or handled in some way that might be hurtful, the person would feel the pain.[28]

By preserving the finger in brandy, a worried mother hoped to protect her son. This, too, was the solitary act drawing on folk wisdom. We know what Mathews did because she mentions it in her published memoir of her life in Nevada during the 1870s. By writing about the incident, she assumed her readers would understand the practice, and, indeed, many probably did.

While Mathews had her own ideas about folk medicine, the West offered a range of possibilities. De Quille described an incident in 1861 that illustrates how immigrants, in this case Chinese Americans, made their traditional practices available to others who settled in the West:

A miner in the vicinity of Grass Valley, California, had been for some time afflicted with the rheumatism; he had tried all kinds of patent medicines and every remedy recommended by his friends without experiencing the slightest relief; had consulted a number of the best physicians and applied their prescriptions in vain; nothing seemed to afford him the least relief. At last he was told of a certain Chinese doctor who was "death on rheumatis," at any distance, and to him he sent. The celebrated practitioner forthwith dispatched to him a large bottle of colored glass, filled with a fluid, for which he demanded and received $5. The miner was very agreeably disappointed on taking his first dose to find the medicine extremely palatable—in fact its flavor was precisely similar to that of a good article of brandy.—The sick man took the medicine quite as often and in quite as large doses as the directions required, and in a very short time was perfectly sound. Finding there remained a substance of some kind in the bottle which through the dark glass had the appearance of some sort of bark or roots and being anxious to discover the secret of the Chinese doctor's great medicine, he broke the bottle and found not roots nor bark but the remains of three or four great black lizards which had been pretty thoroughly "smushed" that they might the more readily impart their healing juices to the brandy. He of course felt satisfied that he had discovered the great secret and it is currently reported that he was heard making a noise that sounded a little as though he were trying to shout *eureka!*[29]

Medicines were not the only expression of folklore that reflected diverse traditions in the mining West. As was often the case, humor also played a role in the way people interacted.

DIVERSE ETHNIC GROUPS IN the mining West created an environment ripe for humor. Often this focused on how various immigrants expressed themselves: contemporary newspapers are filled with attempts to capture the way different people spoke, a mainstay of the writings of Mark Twain, for example. Jokes about dialects were amicable or vicious depending on the status and nature of the ethnic group.[30]

Mathews provided an example of dialects, in this case mocking the distinct speech of Cornish miners who misplaced or omitted an initial *h* sound. She recorded what was certainly a joke from the period, in which a Cornishman responded to his superintendent's question about the condition of the mine; the miner answered, "Oh very well, sir, heverything is hall right, but hit is very 'ot there now."[31]

A similar anecdote appeared in 1876 when the *Gold Hill Daily News* published a witticism about a Cornishman's account of an Odd Fellows gathering. This included a popular local, Simon Ogg, a Swiss emigrant and well-known teamster, who was wearing a "nobby hat," a way to refer to a bowler: "I saw the Hodd Fellows' procession all through. The Hencampment was a fine set o' lads, and there was a big string of carriages. Sime Hogg of Gold 'Ill, you know, 'ad the finest rig of 'em all. Hogg druv four fine 'orses, with 'is 'air all slicked down, and nobby 'at on 'is 'ed. Some style about he."[32]

Humorous stories were a favorite genre of oral tradition in early Nevada, and newspapers of the period frequently included them. The comic aspect of the Cornish dialect may be lost on most readers today because they are not encountering a wave of these emigrants. Here, the jokes—such as they were—stand as reminders that the oral tradition of the past does not necessarily play well today, long after it ceased to be relevant. Jokes were fitted for the moment, which easily faded.

Each ethnic group present in a mining community had its own oral traditions while also being a potential subject for others within the community. The popular rhyme "by *Tre*, *Pol* and *Pen* ye may know the Cornish men" was a popular way to identify the Cornish by their distinctive surnames, and while the Cornish dialect was regarded as fair game for everyone, the Cornish miner was acknowledged in industry for having hereditary mining lore.[33] This, in turn, generated a great deal of folklore about these emigrants.

The reputation of the Cornish immigrants granted them special access to the best jobs, but it also elevated the stature of their folk traditions, sometimes inspiring others to borrow from them. Chapter 9, for example, describes how diverse miners adopted stories of the Cornish knocker, the underground mining spirit, even when workers had no roots that led back to Cornwall. That, however, is only one example. R. W. Raymond's 1881 glossary of mining and metallurgical terms includes many words in common usage that are indicated as having Cornish origin.[34] In addition, Cornish technology was widely acknowledged as superior, with the Cornish pump used to dewater mines and their long-handled shovels recognized as part of the unique tools of these miners with millennia of tradition at their fingertips.[35]

While people mocked their dialect, folklore about the Cornish tended to be positive. They were regarded as talented if quaint. The same was not true for many other immigrant groups. Everyone brought traditions, but reactions differed with neighbors, accepted by some, rejected, mocked, or hated by others, for cruelty was too often embedded in the way people interacted.

Newly arrived Irish often found the Cornish to be antagonistic. This was partly an expression of religious differences: the Cornish were typically Methodists, and the Irish who arrived in Nevada were mostly Catholics. Animosity was also a matter of Cornish managers having authority over Irish labor. The opposing perspectives of the two groups serve as a reminder that no matter how someone in the West may have viewed each ethnicity, there were always others who saw things differently. While Irish Americans were a sizable part of early Nevada and many others joined in for the annual St. Patrick's Day celebration, there were those who looked down on the wearing of the green.

De Quille's story of the two Irishman "bustin' the injunction," destroying a valuable piece of survey equipment, underscores how some ridiculed these immigrants. Duncan Emrich, collecting in Virginia City in 1949 and 1950, recorded an older joke dating to decades earlier when there was active underground mining on the Comstock. The historic antagonism between the Cornish—often called Cousin Jacks—and the Irish is at the core of this. There had been an accident in a mine, and they had to haul up the three dead workers, two Cornish and one Irish. Afterward, a Cornishman "went home and there was a Cousin Jinny, that is a Cousin Jack woman, and she said, 'What's the matter tell me over at the mine?' 'Oh,' he said, 'Two poor souls and an Irishman got killed.'"[36] Of course, with the fluidity of ethnic antagonism, the joke could easily be reversed depending on who told it.

California placer miners reputedly thought African Americans were lucky, but if this were the case in the underground excavations of Nevada, the evidence is elusive. Mostly, African Americans were too few to inspire consistent, widespread folklore among others.[37] The same was often the situation for the speakers of Spanish, who also represented a small minority in a larger population.

Nevertheless, there was considerable curiosity about the technology used in the Mexican Mine, which prospered on the north end of Virginia City in the early 1860s. Operated by the Maldonado brothers, they took an older path distinct from the new industrial mining on the Comstock being invented by some of the best engineers of the day. The mine and its Mexican workers employed traditional approaches dating back centuries. This, too, was an expression of folklore, knowledge passed down for generations about how to extract underground ore. Practices included using native rock pillars, left at critical locations to support underground chambers. Workers ascended and descended on ladders, and they hauled ore in sacks that rested on their backs, hung from a strap, taut against the forehead. Ore was processed with arrastras, flat stone structures dependent on the sun to heat a mixture of ore, water, salts, and mercury that was churned by a tethered horse walking around a central pole.[38]

Scarcity of numbers and general curiosity did not prevent expressions of the worst of racism against these groups, but when it came to hateful interaction of cruel popular tradition, few suffered more than Chinese immigrants. Asian folklore itself was rich and complex, preserved in communities that were large enough to sustain their culture in a new world. Those traditions were inexplicable for most in the West who were not of Asian descent and did not know the language. Documentation of Chinese folklore in early Nevada is consequently rare.

Folklore about these immigrants was another matter. Asian arrivals were exotically different from the point of view of others, and they were the subject of beliefs that perpetuated the racism of the majority. Many feared what they perceived as strange diseases and markets with questionable meats. In addition, there was a misunderstanding about how they ironed clothes for customers. Chinese American laundry workers used a mouth-blown apparatus that sprayed atomized starch on fabric as they smoothed it with a hot iron. Others perceived the innocuous practice as evidence that they were spitting on the garments, and stories about this spread, discouraging people from patronizing Chinese American businesses.[39]

While prejudice against Chinese Americans was widespread, archaeologists frequently uncover Asian keepsakes of various sorts in the remains of Euro-American homes. This together with primary source records make it clear that many approached their Chinese American neighbors with curiosity, drawn in by things they perceived as exotic and desirable.[40] The way people dealt with each other could be complex.

As indicated in the introduction, this volume does not attempt to tackle yet another rich world of folklore, traditions held by Native Americans. That said, it is important to note that during the first few decades after the founding of the Nevada Territory, many of the new arrivals expressed fascination with Native American legends and traditions. De Quille wrote extensively on the subject, but clearly there was as much fictionalizing as collecting when it came to his record of stories that Paiutes and other Indigenous people told. The interest held by some came with an element of irony, since racism and brutality dominated the way most treated those who had lived in the Great Basin for countless generations. Much was appropriated but then confused, while other traditions were imagined and projected onto the cultures of the American Indians. A complex process added its own dimension to early Nevada folklore.

THIS ARRAY OF EARLY Nevada traditions includes a story entwined with a belief here, a magical practice there, all mixed with a joke or two. Cruelty was too often ubiquitous. Added to this were the traditional groups that organized to entertain people and to perpetuate customs. Many diverse facets of culture, essential to folklore, are not typically found in compendiums of a region's tales. The following chapter returns to more familiar ground, the popular stories people told. In this case, the narratives feature many of the later characters who filled the repertoire of Nevada raconteurs.

CHAPTER 8

More Legendary Characters

SANDY AND EILLEY BOWERS belonged to the placer-mining phase of the western Great Basin. They were present during the gold and silver discoveries in 1859, but unlike most others who left shortly afterward, they remained as new arrivals swamped the region. This husband-and-wife team was unusual because they lingered and were two of the earliest Comstock millionaires. Previous chapters point out that the departures of many first players encouraged their inclusion in local narratives. Despite staying in the area, Sandy and Eilley Bowers also took their places in local stories, remaining as fixtures of Nevada folklore to this day.

Alison "Eilley" Orrum was born in Scotland in 1826 and was one of a few women living in what would become the Comstock Mining District as the 1859 strikes occurred.[1] She had divorced her second husband when he left her in Washoe Valley to return to Salt Lake City in 1857. His Church of Jesus Christ of Latter-day Saints had summoned him to wait for an anticipated invasion of federal forces, sent to quell perceived issues associated with the religion's militancy. Newly separated, Eilley Orrum Cowan took up humble residence at Gold Hill even as it was establishing itself. She profited from washing clothes and providing a boardinghouse for miners. Local lore maintains that she obtained ten feet of the orebody in Gold Hill as payment for room and board.

Lemuel Sanford "Sandy" Bowers, born in 1833, had come west after working in Missouri. He was one of the Gold Canyon placer miners who was well positioned to take advantage of the January 1859 Gold Hill strike. Bowers possessed ten feet of a claim next to Eilley Cowan's, and according to the story, he was able to purchase an additional ten feet for $100. When the two married, their union gave them command of thirty feet of some of the richest near-surface ore that the Comstock Lode had to offer. While most of the original Comstock claimants sold out within a few months, Sandy and Eilley Bowers kept their holding, which Sandy worked.[2]

Beginning in 1861, Sandy and Eilley built a mansion, reputed to cost several hundred thousand dollars at a time when a fraction of that could buy a substantial house. Over the years, most who acquired remarkable wealth in Nevada mines commissioned large estates elsewhere, notably in California's Bay Area. Sandy and Eilley Bowers were unique in selecting Washoe Valley, not far to the west of Virginia City and Gold Hill. Seeking the finest appointments, the couple traveled to Europe on an extravagant spending spree. Tradition maintains they attempted but failed to meet Queen Victoria. Another account has the couple returning aboard the famous British passenger liner *Persia* and adopting a newborn whose mother had just been buried at sea. They named the girl after the ship, according to an unverifiable flight of fancy. The facts are muddled, and as is often the case, folklore clouds the issue and dominates the narrative.[3]

Upon their return to Nevada in early 1863, Sandy found their orebody depleted and his health diminished. After desperately attempting to locate new ore and to restore his family's wealth, he died in 1868 of lung disease. Sandy Bowers had been a simple, honest miner unable to keep his fortune. Now his widow struggled financially and emotionally. The death of Persia in 1874 punctuated the decline. To remain solvent, Eilley Bowers hosted visitors to the mansion. Eventually, she considered raffling off her furniture and possessions, and with one or another strategy, she managed to keep her home for a while. Nothing, however, could forestall foreclosure, and Reno's Myron Lake obtained the estate in 1876.

Bowers long claimed she had psychic abilities and apparently once asked John A. "Snowshoe" Thompson (1827–76) to bring her a crystal ball; Thompson was famous in the 1850s for skiing across the Sierra Nevada to deliver and retrieve winter mail for the western Great Basin, becoming legendary in his own right. The fact that Bowers and her husband once struck it rich on the Comstock enhanced her reputation for second sight, which she exploited, working as a fortuneteller in Virginia City, Reno, and California.

As De Quille portrayed Eilley Bowers in 1876, she was "now known as the 'Washoe Seeress' on account of her many predictions about fires in the mines and rich bodies of ore."[4] After Virginia City's Great Fire of 1875, some looked back to her prophecies and saw in them an indication that she foresaw the disaster. Henry DeGroot in his 1876 articles published in the *Mining and Scientific Press* explained that Bowers was "reputed to be endowed with something of that occult power that enables the possessor to foresee future events. In the exercise of this faculty she has frequently prognosticated ore developments on the Comstock, some of which are said have been verified by subsequent events."[5]

Drury, who arrived on the Comstock too late to know Sandy Bowers, recounted much of what he had heard about the couple. For example, he credited Sam Davis, another later journalist, with a tale about a wedding gift. According to the story, the prospective couple "worked for a time in a Gold Hill restaurant." Their customers "urged Sandy and Eilley to get spliced, and amid uproarious laughter gave them as a wedding gift 'a million dollars.' This sum was the face value of mining stock, which the jokesters believed virtually worthless." Of course, as the legend unfolds, the feet in the claim proved extraordinarily rich, "and Sandy Bowers unloaded his stock, selling it for about what the hilarious miners had promised him." Drury then maintained that the occasion of selling stock for a million dollars inspired Sandy Bowers to stand "on the porch of the old International Hotel and [proclaim] that he 'had money to throw at the birds.'"[6] As an accurate account of history, the story is problematic on several levels, but it serves as an excellent example of the sort of narratives circulating about the earliest of Comstock millionaires in the final decades of the nineteenth century.

Drury also explored the stories about the couple's palatial residence, Bowers Mansion. At a time when Storey County extravagantly paid $117,000 for a grand courthouse, Drury credited the Bowers couple with spending $300,000 on their home.[7] True or not, the imagined cost of the Bowers estate expresses the fascination Nevadans had with the ultimate expression of wealth and the nouveaux riche. As Drury wrote, "The stories about the doorknobs and hinges made of silver bullion are true, as also are the tales of marvelous prices paid for pictures and statuary, and a bronze piano with mother-of-pearl keys. The library was a chamber of wonders, containing rare books and curios that cost many times what they were worth. The windows were of French plate glass and the entire mansion was most opulent in its furnishings."[8] There is little question that people told stories about the glory days of Sandy and Eilley Bowers and that their mansion, which survives as an expression of their success, became a focal point of legend.

Sandy represented the common man who, through dumb luck, won a fortune and became a millionaire. He did not discover the lode, nor did he craftily obtain a part of it. He owned thirty feet of claim that just happened to be the location of a fabulous concentration of near-surface gold and silver. Apparently drawing on a folklore stereotype about the Scots being good with finances, DeGroot typified Sandy Bowers (whom DeGroot misunderstood to be Scottish) as "a rough, honest fellow and well-liked by his companions, though not so canny and circumspect in his worldly affairs as his countrymen are commonly reputed to be."[9] Despite the folklore that drifted from fact, it is possible to summarize Sandy's life: his simplicity won him many friends, and when his wealth and health failed, his final chapter became a tragic example of whimsical fate. His was at least an uncomplicated ending; for his widow, the decline was protracted and painful. Deaf and impoverished, she died in 1903 in California.

Eilley Bowers survived the "good old days" of the first strike to remain as an extraordinary character for the rest of the nineteenth century. Fascination with wealth was clearly part of why she became a focus of popular attention, but her Scottish accent no doubt added charm to her persona and could only enhance her reputation for having second sight. With all of this, she was someone to talk about, and tales featuring her were common stock in local folklore.

Bowers was interviewed for Myron Angel's 1881 *History of Nevada*, but she muddled specifics of her life, often in a self-serving way. Regardless of her motivation, the foggy details could only contribute to an episode from early Nevada that was destined for the realm of folklore.[10] Matters became even more hazy when Swift Paine published *Eilley Orrum, Queen of the Comstock* in 1929. The Bowers Mansion Regional Park curates a letter from Paine in which he expressed surprise that his book was taken as a history, when it was intended as fiction, resting on some core facts.[11] A misunderstood novel consequently augmented folklore. The story of the early life of Eilley Bowers became part of the distant legendary past, but unlike Henry Comstock, Old Virginny, and even her husband, she endured, remaining in the region. Her reputation for fortunetelling added to her mystique.

Accounts of women winning sudden wealth in the mines were extremely popular in the West, serving as expressions of the perceived capricious nature of Lady Fortune. Too often the heroines in these narratives were celebrated for their transitions from rags to riches to rags. For those who ended their days impoverished, recollections of their lives thrived with an enduring poignancy. The tale of Eilley Bowers combines tragic elements with her reliance on the supernatural, which enhanced the oral tradition associated with her. Indeed, her story remains powerful, one of the few examples of early Nevada folklore that continues to be told.[12]

The millionaire became a fixture of early American mining folklore. Westerners watched closely as striking it rich had its effect on a common man or woman. The fates of these people supported such clichés as "Wealth can't buy happiness," "Wealth will corrupt an evil man and make him worse," and "Wealth cannot corrupt a truly good person." As though they were part of a local morality play, newly minted millionaires fitted into roles that explored sudden affluence and, occasionally, the prospect of losing everything. These were actors in a drama that demonstrated the variations of human nature.

By the time Sandy and Eilley Bowers returned from Europe, the

Comstock had already transformed. Placer miners had long since disappeared, but so had the time when one could realistically stake a new prospect on the Comstock and win a fortune. Virtually everything of true value had been claimed and mostly resold within a short amount of time, and it was nearly—but not entirely—impossible to get rich by obtaining an undeveloped parcel for a low price. This new phase of Nevada history focused on corporate maneuvering and strategies.

TWO OTHER COMSTOCK MILLIONAIRES, both present in this earliest period, reveal how folklore can be unpredictable about who is celebrated. To be fair, actual events affected the process of remembrance, for history can be a coconspirator in selecting the focus of oral tradition. George Hearst (1820–91) was a California gold country placer miner. Realizing the challenges in that occupation, he became interested in prospecting for underground "quartz" veins and developed some expertise in that form of mining. When he heard of the remarkable strike of what would be called the Comstock Lode, he borrowed some money and reached the new mining district in the summer of 1859. There, he purchased a share in the Ophir Mine, site of the original discovery.

Hearst went on to invest in other Comstock claims, gaining a significant share in the profitable Gould and Curry Mine. With his ventures in the district, Hearst made a modest fortune. He began to phase out his Nevada holdings over a few years, sensing the Comstock might be exhausted and always looking to ride the next crest of the wave. He invested his profits in Park City, Utah, and elsewhere, consistently increasing his wealth with diverse mining prospects, weathering storms when times turned tough.[13]

With a career that had Nevada roots, Hearst became one of the more famous millionaires of the Gilded Age. In addition, his family continued to be well known nationally for decades afterward. Despite all of this, Hearst was largely forgotten in early local folklore. While De Quille purported to write a "history" of the mining district and was ever attuned to oral tradition, he was silent on Hearst.

A grand mine superintendent's house at the Gould and Curry Mine could conceivably be celebrated as the first "Hearst Mansion," yet it bears the name of someone else, a man who was a struggling miner when Hearst departed Nevada as a millionaire. This other miner was later a part owner of the Gould and Curry, and he may have stayed at the superintendent's house for a few months after the Great Fire of 1875. Because he remained on the Comstock, the story of John William Mackay (1831–1902) is interlaced with the history and folklore of the region. The manager's house for the Gould and Curry is known as the Mackay Mansion, with the name Hearst all but gone from memory.

Stories about Mackay appear elsewhere in this volume, but here the narrative about his arrival in 1859 deserves to be recounted. Part of that first wave of fortune seekers, Mackay arrived late in that year accompanied by Jack O'Brien, his partner. As Michael Makley explains in the definitive biography of Mackay, "Legend tells that when they reached the head of Six Mile Canyon, O'Brien pulled a fifty-cent piece from his pocket, the last of their joint capital, and threw it far down the canyon, asserting that now they might enter the camp like gentlemen."[14]

True or not, the story of the entrance of Mackay and O'Brien into Virginia City has been repeated endlessly. It captures a widespread perception of the carefree early days and underscores how everything that Mackay built—from his mines to his fortune—was thanks to his own hands. This was unlike Hearst, who used borrowed money to "buy in" near the top and then exploited his first Comstock success to leapfrog across the mining West, repeatedly arriving at just the right time and then abandoning a place before the inevitable decline. Mackay, on the other hand, began as a hard-working miner, and he persisted long after many had given up hope that a subsequent Comstock bonanza would ever be found.

Hearst was fortunate to have a son, William Randolph, who used the financial foundation to propel the family name into the headlines—literally—as he switched from mining to newspapers. Mackay was able to amass a fortune few exceeded at the time, but the following generations lived more quietly. While the nation remembers Hearst, Mackay is typically ignored. In Nevada the pattern was reversed. At times, folklore, like history, can be fickle.

WHILE THE FIRST STRIKES of 1859 were fodder for legends, the subsequent years of day-to-day mining, even when yielding tens of millions of dollars of gold and silver, did not always furnish moments to commemorate with narrative. That changed in 1873 with the discovery of the Big Bonanza, one of the richest single gold and silver strikes in history. Behind-the-scenes calculations and machinations allowed four Irishmen, John Mackay, James Fair, William O'Brien, and James Flood, to secure majority stock holdings of a key, neglected part of the Comstock Lode.[15]

History then recounts the expert tracking of a vein, shifting from the obvious to the barely recognizable, that led to the discovery of an orebody of gargantuan proportions. It had the potential to be a central focus of oral tradition, but again, folklore is unpredictable. Books have been written detailing how it all unfolded, and it is, indeed, a fascinating story, but there is no evidence that an account of what happened spread through the community. Simply labeling something as "legendary" does not automatically mean that it circulated orally. Instead, people seem to have been more fascinated with the consequence of the wealth that was discovered.

The enormous concentration of precious metals transformed Mackay and Fair into multimillionaires within months.[16] How wealth affected them became the subject of local folklore even while they continued to walk the streets of Virginia City. Their stories show the way reality can shape narratives.

The widespread assessment found Mackay to be of such fine character that his success left him unblemished. He remained in Virginia City, where he was known as a common, humble, hardworking miner. In fact, Mackay was held in such high esteem that his very name became a byword for excellence and good fortune. Wells Drury noted that the phrase "It's a John Mackay" signified "the idea of high quality and good luck."[17]

Mackay stuttered and had a quiet, businesslike demeanor. He was known for his quick temper as well as his generosity. This contrasted with Fair: people described him as always at ease with others, quick to laugh and to inspire laughter. Despite his gregarious facade, Fair's role in local folklore demonstrated that obtaining millions could exaggerate the darkness in one's soul. Fair was perceived ironically as "unfair," stingy, mean-spirited, interested in grabbing power, and always seeking a way to pursue his personal interests.[18] Regardless of what was true, the contrast provided by the images of Mackay and Fair answered the question about how sudden wealth would have its influence on someone: a good person would be unaffected, while a bad man would be shown for his shortcomings, and local folklore illustrated this.

The way adults perceived Mackay and Fair was one thing, but where there is a group of children, their folklore also comes into play: stories survive about Mackay paying for penniless boys to attend shows at Piper's Opera House. Another account features boys sledding down the steep slope of Union Street to Mackay and Fair's mine. The kindly Mackay would use his buggy to tow their sleds back to the top. If Fair's carriage was at the mine instead of Mackay's, the children would start the long uphill hike, unassisted. Or so the stories say.[19]

Another of the stories involving Mackay deals with Virginia City's Great Fire of October 26, 1875. The event was so catastrophic, it became a fixture in local folklore. Residents still identify buildings as "prefire" or "built after the fire." When uncovering a thick layer of ash while planting trees or excavating for construction, residents invariably recall the event.[20]

A statue of John Mackay by emerging sculptor Gutzon Borglum was dedicated in 1908, standing in front of the Mackay School of Mines on the quad of the University of Nevada in Reno. Mackay, depicted as a simple miner, looks up in the direction of Virginia City, home of his Big Bonanza. A student polishes the statue during Mackay Week, 1979, an annual springtime celebration of the state's mining heritage. In the autumn homecoming celebration, the Mackay statue, with its own folk traditions, is often painted or dressed in inappropriate ways. Photo by John Newman, courtesy of Special Collections and University Archives Department, University of Nevada, Reno, Libraries.

In an account of the conflagration, Mackay and Father Patrick Manogue are reputed to have had a confrontation over the fate of the Catholic church. Manogue had a formidable reputation, and he attracted his own body of folklore, the match of any bonanza king.[21] He was an Irish immigrant who worked in the California goldfields before being called to the priesthood. Manogue went to France for training and ordination, and then his superiors assigned him to minister to the mining West.

As the 1875 fire progressed downhill, consuming block after block, it threatened E Street where the Catholic church stood. There were also important mine entrances in the vicinity, including the Con Virginia, central to the affluence of Mackay and Fair. Mackay is always key to stories about an argument over the fire, but the other character varies: it is often Father Manogue, but in other manifestations of the legend, someone else takes the role. Mackay's fierce defense of his mine, which he knew to be essential for the well-being of the entire community, was succinctly summarized by Charles C. Goodwin in his retelling of one version of the story:

> In the crisis of the fire, when the miners were dynamiting the houses on the west side of D street, and filling the shafts to a depth of thirty feet to where the cages had been lowered, with bags of sand and covering the floors of the hoisting works around the cages with sand two or three feet deep and Mr. Mackay was everywhere directing the work, a devout old Irish lady approached him and said: "Oh, Mr. Mackay, the church is on fire!" All the answer that he vouchsafed was, "D—n the church, we can build another if we can keep the fire from going down these shafts!"
>
> The old lady went away shocked, but next morning Mr. Mackay called upon Father—later Bishop Manogue and said: "There is a good deal of suffering here, Father. If I try to help personally I shall be caught by two or three grifters and then will be liable to insult some worthy men and women. I turn the business over to you and your lieutenants. Do it thoroughly, and when you need help draw upon me and keep drawing." In the next three months Father Manogue drew upon him for $150,000, and every draft was honored on sight, and the old Irish lady saw, besides a church grow out of the embers of the old one, and it was larger and more beautiful than the one that had been destroyed.[22]

The sum that Goodwin described was sizable at the time and represents only one of many examples in oral tradition of Mackay quietly donating money in the community.

AT LEAST ONE POPULAR narrative about Fair depicts his willingness to play along with a situation. Drury indicated that the account he heard of a tour through a mine involving Fair was likely local folklore. He wrote that it was "a rather good story . . . which may not be authentic—it is recounted sometimes with another set of characters—but which is characteristic of the camp." The statement reveals that Drury had heard variants of this.[23] As he related it, the incident involved the prominent Polish actress Helena Modjeska during a visit in 1877 to Virginia City to perform at Piper's Opera House.

Modjeska asked for a tour of the mines, a common diversion for tourists to the Comstock. Local newspaperman Sam Davis offered to be her guide into the depths of the famous Con Virginia. They put on the required garments and then descended to the six-hundred-foot level, where they met

Fair, by then, according to legend, a US senator as well as one of the wealthiest men in the nation. He would not purchase his seat in the Senate until several years later, but in the realm of folklore the strength of a story is more important than facts. Fair wore overalls and a slouch hat, as was common in the mines. Davis introduced the actress, but he did not tell her the identity of her guide.

> The Senator personally conducted the party through the underground passages, and after they had seen the mine Modjeska asked Davis if she had not better tip her guide in appreciation for his services. Sam unblushingly replied that it was a good idea, whereupon the actress drew a silver half-dollar from her purse and dropped it in the Senator's hand. Noting his look of astonishment, she asked Sam the reason, and he hinted that possibly it was not as large as the man had expected. So another half-dollar was added to the Fair fortune, and the lovely Helena had left before the Senator regained his usual composure.[24]

Goodwin provided a version where the tour was for "a gentleman from Boston with his wife and young lady daughter." They met Fair, whom they took for one of the miners working the shift, and they were delighted by the tour that they received.

> When they reached the cage and were about to be hoisted from the depth, the Boston man tendered the miner a bright new silver dollar. The miner thanked him but declined the gift, remarking that the company paid him for his time and it was easier to show strangers around than to swing a pick.
>
> "But," said the man, "this is for you personally." But still the miner declined, saying that what he had done was no trouble, but rather a pleasure.
>
> But the Boston man persisted and said, "Now, tell me honestly, my man, why do you not wish to take this dollar."
>
> The miner sighed and said, "Well, one reason is that I have $600,000 up in the bank and it has been bothering me all the morning to decide how I had better to invest it."[25]

The fact that this story appears with variations is a strong indicator that it had percolated in conversation before it was recorded by these and other authors.

The account of Fair giving a tour of the mine is only one of several about him. Most others are not so flattering. For example, there is a narrative about Fair and the issue of smoking tobacco underground, something that was strictly prohibited because of the risk of fouling the air and, more important, because of the threat of fire. Again, from the many versions in primary sources, it seems to have circulated widely. The following is how John Waldorf remembered the tale from his childhood, for it appears that even young people heard—and possibly told—these stories:

> One day while Fair was on one of his lower level inspection tours, his keen nose caught the smell of tobacco. Without making any remark as to his discovery, he turned to the miner at his side and said longingly, "I'm dying for a smoke. I'd give anything for a pipeful of tobacco." The miner looked up, but Fair's face gave no hint of suspicion. Fair spoke of his longing again and again. Finally the miner took pity on him, reached behind a timber and brought forth a pipe and tobacco.
>
> Fair took a smoke, but when he got above ground he made it his business to see the foreman and say, "Fire that man; he's smokin' down there." . . . I don't wonder that we kids didn't like him.[26]

In other sources, there are several men that Fair entices into smoking with him. Fair subsequently dismisses them all, even though he coaxed them into breaking the rule. Other accounts tell of Fair having the entire shift fired. Stories consistently have Fair returning to the surface and ordering the shift manager to do the disagreeable deed of terminating the employment of the workers. Some narratives include the motif of Fair contriving to blame Mackay for the dismissal, although the workers knew that could not have been the case and blamed Fair nevertheless.[27]

Goodwin included several other stories about Fair, which usually depict him as affable but capable of inflicting harm on innocent victims. An account featuring Fair in this trickster-like way involves his wife and the stock market. Referring to Fair as "Uncle Jimmie," Goodwin told of the incident as occurring in the 1860s, before the discovery of the Big Bonanza in 1873:

> Mr. Fair, as he got up from the breakfast table one morning, said to his wife: "My dear, have you any money?" Mrs. Fair replied that she had $7,000 in the bank. By this time Uncle Jimmie had put on his hat, and said: "Don't mention the matter to a soul, but I think there are a few dollars in Curry," and went out.

Mrs. Fair thought the matter over for a few minutes. Then she said to herself, "Surely there would be no harm in letting my brother know," and crossed the street. Her brother was away, but his wife was home and Mrs. Fair told her.

She had a brother and like Mrs. Fair, her thought was, that there would be no harm in telling her brother. By noon all Ireland in Virginia City was buying Curry and Uncle Jimmie was unloading it upon them.

By the end of the week the stock had dropped out of sight and in the Fair house there was a thunder cloud in every room. As Uncle Jimmie rose from the breakfast table he said to his wife: "My dear, did you not tell me that you had some money in the bank?"

Here the storm broke. "I had $7,000 and it is all lost in that old Curry," said Mrs. Fair, and she burst into tears.

"My, my, but I am sorry," said Fair then with a deep sigh, he went into his library and a moment later returned with a check for $7,000. Handing it to his wife he sighed again and said, "I will help you out this time, my dear, but I fear you are not constituted just right to successfully deal in stocks."[28]

Although there are variations of the story, they all depend on the fact that Fair needed to unload worthless Curry stock, and he knew he could count on his wife to spread the deception that it was a good investment. The accounts include returning his wife's money while victimizing everyone else. According to the narratives, Fair swindled his neighbors, but at the time, this brand of stock manipulation was not a crime.

OTHER STORIES OF EARLY Nevada come more directly to the point about breaking the law. Although a good part of the image of the Wild West focuses on criminals and violence, outlaws did not generally rise to prominence in early Nevada folklore. While the region celebrates names like Jesse James, Billy the Kid, Joaquin Murrieta, and similar characters who continue to play in the national perception of the West, Nevada came up surprisingly short with this topic. Wells Drury attempted to raise the stature of a few of these local criminals, but they hardly were on a level with other western counterparts.[29] As indicated, there were stories about the victims of robberies, but the accounts lack the heroic outlaw that one finds elsewhere.[30]

In a celebration of a target of crime, Drury cited the local ballad of "Baldy Green," which, he suggests, "used to be the most popular song on the Comstock." He records the lyrics as follows:

" HOLD UP YOUR HANDS!"

De Quille celebrated the rougher aspects of his society, describing robberies and other crimes, but his extensive treatment of early Nevada lacks mention of any specific criminal becoming prominent in the state's folklore. Wright, *History of the Big Bonanza* (1876); from the author's private collection.

I'll tell you all a story,
And I'll tell it in a song
And I hope that it will please you,
For it won't detain you long;
'Tis about one of the old boys
So gallus and fine,
Who used to carry mails
On the Pioneer Line.

He was the greatest favor-ite
That ever yet was seen,
He was known about Virginny
By the name of Baldy Green.
Oh, he swung a whip so gracefully,
For he was bound to shine—
For he was a high-toned driver
On the Pioneer Line.

Now, as he was driving out one night,
As lively as a coon,
He saw three men jump in the road
By the pale light of the moon;
Two sprang for the leaders,
While one his shotgun cocks,
Saying, "Baldy, we hate to trouble you,
But just pass us out the box."

When Baldy heard them say these words
He opened wide his eyes;
He didn't know what in the world to do,
For it took him by surprise.
Then he reached into the boot,
Saying, "Take it, sirs, with pleasure,"
So out into the middle of the road
Went Wells & Fargo's treasure.

Now, when they got the treasure-box
They seemed quite satisfied,
For the man who held the leaders
Then politely stepped aside,
Saying, "Baldy, we've got what we want,
So drive along your team,"
And he made the quickest time
To Silver City ever seen.
Don't say greenbacks to Baldy now,
It makes him feel so sore;
He'd traveled the road many a time,
But was never stopped before.
Oh, the chances they were three to one
And shotguns were the game,
And if you'd a-been in Baldy's place
You'd a-shelled her out the same.[31]

Drury pointed out that the performer would sing the lines "And he made the quickest time / To Silver City ever seen" as rapidly as possible. The assertion that he "was never stopped before" was an inside joke for Comstockers: during the 1860s, Bally "Baldy" Green was well known for being robbed so frequently that Nevadans became suspicious that he was coordinating the thefts with the robbers.[32]

EXCEPT IN EXCESS, DRINKING alcohol was not usually a crime. Nevertheless, many regarded it as a vice. In addition, drunkenness is a natural friend to oral tradition because of its potential for producing outrageous behavior, grist for stories. Alcohol was a common fixture in early western folklore, as people claimed that they drank harder and had more saloons than anywhere else, even when this is not verifiable.[33]

Drury captured a brief anecdote that serves as an example of drinking as a core motif. He wrote of Brutus Blinkenberry of Gold Hill recounting how he "groaned when his wife accused him of being drunk twenty-seven nights in the preceding month, and who, when sharply interrogated by his spouse, explained that by his groans he was expressing sorrow for missing those other three nights."[34]

This story recalls yet another aspect of early Nevada folklore and the characters that fill its stories, namely, the role of women. While it is true that Eilley Bowers had an important place in the period's oral tradition, she stands out when it comes to representation of her gender. Later, Julia Bulette, a sex worker, became famous, but her ascendancy was apparently a twentieth-century phenomenon, as discussed in the final two chapters. In the first decades after her death in 1867, documentation focused on her accused murderer and his hanging.

Folklore included the belief that sex workers were the first women on the scene and that they played an outsize role in the community during its first years. This misconception survives to the present, even though historical research demonstrates the opposite.[35] Nevertheless, women were generally presented in anonymous ways in early Nevada folklore. We do not know the name of Brutus Blinkenberry's wife who berated his excessive drinking, and Antoinette "Aunty" Adams is merely the brunt of a joke. James Fair's wife is manipulated to assist with his stock scam, but she is not the fully developed character that her husband is. Again, folklore tended to focus on the man rather than the woman.

The diminished role of women could be attributed to the fact that there were far more men in the region, and stories were dominated by a masculine perspective. Eilley Bowers does hint at what was possible, but the tendency to reduce women to two-dimensional often nameless characters is still something that cannot go without comment. When it came to mining in general, it took the groundbreaking research of historians, notably Sally Zanjani, to reshape narrative and work against cultural assumptions.[36]

Folklore, however, is grounded in just these kinds of assumptions, and beliefs have more to do with perception than reality.

THE LATER LEGENDARY CHARACTERS who became the focus of Nevada folklore were affected by the same telescoping of the past discussed in chapter 1. This caused events only a few years before to seem to have occurred "long ago." The phenomenon of perceiving history in this way persisted throughout the nineteenth century. De Quille could speak with wonder about the 1860 discovery of the Grosh brothers' furnace, constructed a mere three years before. John Piper established his Virginia City Corner Bar in 1860, and within a few years it became the Old Corner Bar. Maps dating to the 1870s identify sites abandoned the previous decade as though they were revered antiquities from the ancient world.

The transient nature of the mining West enhanced this phenomenon. Few who were in Virginia City in 1860 still lived there by 1880. Those who came to the intermountain mining West invariably moved on, seeking better opportunities, and, as has been noted, each recently arrived group brought the potential for new traditions. Writing on September 20, 1863, after being home in Iowa for almost ten months, De Quille observed dramatic changes in the community. New buildings were part of a city as it sprawled outward. "Worst of all, in the throng of people, . . . not one face was familiar to me."[37] While this is certainly an exaggeration, the point cannot be dismissed. De Quille was documenting a rapid transformation, as it occurred in less than a year, and it happened repeatedly over subsequent decades.

Mobility created a dynamic environment for the formation of oral narratives. Describing the past of only a few years before became not so much getting the facts right as it was an explanation of a distant, unknowable time. Imagination prevailed, and because each period was new to a certain extent, its residents had the freedom to form their own stories about those who lived there before. Ironically, transience could also inhibit the formation of tradition. People often moved before they had a chance to sink deep roots or to leave an imprint on the community's culture. In this way, someone as important as George Hearst could be forgotten, and John Mackay and James Fair but also Eilley Bowers became the focus of accounts that circulated in Nevada folklore of the day.

The following chapter tackles entities that were often without clear personalities, but who nevertheless assumed a place in local story and belief. Tommyknockers and ghosts were a cultural backdrop for the region. The interplay between the two types of entities went a long way toward defining aspects of early western folklore, exceeding the borders of the state.

CHAPTER 9

Ghosts and Tommyknockers

AN ARTICLE IN VIRGINIA City's *Territorial Enterprise* from 1876 tells of a young girl on a tour in a Comstock mine. The newspaper reported that "on observing the tiny creature led along the drifts toward them, the picks fell from the hands of some of the miners and they stared and gazed with startled eyes and relaxed jaws, believing that at last one of the fairies of the mine, about which they had heard so much, had actually been captured by their sagacious superintendent."[1] This whimsical description of an underground visitor includes the key words "the fairies of the mine, about which they had heard so much." The reference suggests that regardless of any degree of belief, miners understood the idea of mines being inhabited by fairylike entities.

By comparison, De Quille commented in the same decade about underground hauntings: "So many men have been killed in all of the principal mines that there is hardly a mine on the lead that does not contain ghosts, if we are to believe what the miners say."[2] In 1883, Eliot Lord similarly indicated how "it would seem that the recovery of a body, merely to lay it in a shallower grave was an uncalled-for service to the dead, but miners are very reluctant to leave a corpse in a mine where they are working."[3]

De Quille and Lord provided unmistakable declarations that miners were familiar with the concept that those killed underground could linger. Working in the late 1970s, historian Paul Strickland recorded Virginia City native Ty Cobb (1915–97) as indicating that there were "all sorts of legends of ghosts being seen in deserted mines."[4] Cobb's testimony is important because he worked closely with the mining industry in his youth in the early twentieth century. Again, belief is difficult to measure, but there is clear evidence of the idea that spirits could remain underground. In popular imagination, fatal industrial accidents filled dangerous, eerie excavations with phantoms of the dead.

The reference to the underground fairy together with these descriptions of fearing the dead in the mines present an opportunity to consider how workers viewed the supernatural in their excavations. The notion that spirits

Mining with heavy equipment and explosives made for a dangerous occupation. Underground accidents were frequent and dreaded. Death was often the consequence. Wright, *History of the Big Bonanza* (1876); from the author's private collection.

lurk in subterranean mines is international. After all, these are intimidating, hazardous settings, and it is easy to imagine unknown forces dwelling there. Complicating the topic, western hard-rock mining attracted a wide variety of emigrants as well as transplants from eastern states. The workplace consequently became fertile ground for the blending of traditions and the growth of indigenous ones.

Grappling with the folklore of the western mine, then, requires the navigation of entwined perspectives documented by sources that require scrutiny. Whatever emerges from an understanding of mining traditions encounters folklore about hauntings on the surface.

NINETEENTH-CENTURY AUTHORS ADDRESSING MINES often mentioned frightening events intended to thrill readers. These included encounters with the supernatural. What is not always clear is whether incidents in the depths were caused by deceased workers or by something that was more elfin in nature. Ghosts were ubiquitous in Victorian-era society, so it is not surprising to find them identified in excavations where men died in industrial accidents. As famed American folklorist Wayland Hand observed in 1942, "Almost every mine of any size has its ghost story."[5] Indeed, there is ample documentation of stories from Hand's time and before about the souls of the dead lingering in excavations of the American West. At the same time, there are references to folklore about the mines that clearly describe elf-like entities.

During the first half of the twentieth century, folklore collectors documented the various traditions as hard-rock underground mining waned in importance. By then, much of the industry was transforming into surface open-pit excavations, so the gathering of oral traditions from older miners was more a matter of looking back than of recording stories associated with current technology. To understand the complexity of beliefs in subsurface ghosts and how they interacted with more elf-like creatures, it is necessary to draw upon diverse primary documents. Despite the need to employ rigorous source criticism, it is possible to cobble together the historical aspects of the occupational folklore during a pivotal period of a region's development.

Tommyknockers, elfin inhabitants of the mines, are one of the more celebrated aspects of early western folklore. Popular tradition maintains they were from Cornwall, where they were known, simply, as knockers. To understand this entity, it is consequently necessary to return to that homeland, to grapple with the tradition of the Old World miners before they emigrated.

The Cornish story "The Fairy Miners—The Knockers" is typical. It first appeared in print in 1865, telling of "an old man and his son, called Trenwith," miners working near Bosprennis on the south coast of Cornwall. They saw some of the "'Smae People' bringing up the shining ore" to the surface. The father-son team were able to negotiate with "the fairy people," promising them "one-tenth of the richest stuff, [left] properly dressed." The expectation was that with this compensation in hand, the otherworldly miners would allow the men access to the rich ore. With the agreement in hand, the father and son became wealthy. For as long as the old man lived, they honored the arrangement, but when he died, his son proved to be "avaricious and selfish." He cheated his supernatural partners by hoarding all the wealth for himself, and his luck turned. "He took to drink, squandered all the money his father had made, and died a beggar."[6]

There are other legends about knockers punishing those who spy on them or show disrespect. With this, they behaved much like the Cornish piskies (a version of the word "pixies") of the surface and were in line with fairies, elves, *huldrefolk,* or any number of other beings of similar nature, which were part of traditions throughout northern Europe. Most feared them because they were powerful and easily offended. When encountered at an opportune time, the creatures could be helpful to people of good character or to those who were simply fortunate not to offend the supernatural beings.[7] In line with this, knockers, or buccas as they were often called, were capricious and dangerous, so miners avoided them for fear of what ill they might bring.

The Cornish knockers were powerful supernatural miners of relatively short stature. Sometimes they were willing to work with their human counterparts, and they rewarded honesty by leading the way to valuable ore, but they punished greed and anyone who would renege on an agreement. For all of this, however, there was an additional important aspect of Cornish tradition, namely, that the knockers warned miners of danger. This detail is essential because it gave the underground fairies their nickname, which referred to the sound of timbers creaking, "knocking" in a certain way that was taken as a signal of trouble, time to flee to the surface.

In addition, Cornish informants often described these otherworldly miners as spiritual remnants of Jews exiled to mines of Britain's southwest two thousand years ago. This is oddly specific, but it is also in keeping with how many northern Europeans viewed fairies and related creatures as remnants of "ancient souls." This was a common perspective when it came to the origin of these and related supernatural beings, regardless of the setting. Even though the many varieties of fairies were likened to ghosts, the world of the fae was very much separate.[8] An archaic pedigree was key in making fairies and their ilk distinct from the way people viewed manifestations of those who died recently or at most within several generations.

How this tradition came to the American West is another matter. A core question about emigration and folklore revolves around how much survived the transition, and more than that, there has always been interest in whether transplanted beliefs and stories were able to thrive. People do not forget the traditions they once embraced, but they do not always express them in a new setting, especially when surrounded by those from elsewhere. Much of one's folklore can consequently endure, but if it fails to become part of the next generation, it does not meet the threshold of flourishing. As previously considered, Doten's journals describe much of what he knew of folk culture from the East Coast, but thriving as a living tradition in the larger community is another matter.

The transference of the Cornish knocker to North America is a remarkable story. There have been repeated attempts to consider other European supernatural beings who have made a similar transition. Scandinavian trolls remained a force in some midwestern emigrant areas. Fairies found a home in places that were, again, dominated by emigrants from a single region: for example, the Scots who settled in Nova Scotia were able to retain their folklore concerning these entities.[9]

Irish supernatural beings found a home in North America, as shown by the banshee and the leprechaun in modern pop culture. Despite this, however, it is important to understand that Irish American examples are not typically expressions of a living tradition with believers. They are often popularized and even commercialized versions of the supernatural beings akin to the idea of the "folkloresque," which is discussed in the following chapters. Here, it suffices to point out that knowing about something is not the same as telling traditional stories or entertaining folkloric beliefs.[10]

Cornish knockers are unique in the unusual way that they endured the trip across the Atlantic. Not only did they survive the death of the first generation, but non-Cornish westerners adopted the tradition, telling stories about these otherworldly miners who earned widespread respect, now called "tommyknockers." Miners of diverse backgrounds viewed the entities with caution, and they listened for their warnings.

It would be easy to assume that the Old World tradition was imported in its entirety, but that was not the case. Even in Cornwall, the folklore was not monolithic. Rather, it appears stories and perceptions changed in response to innovation. Industrialization altered the way miners thought of the knocker. As Cornish labor adapted from small holdings to larger business operations, the Cornish workplace saw small cohorts of largely self-employed miners replaced by wage earners who went deeper for wealthy mine owners.

This affected expectations when it came to the knocker. Directing miners to profitable orebodies was no longer relevant, but the motif of warning of danger survived the transition to the West. In its North American setting, the tommyknocker only occasionally resumed its role of identifying valuable ore, even while it retained the practice of signaling a mine collapse, a motif that endured as the entity's most important service in both hemispheres.[11]

CONSIDERING THESE TRADITIONS CAREFULLY, it becomes clear that the situation is complex because of the way tommyknockers and ghosts shared the environment. Hand began his 1942 essay on underground folklore with seven paragraphs devoted to tommyknockers, but he often included what he had gathered about underground spirits without apparent tommyknocker affiliation. In this way, Hand confused those with clear elfin attributes with what were merely remnants of dead miners.[12]

Of course, both northern Europe and North America have longstanding beliefs and narratives about ghosts that are not affiliated with the elfin world. In Cornwall, knockers were not associated with the dead from recent times. In North America, however, there was a near consensus that the tommyknockers were some sort of residue of men who died underground. That said, not all mining spirits were tommyknockers. Distinguishing between the two provides a means to correct a misunderstanding that affects both scholarly and popular perceptions of mining folklore.

This is not an easy task, since traditions across the expanse of the West and spanning several decades are not easily compartmentalized. Contradictions and hazy boundaries are common. Comparisons with Cornish folklore add to the problem: miners used fairy-related terms such as "knockers," "knackers," and "bucca" ubiquitously. While these words were applied to many situations, searching primary sources in Cornwall for an underground spirit other than these—a ghost of a dead miner—is to hunt for elusive quarry.

In North America, things were easily muddled. For obvious historical reasons, it was not possible to ascribe an ancient Jewish origin to the tommyknocker of the West. Everyone understood that they could not have resided in any given mine longer than the mine existed. Consequently, there was no imported explanation for the origin of supernatural beings in western excavations. This left the door open to blending tommyknockers and spirits of newly deceased miners who were victims of recent accidents.

While the American tommyknockers easily merged with some but not all ghosts, this distinction was not necessarily reflected in folklore studies of the West: in their enthusiastic search for expressions of the transfer and survival of European fairy traditions to the New World, some folklorists were inclined to see any reference to underground apparitions as examples of tommyknockers. Hand's approach, blurring this line, is typical, and he was not alone in seeing a tommyknocker when dealing with other sorts of supernatural occupants of the mines. My early publications share in this misperception. The name "tommyknocker" provided a convenient if not charismatic catchall for any expressions of folklore that seemed even remotely similar. It was all too easy, then, for documentation and analysis of folklore to be confusing on this point. Either it is necessary to separate tommyknockers and similar entities from accounts that deal with non-elfin spirits of the dead, or we must concede that the miners themselves were sometimes vague on this point.

In at least one instance, Hand's informants felt separating the two realms of the supernatural was possible: "One miner quit the Wyoming Mine in Nevada County [California] in a hurry when he heard tapping, which he called a ghost; more seasoned miners chuckled and said it was only a Tommy Knocker."[13] For the uninitiated, the difference might seem subtle. Making that distinction more difficult to perceive, Hand notes that, "like the Tommy Knockers, ghosts are supposed to be spirits of dead miners which continue to inhabit the areas in which the men were killed."[14]

If both are remnants of dead miners, the distinction appears to be without difference. That said, Hand's report of the use of clay effigies of tommyknockers in California, placed in mines and given offerings of morsels of food, is a step removed from ghosts. This is as an example of appeasing the supernatural, something that seems to be an expression of a belief in an underground fairy of some sort. Significantly, the practice appears to be a survivor of a counterpart in Cornwall. In addition, accounts of these entities throwing pebbles at miners or misplacing tools recall an impish attribute.[15]

An 1884 article in the *Virginia Evening Chronicle* features an incident involving invisible underground workers. Miners observed "two striking hammers hard at work on the head of a rusty drill, which was being deftly turned by unseen hands, and though not a soul was in sight except themselves, they heard a lively conversation, but could make out no words." The story describes that when word of what they saw was contested aboveground, they took witnesses below who testified to the strange occurrence. This narrative would be ambiguous as to whether the dead or tommyknockers were intended, but the newspaper chose to provide the headline of "Underground Ghosts: Is It Peter O'Reilly's Ghost, or 'Old Virginny's?'—or Is It Sandy Bowers's, Maybe?" There is no way to determine if this attribution came from miners or the newspaper, but either way, someone decided that these were ghosts, failing to call them tommyknockers.[16]

The clearest way to separate tommyknockers from the souls of lost miners seems related to whether a given manifestation was associated with a specific miner known to have died in the mine or if the miners themselves were making a clear distinction between the two. The tommyknocker was best rooted in ambiguous origin. In short, a miner who died underground and was known to the living by name did not transform into a tommyknocker, but he could become a ghost. In addition, despite Hand's assertion about tommyknockers being remnants of dead miners, there is no evidence that all workers agreed.[17]

FOR ALL THIS CONFUSION, tommyknockers were most likely to be credited with warning of danger. In early Nevada, a dead miner did not typically help his living counterparts in this way, although it is important to point out that elsewhere, even this line was sometimes obscure. Some traditions apparently did describe the deceased playing this role.[18] That said, a much later Nevada account, this one dating to 1992, specifically links ghosts with tommyknockers, together with the idea of warnings about a threat in the mine. Greg Melton, a Nevada artist and sometime underground laborer, told a reporter that the thirty or so miners who lost their lives in the Sutro Tunnel transformed into tommyknockers. He credited one of these with saving his life with a warning to flee the tunnel where he was working. After Melton left, the old supports collapsed. Here, there is a late example of a victim of an industrial accident turning into a tommyknocker and then warning of danger.[19]

Although underground ghosts of miners did not generally lead western prospectors to riches, sometimes ethereal aboveground voices promised just that. As previously discussed, Peter O'Riley, who participated in the first Ophir strike of 1859, claimed to have followed the advice of a haunting as he searched for another possible bonanza. His last mining project was digging an adit, alone and against all odds, in an unlikely part of the Sierra Nevada. The voice promised wealth, and O'Riley persisted without reward.[20] Eventually, the Irish immigrant was taken to a psychiatric hospital where he ended his days, believing he continued to hear the otherworldly urging to return to his excavation.

A second story describes the supernatural working through a medium to direct a man to tap into a huge oil reserve within Mount Davidson, looming above Virginia City. Despite the fascinating details of these anecdotes, the nature of the entities is unclear. In both this and the O'Riley case, the spirits were in keeping with those contacted during parlor-room séances, the way people sometimes sought otherworldly assistance with finances. Tradition maintained that although aboveground ghosts did this sort of thing, those within mines usually did not.

Traditions on the surface complicated what was occurring belowground. Early Nevada was not unique in the way people regarded the dead as being present everywhere. In 1868, Doten noted that a Scottish immigrant told him that there was "a ghost in the Chollar Potosi mine" in Virginia City. Twenty-two years later in 1890, Doten wrote in his journal that "a female ghost has been seen about the big Congregational church" in Reno. From Doten's point of view, there was little to distinguish between the two remarks in his journal. The departed could manifest anywhere.[21]

Despite the common threads shared by stories, there was an important distinction that separated ghost-related folklore on the surface from traditions belowground. Doten described numerous séances, attempts to conjure spirits to open lines of communication with loved ones and others, something that workers would never attempt in a mine, regarding such an undertaking as too risky. Rather, placating the subterranean supernatural while

ENCOURAGED BY REVELATIONS.

De Quille recorded a story about a miner directed by an "old lady and her spirits" to excavate a huge deposit of oil encased within Mount Davidson. Repeated revelations allegedly encouraged the man to persist until he became fearful that the oil might ignite with his blasting, causing a devastation that could engulf Virginia City below. Either the account was part of oral tradition, or De Quille invented it. Either way, the story underscores how some looked to spiritualism for clues about underground deposits. Wright, *History of the Big Bonanza* (1876); from the author's private collection.

keeping it distant was the goal. For example, one did not whistle underground for fear of what might be attracted to the sound.[22] That this prohibition is shared aboveground during the night illustrates a rough equation: the supernatural was thought to be most threatening in a mine's dark underground shadows and during the night on the surface.

Whether the danger underground was from ghosts or tommyknockers remained vague. There was apparently fluidity from one situation to the next and one miner to another. Sometimes strange circumstances evoked thoughts of the spirit of a dead man, and at other times, perception leaned more in the direction of a tommyknocker, with each worker seeing things differently. Folklore does not come in tidy packages, despite the efforts of later writers to provide rigid classifications.

VOLUMES HAVE BEEN WRITTEN on beliefs about hauntings and various ways to understand accounts of them.[23] Chapter 12 deals in part with recent ghost hunting in historic settings, but that aside, documenting similar nineteenth-century traditions in the community is an important step in understanding early Nevada folklore. For the modern world looking back, the séance has become a cliché of how people in the past interacted with those in the afterworld.

Doten's journal documents the role this practice could play at the time, but reality was complex. For many, the notion of the realm of the departed persisted. The spiritualist movement sanitized the afterlife, making it safe to explore, but that had not always been the case. The diary of Timothy McCarthy (1834–1918), an Irish-born blacksmith who worked in Virginia City, provides insight into how at least one person viewed the fate of the soul. Wedded to his Catholic Church, he likely never attended a séance or a meeting of the spiritualist movement.

In 1872, Timothy's wife, Mary, looked forward to the birth of their child, but on September 15, she became sick, and her husband called on Dr. Bertier, who visited their home for the considerable fee of ten dollars. Over the next six days, Timothy, or "Taigh" as he was known by his Irish nickname, asked several other doctors to see his wife, who remained in ill health. On September 21, Mary gave birth to a girl, but the delivery went poorly, and numerous doctors came to visit, each trying to give the new mother a chance at survival. Ultimately, they failed, and on October 6, McCarthy recorded in his diary, "My dear and loving wife departed this life at 10 minutes after 2 in the morning. May her soul rest in peace. Amen."[24]

McCarthy emigrated from County Cork, like many if not most of the Irish in Virginia City. Cork had the only underground mines in Ireland, so emigrants from that area often traveled to the West, where they could obtain respectable wages for their skills. As a blacksmith, McCarthy would not receive the preferred access to a job in the mines, but he settled in Nevada where the pay was nevertheless good and he would be among friends. Like many from western Cork at the time, he spoke Gaelic and English.

As would be expected, McCarthy brought beliefs and traditions from his place of birth. With the death of his wife, he turned to his priest and his community for consolation. The Irish made up the largest immigrant group in Virginia City, more than a quarter of the population at the time. It is no surprise that St. Mary in the Mountains Catholic Church is its most impressive religious structure.[25]

With Mary's death, McCarthy's diary reflects a preoccupation with the afterlife. On November 1, he made a notation about his deceased wife, "This day at 1 1/2 o'clock p.m. that soul took its flight to Heaven and would be there at 20 minutes to 2 o'clock p.m." The exact declaration raises questions about how McCarthy knew the specific details regarding when the ascent would occur and how long it would take, a journey lasting precisely ten minutes. The answer rests with his Irish neighbors. Key to his remarkable insight into the afterworld was a ghostly encounter that caused a stir on the Comstock, reinforcing and affecting belief.

On November 13, twelve days after Taigh celebrated his wife's ascent to heaven, the *Territorial Enterprise* published a lengthy report of a haunting said to have occurred in Virginia City. Agnes McDonough, aged fourteen, claimed she was communicating with her dead father. Others said that whenever Agnes was alone in one of the rooms, they could hear rapping, and she maintained that she could talk to her father only if no one else was near.[26]

Father Manogue plays a role in this story because he was so highly respected throughout early Nevada. As an important church leader, he investigated the claim of contact with the departed. A nod from him would mean that the Agnes McDonough account could be taken as fact. Manogue likely did not want to be in the position of encouraging advocates of the spiritualist movement, viewing it as potentially encouraging false beliefs, distracting the faithful from the true teaching of the Catholic Church.

The coincidence of the McDonough incident with the death of Mary McCarthy reveals the inner workings of oral tradition within the Irish American neighborhoods of Virginia City. The November 13 newspaper article reported on events in October, indicating that McDonough's father told his daughter that the dead were most likely to ascend to heaven on November 1, All Saints' Day. In addition, the apparition indicated that the journey would take place at 1:30 p.m. and that it would last ten minutes, exactly as Taigh McCarthy wrote in his journal.

The date was particularly important for the widower because his wife had died fewer than four weeks before, and the opportunity presented by All Saints' Day meant that she would not have a long wait in purgatory before going to her eternal reward. More important, Taigh wrote about this in his journal nearly two weeks before the newspaper article was published. He apparently received insight about the otherworldly travels of souls from those within his community during conversations about what Agnes McDonough had learned from her deceased father. The juxtaposition of the diary entry and the subsequent newspaper article lends insight into the chattering about the otherworld that was circulating in 1872 in a Nevada immigrant community.

The spiritualism movement contributed new ideas to places like Virginia City, influencing existing concepts of the survival of death, but the advocates could not contradict existing belief without the risk of chasing away potential adherents. For the most part, lectures served to raise interest and make spirituality a topic of conversation, inspiring people to talk about their beliefs and stories. The example provided by Taigh McCarthy allows for a glimpse into the process that unfolded in his community as people talked about manifestations of the deceased. Father Manogue's final part in the story is unclear, but he may have chosen not to challenge what had become a celebrated event.

AGNES MCDONOUGH TOOK HER own approach, contacting her deceased father in private. Many others followed more conventional paths, and in the second half of the nineteenth century, séances and similar methods became commonplace. Among the many topics that Mary McNair Mathews addressed in her memoir of living in Nevada from 1869 to 1878 are observations about séances, prophecies, and fortunetellers, and this provides insight into the range of possibilities.

Mathews did not adhere to the spiritualist movement. Despite this, she did see importance in dreams, and she believed in the efficacy of folk medicines, often considering them to be better than what trained medical professionals offered. With some ambivalence, she read tea leaves in the bottom of cups to predict the future or to cast light on the past. Mathews wrote that she had become known for her accurate predictions. Although she realized being a fortuneteller might have been a profitable path, she confessed, "I never believed in such humbuggery. What I did was a pastime and amusement."[27]

Underscoring her cynicism regarding spiritualism, Mathews described an incident involving a couple, a husband assisting his wife, who served as the clairvoyant. The woman needed to go into a trance to be successful, and Matthews wrote that she "commenced rubbing her hands, and passing them several times over her face. Next, she commenced shaking her head to and fro, and from side to side, winking her eyes, and jerking her hands and feet."[28] Although Mathews was not convinced by the performance, what she documented was clearly standard fare for the day, and it satisfied at least some people, fitting in with how they believed someone in a trance should behave.

After being invited to pose a question, Mathews asked if she could communicate with her brother, for her trip west was with the hope of settling his estate. Through the clairvoyant, her brother allegedly asserted that there was no reason to linger in the region and that he had killed himself with the effects of alcohol. After the woman's trance ended, Mathews said that nothing that had been said was true, that her brother never drank. Despite the failed attempt, the incident illustrates how this aspect of folk belief could unfold in early Nevada. It also serves as a reminder that folk belief is not consistent among people: while some might embrace the idea that the departed attempt to communicate with the living, others approached the efforts with skepticism.[29]

For those who found comfort or amusement in séances, death became more of a curiosity, and spirits were welcomed and encouraged to visit with the living. Some may have experienced a thrill that bordered on fear during these ceremonies, but these people had voluntarily participated in the effort. Either way, trying to communicate with the dead had been discouraged only a few decades before. There were charms and rituals one could use to reach beyond the grave, but earlier legends typically described how horrific the consequences could be. "Lenore," a well-known poem by Gottfried August Bürger (1747–94), appeared in 1773, remaining popular for decades. It is typical of the way many viewed contact with the dead earlier in the nineteenth century and before. Indeed, Bürger was exploiting a widespread oral narrative that is known as "The Lenore Legend," because of the importance of the poem it inspired.[30]

Lenore, the woman at the center of the action, grieved for the absence of her betrothed, who had gone to fight in a foreign war. Many of the variants of the story tell of the young woman engaging in magic to reach out to the man she loved. Unbeknownst to her, he had died, and so her efforts had awful ramifications. The legend, like the poem, featured the return of the betrothed from the otherworld, now determined to take his bride to his grave. Although most versions have her escaping burial, she usually dies in the end because of the incident.[31]

"The Lenore Legend" typifies how Europeans—and Americans—of the early nineteenth century viewed the dead. The spiritualist movement redefined relationships, however. At the midpoint of the century, many began to gravitate to a different perspective, one that saw communication with the dead as a positive thing. Taigh McCarthy apparently made no effort to contact his dead wife. He nevertheless found solace in words from the dead, repeated by Agnes McDonough; McCarthy took comfort in the idea that his wife would be ascending to heaven on All Saints' Day and that the journey would be effortless, taking only ten minutes. This was not Catholic Church–sanctioned insight into the otherworld. Rather, it was information gleaned from a fourteen-year-old who claimed she was talking with her deceased father.

Even for those who had not formally enlisted in the movement, spiritualism was changing people's relationship with the dead. De Quille summarized beliefs in spiritualism at his time: "Comstock was a believer in spirits. Mrs. L. S. Bowers . . . is a Spiritualist, and very many of the early settlers and those who were one way and another connected with the discovery of silver in Nevada, were Spiritualists. Old Virginia was also a believer in 'spirits.' O'Riley was not the only person who did mining in Nevada under the direction of the spirits. Much money has been lost in that country with spirit superintendents in charge of the work."[32] De Quille lent no credibility to the idea that the departed would help with prospecting, but it was worth reporting on news about forces from the otherworld directing people to action.

While some approached the deceased about the quest for wealth, séances were simply entertaining for others. A hint of this can be found in an incident when several people attempted to contact Sandy Bowers, the early Comstock millionaire, who had died in 1868. Two years later, Doten described a séance where participants believed they were communicating with his spirit.[33] The idea that he would visit Doten's séance is an expression of the legendary status that Bowers had achieved in the community.

EARLY NEVADANS, LIKE THEIR contemporaries throughout the nation, tended to approach the deceased in ways that were different from previous generations. Indeed, their thinking about spirits is also distinct from what has occurred more recently. Today, ghost hunters seek remnants of the dead, hoping to capture them on film. These once dangerous entities have been domesticated. They are like threatening predators, now exhibited in zoos. People gaze at them in safety, reinforcing humanity's false view of itself, in total mastery of the world. A sense of this is present when reading about nineteenth-century séances: people invited the departed to participate in what was little more than a parlor game. No doubt some felt the horror and dread at one point common when dealing with ghosts, but the dead were shifting to their modern stance, the menace they formerly represented now diminished.

Underground, things were different. Danger and dread remained. A mine was not a domesticated space. Any eerie manifestation could inspire spine-tingling panic that threatened to overcome a miner when a groaning timber echoed in the depths. Whether the tommyknocker was a personification of a generic ghost or a separate species of the supernatural, it demanded caution even when being helpful. Although the knocker was regarded with terror in Cornwall, it could be helpful to miners of good character, leading them to valuable ore and warning of possible cave-ins. In the American West, the tommyknocker leaned even more toward the positive attributes, leaving most of the horrific aspects to the underground dead. That said, there was no set dogma, and western miners could speak of tommyknockers with dread or something more lighthearted. Perception was no doubt different from miner to miner and place to place, making a summary of a shared perspective as elusive as the knockers and ghosts themselves.

The following chapter takes folklore in a different direction, bending toward the modern. In this case, the popular legend about Hank Monk and Horace Greeley became fodder for the way westerners perceived themselves and those less familiar with the wilds of the region. How this was adapted by Mark Twain and others hints at a progression toward more recent attitudes. This journey to the present is completed in the two final chapters, which explore the way early Nevada folklore would be viewed by new generations.

CHAPTER 10

Hank Monk and Mark Twain

A BOOK ABOUT LYING in the West begs for a discussion of Samuel Clemens. That famous author, who took his name Mark Twain while working for Virginia City's *Territorial Enterprise,* would seem a natural fit for the subject, given the region's predilection for deception. Astute readers may have noticed how few times Twain's work has figured here, but it is not for his failure to extend himself into the realm of folklore.

An expert on stories with exaggeration, Carolyn Brown suggests that it is possible to see the entirety of Twain's book *Roughing It* as a tall tale. After all, the extravagant account of his life in the West weaves one absurdity with the next. Twain's inclination to tell his "stretchers" has long been maddening for historians seeking accurate details in *Roughing It,* but this also makes it a delight for those who enjoy brilliant literature.[1]

As noted previously, western narratives depending on deceit draw on the region's exploitation of duplicity for humor. A collection of the "folklore of the West" could easily include Twain's gift by quoting his tall tales, but his relationship with oral tradition is much more complex than that. Twain's reaction to a legend that had been circulating in the West in the early 1860s serves as an example of how difficult it is to consider something like *Roughing It* when dealing with the region's folklore.

The account about Horace Greeley was mentioned in chapter 4, furnishing context for other tales about Hank Monk, the famed stage driver, but De Quille purposefully abbreviated the Monk-Greeley episode. A more focused consideration of the story ultimately requires a perspective different from what has been previously employed. The history of this incident can be summarized in simple terms: news of the 1859 encounter between Greeley and Monk spread quickly in the form of a legend, something told to be believed.

As described earlier, Greeley was famous when he traveled to the West, giving numerous lectures advocating the region's development. Often credited with the catchphrase "Go West, young man!" Greeley was well known for his role in helping found the antislavery Republican Party in the 1850s.

Hank Monk had a reputation for being a fine teamster, but his encounter with Horace Greeley in 1859 turned the wagon master into a legend, giving him a degree of national fame. Wright, *History of the Big Bonanza* (1876); from the author's private collection.

As editor of his *New York Tribune,* he became a powerful eastern voice for reform-minded social and political causes, seeking to rally a nation in support of issues including the abolition of slavery. He was a proponent of a transcontinental railroad, and he looked to the development of the West to lift the fate of the nation. As Greeley set out for the frontier, it would have been hard to imagine that a welcomed national celebrity would transform into the victim of a biting, comic narrative.[2]

On July 30, 1859, while in Genoa in present-day Nevada, Greeley asked the manager of a stage company for transport over the Sierra Nevada so he could give a presentation in Placerville on the western, Californian slope. Greeley was assigned to Hank Monk, with the promise to arrive at his destination in time for his lecture. Since Monk was one of the best teamsters in the region, the famous journalist was in capable hands.

According to the legend, Monk's slow progress uphill inspired an imperious Greeley to demand a faster pace. The journalist was worried he would miss the appointed hour, but Monk gave little response as they ground their way upward. He knew his route better than most, and he understood what he could achieve with a good team: since the trip began with a steep ascent, it was necessarily sluggish at first. When a frantic Greeley repeated his demand for haste, a laconic Monk replied that he had his orders to get him there on time, leaving the New Yorker with the impression that his driver did not understand the urgency of the situation.

Finally, they reached the summit, and the teamster turned his horses loose to race down the remainder of the route, making up for lost time. Monk coaxed everything he could from his team, leaving the petrified journalist to protest the speed of their daredevil descent, often at cliff's edge. In answer, the experienced teamster merely shouted back, "Hang on, Horace, I'll get you there on time." Of course, Monk delivered his charge to Placerville by the appointed hour, but it was a frightened, badly shaken Greeley who faced his audience. Or so says the legend.

Accounts of the incident circulated, reflecting the popular idea of what it was to be a westerner and how an effete newspaperman was no match for someone like Monk. The story delighted regional audiences for several reasons. At the beginning of the tale, Monk seems to be an incompetent, buffoonish simpleton. Greeley assumes the role of an arrogant, know-it-all easterner, a western cliché, even if unfair. With the shockingly wild second half of the trip, traversing one of the West's more dramatic landscapes and dangerous routes, Monk reveals his expertise, and his assurance to Greeley adds an understated punch line that is both effective and memorable.

Western audiences likely enjoyed how Monk, a common worker, presumed to refer to his passenger as Horace rather than Mr. Greeley, despite his national stature. Using a personal name celebrates regional ideals of informality and equality, combined with a desire to put eastern pretenses in their place. As the story concludes, this true westerner showed his skill and mastery of the wilderness, outfoxing the presumed intellectually superior easterner even while Monk pretended to be a fool.

By initially convincing Greeley that he does not know his trade and then by demonstrating that he is, in fact, an expert wagon master, Monk dupes his deceived victim, who becomes a quivering mass of fear.[3] For his part in the story, Greeley boards the stage with absolute, unflinching supremacy, but he leaves it humbled and shaken, having his own manhood called into question by the standards of the time. In fact, the plot describes what amounts to a practical joke.

Over subsequent years, the description of Greeley's naive reaction to western geography exposed him to lasting ridicule. Accuracy aside, there is ample evidence that the account circulated quickly. Writers allude to having heard it beginning in 1860. On one level it is valuable to identify a thriving expression of early Nevada folklore. It is useful to understand its life cycle and to consider the implication here that there may have been other stories that arrived on the scene only to disappear without having been recorded.

That said, the Monk-Greeley legend did not fade entirely: later authors recorded the story, which continued to resonate even if with less enthusiasm. In addition, this part of western folklore inspired two of the greatest American humorists of the time.

The success of the account was partly due to Greeley's national fame when he arrived in the West. Before the incident, Monk had a reputation in the area for being a capable teamster, but that was the limit of his renown. Afterward—as previously discussed—he became the subject of still other regional legends.[4]

To provide additional context, it is important to remember that Greeley's encounter with Monk occurred only a few weeks after the discovery of gold and silver at the nearby Comstock Lode. It was a dynamic time. Primitive roads across the Sierra Nevada served fortune seekers as well as teamsters and packers delivering supplies to scattered emerging settlements. In a few months, the mass movement heading to the Comstock and newly founded Virginia City would inspire improvements to the region's roads. In the summer of 1859, most of these routes through the wilderness remained little more than trails.[5]

HORACE GREELEY WROTE THE earliest published version of his trip across the mountains, set to paper on August 1, 1859, two days after he rode with Monk; it appeared in his New York newspaper on September 7. He described the vistas, the various species of trees, and how they passed around the southern shore of Lake Tahoe. For Greeley, the road from there to the western foothills of the Sierra Nevada anticipated as it is yet today, "eaten into the side of a steep mountain, with a precipice of from five to fifteen hundred feet on one side and as steep an eminence on the other."

Greeley suggested that the rate of travel along "this mere shelf" was "of ten miles an hour (in one instance eleven), or just as fast as four wild California horses, whom two men could scarcely harness, could draw it." He declared that "our driver was of course skillful," and he mentioned that there was some risk in the journey given the road and the speed. "Yet at this break-neck rate we were driven for not less than four hours or forty miles, changing horses every ten or fifteen, and raising a cloud of dust through which it was difficult at times to see anything." At journey's end, Greeley observed how happy he was "to find myself once more among friends, surrounded by the comforts of civilization, and with a prospect of occasional rest. I cannot conscientiously recommend the route I have traveled to Summer tourists in quest of pleasure, but it is a balm for many bruises to know that I am at last in CALIFORNIA."[6]

The journalist's account only hints at the ride being wild, and he offers no indication that he was terrified or that his driver uttered the comic retort that became so famous. In fact, Monk remains anonymous in the article, appearing merely as a skillful driver. Either Greeley sidestepped his panic and anything that would be embarrassing, or the journey was far more subdued than the legend would later indicate. Either way, the *New York Tribune* article was far removed from the oral narrative that would take shape.

In 1942, historian Richard Lillard suggested that the embellished story of the Monk-Greeley wild ride was "widely circulated within less than six months" and "became 'the topic of the entire coast country.'" Lillard cited an article published on April 15, 1860, in San Francisco's *Golden Age:* a correspondent using the pen name "Cornish" had interviewed Monk and reported the teamster as describing Greeley with "his bare head bobbing, sometimes on the back and then on the front of the seat, sometimes in the coach and then out and then on the top and then on the bottom, holding on to whatever he could grab." Cornish also captured the dialogue that became key, with Greeley calling out, "Driver. I'm not particular for an hour or two!" with Monk answering, "Horace . . . keep your seat! I told you I would get you there by 5 o'clock, and by G—I'll do it, if the axles hold!"[7]

The story began to take shape between the ride in late July 1859 and the interview of Monk before April 1860. Little in Greeley's unremarkable published account would seem inspirational to become the core of a legend, nor would it have likely attracted the attention of the author for the *Golden Age.* Perhaps Monk told of the ride across the Sierra Nevada with embellishments, but that cannot be certain. At some point, the first-person recollection was repeated by others. Within months, it attracted Cornish's attention, but this transition occurred without documentation.

Twain, in his 1872 *Roughing It,* recalled the Monk-Greeley legend as widespread by the summer of 1861 when he journeyed overland from Missouri to Nevada.[8] While Twain always warrants caution when it comes to the facts, this evidence seems sound, and it is supported by famed comic writer and performer Artemus Ward (Charles Farrar Browne; 1834–67), who came to the West in 1863. While traveling the expanse of the continent to reach previously untapped markets, he recorded a version of the Monk-Greeley story.

Elaboration enhanced the tale. Repetition smoothed its edges. There can be little question that the narrative belonged to regional folklore and remained in circulation for at least several years. Twain would eventually describe fatigue associated with the legend, but other evidence points to its ongoing popularity. In addition, all the attention made Monk something of a tourist attraction.

Traveling the West in 1866, British statesman Sir Charles Wentworth Dilke, 2nd Baronet, wrote of his journey, recalling how he rode the stage route well known for its driver. "When we were nearing Hank Monk's 'piece,' I became impatient to see the hero of the famous ride." Dilke was then disappointed to see another driver assume the seat, as the British traveler wanted to meet the man "who drove Greeley." Then, finally, Monk replaced the driver, and Dilke was honored to ride in the seat next to the famed teamster. Sadly, the hero of legend spoke few words, just as the story captured him, providing Dilke with an opportunity to record no more than a snippet or two.[9]

There are many examples of the Monk-Greeley anecdote in print from the 1860s, but the way Twain and Ward, the two great comic writers of their time, handled it reveals something about creative options when exploiting nineteenth-century oral tradition. By the late 1850s, Ward had become a national icon as a columnist. By taking his character to the stage, his legacy grew as a pathbreaking humorist. He became the delight of the English-speaking world, his fame even reaching Britain.[10]

Ward made a career of poking fun at people, and stilted eastern contemporaries were easy targets. It was natural, then, for him to embrace the Monk-Greeley tale, which appeared in his 1865 book *Artemus Ward (His Travels) Among the Mormons.* This early opportunity for a national audience to know of the incident mismatched its basic facts.[11] For Ward, Greeley traveled from Folsom to Placerville, both on the California side of the mountains, where the harrowing episode of riding on the edge of a cliff could not have occurred. It is unknowable if Ward heard the story that way or if he confused the details.

In 1872 when Mark Twain wrote of coming west a decade after arriving, he claimed that the Monk-Greeley legend was already a tired anecdote, but that was likely an exaggeration. It seems more probable that Twain sensed that the story was overused by sometime later in the 1860s. The emerging author then exploited this weakness for stage and print.

Twain would have known the way Ward handled the account of Greeley and Monk in his 1865 book. Although Ward had befriended his colleague and had opened doors for his early publications, Twain was competitive, and he no doubt saw an opportunity to set a radically different tone from that of Ward. Reaching beyond a simple retelling, he manipulated the story to suit his purposes.

Twain first drew on the anecdote in 1866. In his autobiography, he explained that he used Monk and Greeley to test ways to address an audience, even as his career on the stage was beginning. Twain wrote that an earlier presentation lacked a funny start, so he "felt the necessity of preceding it with something which would break up the house with a laugh, and get me on pleasant and friendly terms with it at the start." He then added, "I prepared a scheme of so daring a nature that I wonder now that I ever had the courage to carry it through. San Francisco had been persecuted for five or six years with a silly and pointless and unkillable anecdote which everybody had long ago grown weary of—weary unto death. . . . I resolved to begin my lecture with it, and keep on repeating it until the mere repetition should conquer the house and make it laugh."[12]

Although Twain indicated that his first use of this "scheme" occurred in San Francisco, evidence suggests that he initially exploited the risky preface in Virginia City, in early November 1866. Nevertheless, a reporter for the *Alta California* described Twain's first audacious comic assault on the audience at Platt's Hall in San Francisco, on November 16, 1866. According to the newspaper, "The lecturer commenced with a story he had heard about the Overland Mail service, and didn't want to hear any more." Faced with an audience of fifteen hundred, many his friends, Twain determined to "grieve them, disappoint them, and make them sick at heart to hear me fetch out that odious anecdote with the air of a person who thought it new and good."[13] In his autobiography, the author remembered how he stood before the packed hall and recounted the first day of his journey overland in 1861 when a man joined them in their stage at one of the stops. A passenger told Clemens and the others of "a most laughable thing," the tale of the encounter of Monk and Greeley.

The way Twain told the Monk-Greeley narrative was to strip it of much of the content, particularly how the slow ascent contrasted with the rapid descent. Leaving as little flavor as possible, he distilled the story: "Hank Monk cracked his whip and started off at an awful pace. The coach bounced up and down in such a terrific way that it jolted the buttons all off of Horace's coat and finally shot his head clean through the roof of the stage, and then he yelled at Hank Monk and begged him to go easier—said he warn't in as much of a hurry as he was a while ago. But Hank Monk said 'Keep your seat, Horace, I'll get you there on time!'—and you bet he did, too, what was left of him!"[14]

Twain further described the performance in his autobiography:

I told it in a level voice, in a colorless and monotonous way, without emphasizing any word in it, and succeeded in making it dreary and stupid to the limit. Then I paused and looked very much pleased with myself, and as if I expected a burst of laughter. Of course there was no laughter, nor anything resembling it. There was a dead silence. As far as the eye could reach that sea of faces was a sorrow to look upon; some bore an insulted look; some exhibited resentment, my friends and acquaintances looked ashamed, and the house, as a body, looked as if it had taken an emetic.

I tried to look embarrassed, and did it very well. For a while I said nothing, but stood fumbling with my hands in a sort of mute appeal to the audience for compassion. Many did pity me—I could see it. But I could also see that the rest were thirsting for blood. I presently began again, and stammered awkwardly along with some more details of the overland trip. Then I began to work up toward my anecdote again with the air of a person who thinks he did not tell it well the first time, and who feels that the house will like it the next time, if told with a better art. The house perceived that I was working up toward the anecdote again, and its indignation was very apparent.[15]

A summary is sufficient here to avoid the tedium inflicted on the nineteenth-century audience: Twain told how he heard about the incident a second time, again speaking in as flat a way as possible. The audience remained silent. Twain recalled that "I looked embarrassed again. I fumbled again. I tried to seem ready to cry."

Then, for a third time, Twain began to tell the story, pretending to be desperate for his audience to see the charm and wit in the tired anecdote. Again, he described his presentation in his autobiography,

All of a sudden, the front ranks recognized the sell, and broke into a laugh. It spread back, and back, and back, to the furthest verge of the place; then swept forward again, and then back again, and at the end of a minute the laughter was as universal and as thunderously noisy as a tempest. . . . It was a heavenly sound to me, for I was nearly exhausted with weakness and apprehension, and was becoming almost convinced that I should have to stand there and keep on telling that anecdote all night, before I could make those people understand that I was working a delicate piece of satire. I am sure I should have stood my ground and gone on favoring them with that tale until I broke them down, for I had the unconquerable conviction that the monotonous repetition of it would infallibly fetch them some time or other.[16]

GREELEY'S RIDE.

"Greeley's Ride" from Mark Twain's *Roughing It* (1872) made light of the story about Monk and the journalist from the East. This lithograph is consistent with oral tradition, which transformed an ambling wagon into a swift ride in a stagecoach. Courtesy of Special Collections and University Archives Department, University of Nevada, Reno, Libraries.

Because this approach required an audience that was ignorant of the strategy, Twain could not abuse the Monk-Greeley legend everywhere. He had succeeded in turning folklore on its head, but surprising the unwary was key to his success.[17]

The great man of American letters had manipulated folklore for use on the stage, but that was not the end of it. Instead, Monk and Greeley stood ready to be exploited in writing as well. In *Roughing It,* Twain wrote about how he accompanied his brother Orion Clemens, appointed by President Abraham Lincoln to serve as the first secretary-treasurer of the newly organized Nevada Territory.[18] His account of the overland trip included the Monk-Greeley story, introduced much as it was in his 1866 lectures: strangers repeatedly told the anecdote to the two brothers. After that, the written word called for a new ploy, a literary solution.[19]

Twain then described how while crossing a desert, he and his fellow travelers encountered "a poor wanderer who had lain down to die. . . . Hunger and fatigue had conquered him."[20] He and the others carried the unfortunate man to the stagecoach and nursed him back to life. With "a feeble voice that had a tremble of honest emotion in it, he thanked his rescuers," apologizing for his inability to repay their compassion. The rescued man then suggested that he could at least offer something to serve as modest compensation:

> "I feel that I can at least make one hour of your long journey lighter. I take it you are strangers to this great thoroughfare, but I am entirely familiar with it. In this connection I can tell you a most laughable thing indeed, if you would like to listen to it. Horace Greeley—"
>
> I said, impressively:
>
> "Suffering stranger, proceed at your peril. You see in me the melancholy wreck of a once stalwart and magnificent manhood. What has brought me to this? That thing which you are about to tell. Gradually but surely, that tiresome old anecdote has sapped my strength, undermined my constitution, withered my life. Pity my helplessness. Spare me only just this once, and tell me about young George Washington and his little hatchet for a change."
>
> We were saved. But not so the invalid. In trying to retain the anecdote in his system he strained himself and died in our arms."[21]

Twain then expressed his regret, acknowledging that he should not have forced the stranger to keep "that anecdote in." This, however, merely established an opportunity to transition into a rant against the legend that had been circulating without restraint. Twain suggested that during his six-year western sojourn,

> I crossed and recrossed the Sierras between Nevada and California thirteen times by stage and listened to that deathless incident four hundred and eighty-one or eighty-two times. I have the list somewhere. Drivers always told it, conductors told it, landlords told it, chance passengers told it. . . . I have had the same driver tell it to me two or three times in the same afternoon. It has come to me in all the multitude of tongues that Babel bequeathed to earth, and flavored with whiskey, brandy, beer, cologne, sozodont, tobacco, garlic, onions, grasshoppers—everything that has a fragrance to it through all the long list of things that are gorged or guzzled by the sons of men. I never have smelt any anecdote as often as I have smelt that one; never have smelt any anecdote that smelt as variegated as that one. And you never could learn to know it by its smell, because every time

you thought you had learned the smell of it, it turned up with a different smell.[22]

In tall-tale fashion, Twain suggested that he had "heard that it is in the Talmud. I have seen it in print in nine different languages; I have been told that it is employed in the inquisition in Rome; and I now learn with regret that it is going to be set to music. I do not think that such things are right." With a footnote, Twain claimed that the story was not even true and was consequently deprived of even the value of veracity. He further invoked "the thirteenth chapter of Daniel," a biblical passage demanding the death penalty for lying, not without irony since it came from a celebrated liar.[23]

Despite Twain's assertion, the event did occur, but through the process of oral transmission, details drifted from reality, something likely under way as early as 1860 when Hank Monk talked to Cornish, the author of the *Golden Age* article. In 1883, A. H. Hawley, looking back on his life at Lake Tahoe, wrote, "I was there when Horace Greeley passed through the [Lake] Valley in a miserable little old four horse team and small mud wagon instead of the high toned outfit that is so much talked about."[24] This detail about the vehicle matches Greeley's version. Oral tradition transformed the rambling, humble wagon—suited to the rough mountain trails in the summer of 1859—into a sleek, racing stagecoach in keeping with the glamour of the Wild West. It is also likely that exaggeration of the abuse sustained by Greeley coincided with the amplification of the speed and danger of the journey. These changes may have raised Twain's suspicions. At the same time, this revision was central to why people told the account.

TWAIN MAY HAVE DONE what he could to extinguish enthusiasm for the Monk-Greeley legend, but it continued to appear in print for decades, an apparent echo of ongoing oral circulation. Drury recounted the narrative in his memoir, published in 1936; he described it as "a-thousand-times-told, in variant form."[25] As evidence of its enduring popularity, the Monk-Greeley story even inspired the work of noted Comstock composer J. P. Meder, whose 1878 "Hank Monk Schottische" transformed the tradition into music: Twain's stated fear had come true.[26]

In 1914, Reno's pageant for the fiftieth-anniversary celebration of Nevada statehood included a skit of the Monk-Greeley ride. Actors spoke Greeley's celebrated words, "Go easy, Hank, go easy," with the teamster's answer, "Keep your seat, Horace, I'll get you there on time."[27] In his history of the Comstock appearing in 1943, Grant H. Smith recorded the phrase in rhyme as "Keep your seat, Horace! I'll get you there on time if I kill every horse on the line."[28] Variation hints at diversity in oral tradition, but at the very least, repetition is evidence of endurance.

The Monk-Greeley story entered the realm of political discourse when New York congressman Calvin Hulburd read Ward's version of the incident on the floor of the House of Representatives, entering it into the official *Congressional Record* on March 29, 1866.[29] Hulburd sought to tarnish Greeley's reputation, but the journalist nevertheless went on to challenge President Ulysses S. Grant in his bid for reelection in 1872. It is impossible to know if the western legend affected the campaign, since Greeley faced a fierce political headwind. Grant, a national hero of the Civil War, easily won a second term. Before the month of the election ended, Greeley died.

Further testimony to Monk's celebrity manifested in 1882 when he was offered $250 per month to tour large eastern cities "as the man of Horace Greeley Fame." Virginia City's *Territorial Enterprise* reported, "Hank says that he has not seen a place larger than Virginia City in over twenty years. Hank don't want to be hauled about the country in a dry goods box, and exhibited between a fat woman and a big 'snaik.'"[30] By using poor grammar and employing a provincial pronunciation, the newspaper emphasized Monk's rustic character.

Here again, Monk is the sly westerner, whose simple wit was enough to dethrone the monarch of eastern journalism and who knew enough to avoid being featured as a curiosity in a carnival show. The potential fate of being exhibited between a large woman and a big "snaik" would be immediately recognized by *Enterprise* readers as a reference to the work of Artemus Ward, who was known for his comic misspellings and for describing the display of remarkable things, including a big "snaik." More important, here is additional evidence that the Monk-Greeley story continued to have national currency in the early 1880s.

DESPITE TWAIN'S EFFORT TO assassinate the legend, it persisted. He had considered what he had on hand and transformed an example of early western folklore into something new, a legend fitted into two other genres: his treatment considered the story from outside itself and twisted it into a satire that allowed for distinct approaches to wit, one onstage and the other in print. This great American author was not satisfied with simply repeating a popular humorous narrative in the way that Ward did in 1865.

By arriving at creative ways to manipulate the legend, Twain's innovations meet the definition of a new approach to folklore studies. Michael Dylan Foster and Jeffrey Tolbert recently embraced various adaptations of and allusions to folklore with the term "folkloresque."[31] They use this word to discuss how modifications and imitations of oral tradition yield new forms in various media. In an increasingly media-savvy world, the idea of the folkloresque addresses aspects of culture that folklorists have long considered, but not always satisfactorily. The idea of the folkloresque is particularly valuable for understanding early—and later—Nevada.

In 1950, American folklorist Richard Dorson coined the word "fakelore" for what he identified as "nonsense and claptrap collections," produced by a literate culture and passed off as drawing from folk tradition.[32] This inspired some to engage in "myth busting," an exercise that rightly corrected the historical record, but the effort too often sterilized a flavorful past. A great deal of color has been thrown on the trash heap as unwanted cultural debris, undesirable, at least, for some.

Foster and Tolbert's folkloresque embraces many more cultural expressions than what Dorson was addressing when he put forward the idea of fakelore. This new term is also intended to apply to literary and other adaptations of folklore as well as inventions that have the appearance of popular narrative yet lack actual roots in oral tradition. At the heart of this new term is that it is not judgmental; as Foster points out, "The very act of relabeling asserts that these products, and the processes associated with them, are as culturally revealing and valuable as 'genuine' folklore."[33]

Because Twain's intent became all too clear, his exploitation of the Monk-Greeley legend could not be confused with what was circulating orally. This was parody, and as such, it would not have fallen under Dorson's fakelore.[34] While satire influenced much of Twain's work, the example explored here fits the specific definition of parody within the context of the folkloresque. Of pivotal importance is the twisting of a well-known story while stepping into the realm of folklore about folklore.[35] His treatment of oral tradition looks at itself from outside while turning the narrative itself into the brunt of a joke. Foster describes this species of parody and the folkloresque as "simultaneously a form of metafolklore and also a popular culture appropriation of the power of folklore and its assumed association with 'authentic' tradition."[36]

While the flow between folklore and literature has ancient roots, the practice of dipping into an international library of oral tradition for various purposes has many manifestations in a modern world. Foster and Tolbert have put forward a means to grapple with these cultural expressions comprehensively. In the context of the legend of Greeley and Monk, they also provide a way to understand the genius of Twain in the context of early western folklore.

IN THE TWENTIETH CENTURY, Nevadans and their visitors came to interact with local folklore in diverse ways. While constant change and upheaval affected the coalescing traditions, still more was in store for westerners. Looking specifically at the Comstock, it is possible to see a place that had dominated the early traditions of the region with its repeated cycles of bonanza and borrasca. By the 1930s, those few remaining in the mining district were forced to find new ways to deal with shifting circumstance.

Most of Nevada found its own path—or paths—to address the decline in mining that depressed the economy in the final years of the nineteenth century. With every decade that followed, even more new people arrived. Much as happened with the waves of fortune seekers affecting the territory in the 1860s, the region was redefined with the many who came to exploit fresh economic opportunities, closing the early chapter of Nevada folklore.

For the Comstock, however, things were different. With a population dwindling to several hundred, the economic promise of the former capital of mining rested in its past. Heritage tourism became an increasingly important part of its survival, and as such, residents of the mining district needed to address what went before. This often entailed reworking older traditions to suit a new century. What Twain began with his manipulation of the legend of Greeley and Monk, Comstockers would perpetuate. Whether referred to as fakelore or the folkloresque, the story they told about their past was often a jumble of history, lore, and fabrication. And it worked well.

How later Nevadans addressed the region's earlier folklore is the subject of the following concluding chapters. This includes the several ways people have recently considered the remnants of early Nevada, principal among these being the Virginia City National Historic Landmark District. Just as traditions affected perception, those who visited the remnants of the past applied their own folklore to what they found. Stories gave life to a past that was at times increasingly misunderstood.

CHAPTER 11

Sex, Murder, and More Monumental Lies

IN THE SUMMER OF 1960, at roughly the same time I heard the legend of the underground river discussed in chapter 7, I joined an honored folk tradition by telling my first Comstock lie. It was about Julia Bulette, a sex worker who had transformed into a fixture of the Wild West. I had just turned five years old.

Inspired by the television show *Bonanza,* my parents took my older brother and me to Virginia City, where the fictional Cartwrights rode into town for supplies, a drink, and some trouble. A coin-operated telescope in the Bucket of Blood Saloon enticed tourists to pay the price so they could see the grave of the famed Julia Bulette. My father answered the siren call and fed a nickel into the device, quickly found the site, and then yielded it to my mother. She, too, saw the gleaming painted wood around Bulette's memorial, the object of so much mythical awe. Then it was the turn of my brother, who also caught a glimpse of the grave site.

When it came to be my chance, I failed to see anything. The telescope's timer was clicking down to zero, and we all knew it would shortly go dark, demanding another coin, which my father certainly would not spend. "Do you see it? Do you see it?" my parents pressed me. Seeking to end the harassment, I finally answered, "Yes." I had lied about the legendary sex worker. Although lacking the artistry of De Quille or Twain, my sadly simple fabrication leaned toward a tradition that has contributed to the stature of the Wild West.

How Bulette and I came to that place at that time is key to understanding the twentieth-century interaction of history and folklore about the 1860s. Six years earlier, Lucius Beebe wrote that Bulette was drawn to Virginia City in 1859: "In far-off New Orleans, a dusky beauty . . . who was soon to fill columns of space in *The [Territorial] Enterprise,* read about the Comstock in the *Picayune* and took passage for Panama en route to the new golconda." He added that she was "Virginia City's first and easily most publicized courtesan."[1]

Some twenty years before that, George Lyman published a book about the glory days of Virginia City and the great Comstock Lode. He described an epidemic in 1859 and how Bulette, having built a magnificent brothel, "turned her palace into a hospital. Caldrons of broth and steamers of rice stewed on her stove. Night and day she went from bed to bunk in cabin and tent on her mission of mercy, soothing and comforting, feeding and nursing like a white angel."[2] Gosh, what a gal, to use the day's vernacular. Proving how remarkable she truly was, Bulette accomplished all this, four years before she even arrived on the scene. Not to mention that there was no epidemic.

Bulette came to Virginia City in 1863, one of dozens of sex workers from California. These women often faded from the historical record and were typically ignored as individuals in local folklore. All except Julia Bulette, who was eventually resurrected in oral tradition.[3] While still alive, she gained some attention as a favorite of Tom Peasley, mentioned previously for wanting his boots removed before he died. He was a popular saloon owner and the captain of the volunteer firefighters, Virginia Engine Company No. 1. Bulette even became an honorary member, but with Peasley's death, her fortunes declined.

Although disease dogged Bulette's final steps, it was a grisly murder that extinguished her life. On a cold night in January 1867, she was bludgeoned and then strangled in her two-room crib. It became the best-documented part of her existence. Newspapers published details of her death and funeral, and then the crime receded from public view, replaced with subsequent cycles of news. When Bulette's estate was probated, her limited assets could not cover her debts.[4]

Tracing the roots of Bulette's legend is a challenge for want of sources. Several writers—all men—were in positions to remember her, but they gave her barely more than a passing nod: Doten mentioned her a few unremarkable times in his journal. Months after her murder, he wrote about her newly captured killer.[5] This event was crucial for Bulette's story. Because a man was tried and hanged for the killing, the community could revisit the slain sex worker. Despite this, her legacy sputtered. A few years later, Dan De Quille was silent on Bulette when he published a mammoth overview of Virginia City and its history.

Mark Twain lived in Virginia City when Bulette arrived, yet she is invisible in his *Roughing It*.[6] In 1868, Twain returned to Virginia City to give a lecture, his visit coinciding with the hanging of Bulette's murderer.

In a column for the *Chicago Republican*, Twain focused on his repulsion at the sight of the execution, but he wrote of Bulette only in the context of the killer: "He secreted himself under the house of a woman of the town, and in the dead watches of the night, he entered her room, knocked her senseless with a billet of wood . . . , and strangled her." So ended Bulette, a nameless, featureless "woman of the town."[7]

In 1908, an interviewer asked Joe Goodman about Bulette. Like others, the retired Comstock newspaper editor fixated on the murderer's crime, trial, and hanging—events he knew firsthand. More than forty years after her death, Goodman described Bulette with vague, incorrect details: "She was a tall, slim Frenchwoman, and a very popular character in those free-and-easy times; for she was kind-hearted and public-spirited."[8] With his summary, Goodman hinted at a turn-of-the-century oral tradition about Bulette, something percolating from below.

During the twentieth century, the image of Bulette changed. The previously quoted Lyman novel, published in 1934, advanced an extravagant image of her, far removed from fact. Bulette had become a madam, elevated to "soiled dove with a heart of gold," wealthy beyond imagination and exhibiting the generosity of a saint. Whether Lyman drew on folklore is impossible to say, but his image of Bulette anticipated and likely shaped later oral tradition.[9]

In 1958, a volume appeared, written by Zeke Daniels, the pen name of local historian Effie Mona Mack, the first woman to take on Bulette. Likely drawing on Lyman, Mack described her heroine as living in a palace, riding in a gilded carriage, wearing costly jewelry, and having earned as much—or more—than the richest silver barons of the Comstock.[10] It is not clear when the fabulously conceived Bulette became part of local folklore, but her story was in full force by the mid-twentieth century even before Mack wrote. In 1945, the Virginia and Truckee Railroad restored a coach-caboose, giving it the misspelled name *Julia Bullette*, evidence that the long-dead sex worker was winning acclaim in the popular mind.[11]

In the late 1940s, American folklorist Duncan Emrich was hot on Bulette's trail during his many visits to Virginia City, what the Library of Congress referred to as his "summertime rambles through the American West." Chief of the Library of Congress's Folklore Section from 1945 to 1955, he recorded in Virginia City's Delta Saloon, documenting aspects of her legend.[12] She was no longer the forgotten murdered sex worker, a sideshow to a hanging. Bulette had taken center stage in the drama.

When Emrich asked Joe Farnsworth, a Virginia City resident, about Julia Bulette, he answered, "What I heard, she's a swell woman. . . . [S]he had plenty of money and she was a fine spender. She was good to the down-and-outers. You see, she'd take you up and buy you a pair of shoes or a suit of clothes and rig you out fine."[13]

Similarly, Tommy Dick told Emrich how during the first winter of 1860, people were running out of food because the passes over the mountains were closed. Dick asserted that Eilley Bowers had plenty of food because she was running a well-stocked boardinghouse. Julia Bulette went to Bowers on behalf of the starving miners and said, "Now you share this with the folks around here," but Bowers refused. Dick concluded that Bulette "was a wonderful gal in her way."[14]

Bulette was transforming into a legend, and Emrich was able to document a folk tradition as it was taking hold. In his 1949 book *It's an Old Wild West Custom*, Emrich described the story of Bulette, including the trial of her assailant. Much of his text appears to be borrowed from Lyman's 1934 novel. Nevertheless, there is evidence that Emrich had done additional research: Where Lyman placed her in Virginia City in 1859, Emrich correctly indicates she moved there in 1863. In addition, Emrich offers details that cannot be found elsewhere.[15]

Popular enthusiasm for Bulette was likely coalescing in the first half of the twentieth century, but lacking an Emrich or a De Quille collecting at the time, all that remains is speculation. The existing evidence indicates that by the time Emrich was recording in 1949 and 1950, some of that tradition existed. Thanks to novelist George Lyman and the quasi-historians Lucius Beebe, Charles Clegg, and "Zeke Daniels," aspects of a complete Bulette story emerged in print. These literary legend-like treatments were examples of the folkloresque, and in these cases, they likely affected folklore as it was taking form.

All this was happening just as Virginia City shifted from mining to tourism. Promoting the myth of the Wild West was essential to the economy. Celebrating local folklore in the 1950s, the Delta Saloon hung a photograph with the label "Julia Bulette" above the bar.[16] It depicted an attractive mixed-race woman from the nineteenth century, an homage to Beebe's "dusky beauty," an attribute based on no historical information. In addition, Don McBride of the Bucket of Blood Saloon, together with other members of E. Clampus Vitus, began a process of caring for a faux commemorative grave site for Bulette in the Flowery Hill Cemetery, her actual place of repose somewhere nearby but long since lost. The community had used Flowery Hill for burials until the late 1860s when another cemetery replaced it, leaving the older graveyard to fall into disrepair.[17]

For folklore, however, things were imagined differently. Bulette's newly

The invented location of Julia Bulette's final resting place includes wood likely taken from another grave. The chain-link fence protects the focus of veneration from wild horses who would trample it. Photograph by Ronald M. James.

created cenotaph rested on a lonely hill across the ravine from the respectable cemetery. Legend now maintained that Bulette, shunned in death, could find eternal repose only within the bounds of a notorious fictionalized Boot Hill. As Beebe and Clegg described it in 1950, "Burial within holy ground was not to be considered, so Julia was laid away on a Nevada hillside," a place of sorrowful abandonment.[18] For twentieth-century residents, however, neglect would not be tolerated. Now, her invented grave with its bright-white fence could be seen through a coin-operated telescope at the back of the Bucket of Blood Saloon. For a nickel, anyone could glimpse the myth of the Wild West. The focus of my first Comstock lie.

Providing an authoritative statement from national media, Bulette appeared on the popular television show *Bonanza*, the hit series that premiered in celebration of the centennial of the original 1859 gold and silver strikes. Episode 6, aired on October 17, 1959, featured Jane Greer in the title role of "The Julia Bulette Story." She wore a dress with a distinctive neckline, patterned after what appeared in the photograph, now hanging in the Bucket of Blood. Greer played the part of a love interest of "Little Joe" Cartwright, ensuring the fame of the murdered "woman of the town."[19]

The Bulette legend, partly begun in media in the realm of the folkloresque, thrived as a tradition where it lingered until locals wove those threads together. While it is possible that at least some details about her were "imposed from above," what emerged likely included some of its own homegrown motifs, popular among those who called the Comstock home. The resulting tapestry was presented to tourists attracted to Virginia City in the wake of *Bonanza.* Untangling all the beginnings of those threads associated with Julia Bulette is likely impossible, but the outcome is easily documented.

In the twenty-first century, one can still hear shopkeepers embellishing Julia Bulette's life for eager tourists just as they have done for decades. Speakers on tour trolleys and on the V&T Railroad continue to boom hourly with tales of this imaginary West, complete with stories about the woman who has become a legendary "courtesan," far removed from reality. To be fair, some of these popular tour guides do very well and have commendably attempted to present only the verifiable facts, but "busting myths" is never easy and seldom effective. The enduring forces that create and sustain folklore are often irresistible.

For example, in 2007 a guide for an evening ghost tour described a local undertaker who refused to yield Bulette's body, keeping poor Julia on ice for whatever nefarious purpose until he finally surrendered the object of his adoration. Janice Oberding recorded the tale not long before, indicating that "a story has been told for many years about an undertaker who so fell in love with Julia he couldn't bear to see her buried."[20] Oberding observed further that the "undertaker who prepared her for burial was enamored with the attractive woman. He couldn't bear the thought of her being buried out on Flowery Hill, so he filled an empty coffin with sand and rocks and sent it on its way to the cemetery. Then, to keep Julia ever near, he buried her in his basement."[21]

Without citation or context, it is not possible to know the origin of this, but it was clearly diffusing. It appeared the next year in Brian David Bruns's collection of ghost stories.[22] As with so many of the details now attached to Bulette's life and death, no historical document even hints at such a thing. It seems the notion of the undertaker is being shaped as tradition weaves the written and spoken words together.

Yet another element of folklore associated with Bulette came in the form of a custom dating at least to the 1990s: some have taken to decorating Bulette's fictional final resting place and a nearby tree with keepsakes.[23] Local residents attribute the items either to a Virginia City Wiccan coven or to regional sex workers who have reputedly adopted Bulette as an icon of their profession. Her fake grave site has fitted into local legend, becoming the object of its own tradition. Folklore thrives as the community repeatedly reconsiders events from long before.

In 1984, Susan James, my wife, wrote the first real attempt to "bust" the myth of Julia Bulette.[24] At the time, I was concerned. As a historian, I have also corrected the record, colored with the fantastic wanderings of oral tradition. As a folklorist, however, I celebrate imagination and have no wish to see it dampened. Fortunately, I have repeatedly watched the written word fail to undo myth, and the Bulette story is no different. Her legend endures any effort to be corrected. Folklore has power over history.

There was a real nuanced West of wealth and success, failure and disappointment, filled with people who experienced happiness and sadness, and then exited the stage. In the end, we must not forget that Julia Bulette was a real person whose occupation was too often dangerous and degrading. At the same time, the myth of the Wild West dominates perception.

Bulette historians document a woman who thrived in her own way and then was murdered. Today, the real person has largely disappeared. In contrast, popular tradition remembers the Queen of the Red-Light District, a symbol of glorious wealth, living life to its fullest. Virginia City residents and visitors celebrate a legendary woman who has assumed a role in an imagined Wild West.

THE PREVIOUS CHAPTERS CONSIDER aspects of early western folklore. Because most lived in a small part of northwest Nevada, sources directed the inquiry to that region. Additional volumes could be written about other places. As noted before, within the borders of the state is a vast sagebrush ocean, and each island of habitation has its unique story. Las Vegas, beyond the southern edge of the Great Basin, has its own rich traditions and heritage. That said, the abundance of documents from the area dominated by the Comstock makes it possible to imagine a body of nineteenth-century western folklore.

Again, with limited space, the focus here is on how those who lived in or near the Virginia City National Historic Landmark District have viewed the legacy of a previous time. As residents look back, fresh layers of traditions take shape. Sometimes, this no doubt has been a self-aware process. Dorothy Young Nichols, a third-generation Nevadan born in Gold Hill in 1903, wrote seventy years later, "Stories of the great bonanza days were part of my childhood."[25] The churning away of oral tradition never stopped as people reconsidered their heritage with every generation.

Because Virginia City and its mining district played such an important role well beyond the borders of Nevada, Beebe and Clegg could understandably declare in the 1950s that "for nine decades now the Comstock has been an integral part of the legend of the American West. . . . The legend of the Lode is as completely irresistible to writers as ever the original 'blue stuff' was to James Finney or Pat McLaughlin."[26] The way Bulette emerged in twentieth-century folklore is an example of how modern residents of the region understood the Wild West legacy of early Nevada.

For those looking back at the founding of the West, "wanton women" together with whiskey, drinking, and saloons were essential. Many saw the period of territory and early statehood as a time when men drank and fought hard, women were sex workers, and saloons were ubiquitous. Popular tradition celebrated the violence and vice of the first years, following a national perception that linked the Wild West with pervasive sin, bloodshed, and crime.

Beebe wrote that "the early 'sixties was the archetype of the tumults and lawlessness that characterized all the mining towns of the Old West in greater or less degree," and that 1863 was particularly "a banner year in the annals of assault, mayhem, murder, and, of course, acquittal in Virginia City."[27] This portrait of the Wild West has deep roots no matter how flawed it is historically. J. Ross Browne depicted Virginia City in much these terms during his two visits to the western Great Basin in 1860 and 1863. This was an image that sold to eastern audiences, and a century later, Beebe with his Bostonian roots was keenly aware of the legendary West that the nation imagined to be real and worthy of celebration.

The delight in contemplating early violence extended to the quality and quantity of the "whisky," as described by Emrich: "Early whisky in the frontier West was rightly named—Tangle-Leg, Forty Rod, Tarantula Juice, Rookus Juice, Bug Juice, Lightning, and, more specifically, Taos Lightning. They were villainous compounds, made from barrels of the vilest alcohol, with the addition of burnt sugar and various flavoring extracts, not excluding a chaw of tobacco. And guaranteed to main or kill."[28]

Beebe and Clegg recount the story of James "Old Virginny" Finney baptizing Virginia City with the last remnants in his broken bottle, and for them, the whiskey bore the fictional name of "Old Reprehensible."[29] That was the Wild West that drew the attention of Emrich, Beebe, and others, a Wild West that many insist must have existed. If these writers of the mid-twentieth century could not find documentation of that West in a real past, they would settle for one found in legend, even if it was a tradition they helped conceive.

In truth, the American West quickly became well connected with the international marketplace, and it had the finest of imported beverages.

This is demonstrated by a wide variety of artifacts that archaeologists have uncovered, including bottles that once contained the best of liquors, beers, and wines.[30] Certainly, connections with the rest of the world were not established immediately, but counterfeit whiskey and other near-poisonous drinks were hardly a fixture for long, if ever. Emrich's assertion that the "early whiskies" were dreadful concoctions is removed from accurate history. Rather, this shows how a nationally known folklorist was drawn in by tradition, for folklore can be extremely persuasive.[31]

In addition, there is a widespread belief about the excessive amounts of alcohol consumed, again something that historical evidence does not support: comparing rates of drinking together with the number of saloons puts early Nevada communities on a par with cities nationally. Reality often contradicts legend, but folklore persists. Granted, the first to arrive tended to be young, male, and single, and nature taking its course, a boomtown could have more violence and drinking per capita than elsewhere, but this phase usually passed quickly. Tradition celebrated and exaggerated those early months until they were thought to be an accurate picture for an entire region, lasting for many years.[32]

The issue with the arrival of women was an entirely different matter. As previously discussed, it is widely celebrated that the first women in the mining West were sex workers. This incorrect perception dates to the nineteenth century, a falsehood that endures, embedded in the folklore of the region. Sex workers were some of the most misunderstood people of the West. Folklore clouded the view, placing them in towns before they arrived and turning them into soiled doves. Some graduated to being "white angels," as Lyman would write, bestowing upon them "hearts of gold." This popular perception was so widespread that it convinced many early historians that it must be true.[33]

For Emrich, who was committed to finding the folkloric image of the Wild West, the traditional perception of the past and its sex workers directed his inquiry. While recording the "old timers" gathered in Virginia City's Delta Saloon in the mid-twentieth century, Emrich sometimes shaped conversations rather than allowing his storytellers the freedom to tell their tales. He repeatedly tried to redirect the discussion to capture prurient details about nineteenth-century brothels and the women who worked there. This reflected the interest of the folklorist more than of his informants.

BAD ALCOHOL, VIOLENCE, AND sex workers were only a part of the way later generations viewed the legacy of the Wild West. Stories about stolen and subsequently lost treasure rose as an echo of western legends of lost mines.

Similar tales influenced the perceived legacy of the Grosh brothers, but in the twentieth century, the lure of hidden or misplaced riches enticed a new generation. People thought back on rumors of robberies and began to speculate about where stolen wealth might be.

One account focuses on bullion stashed from a holdup on Geiger Grade. Legend maintains that a robber named Jack Davis developed a reputation for his extravagant series of stagecoach holdups. Wells Fargo agents killed him before he was able to disclose the location of his treasure. Some suggest that he hid it at the top of Sugar Loaf, the large rocky "volcanic plug," a protrusion at the base of the canyon to the east of Virginia City. Many tell of the Davis plunder resting there beneath a stone marked with an *S*. There are also versions about the ghost of Davis guarding his hidden loot.[34]

Even more traditions focused on other aspects of society. The name "tommyknocker" lingers even as tradition wanes. Modern enthusiasm for this underground sprite has inspired names for beers, breweries, and diverse stores throughout the West. Logos focus on the elfin characteristics of the supernatural miners, and, indeed, it is possible to point to many examples where elfin tommyknockers beckon to customers.[35]

Yet another echo of an early tradition took the form of a man and his burro. Late in the winter of 2021, StinkE, a revered Comstock character, died at age seventy, although he was timeless and looked much older. Reprising a role played by others since the 1950s, StinkE spent years posing on Virginia City's main street as the perennial prospector in dirty-red body-length long johns, together with his burro, Burnadeen.[36] The pair were perfect for a capital of mining turned tourist attraction, offering an opportunity for visitors to touch the past, feed Burnadeen a carrot, and have a picture taken with an icon. All for a price.

StinkE (Danny Eugene Beason) and Burnadeen offered a humble example of how people looked back and imagined a legendary image from early Nevada. Lest there be a concern that this tradition ended with the passing of StinkE, his grandson, Connor Nichols, has emerged as PokE, together with the beloved Burnadeen. Folklore is not easily extinguished.[37]

Modern tradition also reconsidered animals of the past by giving camels a new role in the folklore of the region. Majestic "ships of the desert," camels were used experimentally in some parts of the West to haul supplies from salt mines to centers of milling.[38] Those who imported the beasts thought that they would be well suited for the environment, but as it turned out, the idea largely failed. Camels could not cross terrain with sharp rocks, and they frightened horses. In 1875, the Nevada legislature passed a law prohibiting camels on public highways, and Virginia City had an ordinance restricting

By 1979, Virginia City had been celebrating annual camel races for two decades, more or less, depending on whose story one believed. The festivities had become and continue to be a well-established fixture of the Comstock calendar. Courtesy of Michael "Bert" Bedeau with thanks to Joe Curtis.

the creatures in town to after dark.[39] Eventually, camels fell out of use, and for decades, stories circulated about sightings of the abandoned animals wandering in the Nevada desert.[40]

The role of camels in local folklore blossomed fully in a twentieth-century rebirth of the earlier tradition of the hoax perpetrated by the likes of Mark Twain and Dan De Quille. Beebe and Clegg, in their effort to resuscitate Comstock institutions and to return the mining district to its glory days, reestablished the *Territorial Enterprise*. They were able to transform the abandoned institution into an impressive, nationally recognized weekly publication, often featuring acclaimed writers. To give the *Enterprise* its full texture from the previous century, the new owners tried their hand at the journalistic hoax. Their editor, Robert "Bob" Richards, began a series of articles that falsely alluded to failed annual efforts to hold a camel race in Virginia City.

The famed hoaxes of De Quille and Twain required a degree of sorting out by both local readers and those in California. In this case, Comstock residents would immediately understand that this story was false because there were no efforts to hold such an event. What is more, locals would have recognized that the newspaper was celebrating the institution of the hoax. Many, no doubt, were delighted when other newspapers republished these articles, even though some in California may have also appreciated the underpinning spoof.[41]

Of course, the joke backfired in 1960 when the *San Francisco Chronicle* offered to sponsor a camel in the next annual camel race and famed film director John Huston told the people of Virginia City that he wished to ride the beast. He was in the area directing the film *The Misfits,* starring Marilyn Monroe and Clark Gable. Huston, being an adventuresome thrill seeker, would not miss the opportunity to race a camel in the Wild West. What had begun as a nod to historical camels, combined with the celebration of a hoax, transformed into a real event.

Here again was an example of the folkloresque, something presented in imitation of folklore, forcing its way back into tradition. Now there was a real effort to secure two camels so an actual event could be held. The first camel race, held on Labor Day, September 5, 1960, was a success. Huston won the contest and was satisfied, and with that, the camel race became its own institution. The community has held the contest every year since then, now an honored celebration of the Wild West.[42]

BEEBE AND CLEGG'S PENCHANT for deceit reached beyond hoaxes and camels. They also invented histories of their real-estate holdings that would match their vision of what was best about Virginia City. Their house uphill from Piper's Opera House became John Piper's home. The building had only a thin link to one of Piper's children and the theater. Nevertheless, with Beebe and Clegg's tinkering, their property gained an exalted theatrical pedigree, now claimed to be previously occupied by a theater impresario who had hosted all the world's greatest performers.[43] Facts did not matter.

Similarly, Beebe and Clegg were not satisfied to own the place where the *Territorial Enterprise* moved after 1875. The Great Fire of that year destroyed the building where the newspaper was published from 1863. To give the surviving home of Virginia City's newspaper a more illustrious lineage, Beebe wrote *Comstock Commotion.* Published by the prestigious Stanford University Press, the book included an invented past for his structure, described incorrectly as a "two-story brick building into which *The Enterprise* moved in 1863 and from which it is still published." This falsely became, then, the setting where Samuel Clemens took the name "Mark Twain" and Dan De Quille crafted some of his earliest work, even though clear evidence indicates that the home of the newspaper at that time had been elsewhere.[44]

Part of Beebe's fabrication included a piece of furniture: within the

Enterprise building is an old desk whose wood had supported the pen and elbows of Twain and "other famous characters" as they wrote their articles. This is shown to be true (even though it is not) because someone wrote this "fact" on a photograph by Eastman's Studio. It is an image reproduced not without irony in Lynda Walsh's expert discussion of nineteenth-century hoaxes, a photograph she identifies as "Composing Room at Territorial Enterprise showing desk used by De Quille and Twain."[45] While De Quille may have sat there to write articles in the final years of his career, there is no way to be certain of even that. The piece of furniture has an unknown provenance other than Beebe's claim that it is "the desk" of the great nineteenth-century reporters. This complemented his falsification of the role of the *Enterprise* building in the early 1860s, adding fabric to a newly woven tapestry of deceit.[46]

No blame should be heaped on Walsh or countless others who accept the building and "the desk" as the place where Clemens transformed into Twain. This was no western hoax with clues embedded to be discovered by shrewd readers, leaving only the gullible holding the bag. Nor was this an eastern hoax, something so outlandish that even though it was presented with a straight face, the truth was certain to be found out eventually.

When Beebe and Clegg created the camel-race hoax, locals knew it was false and reveled in the deception as an homage to earlier hoaxes. Something else was occurring when Beebe and Clegg promoted the genealogy of their house and the surviving *Territorial Enterprise* building, together with the desk. In this instance, they were not engaging in a hoax, a tall tale, or a burlesque lie. This deception may have included an element of self-deceit, but it may also have been a marketing ploy, intended never to be found out. It is impossible to fathom the motives of Beebe and Clegg.

As is often the case, falsehoods entered local tradition, which now embraces invented history as fact. The *Enterprise* building and its desk continue to be presented to visitors as the place where the magical birth of Mark Twain occurred. Despite careful research, some stories are too good not to repeat. As Mark Twain himself once said, "A lie can travel halfway around the world while the truth is still putting on its shoes." Except that is false: Twain is not the source of that quote no matter how frequently it is attributed to him. It is an assertion that has found its own path into folklore.[47]

There is no lie more believable than a lie attributed to a liar. Once again, folklore is a powerful thing, not to be turned aside by facts and the mere written word. Readers who forget everything asserted here will do a service to folklore!

The specifics about camels, buildings, and a desk aside, what is curious about a retrospective of Nevadans' view of their Wild West past is the way they cling to hoaxes, tall tales, and burlesque lies. Carolyn Brown in her classic treatment of the tall tale describes how proponents of the genre frequently lie to strangers and tourists, and this is something that local Comstockers sometimes do with pride.[48] It is simply too easy—and too much fun—not to expound on absurdities projected onto the past. Many locals find inspiration when tourists ask about the Cartwrights and other fictional aspects of the television show *Bonanza*. The response is often a fabulous tall tale woven on the spot for the occasion.

From the mining district's start in 1859, Comstockers have celebrated tall tales. To this day, the tradition persists as Virginia City residents attempt to outstretch one another when talking about early Nevada. Exaggeration feeds the popular perception of a once "Wild" West, sending tourists on their way believing they have touched the real thing. One can have history and one can have folklore, but sometimes the two are mutually exclusive. Nevertheless, the blending of fact and legend keeps the Wild West a vibrant, ever-expanding domain of oral tradition.

THE ENTWINING OF FOLKLORE and history has maddened those who seek the truth and wish to correct the record. Historians have been known to howl indignantly at the persistent folk belief that Nevada was admitted to the Union so its gold and silver could help win the Civil War. The coincidence of the development of the Comstock Lode with the conflict of the early 1860s encourages this tradition.[49] Legend sidesteps the fact that Washington's access to Comstock riches did not change with statehood; if anything, a state government could claim some of the profits with taxes, keeping revenue in the West. That did not happen, but neither did statehood improve the situation for Lincoln's treasury.

A similar tradition maintains that Nevada's gold and silver were essential for making San Francisco a great city. As is often the case, folklore can offer conflicting lines of thought—the wealth went to California and made the Bay Area glorious, but it was also needed in the East to save the Union.[50] Comstock bullion helped the federal government balance its budget and no doubt funded some of the building in San Francisco. That said, even without the Comstock, the United States would have defeated the rebellion and San Francisco would have become a great city.

As often happens, popularized histories of early Nevada act like a spider's web, capturing folk traditions as they fly about in search of a place to alight. Phyllis Zauner's self-professed "mini-history" of Virginia City serves up some of the folklore that gathered around the Comstock Historic District in the twentieth century:

> Virginia City would become a city as big as San Francisco, populated by millionaires who demanded the finest in everything.
>
> The thunderous wealth promulgated by the mines would bring an unprecedented opulence to the city of San Francisco, where most of the Comstock silver was diverted to build that city's finest hotels and civic buildings.
>
> A mining town of 30,000 would figure briefly in the destiny of the nation. And the rise and fall of fortunes would occasion suicides, bankruptcies and heartbreak.[51]

Folk belief overstates reality.

Popular assessments often exaggerate the maximum size of Virginia City with some preposterous claims asserting that there had been a quarter-million residents on the Comstock. More important, tradition has it that Virginia City was the largest city between the St. Louis on the Mississippi and San Francisco.[52] In 1870, the US Census recorded a population for Storey County, which included Virginia City, Gold Hill, and other smaller communities, as 11,359. At that time, there was Sacramento (16,283), Kansas City (32,260), and Salt Lake City (86,336). Claims about the size of Virginia City also ignore the difference in scale represented by St. Louis, weighing in at nearly 311,000, and San Francisco, with more than 149,000 that year. As indicated before, the peak population of Virginia City in the mid-1870s was perhaps as much as 16,000, with Gold Hill reaching as many as 8,000. This approached but did not exceed a combined total of 25,000. By 1880, Denver had grown to more than 35,000. Together, Virginia City and Gold Hill represented a sizable community for the time, but it was hardly the largest in the region.

Regardless of the facts, popular belief persists that Virginia City was enormous, influential, and sophisticated. For many, population size becomes a way to express an important truth that for a smaller city, it was incredibly cosmopolitan with technology that influenced mining for the next several decades. It was also opulent, although most bullion left the community for the benefit of other places.

Mine owners consistently took Nevada wealth out of state, yet there was a persistent tradition that Virginia City paved its streets with silver. This was an extension of the old narrative about the silver-laden blue mud in 1859. For modern folklore, the mud was used on the roadways. Sometimes the idea that the streets of Virginia City were covered in silver is changed. In this version, people suggest the roads are covered with mill tailings that still contained both gold and silver. That, however, contradicts the popular belief, which focuses on the silver in the mud that was discarded for a few weeks in the early summer of 1859. Lyman's 1934 novel, *The Saga of the Comstock Lode,* asserts that rich ore was so commonplace that anything that "ran fifty dollars a ton or less was utilized in grading 'A,' 'B' and 'C' streets."[53] This may have contributed to recent stories about the streets.

As with wealth, so too with sophistication: Virginia City's International Hotel, rebuilt in 1877, did have a commercial elevator, but that was not the first west of Chicago, as one of the old timers told Emrich when he was recording in the Delta Saloon in the mid-twentieth century. Although this Nevada folk tradition is ubiquitous and impossible to quash, it is not even close to being true.[54] The elevator was the first to serve the public in Nevada, but other aspects of the community—its theater, fashion, restaurants, newspapers, and schools, not to mention its mines—were all cutting edge on a grander scale.

THESE, THEN, ARE A few of the ways modern Nevadans use the lens of folklore to view the past. Another aspect of this process is reflected in how people consider the spiritual remnants of those earliest years. A fascination with ghosts matches that of the nineteenth century, but in modern times, interest shifted from lingering loved ones to the ethereal inhabitants of old buildings. It is, perhaps, remarkable that there were so many stories of hauntings from a time when the state was young. Nevertheless, ghosts were part of the fabric of early Nevada folklore from nearly the start. How the souls of the departed became part of the traditional way to consider the Wild West is the subject of the following final chapter.

CHAPTER 12

Ghosts of the Past

THE VIRGINIA CITY GHOST tour, on August 18, 2007, included an account set in abandoned apartments above the historic Werrin grocery store on South C Street. During a restoration of the two-story masonry building, a welder installed steel beams for reinforcement. While working upstairs, he felt the presence of an entity named "Margaret" and wrote her name on one of the girders. Apparently, he gained an impression of the woman's biography, believing in all this without hearing anyone else talking about her. The tour guide used this anecdote, based on one man's psychic impression, as evidence that the apartments are haunted, potentially adding an element of folklore to a structure dating to the 1870s.[1]

A caveat is needed when discussing ghost stories in this context, but a similar caution is warranted when dealing with any folk legend. The application of the term "folklore" can be taken to mean that a story should not be believed, relegating it to silly superstition. Folklorists make no judgment about the truthfulness of what they study. The lack of a South American home for the cui-ui fish is a clue when identifying the folkloric nature of an underground river from Pyramid Lake. Nevertheless, falsehood is not required before employing the term "folklore."

The study of ghost stories as folklore does not mean to imply that believers are gullible. Folklorists are not authorities on the possibility of an afterlife or on any other extraordinary beliefs. The anecdote about "Margaret" reveals a willingness to entertain the idea of lingering souls. To document this is sufficient in the realm of folklore studies.

With that, considering the tour of 2007 can resume. Heading north from the Werrin building, the Virginia City guide told us about six ghosts in the tall wooden Chapin Boarding House built in 1862. The owner of the property spoke of hauntings she had encountered, including a mischievous child, a maid, a Civil War widow, and a miner.

In her published collection, Janice Oberding documents tales from this former boardinghouse, including a Civil War veteran named John W. "Jack" Reed. He is reputed to have returned from the dead to visit those now staying at the establishment, "to gallantly kiss the ladies, or even tuck them in at night, especially if they are staying in his room." According to the narrative, Reed was heartbroken when he came back from war and found his wife with someone else. At the same time, Oberding tells of a woman who lost her fiancé in the war. Legend describes her as still dwelling in the Chapin house long after death. Sometimes she asks if there is any news, apparently hoping her groom-to-be will return someday.[2]

The insights shared by the tour guide likely came from Oberding's 2003 book about Comstock spirits. Overlaps occur elsewhere, and sorting out the effect of literature on tradition is often difficult. The evidence of the tour and various local ghost books suggests that regardless of original sources, many of these accounts have been circulating in recent times.

In the case of the Virginia City Visitor's Center building, there are fewer similarities in the stories, making it easier to recognize that different sources were being used. Oberding writes of vague encounters there, while the tour guide identified a specific one, a little girl standing on the boardwalk and crying.[3] For example, a woman at the Visitor's Center said that once a child asked about the little crying girl who was there, but no one else could see her. Indeed, the ghost tour revealed a good sample of attitudes toward the eerie inhabitants of the Virginia City National Landmark Historic District.

From their earliest days, Nevadans have entertained the idea of ghosts. Journalist Alfred Doten documented his when he recalled his many attempts to contact the spiritual world. Other early residents of Nevada also recorded efforts to communicate with apparitions of those known to them. The subjects of inquiry were typically deceased family members, but in a similar way, miners watched for underground remnants of fellow miners who had died in the works.

When there was not this degree of familiarity, most at least understood that hauntings had been occurring for only a short time since the community was still young. With the passing of the decades, it eventually became possible to entertain the notion of spirits from long ago, souls of dead unknown to a new generation of storytellers. How and when that transition occurred is not clear. Even in modern times, people continue to describe seeing deceased loved ones, but now, the repertoire includes specters from a former century.

To understand the recent array of legends dealing with the supernatural, numerous self-published collections of stories exist. For example, in *Ghosthunter's Guide to Virginia City*, Oberding records what she "gleaned from some of those citizens who've either experienced their own encounters with the supernatural, or been told about those of others."[4] That is to say, she has collected folklore.

One story in Oberding's book is about a contemporary incident involving a man and his dog who died, leaving the widow to live alone in their house. A new neighbor told the widow about seeing a dog in her backyard with a man calling to it. The widow said she had not seen any sign of the visitors, and her fence seemed secure, so she doubted that it had happened. At one point, the widow's new neighbor came into her house and saw a photograph of the woman's deceased husband and his dog. She remarked, "Why that's the little dog, and the man I've seen in your backyard." To that, the widow said that she must be mistaken, for "they've been dead going on five years."[5]

In 2004, Brian David Bruns published a similar collection about ghosts associated with various historic buildings and sites in Virginia City and Gold Hill.[6] Like Oberding's material, the Bruns book includes undated observations without attribution to the storytellers. Nevertheless, most of the narratives clearly date to the turn of the twenty-first century, and it is apparent that they were collected locally. His text wanders between the notes of a ghost hunter and tales collected from others. Both authors preserve stories intended to thrill modern readers interested in hauntings and the nineteenth-century Wild West. Accounts of the recently departed aside, these sources share a sense that those who return from the grave generally belong to the first few decades of the Comstock Mining District.

For the most part, Oberding's and Bruns's published material is not drawn from commonly held folklore. Instead, most of the stories are what folklorists call "memorates." These are legends in the sense that they are told to be believed, but they describe individual experiences, not likely repeated by others. Bruns and Oberding afford readers an opportunity to consider belief and experience in the historic setting. With these collections in hand, it is apparent that at least some people regard old places as the abodes of the departed.

Firsthand recollections may not transform into widespread accounts, what folklorists refer to as "migratory legends." In the modern world, they are often called "urban legends." Regardless of the name, most Nevada ghost stories belong to the realm of the memorate. Some stories, ranging from that of the underground river or the older ones about Hank Monk, far afield from spirits, diffused and took on lives of their own as urban or migratory legends.[7]

One of the modern motifs that has become traditional and widespread features the spirit of the crying girl. In 2004, Bruns documented a girl who is apparently the same one identified three years later in the 2007 ghost tour of Virginia City. He suggests that the little girl represents "the most common thread of any ghostly encounters in Virginia City." Bruns notes that while the stories he found were often different, there was agreement that she died because of "an accident on C Street involving a cargo-laden stagecoach that ran her down and crushed her."

Beyond that core motif, other details vary, and people describe the girl as associated with an assortment of structures. There is also an unverified account linked to her remains: in this case, workers for an electric company allegedly uncover the bones of a child behind the Old Washoe Club on C Street, a supposed event that was taken to support if not explain the idea that the youngster haunts the community.[8]

The girl represents one of four of the most common motifs associated with spirits that can be collected in Virginia City. A second legend concerns sightings of a sex worker sometimes attributed specifically to Julia Bulette. In addition, people tell of encounters with a maid, who often manifests with only the scent of perfume. The fourth motif is also related to an odor, this being the smell of cigar smoke.

Stories of cigar-smoking spirits are associated with several places. Visitors describe the smell in the Gold Hill Hotel, perceiving it as evidence of a ghost popularly named "William." A similar scent at Virginia City's opera house conjures the name John Piper: some have detected the scent of his cigars on opening night with a belief that he is checking on the performance. The shadow man of the Mackay Mansion, sometimes identified as Senator James Fair, includes the motif of cigar smoke, as does an uncanny janitor at the Fourth Ward School.[9]

When it comes to perfumes associated with unearthly maids, perhaps no one is more celebrated than "Rosie" of the Gold Hill Hotel. Legends tell of various encounters, but the smell of roses or rosewater is her most common attribute.[10] The process here reveals something about the way people project onto ambiguous clues. Someone smells the scent of roses and, because of the stories, assumes this indicates the presence of the maid. The equally plausible explanation would look to a former patron, but this is set aside. Folklore finds its way, and having determined a path, the force of that direction is at times irresistible.

Most accounts about female apparitions on the Comstock are about sex workers. During the nineteenth century, these women represented a small group compared with other women, but their profession won them a disproportionate role in later folklore, just as it does in many histories of the

West.[11] Echoing this, people look back on the spiritual remnants of the past and perceive the ghosts of sex workers, who play a large part in these stories.

Oberding includes a section on sex workers in her 2003 book.[12] Of course, from a folkloric point of view, Julia Bulette emerged as the most famous of those who participated in this part of the economy, and her importance grew throughout the twentieth century. It apparently was only within the past few decades, however, that Bulette became the subject of legends about visits from beyond.

There are next to no surviving structures in Virginia City that can be linked to Bulette's life, and her supposed grave is in a remote cemetery, so there are no obvious locations that can be connected to her ethereal residue. For these reasons, perhaps, the community has been slow to talk of her hauntings. In 1969, Dolores K. O'Brien wrote of a ghost associated with Bulette's supposed resting place, but she concluded that what she saw could not have been Bulette because it was "too frail [and] lithe."[13] O'Brien asserted that a visit to the grave site was not worth the effort. As is often the case, it is unclear if this corresponded to anything circulating in the 1960s.

More recent stories associated with Bulette's apparition are wrapped up with the undertaker who, according to legend, refused to relinquish her body. At that point, folklore was tied to a specific site. Ever the source of recent folklore, Oberding describes how Bulette still lurks in the rooms on North C Street where the undertaker conducted his business. "A woman who once worked in the building said she had seen Julia's spirit one evening just before she closed the shop. Believing the woman who stood near the counter was of the flesh and blood variety, she quietly informed her that the store was offering a sale on some of the items she seemed to be gazing at. To her amazement, the woman turned from her and slowly dissolved."[14]

A similar narrative in Oberding's collection includes Bulette appearing in the undertaker's building, but the author also indicates that her presence can be sensed near "the site where her little house stood at Union and D Streets, and the isolated spot out on Flowery Hill where her lonely grave is located."[15] In addition, Oberding records a second account of Bulette associated with the undertaker's place of business:

A former owner of this building encountered the ghostly Julia early one summer morning. It was still too early for tourists to be out and about on the boardwalk so she decided to give the three glass counters in her shop a good cleaning.

She was halfway through the job when she noticed a tall woman standing in the far corner of the store. Acknowledging the woman, the shop owner apologized for not seeing her sooner.

"Is there anything I can help you find?" She asked, noticing that the woman seemed to be looking around intently.

Suddenly the air turned icy; the shop owner gasped as the woman in the corner slowly vanished into thin air. Later she would say it was the apparition of Julia Bulette she saw in her shop that morning.[16]

Legends of her ghost bring the folklore about Julia Bulette full circle. When alive, she was a midrange sex worker who became well known because of her murder in 1867. The hanging of her accused assailant the following year reminded the community about her, but it apparently was not until the following century that she emerged as part of local folklore. Indeed, it was several more decades before people told of Bulette reappearing long after her death.

These and similar accounts provide a means for people to animate the historic fabric of the district, allowing those who once lived there to thrive if only in spirit form. Most of the ghosts from early Nevada have vague identities. While it is true that people have tentatively ascribed the name James Fair to an entity in the Mackay Mansion, there are few other examples of this sort. Bulette has earned the distinction of being someone who is better known today than when living: folklore elevated a woman of modest circumstance, giving her prominence she had not enjoyed when alive, and now she is also celebrated with stories about her spectral appearance.

LEGENDS OF REVENANTS RANGING from sex workers, men smoking cigars, maids with charming scents, and young girls on the boardwalk, together with all the rest, are entwined with perceptions of early Nevada, providing a bridge to the past. By the nature of their folklore, ghosts from the first decades of Nevada are linked to specific places. According to popular belief, the dead remain in historic structures, maintaining their existence next to the living.

One of the more famous hauntings in Virginia City is in the Old Washoe Club Saloon. Its spiral staircase provides a special focal point in this regard. Many describe seeing a woman descending the stairs or standing nearby. Oberding indicates she is often named Lena, and she "appears in a shimmering blue dress in the style of long ago, and her hair is elegantly coifed. The apparition is most often seen standing near the spiral staircase or gazing sadly out from a mirror."[17]

In 1993, Doug Truhill, owner of the Washoe Club, propelled his property to national prominence by promoting its eerie reputation. He advertised for ghostbusters to help him, suggesting that the "spirits that haunt this old mining town are getting pushy and scaring people."[18] Truhill complained of frequent otherworldly pranks, but for all the hype, which was clearly good for business, no one busted any ghosts.[19]

Staircases and saloons are one thing, but cemeteries are by their nature especially evocative of the dead. When walking at night among upright tombstones in a graveyard, markers can take on the illusion of movement as they eclipse one another. This is something that German folklorist Elisabeth Hartmann noted about European cemeteries in 1936, and Bruns echoes this observation in his twenty-first-century look at ghost stories in Virginia City.[20]

Aside from the unnerving nature of these places, there is also a widespread belief that cemeteries can be the source of a curse for vandals and thieves. The pervasive nature of this tradition is demonstrated by the steady stream of cemetery-related artifacts that people return to the Comstock Cemetery Foundation. For decades, people have secretly left objects at the doorstep of the Comstock Historic District Commission.

Others bring artifacts inside to explain their story, often claiming that a relative had recently died and the next generation wished to return something that had been stolen. At other times, there is a frank admission of guilt, with the explanation that since the object had been taken, bad luck had followed. Many were tourists who thought the cemetery was abandoned and there would be no harm in taking a keepsake. Of course, the Comstock cemeteries are an important part of the landmark district, listed by the National Park Service for its many buildings as well as its archaeology and cemeteries. Any theft or act of vandalism diminishes an internationally acclaimed national treasure. Relocating stolen tombstones and other objects can be extremely difficult when photographs or documentation are lacking, but local volunteers actively care for the resource and do their best to tend to these matters.

In the context of folklore, what is important is the idea that stealing from a grave or damaging places of final repose can be the source of persistent bad luck, a curse of the dead vested upon the living. The fact that objects taken from the cemeteries find their way back from throughout the nation together with word of a curse is evidence of the pervasive nature of the tradition, reaching far beyond Nevada or even the West. Oberding referred to this in 2003: "Even though Virginia City legend warns against it, vandals have callously destroyed much of the older headstones and ironwork. Perhaps these people don't mind being haunted by the occupant of a grave whose headstone they've toppled."[21] Although belief in this type of bad luck is likely widespread, the Comstock Cemetery Foundation promotes word of the curse even more because it encourages preservation.

Along with the celebrated supernatural affliction associated with the theft of items, there is also a tradition associated with a specific burial. Many report seeing a glowing tombstone. As Brun indicates, "It's common knowledge that a tombstone glows at night. Not every time, of course, but I can think of a dozen people who've seen it . . . at *least.* Especially from the RV park near there . . . a lot of people claim to see it who don't even live there. You can see it from C Street, too."[22] The source of the light is elusive, however. It can be seen only from a distance. This has inspired some to insist that a spirit is responsible for the glow, sometimes recalling the ghost of the little girl, tradition now placing her in the cemetery, wandering among the tombstones.[23]

For the most part, recent Comstock ghost stories are set in the present, describing sightings of souls from a former time. Oberding, however, documents something that does not fit this pattern. It is unclear whether this is an old legend that people continue to tell or a modern one projected into the past. While spirits associated with old buildings and cemeteries are by nature perceived to be from a previous century, Oberding's tale is about miners who died in the early days when underground mining was the standard of the day. Although she notes that "residents of Virginia City still tell the story of the lucky miner," this only hints of older examples of this narrative.[24]

As Oberding recounts, a group of men, including one designated as the "lucky miner," was riding in a wagon to work underground. They were confronted with "a ghostly man [who] darted out in front of their wagon. The specter stopped and smiled sadly at the men; then ran to the other side of the street and quickly dissolved into thin air. The horses were so startled that it took the driver several minutes to calm the terrified animals." The lucky miner regarded this as an omen, and he jumped from the wagon, indicating that he did not plan to report for the day's shift. The others laughed at him and went on their way. "He was right. That very afternoon there was a terrible cave in at the mine and all of those who'd been in the wagon with him perished."[25]

This legend is different from accounts about incidents involving the "miners' cabin" behind the Gold Hill Hotel. This industrial structure is associated with a mine's hoist work, the site of the infamous Yellow Jacket disaster of 1869. The accident caused more deaths than any of its kind in Nevada

THE BURNING MINE.

The worst mining accident in Nevada history occurred on April 9, 1869, when a fire broke out in Gold Hill's Yellow Jacket Mine. Smoke filled the works of the neighboring Kentuck and Crown Point, resulting in roughly three dozen deaths. The scene on the surface was one of pandemonium, a tragedy that continues to resonate. Wright, *History of the Big Bonanza* (1876); from the author's private collection.

history, and the surviving structure is often seen as a spiritual focus of the many fatalities and the grief of loved ones. The Gold Hill Hotel has retrofitted the building to serve as a rental cabin, now a favorite for ghost hunters and thrill seekers. Descriptions of their experiences are distinct from the tale of the "lucky miner." While that, too, is set in the past, the story remains there: the incident of miners encountering the apparition is said to have occurred long ago, but observations of victims of the 1869 accident in the miners' cabin are modern.[26]

OTHER EXPRESSIONS OF INTEREST in ghosts return to the tradition of the hoax. A clear example of a fabricated tradition dates to 2002 or 2003—records are unclear. For Halloween, Barbara Mackey, then director of Virginia City's Fourth Ward School Museum, entertained children by telling of Suzette, a student whose father was killed in the mines, or so the story went. With the girl's subsequent death, her spirit remained in the school's halls, looking for her father. The building was not known for hauntings, so the director created this "legend" to fill the void on that spookiest of nights. Within months, Suzette gained a local following, and by the reopening of the museum the following spring, people arrived hoping to see the ethereal girl.[27]

Suzette continues to thrive in the community, but it is more complex than one might think. In 1994, before the invention of Suzette the student, Phyllis Zauner published a booklet titled *Virginia City: Its History . . . Its Ghosts*. She wrote about a couple who were driving into town during the night. They gave "a ride to a woman they met on the road. She was dressed in an old-fashioned outfit, said her name was Suzette, and asked to be left off at the Fourth Ward School. It seemed a strange request after dark, since the school is unoccupied. But they watched her as she walked across the yard to the school steps, and were dumbfounded when she suddenly just disappeared."[28] This is a variant of the widespread urban legend of the Vanishing Hitchhiker: examples usually have someone driving at night who picks up a young woman who is later revealed to be an apparition. Now presumably a teacher, Suzette fits into the tangle, but whether this is a literary contrivance or something drawn from local oral tradition is unclear.[29]

Mackey's young student named Suzette, then, has a complicated origin, reaching beyond an incident involving the invention of the little girl, which then inspired stories about her sightings. It is possible only to speculate how the director of the museum arrived at the name Suzette, but the coincidence with the earlier publication by Zauner cannot be overlooked. Zauner presented her anecdote as though it was from oral tradition, even though that is not clear. Nevertheless, the dual Suzettes, one a young girl and the other a teacher, are apparently entwined yet distinct.

In 2015, the *Reno Gazette-Journal* published an article on the "11 eerie places to see this Halloween" in Virginia City. This included the old school turned museum: "It is also said that a teacher only known as Suzette haunts the school. If you're driving by the building late at night, you might just catch a glimpse of her standing outside the building looking to hitch a ride home."[30] It is not known if Zauner inspired the newspaper reference. A later book by Oberding on Virginia City, also dating to 2015, introduces Suzette in a paragraph that had originally appeared in her 2003 book. The earlier version had merely mentioned an anonymous schoolteacher. In 2015, Oberding names the ghost of the teacher, referring to her as Suzette, but whether this is from tradition or a borrowing from other written sources is, again, unclear.[31]

What is apparent is that Mackey had people coming to the school turned museum, asking about sightings of the little girl. At the same time, references to the teacher named Suzette remain in print. Some publications

The Fourth Ward School is an imposing Second Empire Victorian-era building that has long attracted the attention of ghost hunters. To its right, in the distance, is St. Mary in the Mountains Catholic Church. Photograph by Ronald M. James.

fail to inspire folklore, while in this case, a performance on a Halloween night set a legend in motion. This example begs the question about how long a story must be repeated—particularly when it is what Foster and Tolbert would call "folkloresque"—to become genuine oral tradition. Folklorist Dorson would condemn the student Suzette as "fakelore" because she lacks organic roots among the "folk." Nevertheless, what began as innocent invention has become folklore by any sensible definition of the term. Dorson wielded "fakelore" as a club to bash fraud, but the gentler term "folkloresque" allows for less harsh consideration of many possibilities.

The popularity of Suzette the student may in part be because of her similarity to the ubiquitous crying girl. After all, the otherworldly student of the Fourth Ward School reiterates a widely circulating local motif. Given the popularity of the ghostly girl, it is not surprising that a young student named Suzette has become a fixture of Virginia City legends.[32]

BESIDES THOSE OF LITTLE girls, cigar-smoking men, sex workers, and delightfully scented maids, other apparitions have become part of local tradition. In Piper's Opera House, there are observations of a deceased patron appearing in one of the box seats on either side of the stage.[33] In addition, a nun, long since departed, is reputed to walk the halls of St. Mary Louise

Hospital, now known as St. Mary's Arts Center. Tradition incorrectly refers to members of her order as nuns; although they wore the habit and flowing robes that are popularly linked with a word for women who have taken religious vows, these were "Daughters," specifically Daughters of Charity, with an active vocation as they sought to relieve suffering and to help build a better community. Regardless of the term used for them, people claim to see the spiritual remnant of one of their number in the place where she cared for the sick and dying.[34]

There is a specific focus on a hospital room on the fourth floor. Reserved for mental patients, the window is protected with an iron cage, and originally the small space was furnished in ways to prevent occupants from harming themselves. As Rich Moreno describes in his *Backyard Traveler* blog, a story persists that "a patient in the psychiatric ward started a fire that killed him and a nun on duty. It is said that she continues to wander the building looking for patients to help and frequently musses the sheets and blankets on the bed in her former room." For some, the attending Daughter of Charity is referred to as the "white nun," after her all-white garb, and tales of her date to as early as 1969.[35]

Among the various hauntings from the past, there are even reports of apparitions of camels. As discussed in the previous chapter, these exotic beasts of burden were a rare but renowned fixture of nineteenth-century Nevada, and they gained a place with the Comstock's celebration of its past beginning in the 1960s. It is perhaps fitting that there should also be stories of a ghost camel that can be seen climbing "over the top of Mt. Davidson on certain nights when a full moon is high in the sky," as Oberding describes, adding that occasionally "riding the beast is a grinning skeleton."[36] This had appeared earlier, in 1983, in what was likely the source: Douglas McDonald, who wrote of the camels, "Eventually they all perished, either from the elements or predators, until all that remain are the legends. A large red camel supposedly jaunts the steep slopes of Sun Mountain above Virginia City and is only visible on nights of a full moon. Another legend has a ghost camel train roaming the various Nevada salt flats with a skeleton lashed to one of the animals."[37]

A hint of an earlier tradition of otherworldly camels is preserved in testimony collected from native Comstocker Ty Cobb, but details are lacking.[38] Here then is the persistent problem, namely, sorting out documentation of similar recent stories. The ghost genre perhaps more than others attracts popularized written treatments, intended for likely believers who want to be titillated. That, however, can come up short as evidence of folklore.

Often, authors including Janice Oberding have recorded what they have been told, but at other times, the origin of a narrative is unclear. Her publication of the two motifs related to ghost camels—the red one of Mount Davidson and the creature ridden by a skeleton—is presented without citation. Unless one stumbles upon similar accounts—in this case the obscure self-published booklet by McDonald—speculation about the source remains unverified. Even then, it is difficult to say how Oberding came by these two ghostly camels, since there may be an unidentified intermediary source, or she may have heard them from someone repeating the McDonald text. Popularized publications about modern hauntings are problematic in this way, even as they are invaluable for what they disclose about current belief and story.

MANY PEOPLE VIEW OLD buildings, landscapes, and cemeteries as visible legacies of the Wild West, providing a context together with a setting where it is possible to touch the past. Of course, when using the lens of folklore, remnants of the region's beginnings often take on attributes that are removed from what can be documented with historical research. When Nevadans look back on their nineteenth-century heritage, eyes invariably fall upon Virginia City and the Comstock Lode, which made the territory and statehood possible in the early 1860s. Surviving relics of the past also bestowed upon later decades a popular tourist attraction and the largest national historic landmark in the United States.[39] Except that is not true, but like all else, no matter how many times the facts are presented to people, folklore persists, and the landmark will remain the largest in folk belief.

Tourists exploring the Comstock find remarkably well-preserved houses and other structures dating to the last four decades of the nineteenth century. Once the height of architectural style, these Victorian-era buildings survive from a different world. Many people delight in the opportunity to visit the past, to walk amid these traces of a former time. In recent decades, old mansions are more commonly seen as expressions of decay. As art historian Sarah Burns notes, once imbued with hope and aspiration, these buildings increasingly evoked death.[40]

Historic structures and places are a natural habitat of apparitions. For many today, a pivotal way to approach the past is by contemplating its spiritual residue. Whether as active ghost hunting or the more passive means of encountering stories and enjoying the thrill of what lurks in the shadows, folklore offers a bridge to consider this dimension of the early West.

With all of this said, it is important to note that nearly all the modern Comstock ghosts cannot be linked to people identified with historical research. There are exceptions, including John Piper, Julia Bulette, and James

Fair, but these are rare. Whether the little girl on the boardwalk or "William" smoking cigars and "Rosie" cleaning rooms, both in the Gold Hill Hotel, these players are untethered to history, without documented lives. For those who explore a legendary past, the alchemy of folklore conjures flesh for weather-whitened bones.

Conclusion

Virginia City's statue of Lady Justice is well known as one of two in the nation without a blindfold.[1] Residents will helpfully explain how Storey County commissioners purchased the statue for their new courthouse in 1876 as a commentary on the fierce, unflinching way frontier courts should seek and punish criminals. Like most people, Nevadans are committed to the idea of presenting the truth about their past, even when it is not supported by the facts.

In 1985, I sought to verify that the unblindfolded Lady Justice of the Storey County courthouse was, indeed, this rare. Hearing that I had written to my counterparts across the nation for other examples, a few residents hedged their bets and said the statue was perhaps one of three with eyes exposed. Either way, proving the scarcity to be true would underscore the significance of Virginia City's statue.

As it turns out, I found more than two dozen unblindfolded versions in the United States and several more internationally. In fact, it was common to depict Lady Justice with unobstructed eyes in the nineteenth century. Documents in the county recorder's office reveal that Storey County authorities had the choice of purchasing the statue with or without a blindfold. This specific version came from a foundry in Williamsburg, New York. Justice cost $236, and shipping was included.

Then there was a question about what to do with what I realized was an expression of Nevada folklore, accidentally uncovered and disproven by my research. When I began investigating Lady Justice, I initially assumed that Comstockers were merely recounting part of the legacy that surrounds them. After all, they celebrate many aspects of their past, and it would be awkward to classify everything they say about their heritage as oral tradition. Some people have simply read a lot of books and enjoyed the local history, but in this case, finding out that the unblindfolded Justice was not rare helped me to identify her story as folklore.

With this insight, I began asking residents where the second unblindfolded statue could be found, and I received different reports. Many

Virginia City's statue of Lady Justice lacks a blindfold, inspiring folklore to explain the omission. This photograph, by Walt Mulcahy (1907–91), likely dates to the 1950s, well before the statue was restored in 1987. Most of the original gold leaf had fallen away, replaced by silver and maroon paint for skin and robes. The paint began to peel, but the statue remained a local icon, reinforcing a popular perception of frontier justice. Courtesy of the Comstock Historic District Commission.

indicated Aspen, Colorado, but other places also surfaced. It seemed to me that having "one other statue" was a way to accommodate travelers who reported finding another elsewhere. The "other location" could be forgotten, leaving the caveat to serve the next revelation.

Still, I faced the problem of how to deal with what my research had revealed. I was preparing to publish a book on the history of Nevada courthouses, and if it were to include the fact that there were many similar statues, it might extinguish a colorful aspect of local folklore. There was little choice but to state the truth, yet the consequence of publishing my research remained a concern.[2]

Eventually, I was pleased to find out that the disclosure in my publication had no effect on local oral tradition. Over the years, I found that

Comstockers celebrated my book, which included an image of their court-house on its cover. One resident gave copies of my volume as Christmas presents, being particularly enamored by the depiction of her building. Once, while touring Virginia City with students, I was at the courthouse, and that same woman told my class, "You know, our statue of Justice is one of only two in the nation without a blindfold." She then described how the county commissioners had wanted the statue that way because frontier jus-tice demanded constant vigilance.

Folklore survived the written word of history. I was delighted. I have published many things on the West, but as a folklorist, I have always hoped that my work would not smother local tradition. With this example, I put aside my concerns. In the same way, this book represents an opportunity to place "the facts" in perspective while exploring how early Nevadans defined their own truths and how some of that process continues to shape regional folklore. I remain concerned that this book will dampen the stories people tell, inspiring me to hope that what I have written will be ignored.

REMARKS ABOUT THE STATUE of Justice derive from both historical research and folklore collecting from Virginia City residents in the 1980s. Although some personal stories in this volume date to as early as 1960, many other observations draw from interviews over three decades beginning in the 1980s. Most of this book, however, relies on written sources, all of which require scrutiny. Historians will understand this, but some folklorists may balk at the effort, regarding it as hopeless.

In the 1940s, two giants of western folklore offered conflicting views of the printed record. Writing in the mid-twentieth century, C. Grant Loomis observed, "The folklorist is finally realizing that the early newspapers of pioneer days are records as valuable to him as to the historian, economist, student of social institutions, or genealogists. It is true that the modern newspaper does not suggest to the collector of folklore that he will be very well repaid for the trouble of turning its pages. However, the contents of the early journals included as a part of the regular items much material which belongs to the province of folklore."[3] Based on these written docu-ments, Loomis authored several groundbreaking articles on the folklore of the nineteenth-century West.

In contrast, Wayland Hand practiced as an important folklorist of the region at roughly the same time, but he used a different approach. He com-mented on his reluctance to rely on published sources. Introducing his two-part series on California miners' folklore, Hand wrote, "I have cen-tered almost the whole weight of this study upon material collected among miners themselves. Printed material has been relegated to the notes, in order to afford insight into geographical distribution and earlier historical occurrence. Among the scores of miners, active and retired, interviewed throughout the mining camps of the State, are numbered several old timers whose memories run back fifty, sixty, and even seventy years."[4]

Collecting in the 1930s, Hand had the luxury of speaking with miners who remembered as far back as the 1860s. His was the ideal method of the modern folklorist, but Loomis's contributions are no less worthwhile. Attempting to perceive traditions beyond living memory requires the consultation of imperfect sources. Again, some folklorists may assert that such an undertaking is inherently flawed, but then, walking away would be the only option. Short of abandoning the topic, key is a careful reading of sources combined with the realization that some things will not be known clearly.

A CORNERSTONE OF THIS study is the importance of deception, an aspect of folklore that has consistently entwined itself into the story of the region. Because deceit is by its nature regarded as something to avoid, it is easy to misunderstand the role it has played in western culture. Appreciating how tall tales and hoaxes contributed to Nevada's character serves as a reminder that folklore sometimes embeds itself in the unlikeliest of places, and the process is ongoing.

In 1959, Richard Dorson wrote, "The idea that folklore is dying out is itself a kind of folklore."[5] The truth in that statement persists. Every generation tends to see itself as less gullible, less prone to folk beliefs, than those who went before. While it is easy to look down on the superstitions of other cultures and of previous generations, there is a tendency to fail to recognize traditions held by one's peers—or by oneself. Many people who came to early Nevada may not have understood that their emerging society included customs, beliefs, and stories that were taking root. Nevertheless, the adage is worth repeating: everyone has folklore. This was true in the 1860s, and it is true today as people consider the past.

As historians began the task of writing about the state, they were confronted by the deceit that had created a legacy of exaggeration and fabrication.[6] Attempting to sort out facts from falsehoods was nothing short of heroic. Nevada historians often excavate in a complex matrix of ore to extract gold nuggets and to dispose of the rest, lies to be scorned. Rigorous researchers often curse the waste rock that they cast aside, in the same way that the first placer miners reacted to the famed "blue mud."

While the ever-present nature of folklore challenges even the best of

historians, publications of careless writers have also affected the story of
early Nevada. George Lyman's 1934 novel, *The Saga of the Comstock Lode*,
was particularly persuasive, and his influence is tracked throughout these
pages. More fantastic than fact, his work drew on imagination and tradition,
adhering loosely to history. Because of prolific citations, his inventive fiction
influenced a generation of historians who too often assumed that much of
what he wrote was the truth.

Folklorist Carolyn Brown addresses this process in her book on tall
tales: "Folklore inspires subliterature; folklore and subliterature inspire literature; and subliterature and literature in turn re-inspire folklore. Within
this complex relationship there is constant changing, shifting; but there is
also continuity."[7] Lyman's *The Saga of the Comstock Lode* is an example of
how the folkloresque of a novel can draw on history and folklore and then
affect both, with reverberations through the decades.

It was up to subsequent historians to test the assertions of folklore—and
of Lyman among others—one by one. The best of those who wrote of Nevada's earliest decades discarded the false while painting a portrait of the past
that was closer to reality. Here, the effort is to salvage some of what has been
discarded. Considering the dimension of early folklore in the region allows
for an appreciation of the facts of Nevada history while also understanding
the significance of what is left behind. The "blue mud" of this process represents something no less essential to understanding Nevada and the West.
The "Silver State" is silver, after all, because of the blue mud.

Although deceit is fundamental to Nevada folklore, one should not
automatically equate false narratives with the tall tale and its ilk. Inaccura-
cies embedded in the story of the West do not automatically lead to folklore.
Sometimes incorrect depictions of the past simply persist and have nothing
to do with tradition. Intention is key, but determining if trickery originated
as folklore can be difficult to assess in historical documents. Sorting this out
allows for a celebration of deliberate deception, the first cornerstone of early
Nevada folklore. Understanding the role of deceit refreshes the perception
of the past and of the character of the region. It was—and is—a folk tradition of the West to toy with the intersection of deceit, absurdity, and humor.

A SECOND CORE FACTOR has been equally important in the development of
early Nevada folklore. This is, namely, the fact that the population has been
in perpetual flux. Impermanence has always been an issue as people have
come and gone. The waves of arrivals and departures shaped the state's history and culture. Nevada may set a record for the number of times the title
of largest population center has been changed: The settlement that would be

known as Dayton yielded to the town of Genoa (originally Mormon Station) in the early 1850s; Genoa was then eclipsed by Carson City by the end of the decade. In short order, Virginia City took the title from Carson City, all this occurring even before the Nevada Territory was created. Then, as the century ended, Reno could claim to be the largest community in the state.

After that, Goldfield took the baton from Reno for a few years and then passed it back even before the first two decades of the twentieth century had yet to close. Finally, Reno ceased to be the largest community, with Las Vegas outpacing it by 1960. Despite the surges in one direction and then the next, Nevada has often been one of the fastest-growing states as reported by the US Census. This process has not been merely a matter of uneven growth in various places. Instead, people leaving the state continues to be a factor. The depletion of the population at various times, reflecting failed mines and other factors, resulted in Virginia City being reduced to only several hundred people in the 1930s. Much the same happened to Goldfield. Even Las Vegas in the booming Southwest has experienced episodes of decline as well as prosperity.

While individual communities rose and fell at their own pace, so too did the region, causing even more disruption in the formation of traditions. The next decade's newcomers often had no connection with those who had once lived in Nevada and then left. Those belonging to each of these waves of settlement naturally looked back at earlier times with curiosity. People told stories about their new home and about those who had shaped the state.

The turmoil caused by arrivals and departures breed imperfect perceptions of the past. History yielded to folklore in a way that did not necessarily happen in more stable communities. When mixed with the cultural bedrock of deceit, the result was a legendary past that often reached the monumental height of the tall tale, but at other times, stories simply captured the charm of the burlesque lie. Bewildered strangers could not always distinguish falsehood from truth, folklore from verifiable history.

WHILE DECEIT AND DEMOGRAPHIC upheaval served as cornerstones of early Nevada folklore, mining provided yet another pivotal piece of its foundation. The influential industry was at the heart of the transformations in early Nevada. Ranching became an emerging bedrock that allowed stability for many parts of the vast Nevada landscape, but gold and silver strikes defined much of the state for the first several decades. Not surprisingly, mining was a key topic of the Intermountain West's folklore. People not connected to mining nevertheless lived with the industry and told stories about it. There were also those who worked in the excavations: miners possessed their own labor traditions.

Tommyknockers, lost mines, prospectors touching wealth only to lose it, these are examples of motifs that gave mining its dynamic place in western folklore. The industry also created a historical anomaly for the West, defying the stereotypical image of the rural American frontier. While there was usually an early period of scattered prospectors and placer miners, the need to go underground soon pointed the region in a different direction. The mining West emerged industrial, international, and with people living in quickly established towns. This circumstance fostered a unique body of folklore and provided much of the subject matter for nineteenth-century legends. At the same time, mining was at the heart of the very demographic turmoil that affected how traditions formed.

Despite its glory days and notwithstanding a few surviving communities, the importance of mining has faded in much of the state. The annual National Cowboy Poetry Gathering in Elko commemorates the legacy of ranching culture. Coincidentally, because people tended to linger longer in areas that depended on the stability of ranching, its local traditions took on the patina of age. This attracted the attention of some of the first professional folklorists working in Nevada.[8] Various local festivals may feature drilling and other mining contests, but for the most part, the legacy of the industry has nothing on the scale of what occurs in Elko.

Although Nevada remains the "Silver State," for most residents mining heritage lingers as little more than a quaint aspect of a distant past. During the first decade of the twenty-first century, the debate over what would be depicted on the US Mint's "state quarter" for Nevada saw little value in images of mining, settling instead on a depiction of galloping wild horses. The perceived role of mining has declined.

Diversity represents a fourth cornerstone of early Nevada folklore. A complex variety of emigrants each brought their own traditions, some held privately, and others shared and transformed by the exchange. Had a team of multilingual folklorists aggressively collected in Nevada during the 1860s and 1870s, it would have been possible to gather volumes that would reveal both international traditions as well as those that were taking form as the state found its footing. This book hints at possibilities, but the unknowable is far greater than what is discussed here.

New arrivals, attempting to understand local history, placed their stamp on early Nevada folklore. People shaped the story even as many departed. This process continues as a fundamental aspect of regional culture. Today, there is a rich body of folklore of a diverse population, some newcomers and others with deeper roots, but a consistent thread is tangled with the perception of those first decades filled with giants of mythic proportions.

Certain expressions of this early western folklore persist. Even as communities have been buffeted by demographic tidal forces and economic transformations, the tall tale remains essential to Nevadans. It is still employed in Virginia City, even though only a handful of residents can claim ancestors among those in the area in the nineteenth century. Somehow the core cultural bedrock of deception survives. Indeed, it thrives. Understanding that tradition enriches our forays into former times and helps us to grasp the West of today.

The process of imagining and reimagining Nevada's past is not merely a matter of transforming oral tradition. Writers from Mark Twain and George Lyman to would-be historians including Lucius Beebe, Charles Clegg, and Effie Mona Mack have had their way with the perception of Nevada's first decades. At times, the role of deceit was in full bloom in their publications, and the effect of the written word on Nevada folklore cannot be underestimated. For some, this has represented myths to be busted, scorned "fakelore" to be cast aside. The more recent term of Foster and Tolbert, the "folkloresque," allows for a celebration of western falsehoods and exaggerations. Given the importance of monumental lies in Nevada folklore, it is certainly time to come to terms with this aspect of the state's culture and perception of its past.

THROUGH ALL OF THIS, there are the heroes of early folklore collection, those who purposefully or accidentally documented the stories of their times. Chief among them is Dan De Quille, or William Wright as his family knew him. Like so many others, this Iowan came to the West in search of fortune, lingered, and then left Nevada, in his case returning home for his final months. Although De Quille can be hailed as Nevada's first folklorist, he would not have recognized himself in this way. Still, his legacy stands above all others for his ongoing fascination with oral narrative. Without his publications, this book would be brief.

Despite what De Quille accomplished, a core problem remains. It is difficult to forge an understanding of early Nevada folklore using documents not created with that in mind. With the participants dead before professional recording was possible, all that remains are imperfect sources.

Complicating matters, a fascination with deception no doubt affected what authors wrote as much as it changed the stories themselves as they were repeated. Expert of the journalistic hoax Lynda Walsh criticizes Lawrence Berkove's assertion that De Quille sought simply to entertain.[9] Walsh sees hoaxing as serious business with political and other motives, and clearly this has often been the case. Berkove, an authority on the literary legacy of early Nevada writers, nevertheless understood that western deceit was not necessarily malicious. Western hoaxes like tall tales and burlesque lies were opportunities to add humor to life. The malevolent aspects of lying should not be underestimated, and clearly fraud is ubiquitous wherever money or various passions come into play. Nevertheless, De Quille, Lyin' Jim Townsend, Mark Twain, and all the rest were far more interested in the pleasure of a good joke than anything nefarious.

REGARDLESS OF THE MOTIVES of writers in the first decades, most traditions discussed here have long since faded away. The famous ride of Hank Monk and Horace Greeley exists only in the fossilized form of aging publications. What, then, can be done with evidence of an earlier oral tradition? Fortunately, it is possible to hear whispers of tales from the lips of westerners as they settled the region. Their traditions survive in documents.

What is presented here, then, is a consideration of early Nevada folklore. If this were a history, the term "Wild West" might not appear here except as a matter of scorn, since it refers to a mythic land. That said, the wild aspects of the West have always been key to how residents and outsiders alike have viewed the region. From the earliest days, the West was wilder, harder hitting, harder drinking, and harder . . . everything . . . than elsewhere. We know this to be true because legends confirm it. Early on, reality became blurred and folklore celebrated. All this was enhanced by the joyful embrace of the monumental lie, for westerners seldom miss a chance to exaggerate or deceive, all in the name of a hearty laugh.

Notes

Acknowledgments

1. Ronald M. James, "A Year in Ireland: Reflections on a Methodological Crisis," *Sinsear: The Folklore Journal* 4 (1982–83): 4–5, 83–90; Ronald M. James, "Knockers, Knackers, and Ghosts: Immigrant Folklore in the Western Mines."

2. Ronald M. James, *Temples of Justice: The County Courthouse in Nevada*.

3. Ronald M. James, "Monk, Greeley, Ward, and Twain: The Folkloresque of a Western Legend"; Ronald M. James, "In Search of Western Folklore in the Writings of Alfred Doten and Dan De Quille"; Michael Dylan Foster and Jeffrey A. Tolbert, eds., *The Folkloresque: Reframing Folklore in a Popular Culture World*.

4. Richard Erdoes, ed., *Legends and Tales of the American West*.

Introduction

1. G. Grant Loomis, "The Tall Tales of Dan De Quille," 26. For an overview of Loomis, see M. S. Beeler, "C. Grant Loomis (1901–1963)," *Western Folklore* 22, no. 4 (1963): 229–30.

2. For the earliest period, see Sally Zanjani, *Devils Will Reign: How Nevada Began;* and Michael J. Makley, *Imposing Order Without Law: American Expansion to the Eastern Sierra, 1850–1865.*

3. Eliot Lord, *Comstock Mining and Miners;* William Wright [Dan De Quille], *History of the Big Bonanza.* De Quille's book was partly inspired by Mark Twain, whose own portrait of the West, *Roughing It,* appeared in 1872. In addition, Twain assisted with the publication of De Quille's treatment of Virginia City and the region.

4. Ronald M. James, *The Folklore of Cornwall: The Oral Tradition of a Celtic Nation*; William Bottrell, *Traditions and Hearthside Stories of West Cornwall* (Penzance: Beare and Son, 1870, 1st ser.); William Bottrell, *Traditions and Hearthside Stories of West Cornwall* (Penzance: Beare and Son, 1873, 2nd ser.); William Bottrell, *Stories and Folk-Lore of West Cornwall* (Penzance: F. Rodda, 1880).

5. Lawrence I. Berkove, *Dan De Quille* (Boise: Boise State University, 1999); Lawrence I. Berkove, ed., *The Sagebrush Anthology: Literature from the Silver Age of the Old West;* Lawrence I. Berkove, "Life After Twain: The Later Careers of the *Enterprise* Staff."

6. See Alan Dundes, ed., *International Folkloristics: Classic Contributions by the Founders of Folklore,* 9–14, which includes a discussion of the definition of the word "folklore" as well as the original text of the 1846 article by William Thoms proposing the term, reprinting the text from *Athenaeum* 982 (August 22, 1846): 862–63.

7. Chapter 1 draws on the author's "Lost Mines and the Secret of Getting Rich Quick," Folklore Thursday website, July 18, 2019.

8. Chapter 3 draws on the author's "In Search of Western Folklore."

9. Chapter 4 also draws on the author's "In Search of Western Folklore."

10. Chapter 9 draws on publications by the author, based in part on research in Cornwall in 1982: R. James, "Knockers, Knackers, and Ghosts." The subject receives a fuller treatment in the more recent R. James, *Folklore of Cornwall*.

11. Chapter 10 draws on the author's article "Monk, Greeley, Ward, and Twain." A version of the article is also planned for Michael Dylan Foster and Jeffrey A. Tolbert, eds., *Möbius Media: Popular Culture, Folklore, and the Folkloresque*.

12. Chapter 11 draws on the author's article "Sex, Murder, and the Myth of the Wild West: How a Soiled Dove Earned a Heart of Gold"; and Folklore Thursday website, November 12, 2020, presented at the virtual conference "Business as Unusual: Histories of Rupture, Chaos, Revolution, and Change" (September 15–17, 2020), of the Reddit AskHistorians.

13. Jo Ann Nevers, *Wa She Shu: A Washo Tribal History* (Reno: Inter-Tribal Council of Nevada, 1976); Warren L. d'Azevedo and Catherine Fowler, eds., *Handbook of North American Indians*, vol. 11, *Great Basin* (Washington, DC: Smithsonian Institution, 1986). For nineteenth-century Native Americans on the Comstock, see Eugene M. Hattori, "'And Some of Them Swear Like Pirates': Acculturation of American Indian Women in Nineteenth-Century Virginia City," in *Comstock Women: The Making of a Mining Community*, ed. Ronald M. James and C. Elizabeth Raymond, 229–45.

14. Alfred Doten, *The Journals of Alfred Doten: 1849–1903*.

15. Hal Cannon, ed., *Cowboy Poetry: A Gathering*. Duncan Emrich, *In the Delta Saloon: Conversations with Residents of Virginia City, Nevada*, 309–18, provides some recordation of songs and poems in his mid-twentieth-century recordings in Virginia City, but this type of evidence for early Nevada folklore is scarce.

16. Duncan Emrich, *It's an Old West Custom*, 243–45. C. W. Bayer echoes this observation about mining versus ranching songs. See his *Rhymes from the Silver State—Historical Lyrics*, 6. The Bayer book addresses early western songs, but much of what it reprints was composed by professional musicians and may not have entered the "folk" repertoire.

Chapter 1. Lost Mines and the First Strikes

1. For an overview of the work and perspectives of early folklore scholars, see Dundes, *International Folkloristics*.

2. Underground veins in California eventually inspired larger mines like those on the Comstock, but placer mining persisted. Otis E. Young Jr., with technical assistance of Robert Lenon, *Western Mining: An Informal Account of Precious-Metals Prospecting, Placering, Lode Mining, and Milling on the American Frontier from Spanish Times to 1893* (Norman: University of Oklahoma, 1970); J. S. Holliday, *The World Rushed In: The California Gold Rush Experience*; Grant H. Smith and Joseph V. Tingley, *The History of the Comstock Lode, 1850–1997*.

3. Ronald M. James and Robert E. Stewart, eds., *The Gold Rush Letters of E. Allen Grosh and Hosea B. Grosh*, 11; Zanjani, *Devils Will Reign*, 42, 44, 46; Charles Howard Shinn, *The Story of the Mine as Illustrated by the Great Comstock Lode of Nevada*, 29. An early overview of the period and the Grosh brothers is provided by Austin E. Hutchinson, ed., *Before the Comstock, 1857–1858: Memoirs of William Hickman Dolman*. Despite the importance of Frank Antonio's tip, local narratives often neglected to mention him, giving Hosea and Allen Grosh recognition as the first to seek silver in the area.

4. Wells Drury, *An Editor on the Comstock Lode*, 10–11; Wright [De Quille], *History of the*

Big Bonanza, 33–34; Henry DeGroot, *The Comstock Papers,* 5–6. For fanciful descriptions of the Grosh brothers and the early discoverers, see George D. Lyman, *The Saga of the Comstock Lode: Boom Days in Virginia City,* 16–23; and Lucius Beebe and Charles Clegg, *Legends of the Comstock Lode,* 10–14.

5. Wright [De Quille], *History of the Big Bonanza,* 35–36, with De Quille's emphasis.

6. The definitive treatment of the Arizona lost mine legends is Byrd Howell Granger, *A Motif Index for Lost Mines and Treasures Applied to Reaction of Arizona Legends, and to Lost Mine and Treasure Legends Exterior to Arizona.* See also Gerald T. Hurley, "Buried Treasure Tales in America"; and Wayland D. Hand, "The Quest for Buried Treasure: A Chapter in American Folk Legendry." See also Thomas E. Clover, *The Lost Dutchman Mine of Jacob Waltz;* John D. Mitchell, *Lost Mines of the Great Southwest;* J. Martin Lottritz, "Lore of Lost Mines," *New Mexico Magazine* 15, no. 10 (1937): 12; and Richard A. Pierce, *Lost Mines and Buried Treasures of California: Fact, Folklore and Fantasy Concerning 110 Sites of Hidden Wealth* (Berkeley, CA: R. A. Pierce, 1964).

7. Wayland D. Hand, "California Miners Folklore: Above Ground," 39–44.

8. Caroline Bancroft, *Colorado's Lost Gold Mines and Buried Treasure.*

9. Kenneth Silverman, *Edgar A. Poe: Mournful and Never-Ending Remembrance* (New York: Harper Perennial, 1991).

10. Caroline Bancroft, "Lost-Mine Legends of Colorado."

11. Myrtle T. Myles, "Jim Butler: Nevada's Improbable Tycoon."

12. George S. Baker, "Cousin Jack Country," 10; Wright [De Quille], *History of the Big Bonanza,* 17; Kent C. Ryden, *Mapping the Invisible Landscape: Folklore, Writing, and the Sense of Place* (Iowa City: University of Iowa Press, 1993), 148–51; A. K. Hamilton Jenkin, *The Cornish Miner: An Account of His Life Above and Underground from Early Times,* 44; Western Mining History, "Lost Burro Mine—Death Valley," https://westernmininghistory.com/4809/lost-burro-mine-death-valley/?fbclid =IwAR3n9EiyR36IXoVLDeoxOC7D-IrvLgNyvGbztvrqDBqN2joChZOHNxCX-TU (accessed October 22, 2021). Many other creatures figure into this complex of stories. See Hand, "California Miners Folklore: Above Ground," 26–31.

13. Shinn, *Story of the Mine,* 29.

14. Smith gave voice to this pearl of wisdom during one of the annual mining history conferences at the end of the twentieth century.

15. Wright [De Quille], *History of the Big Bonanza,* 41–42. For a history of this early period, see the first chapters of Lord, *Comstock Mining and Miners;* and Ronald M. James, *The Roar and the Silence: A History of Virginia City and the Comstock Lode,* 1–44.

16. Wright [De Quille], *History of the Big Bonanza,* 48–52.

17. Axel Olrik, "Epic Laws of Folk Narrative," in *International Folkloristics,* ed. Dundes, 94–95, with Olrik's emphasis. For a recent discussion of Olrik and the idea of laws, see Elliott Oring, "Four Laws of Folklore," *Western Folklore* 81, no. 1 (2022): 71–74.

18. Lyman, *Saga of the Comstock Lode,* 11–15, 130, claims that the streets were paved with less valuable ore. Guy Rocha, "Virginia City's Silver Streets; Myth #48," (website no longer extant; accessed December 16, 2003). An assertion that it took ten years was part of the narration of a Virginia and Truckee Railroad tour of Virginia City, July 18, 2014.

19. Wright [De Quille], *History of the Big Bonanza,* 55–59.

20. Wright [De Quille], *History of the Big Bonanza,* 60.

Chapter 2. The Earliest Characters

1. R. James, *Roar and the Silence*, 1–44.

2. Record Book C (1859), Storey County Recorder's Office, Virginia City, NV.

3. Lord, *Comstock Mining and Miners*, 53–54.

4. Wright [De Quille], *History of the Big Bonanza*, 62.

5. Dorothy Schwieder, *Iowa: The Middle Land* (Ames: Iowa State University Press, 1996).

6. De Quille mentioned that "I start for Washoe, tomorrow morning" in a letter dated June 2, 1860. Donnelyn Curtis and Lawrence I. Berkove, eds., *Before the Big Bonanza: Dan De Quille's Early Comstock Accounts*, 22.

7. Clarence D. Basso, *Silver Walled Palace: Dan De Quille's "Waifs from Washoe" Originally Published in San Francisco's "The Golden Era"—1860–1865*, 1 (emphases in the original).

8. R. James and Stewart, *Gold Rush Letters*, 202.

9. Wright [De Quille], *History of the Big Bonanza*, 39–40.

10. DeGroot, *The Comstock Papers*, 17, 58–59.

11. Record Book C (1859), Storey County Recorder's Office, Virginia City, NV, p. 78 (September 3, 1859), preserves an example of a transaction authorized by Finney with an *X* and the notation "his mark." Lyman, *Saga of the Comstock Lode*, 11, 360n1, oddly seemed to question whether he came from the state of Virginia, while creating an elaborate fictionalized biography for him.

12. Drury, *Editor on the Comstock Lode*, 12. See also Wright [De Quille], *History of the Comstock Lode*, 59. See also 84–87 for the account appearing in a rambling self-serving largely fictional letter from Comstock. Since the naming of Virginia City had no effect on Comstock's stature, it can be taken that he believed it to be true. For a colorful recounting of the story, see Beebe and Clegg, *Legends of the Comstock Lode*, 12–13. The story of the christening also appears in a mid-twentieth-century tourism pamphlet: Geryl Gould, *Guide of Virginia City: The Cover of the "Pot of Gold" and Silver*. In addition, it appears in Lyman's fantastic imagining, *Saga of the Comstock Lode*, 37.

13. Duncan Emrich, *Folklore on the American Land*, 105–8.

14. Wright [De Quille], *History of the Comstock Lode*, 54; Beebe and Clegg, *Legends of the Comstock Lode*, 13. There were subsequent printings of the Beebe and Clegg book, so the date for this quote could have been later than 1950, although it would necessarily be within the decade. The price paid to Finney, including the blind mustang, is also mentioned by Lyman, *Saga of the Comstock Lode*, 34. In this case it is Henry Comstock who buys the claim, but there is no reason to believe this is from oral tradition since Lyman frequently created his own version of history.

15. DeGroot, *The Comstock Papers*, 50.

16. DeGroot, *The Comstock Papers*, 9.

17. Wright [De Quille], *History of the Comstock Lode*, 54; DeGroot, *The Comstock Papers*, 9. As early as 1861, the *Sacramento Daily Union*, July 8, 1861, documents the sale of a claim by Finney for "an old horse, worth about $40, and a few dollars in cash."

18. Samuel Clemens [Mark Twain], *Roughing It*, 301.

19. Wright [De Quille], *History of the Comstock Lode*, 54; Lyman, *Saga of the Comstock Lode*, 152, in his usual fictional meandering, absurdly transforms this simple story into a pivotal moment that would decide whether the Comstock would belong to the North or the South in the Civil War, a legend transformed into a mythic component of a national epic.

20. Drury, *Editor on the Comstock Lode,* 12; Lord, *Comstock Mining and Miners,* 411; DeGroot, *The Comstock Papers,* 9, 30; *Alta California,* July 22, 1861.

21. Wright [De Quille], *History of the Comstock Lode,* 56.

22. Wright [De Quille], *History of the Comstock Lode,* 77.

23. Wright [De Quille], *History of the Comstock Lode,* 77–78.

24. Wright [De Quille], *History of the Comstock Lode,* 79.

25. Wright [De Quille], *History of the Comstock Lode,* 79. This is oddly recounted by Lyman, *Saga of the Comstock Lode,* 34–35, but as always, Lyman's literary leanings are more likely in evidence than the influence of oral tradition.

26. This inspired the title of David Lowenthal's book *The Past Is a Foreign Country* (Cambridge: Cambridge University Press, 1985), and see his *The Past Is a Foreign Country—Revisited* (Cambridge: Cambridge University Press, 2015). The original quote serves as the opening of Leslie P. Hartley's novel *The Go-Between* (London: Hamish Hamilton, 1953).

27. Mary McNair Mathews, *Ten Years in Nevada; or, Life on the Pacific Coast,* 292–93.

Chapter 3. The Kaleidoscope of Western Folklore

1. "Doten Journals," bk. 72, p. 79, July 20, 1896, Special Collections, University of Nevada, Reno, Libraries.

2. Robert M. Lawrence, "The Folklore of the Horseshoe," *Journal of American Folklore* 9, no. 35 (1896): 288–92; Jacqueline Simpson and Steven Roud, *A Dictionary of English Folklore,* 188–89. Wayland D. Hand, "California Miners Folklore: Below Ground," 142–43, discusses luck associated with horseshoes in the context of mining.

3. R. James, *Roar and the Silence,* 143–66. Although often unreliable in specific information and even observations, this point is valid in Wilbur S. Shepperson, *Restless Strangers: Nevada's Immigrants and Their Interpreters.*

4. Clemens [Twain], *Roughing It,* 309.

5. Gleaning folklore from the written record is an approach used recently to demonstrate how British historian A. L. Rowse (1903–97) recalled the setting of his youth, growing up in turn-of-the-century Cornwall. A. L. Rowse, *A Cornish Childhood* (1942; reprint, London: Cardinal, 1975); R. James, *Folklore of Cornwall,* 36–37.

6. The classic work by J. S. Holliday, *World Rushed In,* is aptly named for this point.

7. "Doten Journals," bk. 72, p. 41, May 7, 1896.

8. "Doten Journals," bk. 73, p. 90, April 23, 1897; bk. 73, p. 141, July 30, 1897.

9. "Doten Journals," bk. 55, p. 58, March 14, 1882; bk. 57, pp. 62–63, March 22–23, 1887; Jill F. Austin, "Equinoctial Gales: Fact or Fiction?," *Weather: Royal Meteorological Society* 50, no. 10 (1995): 330–36; Arthur Newton Pack, "Equinoctial Gale a Myth," *New York Times,* November 3, 1925; Michael Allaby, *A Dictionary of Earth Sciences,* 4th ed. (Oxford: Oxford University Press, 2010).

10. "Doten Journals," bk. 66, p. 56, May 12, 1891; A. D. Bajkov, "Do Fish Fall from the Sky?," *Science* 109 (April 22, 1949): 402; Waldo L. McAtee, "Showers of Organic Matter," *Monthly Weather Review* 45 (May 1917): 217–24; Jerry Dennis, *It's Raining Frogs and Fishes: Four Seasons of Natural Phenomena and Oddities of the Sky* (New York: HarperCollins, 1992); William Bascom, "The Forms of Folklore: Prose Narratives," *Journal of American Folklore* 78, no. 307 (1965): 3–20.

11. "Doten Journals," bk. 31, p. 200, March 2, 1866. Joe Goodman, editor of the *Territorial Enterprise* in Virginia City, authored a three-column article, "How Tom Peasley Died,"

for the *San Francisco Chronicle,* February 21, 1892. He mentioned Peasley's wish to have his boots removed as he was dying, and a drawing of the pivotal moment shows a man pulling at Peasley's boot. See also a mention of the issue of dying while wearing boots in Wright [De Quille], *History of the Big Bonanza,* 132.

12. Ramon F. Adams, *Western Words: A Dictionary of the American West;* Christine Ammer, *The American Heritage Dictionary of Idioms,* 2nd ed. (Boston: Houghton Mifflin Harcourt, 2013); John Ayto, Judith Siefring, and Jennifer Speake, eds., *The Oxford Dictionary of English Idioms,* 3rd ed. (Oxford: Oxford University Press, 2009); *Farlex Idioms & Slang Dictionary* (n.p.: Farlex International, 2017).

13. "Doten Journals," bk. 31, p. 201, March 2, 1866.

14. James E. Crombie, "Shoe-Throwing at Weddings," *Folklore* 6 (1895): 258–81; T. Sharper Knowlson, *The Origins of Popular Superstitions and Customs* (London: T. Werner Laurie, 1910). Compare many Middle Eastern cultures where a thrown shoe is an insult.

15. "Doten Journals," bk. 33, p. 121, March 26, 1867; Simpson and Roud, *Dictionary of English Folklore,* 217–18, 383; Simon Charsley, *Wedding Cakes and Cultural History* (New York: Routledge, 1992); Simon Charsley, "The Wedding Cake: History and Meanings," *Folklore* 99, no. 2 (1988): 232–41.

16. "Doten Journals," bk. 47, pp. 128–29, July 24, 1874. Although references to this tradition are rare, the motif occurs in at least one other example: An incident in Ladoga, Indiana, at the turn of the twentieth century involved a man who slipped while installing telephone wires. He was wearing his wedding coat because of the cold, and the coat caught on a nail, saving him from the fall. The coat tore and was consequently worn out, and as the recollection reads, "He said that he had always heard that a person should wear out his wedding clothes before he had good luck." http://streetsofladoga.blogspot.com/2012/08/the-streets-of-ladoga-in-40s-and-50s.html (accessed July 5, 2021), with thanks to Jeremy Harte, curator, Bourne Hall Museum. See also George Monger, *Discovering the Folklore and Traditions of Marriage* (London: Shire, 2011).

17. "Doten Journals," bk. 65, p. 76, April 20, 1890; bk. 78, p. 163, December 21, 1902. See also Doten's reference on April 20, 1890, to a letter sent about divining rods; Gaston Burridge, "Does the Forked Stick Locate Anything? An Inquiry into the Art of Dowsing," *Western Folklore* 14, no. 1 (1955): 32–43; R. A. Foulkes, "Dowsing Experiments," *Nature* 229 (1971): 163–68; Leonard Zusne and Warren Jones, *Anomalistic Psychology: A Study of Magical Thinking* (Hillsdale, NJ: Lawrence Erlbaum, 1989); Lydia Fish, "The European Background of American Miners' Beliefs," 158; and Hand, "California Miners Folklore: Above Ground," 34–36.

18. Berkove, *Sagebrush Anthology,* 234.

19. "Doten Journals," bk. 72, p. 148, December 5, 1896; Jan Harold Brunvand, *Too Good to Be True: The Colossal Book of Urban Legends;* Mike Dash, *Borderlands;* Ron Genini, "Close Encounters of the Earliest Kind," *American Heritage* (December 1979): 94–99; Ron Genini, "The Airship of '96: Flight of Fancy or Flight of Fact?," *Californians: The Magazine of California History* (May 1983): 6–15; *San Francisco Call,* November 19, 22, 23, 24, 29, 1896; *San Francisco Chronicle,* November 22, 24, 28, December 1, 2, 5, 1896. For a recent study of nineteenth-century urban legends, see Simon Young, *The Nail in the Skull, and Other Victorian Urban Legends.*

20. "Doten Journals," bk. 78, p. 60, May 22, 1902; Edwin Radford and Mona Augusta Radford, *Encyclopedia of Superstition,* ed. Christina Hole (New York: Barnes and Noble,

1961), 142; Edward M. Nebinger, *Growing Up in a Pennsylvania Steel Town During the Great Depression* (n.p.: Lion by Lion, 2012), 100; Edgar Allen Poe, "The Mystery of Marie Rogêt," *Ladies' Companion* 18, no. 1 (1842).

21. "Doten Journals," bk. 73, p. 87, April 18, 1897; Richard M. Dorson, *Bloodstoppers and Bearwalkers: Folk Traditions of Michigan's Upper Peninsula*, 236–38; Mark Robinson, "Fact Checker: Is Lake Tahoe Filled with Hundreds of Preserved Bodies," *Reno Gazette-Journal*, August 22, 2011; Edward B. Scott, *The Saga of Lake Tahoe* (Crystal Bay, NV: Sierra-Tahoe, 1957), 219, 319, 456–57; C. F. McGlashan, "Wonders of Lake Tahoe," *Sacramento Union*, May 9, 1875; Warren L. d'Azevedo, *Two Worlds of Lake Tahoe: A Report on Cave Rock*, Anthropological Papers no. 26, ed. Eugene M. Hattori (Carson City: Nevada State Museum, 2008), 38; Reidar Th. Christiansen, *The Migratory Legends: A Proposed List of Types with a Systematic Catalogue of the Norwegian Variants*, ML 4065. See also a mention of Tahoe not giving up its dead in Wright [De Quille], *History of the Big Bonanza*, 415.

22. "Doten Journals," bk. 31, p. 177, January 28, 1866; bk. 32, p. 26, June 4, 1866; Simpson and Roud, *Dictionary of English Folklore*, 161–62.

23. David K. Nartonis, "The Rise of 19th-Century American Spiritualism, 1854–1873," *Journal for the Scientific Study of Religion* 49, no. 2 (2010): 361–73; Bernadette S. Francke, "Divination on Mount Davidson: An Overview of Women Spiritualists and Fortunetellers on the Comstock"; Daniel Herman, "Whose Knocking? Spiritualism as Entertainment and Therapy in Nineteenth-Century San Francisco," *American Nineteenth Century History* 7, no. 3 (2006): 417–42; Molly McGarry, *Ghosts of Futures Past: Spiritualism and the Cultural Politics of Nineteenth-Century America* (Berkeley: University of California Press, 2008); Christopher M. Moreman, *The Spiritualist Movement: Speaking with the Dead in America and Around the World* (Westport, CT: Praeger, 2013). For the use of a dial, which Doten mentions in this context, see Stan McMullin, *Anatomy of a Seance: A History of Spirit Communication in Central Canada* (Kingston, ON: McGill–Queen's University Press, 2004), 27.

24. "Doten Journals," bk. 35, pp. 78–79, October 24, 1867.

25. "Doten Journals," bk. 36, pp. 16–17, December 11, 1867; Francke, "Divination on Mount Davidson."

26. "Doten Journals," bk. 34, p. 109, July 23, 1867.

27. Folklorist C. Grant Loomis, for example, republished a list of elements from folklore that he found in the *Territorial Enterprise*. These were older traditions that the newspaper published as curiosities, but their appearance in print provides a clue about how a popular fascination with folklore was emerging in the nineteenth century. See his "Some American Folklore of 1880," *California Folklore Quarterly* 4, no. 4 (1945): 417; and *Territorial Enterprise*, January 20, 1880.

CHAPTER 4. DAN DE QUILLE THE FOLKLORIST

1. Curtis and Berkove, *Before the Big Bonanza*, 115, from *Cedar Falls (IA) Gazette*, July 26, 1861.

2. Curtis and Berkove, *Before the Big Bonanza*, 115.

3. Curtis and Berkove, *Before the Big Bonanza*, 115–16.

4. Assessments of Wright's early career often suggest that Wright selected his pen name while working for the *Territorial Enterprise*. Curtis and Berkove's collection of earlier articles, *Before the Big Bonanza*, makes it clear that Wright was signing journalistic correspondence as "Dan De Quille" by May 1860, more than a year before being hired by the *Enterprise*.

5. Curtis and Berkove, *Before the Big Bonanza;* Lawrence I. Berkove, *Dan De Quille* (Boise: Boise State University, 1999); Berkove, *Sagebrush Anthology;* Lawrence I. Berkove, ed., *Insider Stories of the Comstock Lode and Nevada's Mining Frontier, 1859–1909: Primary Sources in American Social History;* Berkove, "Life After Twain"; Richard A. Dwyer and Richard E. Lingenfelter, *Dan De Quille, the Washoe Giant: A Biography and Anthology;* Richard E. Lingenfelter and Karen Rix Gash, *The Newspapers of Nevada: A History and Bibliography, 1854–1879;* Jake Highton, *Nevada Newspaper Days: A History of Journalism in the Silver State;* C. C. Goodwin, *As I Remember Them,* 213–17; Chic Di Francia, *The Life and Times of Dan DeQuille, Chronicler of the Comstock and Reporter for the "Territorial Enterprise" in Virginia City, Nevada;* Chic Di Francia, "Comstock Typeslingers and Sagebrush Journalism: 19th Century Newsmen and Their Careers," *Nevada Appeal* (Carson City), March 17, 2002.

6. Linda Dégh, *Legend and Belief.*

7. Curtis and Berkove, *Before the Big Bonanza,* 34, from *Golden Era,* December 30, 1860.

8. William Wright [Dan De Quille], *Washoe Rambles,* 111–22. There are also two other anecdotes possibly taken from oral tradition, 123–32. The first involves "bummers" who manipulate a liquor salesman into obtaining free drinks, and the second describes a "salted" saloon (a business made to appear more prosperous than it was so it could be sold), located in Arbustum City, California. In addition, De Quille recounted what he claimed to be a Paiute legend, 145–46, and he summarized "Judar and his Brethren," from the *Arabian Nights,* 153.

9. Wright [De Quille], *Washoe Rambles,* 111 (emphasis in the original).

10. Wright [De Quille], *History of the Big Bonanza,* 416–17.

11. *Gold Hill Evening News,* March 28, 1876.

12. Wright [De Quille], *History of the Big Bonanza,* 417–18.

13. Wright [De Quille], *History of the Big Bonanza,* 418.

14. Drury, *Editor on the Comstock Lode,* 139; Guy Rocha, "Myth #38: Levi's 501 Jeans; A Riveting Story in Early Reno," *Silver Sage* (Carson City/Carson Valley, NV) (March 1999); Lynn Downey, *Levi Strauss: The Man Who Gave Blue Jeans to the World* (Amherst: University of Massachusetts Press, 2016).

15. Wright [De Quille], *History of the Big Bonanza,* 153.

16. Wright [De Quille], *History of the Big Bonanza,* 149–50.

17. Wright [De Quille], *History of the Big Bonanza,* 148.

18. Wright [De Quille], *History of the Big Bonanza,* 148.

19. Wright [De Quille], *History of the Big Bonanza,* 109–10.

20. Dorson, *Bloodstoppers and Bearwalkers;* Caroline Bancroft, "Folklore of the Central City District, Colorado"; Wayland D. Hand, "The Folklore from Utah's Silver Mining Camps."

21. Wright [De Quille], *History of the Big Bonanza,* 213–14.

22. Wright [De Quille], *History of the Big Bonanza,* 214.

23. Wright [De Quille], *History of the Big Bonanza,* 360.

24. A rare example of one people's tradition diffusing among others in North America is provided by the belief in the underground mining spirit, the knocker of Cornwall. This entity transformed into the western tommyknocker, common property of regional miners regardless of their place of origin. See chapter 9 and R. James, *Folklore of Cornwall,* 148–62.

CHAPTER 5. THE HOAX AS FOLKLORE

1. Ronald M. James, "Mark Twain in Nevada." Although Ron Powers repeatedly misunderstands Twain's Nevada sojourn, see his recent important biography, *Mark Twain: A Life* (New York: Free Press, 2005).

2. Samuel Clemens [Mark Twain], *The Works of Mark Twain, Early Tales and Sketches,* 155–59. The original text of the newspaper article does not exist, but it was reprinted by other newspapers and attributed to the *Territorial Enterprise,* October 4, 1862. For his own assessment of the hoax, which strays from what is known historically, see Samuel Clemens [Mark Twain], "A Couple of Sad Experiences." Kerry Driscoll, "The Fluid Identity of 'Petrified Man,'" *American Literary Realism* 41, no. 3 (2009): 214–31, points out that Twain's *Galaxy* article "is so exaggerated that it qualifies as a meta-hoax."

3. Clemens [Twain], *Works of Mark Twain,* 158. Relying on what Twain would later write about this and other hoaxes becomes a treacherous path since everything must be evaluated in context, understanding that any of the author's comments may be a deception or may simply be shaded even slightly to suit him at the moment.

4. Loomis, "Tall Tales of Dan De Quille." Hand, "California Miners Folklore: Above Ground," 24, discusses the paradox of a traditional genre with an individually crafted text.

5. Henry B. Wonham, *Mark Twain and the Art of the Tall Tale,* 26–28; Carolyn S. Brown, *The Tall Tale in American Folklore and Literature,* 60–61. For an excellent overview of the journalistic hoax from a point of view other than folklore, see Lynda Walsh, *Sins Against Science: The Scientific Media Hoaxes of Poe, Twain, and Others.*

6. *Oxford English Dictionary* [*A New English Dictionary on Historical Principals*] (Oxford: Clarendon Press, 1901), 5:314.

7. Walsh, *Sins Against Science,* 24–25; Matthew Goodman, *The Sun and the Moon: The Remarkable True Account of Hoaxers, Showmen, Dueling Journalists, and Lunar Man-Bats in Nineteenth-Century New York.*

8. Walsh, *Sins Against Science,* 140, 207. Walsh astutely distinguishes De Quille's tall tales from his hoaxes, underscoring the difference between clearly absurd tales and hoaxes where the absurdity is less obvious to increase profit. Julien Gorbach, "Not Your Grandpa's Hoax: A Comparative History of Fake News," *American Journalism* 35, no. 2 (2018): 236–49, does not offer the same clarity in differentiating between satire and profit as motive.

9. Poe had previously written a story about a balloon trip to the moon, but in that earlier effort, it is not clear if he meant for people to believe what was apparently intended as fiction. *New York Sun,* April 13, April 15, 1844; Walsh, *Sins Against Science,* 60, 90–97, 117; Goodman, *Sun and the Moon;* Arthur Hobson Quinn, *Edgar Allan Poe: A Critical Biography* (Baltimore: John Hopkins University Press, 1998).

10. Walsh, *Sins Against Science,* 25, 51–97. Walsh distinguishes hoax from fraud, but the difference is not as well defined with hoaxes perpetrated in the East since monetary gain was the goal. Goodman, *Sun and the Moon,* 235–46.

11. Walsh, *Sins Against Science,* 16.

12. Brown, *Tall Tale in American Folklore and Literature,* 61, in her comprehensive book on tall tales is specific about this point; Wright [De Quille], *History of the Big Bonanza,* 36–38; Drury, *Editor on the Comstock Lode,* 212.

13. Clemens [Twain], *Works of Mark Twain,* 320–26; Clemens [Twain], "Couple of Sad Experiences."

14. Clemens [Twain], "Couple of Sad Experiences." See also *Gold Hill Daily News,* October 30, 1863.

15. Edgar Marquess Branch, Michael B. Frank, and Kenneth M. Sanderson, eds., *Mark Twain's Letters*, vol. 1, *1853–1866*, 289n2; Ronald M. James, "Mark Twain's Miscegenation Hoax of 1864: Understanding Context." See also Michael D. Pierson, "Mark Twain and the Women of Carson City: Gendered Politics of Civil War Fundraising," *Nevada Historical Society Quarterly* 64, no. 1 (2021): 4–21; James E. Caron, *Mark Twain: Unsanctified Newspaper Reporter*, 150–57; and Robert E. Stewart, "Mark Twain, Ruel Gridley, and the U.S. Sanitary Commission: Raising Funds to Aid Civil War Soldiers."

16. Sidney Kaplan, "The Miscegenation Issue in the Election of 1864," *Journal of Negro History* 34, no. 3 (1949): 274–343; David A. Hollinger, "Amalgamation and Hypodescent: The Question of Ethnoracial Mixture in the History of the United States," *American Historical Review* 108, no. 5 (2003): 1363–90.

17. Branch, Frank, and Sanderson, *Mark Twain's Letters*, 288.

18. Lucius Beebe, *Comstock Commotion: The Story of the "Territorial Enterprise,"* 93.

19. *Territorial Enterprise*, July 2, 1874.

20. *Territorial Enterprise*, July 2, 1874.

21. Walsh, *Sins Against Science*, 188–94. Regarding De Quille quaints, it is possible to add an account from the *Territorial Enterprise*, February 19, 1876, of eyeless fish found in the near-boiling subterranean water of the Comstock mines. See chapter 7.

22. Drury, *Editor on the Comstock Lode*, 211–12.

23. Loomis, "Tall Tales of Dan De Quille," 37n3, citing Drury, *Editor on the Comstock Lode*, 213; De Lancey Ferguson, *Mark Twain, Man and Legend* (New York: Bobbs-Merrill, 1943), 83; Ivan Benson, *Mark Twain's Western Years* (Stanford, CA: Stanford University Press, 1938).

24. *Territorial Enterprise*, October 26, 1867. Three rods can indicate nearly fifty feet, but the meaning of a rod sometimes varies. Totally confusing the time line, Lyman, *Saga of the Comstock Lode*, 208–10, discusses this and several other De Quille quaints.

25. Walsh, *Sins Against Science*, 194.

26. Walsh, *Sins Against Science*, 195, evaluates the claim that Barnum and German scientists requested samples, concluding that it is possible but not certain.

27. *Territorial Enterprise*, March 31, 1872.

28. Wright [De Quille], *History of the Big Bonanza*, 36–38.

29. Walsh, *Sins Against Science*, 209.

30. *Territorial Enterprise*, November 11, 1879.

31. Richard D. Norris et al., "Sliding Rocks on Racetrack Playa, Death Valley National Park: First Observation of Rocks in Motion," *PLOS ONE* (August 27, 2014), https://doi.org/10.1371/journal.pone.0105948; Robert Evans, "Dancing Rocks: Mysteriously Moving Stones in Death Valley Leave Whimsical Trails. How Do They Do That?," *Smithsonian*, July 1999, 88–94.

32. Susan James, "Blazing a Trail with Blasdel."

33. Walsh discusses the March 6, 1892, article in the *Salt Lake Daily Tribune*. Walsh, *Sins Against Science*, 196–97.

34. Walsh, *Sins Against Science*, 198.

35. Walsh, *Sins Against Science*, 216.

36. Drury, *Editor on the Comstock Lode*, 212.

37. Brown, *Tall Tale in American Folklore and Literature*, 23.

CHAPTER 6. TALL TALES AND OTHER DECEPTIONS AS FOLKLORE

1. An analogue of the smart pill is the oracle pill. See Stith Thompson, *Motif-Index of Folk Literature*: "Motif K114.3.1: Virtue of oracular pill proved. The dupe takes it. 'It is dog's dung.' He says, spitting it out. The trickster says that he is telling the truth and demands pay." Thompson cites D. P. Rotunda, *Motif-Index of the Italian Novella* (Bloomington, IN, 1942); and Albert Wesselski, *Die Begebenheiten der beiden Gonnella* (Weimar, Germany, 1920), nos. 4, 4a, 106, and 9, a discussion of an Italian buffoon dating to the fifteenth century. Gene Hattori was the most recent person to suggest that I would benefit from ingesting smart pills (ca. 1995). He should be ashamed.

2. Richard Bauman, *Story, Performance and Event: Contextual Studies of Oral Narrative*, 23–24.

3. Brown, *Tall Tale in American Folklore and Literature*, 11–12; Thompson, *Motif-Index of Folk Literature*: "Motif X1623.2.1: Lie: frozen words thaw out in the spring"; E. Cobham Brewer, "Frozen Words," in *Dictionary of Phrase and Fable* (London: Cassell, 1898); W. F. Garrett-Petts and Donald Lawrence, "Thawing the Frozen Image/Word: Vernacular Postmodern Aesthetics," *Mosaic: An Interdisciplinary Critical Journal* 31, no. 1 (1998): 143–78. See a similar account about words in Virginia City being blown away so that people blocks away heard them: Emrich, *It's an Old West Custom*, 274–75.

4. Wonham, *Mark Twain and the Art of the Tall Tale*, 21; Rudolf Erich Raspe [anonymous], *Baron Munchausen's Narrative of His Marvellous Travels and Campaigns in Russia* (Oxford: Booksellers, 1786); John Patrick Carswell, *The Prospector: Being the Life and Times of Rudolf Erich Raspe (1737–1794)* (London: Cresset Press, 1950); Brown, *Tall Tale in American Folklore and Literature*, 11–12. Munchausen syndrome, more properly "Factitious disorder imposed on self (or others)," takes its name from the literary character to diagnose people who suffer from a condition that causes them to claim nonexistent conditions to gain attention or sympathy.

5. *Public Advertiser*, May 22, 1765. For a historical overview of the American tall tale, see Brown, *Tall Tale in American Folklore and Literature*, 40.

6. Wonham, *Mark Twain and the Art of the Tall Tale*, 4–8, citing several letters from 1765 in the *Public Advertiser*, reproduced in Benjamin Franklin, *Benjamin Franklin's Letters to the Press*, ed. Verner W. Crane (Chapel Hill: University of North Carolina Press, 1950), 30–35.

7. Erdoes, *Legends and Tales of the American West*, xv. Brown's book *Tall Tale in American Folklore and Literature* deals almost entirely with eastern and southern examples.

8. Walsh, *Sins Against Science*, 25–26.

9. Many have observed that the tall tale tended to be the domain of male storytelling, fitting the masculine bravado of whopping fish stories, and again, in a male-dominated early West, the genre found the perfect place to flourish. Bauman, *Story, Performance and Event*, 13–14; Wonham, *Mark Twain and the Art of the Tall Tale*, 181n13. For an excellent treatment of women telling exaggerated narratives, see Vera Mark, "Women and Text in Gascon Tall Tales," *Journal of American Folklore* 100, no. 398 (1987): 504–27. See also Nancy A. Walker, *A Very Serious Thing: Women's Humor and American Culture* (Minneapolis: University of Minnesota Press, 1988).

10. Drury, *Editor on the Comstock Lode*, 197. Hand, "California Miners Folklore: Above Ground," 24, indicates that tall tales were also called "whizzers." See also Richard Moreno, *Frontier Fake News: Nevada's Sagebrush Humorists and Hoaxers*, 71–79.

11. Richard A. Dwyer and Richard E. Lingenfelter, *Lying on the Eastern Slope: James Townsend's Comic Journalism on the Mining Frontier*; *Territorial Enterprise*, August 23, 1900;

Chic Di Francia, "Comstock Typeslingers and Sagebrush Journalism: 19th Century News-men and Their Careers," *Nevada Appeal* (Carson City), March 17, 2002. Twentieth-century journalist Lucius Beebe, who valued the truth as much as Townsend, also addresses the story of Lying Jim. Beebe, *Comstock Commotion,* 57–58; Emrich, *It's an Old West Custom,* 284–85.

12. Lawrence I. Berkove and Michael Kowalewski, "The Literature of the Mining Camps," 111; Clemens [Twain], *Roughing It,* 634n229.26–230.17.

13. Benjamin Griffin et al., eds., *Autobiography of Mark Twain* (Berkeley: University of California Press, 2015), 3:597n287.40; Edgar Marquess Branch, Robert H. Hirst, and Har-riet Elinor Smith, eds., *The Works of Mark Twain, Early Tales & Sketches,* vol. 2, *1864–1865* (Berkeley: University of California Press, 1981), 264.

14. *Virginia Chronicle,* May 27, 1882.

15. *Virginia Chronicle,* May 27, 1882.

16. Berkove, *Sagebrush Anthology,* 276–79; Dwyer and Lingenfelter, *Lying on the Eastern Slope,* 42.

17. Drury, *Editor on the Comstock Lode,* 198.

18. Brown, *Tall Tale in American Folklore and Literature,* 19; Emrich, *It's an Old West Custom,* 269–81.

19. Fred H. Hart, *The Sazerac Lying Club: A Nevada Book;* Loomis, "Tall Tales of Dan De Quille"; Emrich, *It's an Old West Custom,* 285.

20. Highton, *Nevada Newspaper Days,* 43–45. Moreno, *Frontier Fake News,* 8–10, 82–88, provides an excellent treatment of Fred Hart and his account of the lying club.

21. *Territorial Enterprise,* March 21, 1876, attributed to the *Reese River Reveille* (Austin, NV).

22. Hand, "California Miners Folklore: Above Ground," 24, notes the paradox of fitting in material that was individually crafted into a traditional genre when it came to hoaxes, tall tales, and practical jokes.

23. Brown, *Tall Tale in American Folklore and Literature,* 12–13; Robert G. Deindorfer, *America's 101 Most High Falutin', Big Talkin', Knee Slappin', Golly Whoppers and Tall Tales: The Best of the Burlington Liar's Club* (New York: Workman, 1980). For a modern liar's competi-tion in Goldfield, Nevada, see *Comstock Chronicle,* August 4, 1989. See also the annual Big-gest Liar competition in England's Santon Bridge, *Wall Street Journal,* November 25, 2011.

24. Drury, *Editor on the Comstock Lode,* 47. For a simple joke, attempting to convince a miner who fell asleep underground that he was dead, see "Mike Harrington's Wake," *Vir-ginia Evening Chronicle,* August 17, 1875.

25. See chapter 10.

26. Curtis and Berkove, *Before the Big Bonanza,* 82–83, with De Quille's emphases.

27. Goodwin, *As I Knew Them,* 43–46. Lyman, *Saga of the Comstock Lode,* 228, is always a questionable source, but here his comment that a group of students "hailed from Pike" can be taken as an indication that the name continued to have resonance into the twentieth century.

28. Curtis and Berkove, *Before the Big Bonanza,* 83, 168n5, 292.

29. Wright [De Quille], *History of the Big Bonanza,* 535.

30. Wright [De Quille], *History of the Big Bonanza,* 536.

31. Wright [De Quille], *History of the Big Bonanza,* 542–43.

32. Wright [De Quille], *History of the Big Bonanza,* 542–56.

33. Clemens [Twain], *Roughing It,* 537–42, 744–45n540.17–19; *Territorial Enterprise,* November 11, 1866; *Alta California,* December 14, 1866.

34. Drury, *Editor on the Comstock Lode,* 48.

35. Drury, *Editor on the Comstock Lode,* 49.

36. Drury, *Editor on the Comstock Lode,* 52.

37. Drury, *Editor on the Comstock Lode,* 52.

38. Emrich, *It's an Old West Custom,* 98–105.

39. Emrich, *In the Delta Saloon,* 83; Drury, *Editor on the Comstock Lode,* 41–46. Lyman, *Saga of the Comstock Lode,* 199–201, picks up the story, and although he might be the source of subsequent folklore, he cites a newspaper article that appears to have been written by Drury. For Washoe canaries as mules or donkeys, see the following chapter.

40. Drury, *Editor on the Comstock Lode,* 41–46.

41. Drury, *Editor on the Comstock Lode,* 41–46

42. Drury, *Editor on the Comstock Lode,* 41–46

43. Drury, *Editor on the Comstock Lode,* 41–46

44. Drury, *Editor on the Comstock Lode,* 41–46

45. "Doten Journals," bk. 28, p. 163, April 1, 1864; bk. 31, p. 224, April 1, 1866; bk. 34, p. 7, April 1, 1867, Special Collections, University of Nevada, Reno, Libraries.

46. Hart, *Sazerac Lying Club,* 18.

47. Brown, *Tall Tale in American Folklore and Literature,* 9.

CHAPTER 7. A SEVERED FINGER AND OTHER DISJOINTED ITEMS

1. My wife, Susan Dakins James, heard a story ca. 1962–63 about cui-ui that would vanish from Pyramid and reappear in the Red Sea, only to return. The author gathered information on similar legends beginning on September 11, 2021, with a post on Facebook, reviewed by 249 "friends," many of whom were living in Nevada in the 1950s and 1960s. Results provided analogous stories, often without the corpse and featuring only the boat. These confirmed the South America destination, but others placed the boat in Egypt, South Africa, and Ireland. Additional testimony discussed underground rivers between Pyramid Lake and Walker Lake, Pyramid Lake and California, and generically from northern Nevada to southern Nevada.

2. *Carson City Appeal,* March 18, 1918; Chic J. DiFrancia, "'30' Is Ticked Off for Sam Davis: Sagebrush School Journalist Penned Silver State History," *Nevada Magazine* (March–April 2018); Berkove, *Sagebrush Anthology;* Samuel P. Davis, *The History of Nevada* (Reno: Elms, 1913).

3. Sam Davis, "The Mystery of the Savage Sump," *Black Cat* 75 (December 1901): 1–7. See also Edward B. Scott, *The Saga of Lake Tahoe* (Crystal Bay, NV: Sierra-Tahoe, 1957), 247–48, 343–47; and Warren L. d'Azevedo, *Two Worlds of Lake Tahoe: A Report on Cave Rock,* Anthropological Papers no. 26, ed. Eugene M. Hattori (Carson City: Nevada State Museum, 2008), 38–39. Lyman, *Saga of the Comstock Lode,* 131, alludes to this idea in his 1934 novel. In an unpublished seminar paper, "The Folklore of the Comstock Lode and Surrounding Regions: 1850–1900," December 10, 1978, 14–16, Paul Strickland reports on interviewing Ty Cobb (1915–97), a Nevada journalist who maintained that the core of "The Mystery of the Savage Sump" was a legend circulating "probably back to the 1860s." Strickland transcribed the entire story as recounted by Cobb, which follows the Davis version in many ways, but variation points to how the story likely inspired an oral tradition. See also Ty Cobb, *My Virginia City: A Columnist's Memories.*

4. *Carson City Appeal,* July 31, 1883.

5. *Territorial Enterprise,* February 19, 1876; Walsh, *Sins Against Science,* 198–202. Water at 130 degrees will cause third-degree burns within a thirty-second exposure.

6. *Territorial Enterprise,* February 19, 1876.

7. Walsh, *Sins Against Science,* 202, also documents an admission of the hoax in De Quille's own hand, with an annotation on a note from a secretary of the Smithsonian Institution, requesting a specimen, on which De Quille wrote, "A Sold Professor—The 'Eyeless Fish' biz."

8. Writing in the context of De Quille's hoaxes, Goodwin, *As I Remember Them,* 215, also refers to the prevalent idea of an underground connection linking Lake Tahoe and the Comstock mines. Walsh, *Sins Against Science,* 201–2, sees Goodwin's recollection as an indication that there was another De Quille hoax about the subterranean channel. Goodwin's book is flawed in many ways, being, as the title suggests, "as he remembered them," rather than an authoritative history. It is possible that Goodwin confused the blind-fish hoax with other speculations about an underground passage.

9. Beebe, *Comstock Commotion,* 93.

10. For an early reference to Tahoe not giving up its dead, see d'Azevedo, *Two Worlds of Lake Tahoe,* 37, citing the *Placerville Herald* in July 1853.

11. Mathews, *Ten Years in Nevada,* 191. The Mathews memoir is racist and anti-Semitic, but her work is valuable for its many observations.

12. *Nevada State Journal,* July 6, 1887.

13. "Doten Journals," bk. 52, p. 100, July 4, 1879, Special Collections, University of Nevada, Reno, Libraries. Horribles are also mentioned in the interviews conducted by Duncan Emrich in Virginia City, 1949–50. Emrich, *In the Delta Saloon,* 57.

14. Alfred L. Shoemaker, "Fantasticals," *Pennsylvania Folklife* 9, no. 1 (1957–58): 28–31. Now often having women participation, resurrected traditions include, for example, Andover, Massachusetts: *North Andover (MA) Eagle-Tribune,* July 4, 2019. For the British mummers, see Simpson and Roud, *Dictionary of English Folklore,* 259–53.

15. Mathews, *Ten Years in Nevada,* 234.

16. Mathews, *Ten Years in Nevada,* 160–61.

17. Constance Wakeford Long, *The Book of Children's Games: One Hundred Games for Use in Schools and Play-Centres* (New York: E. P. Dutton, 1852), 22. Long's book describes the game as "King Dido is dead," but this makes less sense.

18. John Taylor Waldorf, *A Kid on the Comstock: Reminiscences of a Virginia City Childhood;* R. James, *Virginia City,* 85–95.

19. Wright [De Quille], *History of the Big Bonanza,* 255; Loomis, "Tall Tales of Dan De Quille," 59.

20. Mathews, *Ten Years in Nevada,* 223. Mathews recorded additional insight into the folklore known to people in early Nevada. See, for example, the legend she heard about Henry Comstock and the wife he purchased (chapter 2) and her observations about prophecies and fortunetelling (chapter 8).

21. Wright [De Quille], *History of the Big Bonanza,* 255–56; Loomis, "Tall Tales of Dan De Quille," 59; Lyman, *Saga of the Comstock Lode,* 88.

22. Miriam Michelson, *The Wonderlode of Silver and Gold,* 54; Beebe and Clegg, *Legends of the Comstock Lode,* 55; Emrich, *It's an Old West Custom,* 190. Perhaps in keeping with Lyman, *Saga of the Comstock Lode,* 87, Beebe and Clegg identified the Washoe Canary as a "mine mule"; convention usually identified the canary—desert or Washoe—as a donkey, but

variation and inconsistency are a hallmark of folklore. See Win Blevins, "Desert Canary," in *Dictionary of the American West* (Fort Worth: Texas Christian University Press, 2001).

23. *Territorial Enterprise,* January 7, 1876. Hand, "California Miners Folklore: Below Ground," 136, discusses the affinity of miners for mules.

24. Lord, *Comstock Mining and Miners,* 23. See also Phillip I. Earl, "Burying the Jinx at Buckhorn Camp," *Reno Gazette-Journal,* November 8, 1981.

25. Kelly J. Dixon, *Boomtown Saloons: Archaeology and History in Virginia City* (Reno: University of Nevada Press, 2005), 66–72. Dixon also reports on a Chinese coin and a small mammal skeleton found on a nearby flat rock, but the evidence was not conclusive that these objects were placed there intentionally.

26. Jessica Axsom, "Yeong Wo Mercantile on the Comstock" (master's thesis, University of Nevada, 2009), with thanks to Axsom for assistance with this text.

27. Julie M. Schablitsky, "The Other Side of the Tracks: The Archaeology and History of a Virginia City, Nevada Neighborhood" (PhD diss., Portland State University, 2002), 223–24. The building was likely constructed after the 1875 fire.

28. Mathews, *Ten Years in Nevada,* 55.

29. Letter to *Cedar Falls (IA) Gazette,* published April 5, 1861, from Curtis and Berkove, *Before the Big Bonanza,* 81–82, with De Quille's emphasis.

30. Richard M. Dorson, "Dialect Stories of the Upper Peninsula: A New Form of American Folklore."

31. Mathews, *Ten Years in Nevada,* 304.

32. *Gold Hill Daily News,* April 26, 1876.

33. References to the rhyme, which manifested in several forms, are ubiquitous in the historical record. See, for example, Drury, *Editor on the Comstock Lode,* 70–71; Charles Howard Shinn, *Mining Camps: A Study in American Frontier Government,* 25–36; and Ronald M. James, "Defining the Group: Nineteenth-Century Cornish on the Mining Frontier."

34. R. W. Raymond, *A Glossary of Mining and Metallurgical Terms.*

35. Jenkin, *Cornish Miner.*

36. Emrich, *In the Delta Saloon,* 278–79.

37. J. D. Borthwick, *Three Years in California,* (Edinburgh: William Blackwood and Sons, 1857), 163–64. See also W. Sherman Savage, "The Negro on the Mining Frontier," *Journal of Negro History* 30 (1945): 30–46; and Dixon, *Boomtown Saloons.*

38. Otis E. Young Jr., with technical assistance of Robert Lenon, *Western Mining: An Informal Account of Precious-Metals Prospecting, Placering, Lode Mining, and Milling on the American Frontier from Spanish Times to 1893* (Norman: University of Oklahoma, 1970), 79, 155–56, 204; Lord, *Comstock Mining and Miners,* 90; Shinn, *Story of the Mine,* 98.

39. Ronald M. James, Richard D. Adkins, and Rachel J. Hartigan, "Competition and Coexistence in the Wash House: A View of the Comstock from the Bottom of the Laundry Pile," *Western Historical Quarterly* 25, no. 2 (1994); Sue Fawn Chung, "Their Changing World: Chinese Women on the Comstock, 1860–1910."

40. R. James, *Virginia City,* 42–53.

Chapter 8. More Legendary Characters

1. This spelling reflects Nevada convention, but the family in Scotland uses "Oram" according to Bowers authority Tamera Buzick.

2. There have been several attempts to write an accurate history of the Bowers family

and their mansion, but untangling the folklore has been a consistent problem, as shown by the combinations of history and oral tradition presented by Gloria Millicent Mapes et al., *Bowers Mansion* (Reno: Washoe County, 1952); and Alice B. Addenbrooke, *The Mistress of the Mansion*. More recently, the work of Tamera Buzick, *Bowers Mansion Remembered: 1862* (Reno: Fortunatus Press, 2013), is to be commended for a careful historical approach.

3. Beebe and Clegg, *Legends of the Comstock Lode,* 23–30, provide an imagined description of Sandy and Eilley Bowers. Lyman, *Saga of the Comstock Lode,* 136, 251–53, also addresses this in his fanciful way, but as always, it is unclear how much he drew from local tradition and how much he contributed to it. Thanks to Tamera Buzick for information about the confused Bowers history.

4. Wright [De Quille], *History of the Comstock Lode,* 100.

5. DeGroot, *The Comstock Papers,* 45.

6. Drury, *Editor on the Comstock Lode,* 26. Beebe and Clegg, *Legends of the Comstock Lode,* 23–30, links the International Hotel episode to the going-away party before the couple departed for Europe. An early expression of this story, and a full treatment of the biography, is provided by Myron Angel, *History of Nevada,* 622.

7. Drury, *Editor on the Comstock Lode,* 27; R. James, *Temples of Justice.* The construction projects were separated by about a dozen years.

8. Drury, *Editor on the Comstock Lode,* 28.

9. DeGroot, *The Comstock Papers,* 44. Lyman, *Saga of the Comstock Lode,* 385, repeats this misunderstanding.

10. Angel, *History of Nevada,* 38–39.

11. Swift Paine, *Eilley Orrum, Queen of the Comstock.* With thanks to Tamera Buzick for insight into this letter.

12. Some of this text is taken from an article by the author appearing in the *Online Nevada Encyclopedia*. For an excellent newspaper article extensively quoting an acquaintance of the Bowers family on the occasion of Eilley's death, see *Sacramento Union,* November 16, 1903.

13. Fremont Older and Cora Miranda Older, *George Hearst, California Pioneer* (1933; reprint, Los Angeles: Westernlore, 1966); Judith Robinson, *The Hearsts: An American Dynasty* (Newark: University of Delaware Press, 1991); Fred N. Holabird, "George Hearst, Comstock Pioneer." Always a source for taking liberties, see Lyman, *Saga of the Comstock Lode,* 8–9, 53, 57, 63, 73–75, 79–80.

14. Michael J. Makley, *John Mackay: Silver King in the Gilded Age,* 16. The incident is told in a typically fanciful way by Lyman, *Saga of the Comstock Lode,* 68–69.

15. James Flood (1826–89) was born in New York of Irish parents. The other three members of the "Bonanza Firm" were born in Ireland.

16. The investors Flood and O'Brien lived in California, so they are not fixtures of early Nevada folklore.

17. Drury, *Editor on the Comstock Lode,* 65. For a look at Mackay with mythic exaggeration, see Beebe and Clegg, *Legends of the Comstock Lode,* 64–70, and specifically see 66 for a fanciful account taken from Lyman, *Saga of the Comstock Lode,* 251. The story describes Mackay traveling east and finding his way through the front lines of the Battle of Chattanooga (November 23–25, 1863) to obtain shares of the Kentuck Mine. While likely fiction, there is insufficient evidence to suggest it was part of oral tradition. Makley, *John Mackay,* 29.

18. R. James, *Roar and the Silence*, 206–7.

19. Smith and Tingley, *History of the Comstock Lode*, 266; Waldorf, *Kid on the Comstock*, 62–63. Thanks to Michael Makley for help with this section.

20. Dorothy Young Nichols, *Views and Vignettes of Virginia City: In My Days*, 1; R. James, *Virginia City*, 25–27.

21. *Sacramento Bee*, February 27, 1995; Lyman, *Saga of the Comstock Lode*, 81–90, and see 230 for mention of a silver bell that became a legendary attribute of the church. See also Drury, *Editor on the Comstock Lode*, 30; and Nichols, *Views and Vignettes of Virginia City*, 27.

22. Goodwin, *As I Remember Them*, 161; William Breault, *The Miner Was a Bishop: The Pioneer Years of Patrick Manogue, California–Nevada, 1854–1895*, 87–88. Those who struggled against the fire dynamited many buildings to prevent burning roof shingles from being taken by the wind to ignite fires elsewhere. In addition, the hulking ruins of a dynamited building could serve as firebreak.

23. Drury, *Editor on the Comstock Lode*, 58.

24. Drury, *Editor on the Comstock Lode*, 58. Compare Henry M. Gorham, *My Memories of the Comstock* (Berkeley, CA: Suttonhouse, 1939), 62–63.

25. Goodwin, *As I Remember Them*, 181.

26. Waldorf, *Kid on the Comstock*, 62.

27. Goodwin, *As I Remember Them*, 180–81. See also the work of John Mackay's granddaughter, Ellin Berlin, *Silver Platter*, 140, 169–70.

28. Goodwin, *As I Remember Them*, 183–84. Berlin refers to the story, suggesting that Fair enjoyed the anecdote when he heard it told. Berlin, *Silver Platter*, 169–70.

29. Drury, *Editor on the Comstock Lode*, 248–63.

30. Chapter 6 describes the feigned robbery of Mark Twain on the Divide south of Virginia City, and chapter 7 includes the account told by Mary McNair Mathews recalling the young man who boasted about how brave he would be if robbed, only to have friends test his courage by faking such an event.

31. Drury, *Editor on the Comstock Lode*, 148–50. Bayer, *Rhymes from the Silver State*, 12–13, includes "Baldy Green," providing a broadsheet, which credits the composition to Charley Rhoades (1865), but given Drury's testimony, it appears the song became popular in early Nevada, repeated by people who were not professional performers. R. Michael Wilson, *Great Stagecoach Robberies of the Old West* (Guilford, CT: TwoDot, 2007), 23–33. Hand, "California Miners Folklore: Below Ground," 146–47, documents a miner's ballad, "The Highgrader," that he dates to the early twentieth century. The piece is set in Nevada but was collected in California.

32. Samuel Clemens, "Presentation," *Sacramento Daily Union*, December 25, 1863. Robert Stewart, "The Carson City Mark Twain Knew" (manuscript provided by author; anticipated 2023, *Mark Twain Journal*), discusses the Twain article about a farcical presentation to Bally Green.

33. Dixon, *Boomtown Saloons*, 24–36; R. James, *Virginia City*, 54–72. See also Drury, *Editor on the Comstock Lode*, 122–27.

34. Drury, *Editor on the Comstock Lode*, 124.

35. Ronald M. James and Kenneth H. Fliess, "Women of the Mining West: Virginia City Revisited." Emrich, *It's an Old West Custom*, 110–11, echoes this tradition, which he accepts as historical fact as he traveled the West in search of folklore.

36. Sally Zanjani, *A Mine of Her Own: Women Prospectors in the American West, 1850–1950*

(Lincoln: University of Nebraska Press, Bison Books, 2000). For European traditions, see Cedric E. Gregory, *A Concise History of Mining* (New York: Pergamon Press, 1980), 221–22. See also R. James and Fliess, "Women of the Mining West."

37. Curtis and Berkove, *Before the Big Bonanza*, 241.

CHAPTER 9. GHOSTS AND TOMMYKNOCKERS

1. *Territorial Enterprise*, January 13, 1876.

2. Wright [De Quille], *History of the Big Bonanza*, 331.

3. Lord, *Comstock Mining and Miners*, 219. A body that could not be recovered in the Chollar Potosi Mine in Virginia City caused concern about a potential haunting: *Gold Hill Daily News*, February 26, 1868. This idea is echoed by Shinn in *Mining Camps*, 29, when he wrote about Britain's southwest: "Mendip miners manifested a mingling of superstitious dread, and of faithful loyalty to each other, in their strict rule that the body of a miner who had been killed in a drift must be dug out, at any cost, and given a Christian burial, before a stroke of work would be done elsewhere by a single miner."

4. Paul Strickland, "The Folklore of the Comstock Lode and Surrounding Regions: 1850–1900," 25. Ty Cobb was a Nevada journalist and not the famous baseball player of the same name.

5. Hand, "California Miners Folklore: Below Ground," 131.

6. Robert Hunt, *Popular Romances of the West of England; or, The Drolls, Traditions, and Superstitions of Old Cornwall*, 90–91.

7. Peter Narváez, ed., *The Good People: New Fairylore Essays*. Many other mining cultures have traditions of underground elf-like spirits, but it was the Cornish knocker that made the migration to the American West. Fish, "European Background of American Miners' Beliefs," 163–65; R. James, "Knockers, Knackers, and Ghosts"; R. James, *Folklore of Cornwall*, 136–62.

8. Katharine Briggs, "The Fairies and the Realms of the Dead"; Elisabeth Hartmann, *Die Trollvorstellungen in den Sagen und Märchen der Skandinavischen Völker*.

9. Simon Young and Ceri Houlbrook, eds., *Magical Folk: British and Irish Fairies, 500 AD to the Present*; Gary R. Butler, "The *Lutin* Tradition in French-Newfoundland Culture: Discourse and Belief" (5–21), Barbara Reiti, "'The Blast' in Newfoundland Fairy Tradition" (284–98), and Peter Narváez, "Newfoundland Berry Pickers 'In the Fairies': Maintaining Spatial, Temporal, and Moral Boundaries Through Legendry" (336–68), the latter three from Narváez, *Good People*.

10. Foster and Tolbert, *Folkloresque*. See also their anticipated second edited volume, *Möbius Media*.

11. Baker, "Cousin Jack Country," 11–12; Nichols, *Views and Vignettes of Virginia City*, 20–21.

12. Hand, "California Miners Folklore: Below Ground," 127–53. See also Jack Santino, "Occupational Ghostlore: Social Context and the Expression of Belief."

13. Hand, "California Miners Folklore: Below Ground," 132.

14. Hand, "California Miners Folklore: Below Ground," 131. For a late example of the blending of ghost and elf from the New World, see "Miners Tell About 'Ghost,'" *Canadian Press* (Ontario), March 9, 1937.

15. Hand, "California Miners Folklore: Below Ground," 128; Jenkin, *Cornish Miner*, 297; Jane P. Davidson and Christopher John Duffin, "Stones and Spirits," *Folklore* 123, no. 1 (2012): 99–109; Fish, "European Background of American Miners' Beliefs," 165.

16. *Virginia Evening Chronicle,* October 8, 1884.

17. Erdoes, *Legends and Tales of the American West,* 173–76, provides stories about miners who died and then became tommyknockers, haunting colleagues for various reasons. Erdoes, however, retells stories as literature, and he may be wandering from his sources, which he does not provide.

18. Jack Santino in his 1988 article "Occupational Ghostlore," 207, 216, points out, "In certain occupations, such as mining and sailing, researchers have documented the belief in ghosts who are said to warn former colleagues and comembers of danger and impending accidents and to help them in times of disaster." The author uses mining and the fishing industry to provide a context for stories about ghosts and the airline industry, and of course Santino may have been projecting inappropriately on mining folklore.

19. Troy Anderson, "Sculptor Keeps History Alive," *Nevada Appeal* (Carson City), June 29, 1992.

20. See chapter 3. Lord, *Comstock Mining and Miners,* 412–13; Wright [DeQuille], *History of the Big Bonanza,* 98–99; Hand, "California Miners Folklore: Above Ground," 44.

21. "Doten Journals," bk. 36, p. 87, February 23, 1868 (this is also mentioned in the *Gold Hill Daily News,* February 26, 1868); bk. 65, p. 169, December 12, 1890, Special Collections, University of Nevada, Reno, Libraries. Also consider a story about the ghost of a four-year-old haunting his former house in Eureka, Nevada: *Territorial Enterprise,* March 16, 1877; *Nevada State Journal,* December 31, 1870.

22. Thompson, *Motif-Index of Folk Literature,* "Motif C480.1.1 Tabu: Whistling in Mine."

23. Owen Davies, *The Haunted: A Social History of Ghosts;* R. C. Finucane, *Ghosts: Appearance of the Dead and Cultural Transformation;* Greg Garrett, *Entertaining Judgment: The Afterlife in Popular Imagination;* John P. Brennan and Jane Garry, "Otherworld Journeys: Upper and Lower Worlds"; Louis C. Jones, *Things That Go Bump in the Night.*

24. Timothy McCarthy, "Diary," copy available at the Comstock Historic District Commission, Virginia City, NV, and at the Nevada Historical Society, Reno. The copies of the diary were donated by John McCarthy, grandson of the diarist. See also Ronald M. James, "Timothy Francis McCarthy: An Irish Immigrant Life on the Comstock." The ten-dollar doctor's fee would be the equivalent of nearly three days of work for the average laborer.

25. The name of the church is popularly referred to as St. Mary's in the Mountains as though it is a reference to St. Mary's Church in the Mountains. The true name officially commemorates a journey of the Virgin Mary while pregnant to visit her relative Elizabeth, who lived in the hills of Judah and was pregnant with the future St. John the Baptist. A painting above the altar commemorates the visit to the mountains. Virgil A. Bucchianeri, *Saint Mary's in the Mountains: Nevada's Bonanza Church* (Gold Hill, NV: Gold Hill, 1997), ix, 17.

26. *Territorial Enterprise,* November 13, 1872. The incident is discussed in Francke, "Divination on Mount Davidson," 172–73.

27. Mathews, *Ten Years in Nevada,* 229–31.

28. Mathews, *Ten Years in Nevada,* 160.

29. Mathews, *Ten Years in Nevada,* 160–62.

30. R. James, *Folklore of Cornwall,* 107–21; Calvin Thomas, *An Anthology of German Literature* (Boston: D. C. Heath, 1906), 387–91. The Lenore Legend appears in the tale-type index as Type 365, even though it was often told to be believed. Antti Aarne and Stith Thompson, *The Types of the Folktale: A Classification and Bibliography* (Helsinki: FF Communications, no. 184, 1961; 2nd rev., 4th printing, 1987), 127; Hans-Jörg Uther, *The Types of*

International Folktales (Parts I–III) (Helsinki: FF Communications, nos. 284, 285, and 286, 2011), 229–30.

31. R. James, *Folklore of Cornwall,* 107–21.

32. Wright [De Quille], *History of the Big Bonanza,* 100; *Territorial Enterprise,* January 9, 1875. See also Emrich, *It's an Old West Custom,* 192–93.

33. "Doten Journals," bk. 43, p. 153, December 22, 1870.

CHAPTER 10. HANK MONK AND MARK TWAIN

1. Brown, *Tall Tale in American Folklore and Literature,* 90.

2. Glyndon G. Van Deusen, *Horace Greeley: Nineteenth-Century Crusader* (Philadelphia: University of Pennsylvania Press, 1953), 230; Erick S. Lunde, *Horace Greeley;* Coy F. Cross, *Go West, Young Man! Horace Greeley's Vision for America* (Albuquerque: University of New Mexico Press, 1995). Greeley may have only adopted the phrase "Go West, young man, go West." Some maintain it was first crafted by the writer John B. L. Soule in 1851. Regardless of the origin of the slogan, which appears in various forms, popular imagination typically associates it with Greeley.

3. Erdoes, *Legends and Tales of the American West,* xiv, wrote, "The Frontier West was macho country."

4. Richard G. Lillard and Mary V. Hood, *Hank Monk and Horace Greeley: An Enduring Episode in Western History.*

5. R. James, *Roar and the Silence,* 26–29; Lord, *Comstock Mining and Miners,* 65.

6. *New York Tribune,* September 7, 1859.

7. The original article by Lillard was expanded and appeared in Lillard and Hood, *Hank Monk and Horace Greeley,* 6, 10–11. See Richard G. Lillard, "Hank Monk and Horace Greeley," *American Literature* 14 (1942): 126–34.

8. Clemens [Twain], *Roughing It,* 131–33. See "Elizabeth F. B. Knowlton Reminiscences," California Historical Society, ms. 128, 1:134, for a reference from early 1861 to "Hank Monk the great stage driver."

9. Sir Charles Wentworth Dilke, *Greater Britain: A Record of Travel in English-Speaking Countries During 1866 and 1867* (London: Macmillan, 1869), 146–49. The Nevada portion was republished in the *Nevada Historical Society Quarterly* 3, no. 4 (1960): 14–29.

10. John J. Pullen, *Comic Relief: The Life and Laughter of Artemus Ward, 1834–1867.*

11. Charles Farrar Browne [Artemus Ward], *Artemus Ward (His Travels) Among the Mormons,* 63–68.

12. Samuel Clemens [Mark Twain], *Autobiography of Mark Twain,* 200.

13. Clemens [Twain], *Autobiography of Mark Twain,* 200, 553.

14. Clemens [Twain], *Autobiography of Mark Twain,* 200.

15. Clemens [Twain], *Autobiography of Mark Twain,* 200–201.

16. Clemens [Twain], *Autobiography of Mark Twain,* 201–2.

17. Clemens [Twain], *Autobiography of Mark Twain,* 202–3, 554. Although Twain employed it again in New York in 1887, it appears that these three performances were unique in the use of this bit of oral tradition in this fashion. Lillard and Hood, *Hank Monk and Horace Greeley,* 12.

18. R. James, "Mark Twain in Nevada."

19. Clemens [Twain], *Roughing It,* 131–33.

20. Clemens [Twain], *Roughing It,* 133.

21. Clemens [Twain], *Roughing It,* 134–35.

22. Clemens [Twain], *Roughing It*, 135.

23. Clemens [Twain], *Roughing It*, 135–36.

24. A. H. Hawley, "Lake Tahoe—1883," *Nevada Historical Society Papers I* (1913–16): 176–77.

25. Drury, *Editor on the Comstock Lode*, 138–40.

26. A copy of the sheet music is available at the Special Collections Library, University of Nevada, Reno.

27. *Nevada Historical Society Papers I* (1913–16): 31; *Nevada Historical Society Papers III* (1921–22): 124.

28. Smith and Tingley, *History of the Comstock Lode*, 11.

29. Guy Rocha, "Myth #111: Riding High; Hank Monk and Horace Greeley," *Silver Sage* (Carson City/Carson Valley, NV, July 2007).

30. *Territorial Enterprise*, January 20, 1882.

31. Foster and Tolbert, *Folkloresque*.

32. Richard M. Dorson, "Folklore and Fake Lore," 335.

33. Foster and Tolbert, *Folkloresque*, 9.

34. It is what Tolbert refers to as "the creative redeployment . . . of folkloric images and motifs." Foster and Tolbert, *Folkloresque*, 175.

35. Simon J. Bronner, ed., *The Meaning of Folklore: The Analytical Essays of Alan Dundes*, 82.

36. Foster and Tolbert, *Folkloresque*, 19.

Chapter 11. Sex, Murder, and More Monumental Lies

1. Beebe, *Comstock Commotion*, 23, 64.

2. Lyman, *Saga of the Comstock Lode*, 90. The notion of an epidemic and Bulette serving as nurse also appears in Beebe and Clegg, *Legends of the Comstock Lode*, 16. This is echoed in Phyllis Zauner, *Virginia City: Its History . . . Its Ghosts, a Mini-History* (Sonoma, CA: Zanel, 1989), 23. Evidence that this may have entered local folklore is provided by the appearance of the story of caring for miners who suffered, not from an epidemic, but from bad water. Brian David Bruns, *Comstock Phantoms: True Ghost Stories of Virginia City, Nevada*, 103.

3. Susan James, "Queen of Tarts"; R. James and Raymond, *Comstock Women*. Beebe, *Comstock Commotion*, 49, erroneously describes the earliest period of Comstock history as a time "when Julia Bulette and her girls were practically the entire female population."

4. Susan James, "Julia Bulette's Probate Records."

5. "Doten Journals," bk. 33, pp. 63–64, January 20–21, 1867; bk. 33, p. 74, February 2, 1867; bk. 34, pp. 52–53, March 26, 1867; bk. 34, pp. 78–80, June 26, 1867, Special Collections, University of Nevada, Reno, Libraries.

6. The assertion that Twain's Buck Fanshaw was based on Tom Peasley is ubiquitous but unsubstantiated (Peasley died after Twain left Nevada). Lyman, *Saga of the Comstock Lode*, 120, asserts this to be true, but he is suspect. Lyman cites Nathaniel P. Langford, *Vigilante Days: The Pioneers of the Rockies; The Makers and Making of Montana and Idaho* (Chicago: A. C. McClurg, 1912), 438, who vaguely claims without source or justification, "Peasley was supposed to be the original of Mark Twain's 'Buck Fanshaw.'" Based on this dubious link, some would further see a reference to Bulette in *Roughing It* with the phrase, "[Fanshaw] had been the proprietor of a dashing helpmeet whom he could have discarded without the formality of a divorce." If we accept the questionable claim that Bulette and Peasley were intended, she nevertheless remains anonymous in the text. Clemens [Twain], *Roughing It*, 308, 668.

7. Samuel Clemens [Mark Twain], "Letter from Mark Twain," *Chicago Republican,* May 31, 1868, http://www.twainquotes.com/18680531.html.

8. Berkove, *Insider Stories,* 521. Bulette was not from France but apparently professed coming from England.

9. Lyman, *Saga of the Comstock Lode,* 90, 347.

10. Effie Mona Mack [Zeke Daniels], *Life and Death of Julia C. Bulette: "Queen of the Red Lights."* Beebe and Clegg, *Legends of the Comstock Lode,* 16, refers to her "palace" as "the cultural center of the community"; they also provide a painting of "Julia's House, Virginia City," 68, allegedly found in an attic in Grass Valley in the mid-twentieth century. Lyman, *Saga of the Comstock Lode,* 198. Emrich, *It's an Old West Custom,* 113, echoes Lyman when it comes to some details about Bulette.

11. http://www.nsrm-friends.org/nsrm27.html (accessed October 9, 2021). Beebe and Clegg, *Legends of the Comstock Lode,* 17, includes a photograph of the railroad car with the misspelling.

12. Emrich, *In the Delta Saloon,* xii; *Library of Congress Information Bulletin* (September 2, 1977): 611–12; James Hardin, "The Archive of Folk Culture at 75: A National Project with Many Workers," *Folklore Center News* 25, no. 2 (2003): 3–13. Emrich's title is cited differently in Library of Congress sources: he was also described as the chief or director of the Archive of the American Folk Song Section. *Washington Post,* August 24, 1977.

13. Emrich, *In the Delta Saloon,* 47.

14. Emrich, *In the Delta Saloon,* 265–66. Emrich sometimes led informants, straying from normal practices in folklore collecting, but his material is nevertheless valuable. Beebe and Clegg, *Legends of the Comstock Lode,* 16, erroneously asserts that Bowers and Bulette were the only women on the Comstock during its first days.

15. Emrich, *It's an Old West Custom,* 117–28.

16. This location is described by Beebe and Clegg, *Legends of the Comstock Lode,* 17, which was first published in 1950; caution must be used here, however, since the text was modified for subsequent printings in the 1950s. At some point the image, or a similar image, appeared in Don McBride's Bucket of Blood Saloon.

17. Candace Wheeler, "Comstock Cemeteries: Changing Landscapes of Death." Emrich, *It's an Old West Custom,* 128, however, describes Bulette's grave in 1949 as "carefully tended, its white picket fence repainted from time to time." Thanks to Candace Wheeler for assistance with the history of the Bulette grave site.

18. Beebe and Clegg, *Legends of the Comstock Lode,* 22. Recording in 1949 and 1950, Emrich, *In the Delta Saloon,* 12, 75, pushed the narrative about the Flowery Hill Cemetery being of a disreputable nature, distinct from the proper cemetery. Joe Farnsworth, Emrich's informant, rejected that assertion.

19. Bruce R. Leiby and Linda F. Leiby, *A Reference Guide to Television's "Bonanza": Episodes, Personnel, and Broadcast History* (Jefferson, NC: McFarland, 2005), 3–30. The source provides a synopsis of the episode, but the summary of Bulette's life, scattered in the first two chapters, reflects the fantastic elements of folklore more than verifiable history.

20. The account was collected by the author from a ghost tour of Virginia City on August 18, 2007. Janice Oberding, *Ghosthunter's Guide to Virginia City,* 33.

21. Oberding, *Ghosthunter's Guide to Virginia City,* 88. In a Facebook post (page for Virginia City), January 4, 2022, Oberding repeated the assertion of the mortician retaining Bulette's body and that he buried "her in the wall and sent a coffin full of rocks off to Julia's

burial spot at Flowery Hill." Oberding included Bulette's "secret family recipe for baked beans," attributed to "an old Virginia City tale."

22. Bruns, *Comstock Phantoms*, 111.

23. Visits to the grave site in the 1990s and through the following decade reveal that the tradition is maintained.

24. S. James, "Queen of Tarts."

25. Nichols, *Views and Vignettes of Virginia City*, i.

26. Beebe and Clegg, *Legends of the Comstock Lode*, 72.

27. Beebe, *Comstock Commotion*, 63. See also Beebe and Clegg, *Legends of the Comstock Lode*, 46.

28. Emrich, *It's an Old West Custom*, 65. For another perspective on the Wild West saloon, see Beebe, *Comstock Commotion*, 26.

29. Beebe and Clegg, *Legends of the Comstock Lode*, 12.

30. Dixon, *Boomtown Saloons*; R. James, *Virginia City*.

31. Emrich, *It's an Old West Custom*, 65.

32. Stewart L. Udall et al., "How the West Got Wild: American Media and Frontier Violence"; R. James and Raymond, *Comstock Women*; R. James, *Roar and the Silence*, 32–33, 167–75; Roger D. McGrath, *Gunfighters, Highwaymen, and Vigilantes: Violence on the Frontier* (Berkeley: University of California Press, 1987); Robert R. Dykstra, "Quantifying the Wild West: Problematic Statistics of Frontier Violence."

33. Gary Kamiya, "Prostitutes from France Charmed S.F. During Gold Rush," *San Francisco Chronicle*, May 9, 2014; Irwin Silber and Earl Robinson, *Songs of the Great American West* (New York: Dover, 1967), 95. See chapter 8 for a discussion of the folklore surrounding the first women in a western town.

34. This is not the only story about stolen wealth: Emrich, *In the Delta Saloon*, 262–64; Oberding, *Ghosthunter's Guide to Virginia City*, 106–7. See also Dave Basso, *In Search of Nevada Treasure*.

35. R. James, *Folklore of Cornwall*.

36. *Reno Gazette-Journal*, March 11, 2021.

37. With thanks to Michelle Connor Nichols.

38. Lyman, *Saga of the Comstock Lode*, 141–43, uses the well-known phrase as a header for a chapter dealing with the camels, filled in this case with his typically extravagant fiction.

39. Wright [De Quille], *History of the Comstock Lode*, 369–70; Charles C. Carroll, "The Government Importation of Camels, a Historical Sketch," in *20th Annual Report*, Bureau of Animal Industry (Washington, DC: Government Printing Office, 1904); Frank B. Lammons, "Operation Camel: An Experiment in Animal Transportation," *Southwestern Historical Quarterly* 61 (July 1857): 20–50; Douglas McDonald, *Camels in Nevada*; "Doten Journals," bk. 74, p. 179, November 28, 1898.

40. Emrich, *In the Delta Saloon*, 262. See also Lyman, *Saga of the Comstock Lode*, 342.

41. Duncan Emrich describes a hoax in the *Virginia City News* in his 1949 book, *It's an Old West Custom*, 296–313. For local perspectives on Beebe and Clegg, see Kathryn M. Totton et al., *Comstock Memories: 1920s–1960s*, 110–18. See also Andria Daley, "Boardwalk Bons Vivants."

42. *Reno Evening Gazette*, September 3, 5, 1960; *San Francisco Bulletin*, November 1, 1961; Beebe, *Comstock Commotion*, 94. Not without irony, the *Territorial Enterprise*, November 15, 1877, described a proposition to hold camel races in the town of Sutro near Dayton. Moreno, *Frontier Fake News*, provides an excellent overview of the camel incident.

43. Beebe, *Comstock Commotion,* 52. Identification of the house as John Piper's residence resulted in a listing in the National Register of Historic Places as the Piper-Beebe House. Besides being a contributing resource within the Virginia City National Historic Landmark District, the structure is individually significant architecturally as well as for its association with Lucius Beebe and Charles Clegg, but not because of the Piper family. Andria Sharon Daley and Michael Richard Taylor, "Piper-Beebe House," National Register of Historic Places nomination, listed August 5, 1993. It is important to admit that the nomination form was signed "Ronald M. James, state historic preservation officer," for I was duped.

44. Special Collections, University of Nevada, Reno, Library, has an 1864 lithographic bird's-eye view of Virginia City by Grafton Brown; its border illustrations depict an expansive three-story *Territorial Enterprise* business block (see fig. 12), far removed from its current location, the place where the newspaper took shelter following the 1875 fire. Beebe, *Comstock Commotion,* 79, 85–86; Bruns, *Comstock Phantoms,* 128; Ronald M. James, "Mark Twain's Virginia City: The 1864 Bird's Eye View of Grafton Brown."

45. Walsh, *Sins Against Science,* 175, 184, fig. 5.3.

46. Beebe, *Comstock Commotion,* 119. Nichols, *Views and Vignettes of Virginia City,* 29, refers to the same building as "where Mark Twain was once on the editorial staff." Nichols published her account in 1973, but she was born in 1903. It is unclear when she may have been told that this is where Twain worked. Beebe may have been the source, but he may have heard it from others. For skepticism about a Twain connection with the desk, see "The Town That Can't Rest in Peace," *Portola (CA) Reporter,* July 13, 1961.

47. Niraj Chokshi, "That Wasn't Mark Twain: How a Misquotation Is Born," *New York Times,* April 26, 2017. See also Garson O'Toole, the Quote Investigator, "A Lie Can Travel Halfway Around the World While the Truth Is Putting on Its Shoes," https://quoteinvestigator.com/2014/07/13/truth/ (accessed September 20, 2021).

48. Brown, *Tall Tale in American Folklore and Literature,* 16.

49. Berlin, *Silver Platter,* 105.

50. Beebe and Clegg, *Legends of the Comstock Lode,* 10, 13.

51. Zauner, *Virginia City,* 12.

52. A postcard printed in 1891 indicated that in 1864, Virginia City "was the second city in size west of the Rocky Mountains": Perry Mason, "Nevada" (Boston: Youth Companion, 1891; author's collection). Emrich, *It's an Old West Custom,* 61, places the maximum population of Virginia City at forty thousand.

53. Guy Rocha, "Virginia City's Silver Streets; Myth #48," (website no longer extant; accessed December 16, 2003); Lyman, *Saga of the Comstock Lode,* 11–16, 130. Perhaps in response to Lyman, see the WPA, Federal Writers' Project, publication *Nevada: A Guide to the Silver State* (Portland, OR: Binfords and Mort, 1940), 275. Hand collected a similar belief attributed to Park City, Utah. Hand, "California Miners Folklore: Above Ground," 29n17.

54. Nichols, *Views and Vignettes of Virginia City,* 16, provides a hint of early-twentieth-century roots of the belief in the elevator being the first in the West. Emrich, *In the Delta Saloon,* 76; Beebe, *Comstock Commotion,* 63; Beebe and Clegg, *Legends of the Comstock Lode,* 48; Bruns, *Comstock Phantoms,* 128.

CHAPTER 12. GHOSTS OF THE PAST

1. R. James, *Virginia City*, 24–25.

2. Oberding, *Ghosthunter's Guide to Virginia City*, 138–39. The structure is also referred to as the Chapin-Cavanaugh Boarding House and as the Nevin House. Many of Oberding's observations about the building are recorded in a pamphlet produced by the owner, titled *True Ghost Stories About the Chapin-Cavanaugh Boarding House* (self-published, revised May 2000; author's collection).

3. Oberding, *Ghosthunter's Guide to Virginia City*, 129–31.

4. Oberding, *Ghosthunter's Guide to Virginia City*, 23.

5. Oberding, *Ghosthunter's Guide to Virginia City*, 23–24.

6. Bruns, *Comstock Phantoms*.

7. For an example of a memorate about spending the night at the Silver Queen Hotel, see Oberding, *Ghosthunter's Guide to Virginia City*, 51–52.

8. Bruns, *Comstock Phantoms*, 121–27. For an account of the girl's ghost haunting the upstairs of the Washoe Club and also of children killed in accidents involving vehicles, see Oberding, *Ghosthunter's Guide to Virginia City*, 99–100.

9. Oberding, *Ghosthunter's Guide to Virginia City*, 53–55, 111, 122–23; Bruns, *Comstock Phantoms*, 37–38. See also Phyllis Zauner, *Virginia City: Its History…Its Ghosts, a Mini-History* (Sonoma, CA: Zanel, 1989), 59, for a pipe-smoke story in another location. In twentieth-century sources from a few decades ago, the cigar- or pipe-smoking ghost of the Gold Hill Hotel was named Clarence.

10. Bruns, *Comstock Phantoms*, 32–35; Oberding, *Ghosthunter's Guide to Virginia City*, 53–55.

11. R. James, *Roar and the Silence*, 31–32, 93–94, 176–78; R. James and Fliess, "Women of the Mining West."

12. Oberding, *Ghosthunter's Guide to Virginia City*, 132–33, 136–37.

13. Dolores K. O'Brien, *Meet Virginia City's Ghosts*, 13.

14. Oberding, *Ghosthunter's Guide to Virginia City*, 33.

15. Oberding, *Ghosthunter's Guide to Virginia City*, 89.

16. Oberding, *Ghosthunter's Guide to Virginia City*, 89.

17. Oberding, *Ghosthunter's Guide to Virginia City*, 98–99.

18. Brendan Riley, "'Weird Things Happen . . . It Does Scare the Tourists,'" *Reno Gazette-Journal*, July 24, 1993.

19. *Comstock Chronicle*, July 30, 1993.

20. Bruns, *Comstock Phantoms*, 156–63; Hartmann, *Die Trollvorstellungen*.

21. Oberding, *Ghosthunter's Guide to Virginia City*, 20.

22. Bruns, *Comstock Phantoms*, 65, 160–61, with the emphasis of the author.

23. Marcella Corona, "Haunted Virginia City: 11 Eerie Places to See This Halloween," *Reno Gazette-Journal*, October 27, 2015; Zauner, *Virginia City*, 63. A simple online search for glowing tombstones reveals that the motif can be found in many cemeteries throughout the nation. The motif in Virginia City also appeared in print as early as 1969. O'Brien, *Meet Virginia City's Ghosts*, 10.

24. Hand, "California Miners Folklore: Below Ground," 139–40, discusses reactions to similar omens, so this motif may indeed have deep roots.

25. Oberding, *Ghosthunter's Guide to Virginia City*, 34–35.

26. Oberding, *Ghosthunter's Guide to Virginia City,* 54–55. See also *Comstock Chronicle,* July 30, 1993.

27. Thanks to Barbara Mackey, former museum director of the Historic Fourth Ward School Museum, for assistance with this account.

28. Zauner, *Virginia City,* 63.

29. Brunvand, *Too Good to Be True,* 234.

30. Rich Moreno, "Virginia City's Lively Ghosts," *The Backyard Traveler* (blog), June 10, 2007, http://backyardtraveler.blogspot.com/2007/06/virginia-citys-lively-ghosts.html; Corona, "Haunted Virginia City."

31. Janice Oberding, *Haunted Virginia City,* 85; Oberding, *Ghosthunter's Guide to Virginia City,* 111–12.

32. Oberding, *Ghosthunter's Guide to Virginia City,* 111.

33. Oberding, *Ghosthunter's Guide to Virginia City,* 122–25.

34. Anne Butler, "Mission in the Mountains: The Daughters of Charity in Virginia City," in *Comstock Women,* ed. R. James and Raymond, 142–64. The order abandoned its mission in Virginia City in 1897.

35. Moreno, "Virginia City's Lively Ghosts"; Corona, "Haunted Virginia City"; Oberding, *Ghosthunter's Guide to Virginia City,* 115–17; O'Brien, *Meet Virginia City's Ghosts,* 11–12; Zauner, *Virginia City,* 60.

36. Oberding, *Ghosthunter's Guide to Virginia City,* 108.

37. McDonald, *Camels in Nevada.*

38. Strickland, "Folklore of the Comstock Lode," 28.

39. This assertion is ubiquitous. See, for example, Bruns, *Comstock Phantoms,* 114.

40. Sarah Burns, "'Better for Haunts': Victorian Houses and the Modern Imagination," *American Art* 26, no. 3 (2012): 2–25. O'Brien, *Meet Virginia City's Ghosts,* has abundant examples throughout of seeing Victorian-era houses as having the appearance of being haunted by virtue of their architecture alone.

Conclusion

1. This assertion is ubiquitous in local oral tradition. For a recent written version, see Bruns, *Comstock Phantoms,* 151.

2. R. James, *Temples of Justice.* An early draft manuscript of the book, including my text about Lady Justice, inspired Phil Earl to write an article on the subject, which explains similarities in his writing. The text as it appears in *Temples of Justice* is my own and was the earlier version.

3. Loomis, "Tall Tales of Dan De Quille," 26.

4. Hand, "California Miners Folklore: Above Ground," 25.

5. Richard M. Dorson, *American Folklore.* This is echoed in perceptions about fairy folklore and how people maintain that belief is in a perpetual state of decline, an idea dating back at least to the time of Chaucer. R. James, *Folklore of Cornwall,* 59.

6. Eliot Lord comes to mind here with his respected 1883 book, *Comstock Mines and Miners.*

7. Brown, *Tall Tale in American Folklore and Literature,* 5–6.

8. Cannon, *Cowboy Poetry: A Gathering;* C. J. Hadley, *Trappings of the Great Basin Buckaroo* (Reno: University of Nevada Press, 1993).

9. Walsh, *Sins Against Science,* 208.

Selected Bibliography

Adams, Ramon F. *Western Words: A Dictionary of the American West.* Norman: University of Oklahoma Press, 1968.

Addenbrooke, Alice B. *The Mistress of the Mansion.* Palo Alto, CA: Pacific Books, 1959.

Agricola, Georgius. *De re metallica.* Translated by Herbert Clark Hoover and Lou Henry Hoover. New York: Dover, 1950. First published in translation, London: Mining Magazine, 1912; page numbers refer to 1950 edition.

Angel, Myron. *History of Nevada.* Oakland, CA: Thompson and West, 1881.

Baker, George S. "Cousin Jack Country." *Gold Prospector: The Magazine of Mining and Adventure* 16, no. 3 (1990): 10–12.

Bancroft, Caroline. *Colorado's Lost Gold Mines and Buried Treasure.* 1961. Reprint, Boulder, CO: Johnson Books, 2002.

———. "Folklore of the Central City District, Colorado." *California Folklore Quarterly* (October 1945): 315–42.

———. "Lost-Mine Legends of Colorado." *California Folklore Quarterly* 2, no. 4 (1943): 253–63.

Basso, Clarence D. *Silver Walled Palace: Dan De Quille's "Waifs from Washoe" Originally Published in San Francisco's "The Golden Era"—1860–1865.* Reno: Clarence D. Basso, 2013.

Basso, Dave. *In Search of Nevada Treasure.* Sparks, NV: Falcon Hill Press, 1980.

Bauman, Richard. *Story, Performance and Event: Contextual Studies of Oral Narrative.* Cambridge: Cambridge University Press, 1986.

Bayer, C. W. *Rhymes from the Silver State—Historical Lyrics.* Carson City: Nevadamusic, 2014.

Beebe, Lucius. *Comstock Commotion: The Story of the "Territorial Enterprise."* Stanford, CA: Stanford University Press, 1954.

Beebe, Lucius, and Charles Clegg. *Legends of the Comstock Lode.* 2nd ed. Stanford, CA: Stanford University Press, 1956.

Berkove, Lawrence I., ed. *Insider Stories of the Comstock Lode and Nevada's Mining Frontier, 1859–1909: Primary Sources in American Social History.* Lewiston, NY: Edwin Mellen Press, 2007.

———. "Life After Twain: The Later Careers of the *Enterprise* Staff." *Mark Twain Journal* 29, no. 1 (1991): 22–28.

———, ed. *The Sagebrush Anthology: Literature from the Silver Age of the Old West.* Columbia: University of Missouri Press, 2006.

Berkove, Lawrence I., and Michael Kowalewski. "The Literature of the Mining Camps." In *Updating the Literary West,* sponsored by the Western Literature Association. Fort Worth: Texas Christian University Press, 1997.

Berlin, Ellin. *Silver Platter.* London: Hammond, Hammond, 1958.

Branch, Edgar Marquess, Michael B. Frank, and Kenneth M. Sanderson, eds. *Mark Twain's Letters.* Vol. 1, *1853–1866.* Berkeley: University of California Press, 1988.

Breault, William. *The Miner Was a Bishop: The Pioneer Years of Patrick Manogue, California–Nevada, 1854–1895.* Rancho Cordova, CA: Landmark Enterprises, 1988.

Brennan, John P., and Jane Garry. "Otherworld Journeys: Upper and Lower Worlds." In *Archetypes and Motifs in Folklore and Literature: A Handbook,* edited by Jane Garry and Hasan El-Shamy. London: M. E. Sharpe, 2005.

Briggs, Katharine. "The Fairies and the Realms of the Dead." *Folklore* 81, no. 2 (1970): 81–96.

Bronner, Simon J., ed. *The Meaning of Folklore: The Analytical Essays of Alan Dundes.* Logan: Utah State University Press, 2007.

Brown, Carolyn S. *The Tall Tale in American Folklore and Literature.* Knoxville: University of Tennessee Press, 1987.

Browne, Charles Farrar [Artemus Ward]. *Artemus Ward (His Travels) Among the Mormons.* Edited by E. P. Hingston. London: John Camden Hotten, 1865.

Bruns, Brian David. *Comstock Phantoms: True Ghost Stories of Virginia City, Nevada.* Hiawatha, IA: Norocos Press, 2004.

Brunvand, Jan Harold. *Too Good to Be True: The Colossal Book of Urban Legends.* New York: W. W. Norton, 1999.

Cannon, Hal, ed. *Cowboy Poetry: A Gathering.* 1985. Reprint, Salt Lake City: Gibbs M. Smith, 2008.

Caron, James E. *Mark Twain: Unsanctified Newspaper Reporter.* Columbia: University of Missouri Press, 2008.

Christiansen, Reidar Th. *The Migratory Legends: A Proposed List of Types with a Systematic Catalogue of the Norwegian Variants.* Helsinki: FF Communications, no. 175, 1958.

Chung, Sue Fawn. "Their Changing World: Chinese Women on the Comstock, 1860–1910." In *Comstock Women: The Making of a Mining Community,* edited by Ronald M. James and C. Elizabeth Raymond, 203–28. Reno: University of Nevada Press, 1998.

Clemens, Samuel [Mark Twain]. *Autobiography of Mark Twain.* Vol. 2. Edited by Benjamin Griffin and Harriet Elinor Smith. Berkeley: University of California Press, 2013.

———. "A Couple of Sad Experiences." *Galaxy,* June 1870, 858–61. http://www.twainquotes.com/Galaxy/187006a.html.

———. *Roughing It.* Edited by Harriet Elinor Smith and Edgar Marquess Branch. 1872. Reprint, Berkeley: University of California Press, 1993.

———. *The Works of Mark Twain: Early Tales and Sketches.* Vol. 1, *1851–1864.* Edited by Edgar Marquess Branch and Robert H. Hirst. Berkeley: University of California Press, 1979.

Clover, Thomas E. *The Lost Dutchman Mine of Jacob Waltz.* Phoenix: Cowboy-Miner Productions, 1998.

Cobb, Ty. *My Virginia City: A Columnist's Memories.* Reno: Historic Fourth Ward School Foundation, 2002.

Curtis, Donnelyn, and Lawrence I. Berkove, eds. *Before the Big Bonanza: Dan De Quille's Early Comstock Accounts.* Columbia: University of Missouri Press, 2015.

Daley, Andria. "Boardwalk Bons Vivants." *Nevada Magazine,* November–December 1992, 20–24, 35–36.

Daniels, Zeke. *See* Mack, Effie Mona.

Dash, Mike. *Borderlands.* Woodstock, NY: Overlook Press, 2000.

Davies, Owen. *The Haunted: A Social History of Ghosts.* New York: Palgrave Macmillan, 2007.

Dégh, Linda. *Legend and Belief.* Bloomington: Indiana University Press, 2001.

DeGroot, Henry. *The Comstock Papers.* Carson City, NV: Dangberg Foundation, 1985.

De Quille, Dan. *See* Wright, William.

Di Francia, Chic. *The Life and Times of Dan DeQuille, Chronicler of the Comstock and Reporter for the "Territorial Enterprise" in Virginia City, Nevada.* Virginia City, NV: Virginia City Press, 1998.

Dorson, Richard M. *American Folklore.* Chicago: University of Chicago Press, 1959.

———. *Bloodstoppers and Bearwalkers: Folk Traditions of Michigan's Upper Peninsula.* 1952. Reprint, Madison: University of Wisconsin Press, 2008.

———. "Dialect Stories of the Upper Peninsula: A New Form of American Folklore." *Journal of American Folklore* 61, no. 240 (1948): 113–50.

———. "Folklore and Fake Lore." *American Mercury* (March 1950): 335–42.

Doten, Alfred. "The Journals of Alfred Doten." Manuscript, Special Collections Library, University of Nevada, Reno.

———. *The Journals of Alfred Doten: 1849–1903.* Edited by Walter Van Tilburg Clark. Reno: University of Nevada Press, 1973.

Drury, Wells. *An Editor on the Comstock Lode.* New York: Farrar and Rinehart, 1936.

Dundes, Alan, ed. *International Folkloristics: Classic Contributions by the Founders of Folklore.* Lanham, MD: Rowman and Littlefield, 1999.

Dwyer, Richard A., and Richard E. Lingenfelter. *Dan De Quille, the Washoe Giant: A Biography and Anthology.* Reno: University of Nevada Press, 1990.

———. *Lying on the Eastern Slope: James Townsend's Comic Journalism on the Mining Frontier.* Miami: University Presses of Florida, Florida International University Press, 1984.

Dykstra, Robert R. "Quantifying the Wild West: Problematic Statistics of Frontier Violence." *Western Historical Quarterly* 40, no. 3 (2009): 321–47.

Emrich, Duncan. *Folklore on the American Land.* Boston: Little, Brown, 1972.

———. *In the Delta Saloon: Conversations with Residents of Virginia City, Nevada.* Edited by R. T. King. 1991. Reprint, Reno: University of Nevada Oral History Program, 2012; recorded in 1949 and 1950.

———. *It's an Old West Custom.* New York: Vanguard Press, 1949.

Erdoes, Richard, ed. *Legends and Tales of the American West.* New York: Pantheon, 1991 (originally *Tales from the American Frontier*).

Finucane, R. C. *Ghosts: Appearance of the Dead and Cultural Transformation.* Amherst, NY: Prometheus, 1996.

Fish, Lydia. "The European Background of American Miners' Beliefs." In *Folklore Studies in Honour of Herbert Halpert: A Festschrift,* edited by Kenneth S. Goldstein and Neil V. Rosenberg, 157–71. St. John's, NL: Memorial University of Newfoundland, 1980.

Foster, Michael Dylan, and Jeffrey A. Tolbert, eds. *The Folkloresque: Reframing Folklore in a Popular Culture World.* Logan: Utah State University Press, 2016.

———, eds. *Möbius Media: Popular Culture, Folklore, and the Folkloresque.* Forthcoming, 2024.

Francke, Bernadette S. "Divination on Mount Davidson: An Overview of Women Spiritualists and Fortunetellers on the Comstock." In *Comstock Women: The Making of a Mining Community,* edited by Ronald M. James and C. Elizabeth Raymond, 165–78. Reno: University of Nevada Press, 1998.

Garrett, Greg. *Entertaining Judgment: The Afterlife in Popular Imagination.* Oxford: Oxford University Press, 2015.

Goodman, Matthew. *The Sun and the Moon: The Remarkable True Account of Hoaxers, Showmen, Dueling Journalists, and Lunar Man-Bats in Nineteenth-Century New York.* New York: Basic Books, 2008.

Goodwin, C. C. *As I Remember Them.* Salt Lake City: Salt Lake Commercial Club, 1913.

Gould, Geryl. *Guide of Virginia City: The Cover of the "Pot of Gold" and Silver.* Pamphlet. N.p., 1941.

Granger, Byrd Howell. *A Motif Index for Lost Mines and Treasures Applied to Reaction of Arizona Legends, and to Lost Mine and Treasure Legends Exterior to Arizona.* Tucson: University of Arizona Press with Helsinki: FF Communications, no. 218, 1977.

Hand, Wayland D. "California Miners Folklore: Above Ground." *California Folklore Quarterly* 1, no. 1 (1942): 24–46.

———. "California Miners Folklore: Below Ground." *California Folklore Quarterly* 1, no. 2 (1942): 127–53.

———. "The Folklore, Customs, and Traditions of the Butte Miner." *California Folklore Quarterly* 7 (1946): 1–25.

———. "The Folklore from Utah's Silver Mining Camps." *Journal of American Folklore* 45 (1941): 132–61.

———. "The Quest for Buried Treasure: A Chapter in American Folk Legendry." In *Folklore on Two Continents: Essays in Honor of Linda Dégh,* edited by Nikolai Burlakoff and Carl Lindahl, 112–19. Bloomington, IN: Trickster Press, 1980.

Handler, Richard, and Jocelyn Linnekin. "Tradition, Genuine or Spurious." *Journal of American Folklore* 97, no. 385 (1984): 273–90.

Hart, Fred H. *The Sazerac Lying Club: A Nevada Book.* San Francisco: Henry Keller, 1878.

Hartmann, Elisabeth. *Die Trollvorstellungen in den Sagen und Märchen der Skandinavischen Völker.* Tübingen: Eberhard Karls Universität Tübingen, 1936.

Highton, Jake. *Nevada Newspaper Days: A History of Journalism in the Silver State.* Stockton, CA: Heritage West Books, 1990.

Holabird, Fred N. "George Hearst, Comstock Pioneer." *Nevada in the West* (Spring 2010): 13–16.

Holliday, J. S. *The World Rushed In: The California Gold Rush Experience.* New York: Simon and Schuster, 1981.

Hunt, Robert. *Popular Romances of the West of England; or, The Drolls, Traditions, and Superstitions of Old Cornwall.* London: Chatto and Windus, 1903, combined first and second series (1865).

Hurley, Gerald T. "Buried Treasure Tales in America." *Western Folklore* 10, no. 3 (1951): 197–216.

Hutchinson, Austin E., ed. *Before the Comstock, 1857–1858: Memoirs of William Hickman Dolman.* Reno: University of Nevada, n.d., reprinted from the *New Mexico Historical Review* (July 1947).

James, Ronald M. "Defining the Group: Nineteenth-Century Cornish on the Mining Frontier." In *Cornish Studies 2,* edited by Philip Payton, 32–47. Exeter: University of Exeter Press, 1994.

———. *The Folklore of Cornwall: The Oral Tradition of a Celtic Nation.* Exeter: University of Exeter Press, 2018.

———. "In Search of Western Folklore in the Writings of Alfred Doten and Dan De Quille." *Nevada Historical Society Quarterly* 64, no. 3 (2021): 241–58.

———. "Knockers, Knackers, and Ghosts: Immigrant Folklore in the Western Mines." *Western Folklore* 51, no. 2 (1992): 153–77.

———. "Lost Mines and the Secret of Getting Rich Quick." Folklore Thursday website, July 18, 2019.

———. "Mark Twain in Nevada." *Nevada Historical Society Quarterly* 51, no. 2 (2008): 99–102.

———. "Mark Twain's Miscegenation Hoax of 1864: Understanding Context." *Nevada Historical Society Quarterly* 64, no. 4 (2021): 395–98.

———. "Mark Twain's Virginia City: The 1864 Bird's Eye View of Grafton Brown." *Nevada Historical Society Quarterly* 51, no. 2 (2008): 140–47.

———. "Monk, Greeley, Ward, and Twain: The Folkloresque of a Western Legend." *Western Folklore* 76, no. 3 (2017): 293–312.

———. *The Roar and the Silence: A History of Virginia City and the Comstock Lode.* Reno: University of Nevada Press, 1998.

———. "Sex, Murder, and the Myth of the Wild West: How a Soiled Dove Earned a Heart of Gold." *Nevada Historical Society Quarterly* 64, no. 1 (2021): 56–61.

———. *Temples of Justice: The County Courthouse in Nevada.* Reno: University of Nevada Press, 1994.

———. "Timothy Francis McCarthy: An Irish Immigrant Life on the Comstock." *Nevada Historical Society Quarterly* 39, no. 4 (1996): 300–308.

———. *Virginia City: Secrets of a Western Past.* Lincoln: University of Nebraska Press, 2012.

James, Ronald M., and C. Elizabeth Raymond, eds. *Comstock Women: The Making of a Mining Community.* Reno: University of Nevada Press, 1998.

James, Ronald M., and Kenneth H. Fliess. "Women of the Mining West: Virginia City Revisited." In *Comstock Women: The Making of a Mining Community,* edited by Ronald M. James and C. Elizabeth Raymond, 17–39. Reno: University of Nevada Press, 1998.

James, Ronald M., and Robert E. Stewart, eds. *The Gold Rush Letters of E. Allen Grosh and Hosea B. Grosh.* Reno: University of Nevada Press, 2012.

James, Susan A. "Blazing a Trail with Blasdel." *Nevada Magazine,* September–October 1989, 19–21, 61–63.

———. "Julia Bulette's Probate Records." In *Uncovering Nevada's Past: A Primary Source History of the Silver State,* edited by John B. Reid and Ronald M. James, 55–59. Reno: University of Nevada Press, 2004.

———. "Queen of Tarts." In *Historical Nevada Magazine: Outstanding Historical Features from the Pages of "Nevada Magazine,"* 47–53. Carson City: Nevada Magazine, 1998 (September–October 1984).

———. *Virginia City's Historic Fourth Ward School.* Virginia City, NV: Historic Fourth Ward School Museum, 2003.

Jenkin, A. K. Hamilton. *The Cornish Miner: An Account of His Life Above and Underground from Early Times.* London: George Allen and Unwin, 1927.

Jones, Louis C. *Things That Go Bump in the Night.* New York: Hill and Wang, 1959.

Lillard, Richard G., and Mary V. Hood. *Hank Monk and Horace Greeley: An Enduring Episode in Western History.* Georgetown, CA: Wilmac Press, 1973.

Lingenfelter, Richard E., and Karen Rix Gash. *The Newspapers of Nevada: A History and Bibliography, 1854–1879.* Reno: University of Nevada Press, 1984.

Loomis, C. Grant. "April Fooling on the Comstock," *California Folklore Quarterly* 4, no. 3 (1945): 208–10.

———. "Hart's Tall Tales from Nevada." *California Folklore Quarterly* 4, no. 3 (1945): 216–38.

———. "More Hart Tall Tales from Nevada." *California Folklore Quarterly* 4, no. 4 (1945): 351–58.

———. "Some American Folklore of 1880." *California Folklore Quarterly* 4, no. 4 (1945): 417.

———. "A Tall Tales Miscellany." *California Folklore Quarterly* 6, no. 1 (1947): 28–41.

———. "The Tall Tales of Dan De Quille." *California Folklore Quarterly* 5, no. 1 (1946): 26–71.

Lord, Eliot. *Comstock Mining and Miners.* 1883. Reprint, Berkeley, CA: Howell-North Press, 1959.

Lunde, Erik S. *Horace Greeley.* Boston: G. K. Hall, 1981.

Lyman, George D. *The Saga of the Comstock Lode: Boom Days in Virginia City.* New York: Charles Scribner's Sons, 1934.

Mack, Effie Mona [Zeke Daniels]. *Life and Death of Julia C. Bulette: "Queen of the Red Lights."* Virginia City, NV: Lamp Post, 1958.

Makley, Michael J. *Imposing Order Without Law: American Expansion to the Eastern Sierra, 1850–1865.* Reno: University of Nevada Press, 2022.

———. *John Mackay: Silver King in the Gilded Age.* Reno: University of Nevada Press, 2009.

Mathews, Mary McNair. *Ten Years in Nevada; or, Life on the Pacific Coast.* 1880. Reprint, Lincoln: University of Nebraska Press, 1985.

McDonald, Douglas. *Camels in Nevada.* Las Vegas: Nevada Publications, 1983.

Michelson, Miriam. *The Wonderlode of Silver and Gold.* Boston: Stratford, 1934.

Mitchell, John D. *Lost Mines of the Great Southwest.* Glorieta, NM: Rio Grande Press, 1990.

Moreno, Richard. *Frontier Fake News: Nevada's Sagebrush Humorists and Hoaxsters.* Reno: University of Nevada Press, 2023.

Myles, Myrtle T. "Jim Butler: Nevada's Improbable Tycoon." *Montana: The Magazine of Western History* 26, no. 1 (1976): 60–69.

Narváez, Peter, ed. *The Good People: New Fairylore Essays.* Lexington: University Press of Kentucky, 1997.

Nichols, Dorothy Young. *Views and Vignettes of Virginia City: In My Days.* Edited by Halmar F. Moser. Carson City, NV: Anthony and Janet Hartmann, 1973 and 1980.

Nylen, Robert. "On the 'Desert Canary.'" *Nevada State Museum Newsletter* 21, no. 2 (1993): 4–5.

Oberding, Janice. *Ghosthunter's Guide to Virginia City.* Reno: Thunder Mountain Productions Press, 2003.

———. *Haunted Virginia City.* Charleston, SC: History Press, 2015.

O'Brien, Dolores K. *Meet Virginia City's Ghosts.* Virginia City, NV: Dolores J. O'Brien, 1969.

Paine, Swift. *Eilley Orrum, Queen of the Comstock.* Indianapolis: Bobbs-Merrill, 1929.

Pullen, John J. *Comic Relief: The Life and Laughter of Artemus Ward, 1834–1867.* Hamden, CT: Archon Press, 1883.

Raymond, R. W. *A Glossary of Mining and Metallurgical Terms.* Easton, PA: Institute, Lafayette College, 1881.

Santino, Jack. "Occupational Ghostlore: Social Context and the Expression of Belief." *Journal of American Folklore* 101, no. 400 (1988): 207–18.

Shepperson, Wilbur S. *Restless Strangers: Nevada's Immigrants and Their Interpreters.* Reno: University of Nevada Press, 1970.

Shinn, Charles Howard. *Mining Camps: A Study in American Frontier Government.* Edited by Rodman Wilson Paul. 1884. Reprint, Gloucester, MA: Peter Smith, 1970.

———. *The Story of the Mine as Illustrated by the Great Comstock Lode of Nevada.* 1910. Reprint, Reno: University of Nevada Press, 1980.

Simpson, Jacqueline, and Steve Roud. *A Dictionary of English Folklore.* Oxford: Oxford University Press, 2000.

Smith, Grant, and Joseph V. Tingley. *The History of the Comstock Lode, 1850–1997.* 1943. Reprint, Reno: University of Nevada Press, 1998.

Stewart, Robert E. "Mark Twain, Ruel Gridley, and the U.S. Sanitary Commission: Raising Funds to Aid Civil War Soldiers." *Nevada Historical Society Quarterly* 60, nos. 1–4 (2017): 18–36.

Strickland, Paul. "The Folklore of the Comstock Lode and Surrounding Regions: 1850–1900." December 10, 1978. Unpublished, copy available in private collection of the author.

Sturges, Philip C. "Utah Mining Folklore." *Western Folklore* 18, no. 2 (1959): 137–39.

Thompson, Stith. *Motif-Index of Folk Literature.* Bloomington: Indiana University Press, 1955–58.

Totton, Kathryn M., et al. *Comstock Memories: 1920s–1960s.* Reno: Oral History Program, University of Nevada, 1988.

Twain, Mark. *See* Clemens, Samuel.

Udall, Stewart L., Robert R. Dykstra, Michael A. Bellesiles, Paula Mitchell Marks, and Gregory H. Nobles. "How the West Got Wild: American Media and Frontier Violence." *Western Historical Quarterly* 31, no. 3 (2000): 277–96.

Waldorf, John Taylor. *A Kid on the Comstock: Reminiscences of a Virginia City Childhood.* 1970. Reprint, Reno: University of Nevada Press, 1991.

Walsh, Lynda. *Sins Against Science: The Scientific Media Hoaxes of Poe, Twain, and Others.* Albany: State University of New York Press, 2006.

Wheeler, Candace. "Comstock Cemeteries: Changing Landscapes of Death." Master's thesis, University of Nevada, 2008.

Wonham, Henry B. *Mark Twain and the Art of the Tall Tale.* Oxford: Oxford University Press, 1993.

Wright, William [Dan De Quille]. *History of the Big Bonanza.* Hartford, CT: American, 1876.

———. *Washoe Rambles.* Edited by Richard E. Lingenfelter. Los Angeles: Westernlore Press, 1963.

Young, Simon. *The Nail in the Skull, and Other Victorian Urban Legends.* Jackson: University Press of Mississippi, 2022.

Young, Simon, and Ceri Houlbrook, eds. *Magical Folk: British and Irish Fairies, 500 AD to the Present.* London: Gibson Square, 2018.

Zanjani, Sally. *Devils Will Reign: How Nevada Began.* Reno: University of Nevada Press, 2006.

Index

Page numbers in *italics* indicate illustrations.

About the Author

RONALD M. JAMES WAS the long-serving Nevada state historic preservation officer, administering the office for three decades and retiring in 2012. He was also appointed to the advisory board for the National Park System and served as chair of the National Historic Landmarks Committee. He is the author of *The Roar and the Silence: A History of Virginia City and the Comstock Lode* and several other books about the American West. In 2014, James was inducted into the Nevada Writer's Hall of Fame.